Song of Cthulhu

Tales of the Spheres beyond Sound

More Titles from Chaosium

Call of Cthulhu® Fiction

The Antarktos Cycle
The Azathoth Cycle
The Book of Eibon (forthcoming)
The Cthulhu Cycle
Cthulhu's Heirs
Disciples of Cthulhu, 2nd Ed.
Disciples of CthulhuII (forthcoming)
The Dunwich Cycle
Encyclopedia Cthulhiana, 2nd Ed.
The Hastur Cycle, 2nd Ed.
The Ithaqua Cycle
The Innsmouth Cycle
Made in Goatswood
The Necronomicon
The Nyarlathotep Cycle
The Shub-Niggurath Cycle
Singers of Strange Songs
Tales Out of Innsmouth
Lin Carter's The Xothic Legend Cycle
R. W. Chambers' The Yellow Sign (his complete weird fiction)
Robert E. Howard's Nameless Cults (his Cthulhu Mythos fiction)
Tani Jantsang's Other Nations (forthcoming)
Henry Kuttner's The Book of Iod
Arthur Machen's The Three Impostors & Other Tales
Arthur Machen's The White People & Other Tales (forthcoming)
Joseph S. Pulver's Nightmare's Disciple (original Mythos novel)

Miskatonic University® Archives

The Book of Dzyan

Call of Cthulhu® Fiction

Song of Cthulhu

Tales of the Spheres beyond Sound

E. P. BERGLUND
RAMSEY CAMPBELL
HUGH B. CAVE
FRED CHAPPELL
M. CHRISTIAN
CAITLIN R. KIERNAN
D. F. LEWIS
THOMAS LIGOTTI
H. P. LOVECRAFT
E. A. LUSTIG
BRIAN MCNAUGHTON
THOMAS F. MONTELEONE
GREG NICOLL
TOM PICCIRILLI
ROBERT M. PRICE
STEPHEN MARK RAINEY
JAMES ROBERT SMITH
ROB SUGGS
WILLIAM R. TROTTER
ROBERT WEINBERG

EDITED AND INTRODUCED BY STEPHEN MARK RAINEY

A Chaosium Book
August 2001

FIRST EDITION

10 9 8 7 6 5 4 3 2 1

Chaosium Publication 6032. Published in August 2001.

ISBN 1-56882-117-4

Printed in Canada.

Contents

INTRODUCTION *Stephen Mark Rainey* xiii

THE MUSIC OF ERICH ZANN
H. P. Lovecraft 1

THE DARK BEAUTY OF UNHEARD
HORRORS *Thomas Ligotti* 8

IN THE RUE D'AUSEIL *Fred Chappell* 14

THE PLAIN OF SOUND
J. Ramsey Campbell 19

THE LAST SHOW AT VERDI'S SUPPER
CLUB *Stephen Mark Rainey* 29

WATER MUSIC FOR THE TILLERS OF SOIL
Tom Piccirilli 37

SHALLOW FATHOMS *M. Christian* 49

HOW NYARLATHOTEP ROCKED OUR
WORLD *Greg Nicoll* 57

LISTEN *James Robert Smith* 69

MUD *Brian McNaughton* 75

PAEDOMORPHOSIS *Caitlin R. Kiernan* 88

INTRUDERS *Hugh B. Cave* 99

CHANT *Robert Weinberg*. 111

GHOUL'S TALE *Robert M. Price*. 121

THE NEXT BIG THING *Rob Suggs* 126

THE FLAUTISTS *Edward P. Berglund* 141

FALL FROM GRACE *D. F. Lewis*. 148

DRUMS *William R. Trotter* 154

THE ENCHANTING OF LILA WOODS
E. A. Lustig 181

YOG-SOTHOTH, SUPERSTAR
Thomas F. Monteleone 201

Introduction

Perhaps some of you may recall an obscure little Mexican B-movie from the 1950s called *The Sound of Horror*, in which an invisible (!) dinosaur menaces a small group of brave and daring consumables holed up in a desert shack. My recollections of this faux-classic yarn are quite vague, since I haven't seen it since I was a wee lad of about six; but more than thirty years later, one thing in particular stands out in my mind, and that is the fairly dreadful *noise* the unseen monster emitted just as it was about to devour its prey. Now, even a moderately sophisticated six-year-old might recognize the monster's invisibility as a disguise for a non-existent budget. But on some primal level, that young mind could also feel a rush of fear, simply by accepting the premise that the thing you couldn't see, only hear, could, and in fact *would*, kill you in terrible fashion. The grim black and white cinematography, the bleak desert landscape, the unearthly voice of the monster; in "The Sound of Horror," all these came together to conjure up a fairly creepy atmosphere that, to the moderately sophisticated but still impressionable six-year-old mind, managed to overcome the more rational recognition of budget limitations.

In 1981, while a senior art student at the University of Georgia, I read "The Music of Erich Zann" for the first time (along with every other Lovecraft story I could get my hands on), and upon turning out the lights on that exuberant night, I found myself experiencing the very same delicious chill I'd known after watching "The Sound of Horror" as a kid. In fact, even having reached the slightly more sophisticated age of twenty-two, I found that the more Cthulhu-ish tales I read, the more deeply my fear of the unseen grew. I found myself feeling that the Old Gent from Providence had somehow reached far into the future, into my own subconscious, and pried from it the very essence of all my most personal nightmares (which in my life have been numerous and often exquisite) that he might weave them into his own classic weird tales. To this day, I don't believe I've ever read another author whose work has so effectively managed to manipulate me on a purely emotional level, that emotion overriding all of the more rational observations I might have regarding style, syntax, historical significance, etc., etc.

It was only natural that, as I began my own ventures into the realm of fiction-writing, I should draw upon the material which in its own way seemed to draw upon the essence of fear already buried inside me. My first real attempt at a Cthulhu Mythos story was probably "Threnody," written in 1986, which drew upon the concept of sound as a means to interact with those "other" beings and forces that were the staple of HPL's fiction. That tale introduced a character named Maurice Zann (presumably one of Erich's siblings) and a grimoire entitled "The Spheres beyond Sound"; the Zann character, in this case, being an offstage presence only, never known except as the author of the book. Being at the time an enthusiastic, if hardly exceptional guitarist, I found the exploration of "mystical" music through both written word and instrument to be both intriguing and exhilarating.

As for the origin of "Maurice" . . .

The very name "Zann" struck a familiar chord with me the first time I read the HPL story. For the longest time, I could not quite figure out why; then one day while exploring through a bunch of old LP records in the attic of my parents' home, I happened upon an album I remembered from my youth, entitled "A Child's Introduction to Music." The composer of the music and album's narrator was named "Maurice *Zam*," the name printed in a flourishing chancery script so that the *m* in "Zam" looked remarkably like two *n*'s. And the recording itself had, I remembered, caused me some measure of panic as a youngster, because a number of the musical selections were quite dark, and Monsieur Zam possessed a rather somber and sometimes caustic style of narrating—almost as if the task of introducing a youngster to music was considerably beneath his dignity. What better way to clue the child in than to unnerve him?

So, the more appropriate form of the name stuck.

I had originally planned on including "Threnody" here, but as it has already seen publication in various other magazines and anthologies dedicated to Lovecraftian lore, I opted instead to include a quite different tale, entitled "The Last Show at Verdi's Supper Club," this one far more loosely connected to the "Zann Cycle," if one will allow the application of such an epithet.

Music, as an external stimulus, certainly touches nerves in human beings unlike any other, reaching into the very realm of the spiritual. Indeed, music is an integral part of virtually every religion that has ever sprung up throughout history. What other sensory stimulus could ever sweep from the heights of exultation to the brink of despair, encompassing every conceivable emotion in between? The feelings catalyzed by music can oftentimes be so moving, so inspiring, that, like the fear catalyzed by HPL's fiction, the only catharsis for the creative mind is to compose; be it music, fiction, poetry, art . . . and for those inclined to be involved in a production such as *Song of Cthulhu*, the results can only be of the darkest variety.

Listen to "Hidden Voices" by minimalist composer Ingram Marshall and at the same time visualize the imagery from HPL's "Dreams in the Witch House." Put on "Sinfonia Antarctica" by Ralph Vaughn-Williams and lose yourself in the horrifying majesty of "At the Mountains of Madness." Delve into "The Dream Quest of Unknown Kadath" to the ebullient strains of "The Summoning of the Muse" by Dead Can Dance. The associations between the music and the imagery of the written words can be powerful indeed. Perhaps even powerful enough to begin painting images in your own subconscious that will follow you into your dreams. . . .

Like any eclectic catalog of dark music, this volume of stories explores many levels of emotion, each writer composing his own unique movement to the symphony. Here, you will find a wide range of voices, some spinning tales of pure, deep dread, much as might be found in the most successful works of HPL himself. Others venture into territory that the Old Gent would never have imagined, or wanted to imagine; yet it is very likely the chords struck by his own pen that brought such works to fruition. There's even a touch of whimsy to be found, yet always mingled with the strain of darkness like that faced by Erich Zann in his garret in the rue d'Auseil. The theme of terror by sound, unifying as it is in this volume, still provides innumerable doors that open into vastly different universes.

Interspersed among the upcoming contents, you may find a few non-aural-based surprises as well—for the purposes of punctuating the overall composition, like a discordant striking of the percussion session . . . to jar you from one state of fear into the next. . . .

Please read on. And enjoy. And by all means, sleep the sleep of the dead tonight, to the eldritch music of the spheres. . . .

The spheres beyond sound.

—Stephen Mark Rainey.
August, 1997

The Music of Erich Zann

by H. P. Lovecraft

I have examined maps of the city with the greatest care, yet have never again found the rue d'Auseil. These maps have not been modern maps alone, for I know that names change. I have, on the contrary, delved deeply into all the antiquities of the place, and have personally explored every region, of whatever name, which could possibly answer to the street I knew as the rue d'Auseil. But despite all I have done, it remains an humiliating fact that I cannot find the house, the street, or even the locality, where, during the last months of my impoverished life as a student of metaphysics at the university, I heard the music of Erich Zann.

That my memory is broken, I do not wonder; for my health, physical and mental, was gravely disturbed throughout the period of my residence in the rue d'Auseil, and I recall that I took none of my few acquaintances there. But that I cannot find the place again is both singular and perplexing; for it was within a half-hour's walk of the university and was distinguished by peculiarities which could hardly be forgotten by anyone who had been there. I have never met a person who has seen the rue d'Auseil.

The rue d'Auseil lay across a dark river bordered by precipitous brick blear-windowed warehouses and spanned by a ponderous bridge of dark stone. It was always shadowy along that river, as if the smoke of neighboring factories shut out the sun perpetually. The river was also odorous with evil stenches which I have never smelled elsewhere, and which may some day help me to find it, since I should recognize them at once. Beyond the bridge were narrow cobbled streets with rails; and then came the ascent, at first gradual, but incredibly steep as the rue d'Auseil was reached.

I have never seen another street as narrow and steep as the rue d'Auseil; it was almost a cliff, closed to all vehicles, consisting in several places of flights of steps, and ending at the top in a lofty ivied wall. Its paving was irregular, sometimes stone slabs, sometimes cobblestones, and sometimes bare earth with struggling greenish-grey vegetation. The houses were tall, peaked-roofed, incredibly old, and crazily leaning backward, forward, and sidewise. Occasionally an opposite pair, both leaning forward, almost met across the street like an arch; and certainly they kept most of the light from the ground below. There were a few overhead bridges from house to house across the street.

The inhabitants of the street impressed me peculiarly. At first I thought it was because they were all silent and reticent; but later decided it was because they were all very old. I do not know how I came to live on such a street, but I was not myself when I moved there. I had been living in many poor places, always evicted for want of money; until at last I came upon that tottering house in the rue d'Auseil kept by the paralytic Blandot. It was the third house from the top of the street, and by far the tallest of them all.

My room was on the fifth story; the only inhabited room there, since the house was almost empty. On the night I arrived I heard strange music from the peaked garret overhead, and the next day asked old Blandot about it. He told me it was an old German viol-player, a strange dumb man who signed his name as Erich Zann, and who played evenings in a cheap theater orches-tra; adding that Zann's desire to play in the night after his return from the theater was the reason he had chosen the lofty and isolated garret room, whose single gable window was the only point on the street from which one could look over the terminating wall at the declivity and panorama beyond.

Thereafter I heard Zann every night, and although he kept me awake, I was haunted by the weirdness of his music. Knowing little of the art myself, I was yet certain that none of his harmonies had any relation to music I had heard before; and concluded that he was a composer of highly original genius. The longer I listened, the more I was fascinated, until after a week I resolved to make the old man's acquaintance.

One night as he was returning from his work, I intercepted Zann in the hallway and told him that I would like to know him and be with him when he played. He was a small, lean, bent person, with shabby clothes, blue eyes, grotesque, satyr-like face, and nearly bald head; and at my first words seemed both angered and frightened. My obvious friendliness, however, finally melted him; and he grudgingly motioned to me to follow him up the dark, creaking and rickety attic stairs. His room, one of only two in the steeply pitched garret, was on the west side, toward the high wall that formed the upper end of the street. Its size was very great, and seemed the greater because of its extraordinary barrenness and neglect. Of furniture there was only a narrow iron bedstead, a dingy wash-stand, a small table, a large bookcase, an iron music-rack, and three old-fashioned chairs. Sheets of music were piled in disorder about the floor. The walls were of bare boards, and had probably never known plaster; whilst the abundance of dust and cobwebs made the place seem more deserted than inhabited. Evidently Erich Zann's world of beauty lay in some far cosmos of the imagination.

Motioning me to sit down, the dumb man closed the door, turned the large wooden bolt, and lighted a candle to augment the one he had brought with him. He now removed his viol from its moth-eaten covering, and tak-ing it, seated himself in the least uncomfortable of the chairs. He did not employ the music-rack, but, offering no choice and playing from memory, enchanted me for over an hour with strains I had never heard before; strains which must have been of his own devising. To describe their exact nature is impossible for one unversed in music. They were a kind of fugue, with recurrent passages of the most captivating quality, but to me were notable for the absence of any of the weird notes I had overheard from my room below on other occasions.

Those haunting notes I had remembered, and had often hummed and whistled inaccurately to myself, so when the player at length laid down his bow I asked him if he would render some of them. As I began my request the wrinkled satyrlike face lost the bored placidity it had possessed during the playing, and seemed to show the same curious mixture of anger and fright which I had noticed when first I accosted the old man. For a moment I was inclined to use persuasion, regarding rather lightly the whims of senility; and even tried to awaken my host's weirder mood by whistling a few of the strains to which I had listened the night before. But I did not pursue this course for more than a moment; for when the dumb musician recognized the whistled air his face grew suddenly distorted with an expression wholly beyond analysis, and his long, cold, bony right hand reached out to stop my mouth and silence the crude imitation. As he did this he further demonstrated his eccentricity by casting a startled glance toward the lone curtained window, as if fearful of some intruder—a glance doubly absurd, since the garret stood high and inaccessible above all the adjacent roofs, this window being the only point on the steep street, as the concierge had told me, from which one could see over the wall of the summit.

The old man's glance brought Blandot's remark to my mind, and with a certain capriciousness I felt a wish to look out over the wide and dizzying panorama of moonlit roofs and city lights beyond the hilltop, which of all the dwellers in the rue d'Auseil only this crabbed musician could see. I moved toward the window and would have drawn aside the nondescript curtains, when with a frightened rage even greater than before, the dumb lodger was upon me again; this time motioning with his head toward the door as he nervously strove to drag me thither with both hands. Now thoroughly disgusted with my host, I ordered him to release me, and told him I would go at once. His clutch relaxed, and as he saw my disgust and offense, his own anger seemed to subside. He tightened his relaxing grip, but this time in a friendly manner, forcing me into a chair; then with an appearance of wistfulness crossing to the littered table, where he wrote many words with a pencil, in the labored French of a foreigner.

The note which he finally handed me was an appeal for tolerance and forgiveness. Zann said that he was old, lonely, and afflicted with strange fears and nervous disorders connected with his music and with other things. He had enjoyed my listening to his music, and wished I would come again and not mind his eccentricities. But he could not play to another his weird harmonies, and could not bear hearing them from another; nor could he bear having anything in his room touched by another. He had not known until our hallway conversation that I could overhear his playing in my room, and now asked me if I would arrange with Blandot to take a lower room where I could not hear him in the night. He would, he wrote, defray the difference in rent.

As I sat deciphering the execrable French, I felt more lenient toward the old man. He was a victim of physical and nervous suffering, as was I; and my metaphysical studies had taught me kindness. In the silence there came a slight sound from the window—the shutter must have rattled in the night wind, and for some reason I started almost as violently as did Erich Zann. So when I had finished reading, I shook my host by the hand, and departed as a friend.

The next day Blandot gave me a more expensive room on the third floor between the apartments of an aged money-lender and the room of a respectable upholsterer. There was no one on the fourth floor.

It was not long before I found that Zann's eagerness for my company was not as great as it had seemed while he was persuading me to move down from the fifth story. He did not ask me to call on him, and when I did call he appeared uneasy and played listlessly. This was always at night—in the day he slept and would admit no one. My liking for him did not grow, though the attic room and the weird music seemed to hold an odd fascination for me. I had a curious desire to look out of that window, over the wall and down the unseen slope at the glittering roofs and spires which must lie outspread there. Once I went up to the garret during theater hours, when Zann was away, but the door was locked.

What I did succeed in doing was to overhear the nocturnal playing of the dumb old man. At first I would tip-toe up to my old fifth floor, then I grew bold enough to climb the last creaking staircase to the peaked garret. There in the narrow hall, outside the bolted door with the covered keyhole, I often heard sounds which filled me with an indefinable dread—the dread of vague wonder and brooding mystery. It was not that the sounds were hideous, for they were not; but that they held vibrations suggesting nothing on this globe of earth, and that at certain intervals they assumed a symphonic quality which I could hardly conceive as produced by one player. Certainly, Erich Zann was a genius of wild power. As the weeks passed, the playing grew wilder, whilst the old musician acquired an increasing haggardness and furtiveness pitiful to behold. He now refused to admit me at any time, and shunned me when we met on the stairs.

Then one night as I listened at the door, I heard the shrieking viol swell into a chaotic babel of sound; a pandemonium which would have led me to doubt my own shaking sanity had there not come from behind that barred portal a piteous proof that the horror was real—the awful inarticulate cry which only a mute can utter, and which rises only in the moments of the most terrible fear or anguish. I knocked repeatedly at the door, but received no response. Afterward I waited in the black hallway, shivering with cold and fear, till I heard the poor musician's feeble effort to rise from the floor by the aid of a chair. Believing him just conscious after a fainting fit, I renewed my rapping, at the same time calling out my name reassuringly. I heard Zann stumble to the window and close both shutter and sash, then stumble to the door, which he falteringly unfastened to admit me. This time his delight at having me was real; for his distorted face gleamed with relief while he clutched at my coat as a child clutches at its mother's skirts.

Shaking pathetically, the old man forced me into a chair whilst he sank into another, beside which his viol and bow lay carelessly on the floor. He sat for some time inactive, nodding oddly, but having a paradoxical suggestion of intense and frightened listening. Subsequently he seemed to be satisfied, and crossing to a chair by the table wrote a brief note, handed it to me, and returned to the table, where he began to write rapidly and incessantly. The note implored me in the name of mercy, and for the sake of my own curiosity, to wait where I was while he prepared a full account in German of all the marvels and terrors which beset him. I waited, and the dumb man's pencil flew.

It was perhaps an hour later, while I still waited and while the old musician's feverishly written sheets continued to pile up, that I saw Zann start as from the hint of a horrible shock. Unmistakably he was looking at the curtained window and listening shudderingly. Then I half fancied I heard a sound myself; though it was not a horrible sound, but rather an exquisitely low and infinitely distant musical note, suggesting a player in one of the neighboring houses, or in some abode beyond the lofty wall over which I had never been able to look. Upon Zann the effect was terrible, for, dropping his pencil, suddenly he rose, seized his viol, and commenced to rend the night with the wildest playing I had ever heard from his bow save when listening at the barred door.

It would be useless to describe the playing of Erich Zann on that dreadful night. It was more horrible than anything I had ever overheard, because I could now see the expression of his face, and could realize that this time the motive was stark fear. He was trying to make a noise; to ward something off or drown something out—what, I could not imagine, awesome though I felt it must be. The playing grew fantastic, delirious, and hysterical, yet kept to the last the qualities of supreme genius which I knew this strange old man possessed. I recognized the air—it was a wild Hungarian dance popular in the theaters, and I reflected for a moment that this was the first time I had ever heard Zann play the work of another composer.

Louder and louder, wilder and wilder, mounted the shrieking and whining of that desperate viol. The player was dripping with an uncanny perspiration and twisted like a monkey, always looking frantically at the curtained window. In his frenzied strains I could almost see shadowy satyrs and bacchanals dancing and whirling insanely through seething abysses of clouds and smoke and lightning. And then I thought I heard a shriller, steadier note that was not from the viol; a calm, deliberate, purposeful, mocking note from far away in the West.

At this juncture the shutter began to rattle in a howling night wind which had sprung up outside as if in answer to the mad playing within. Zann's screaming viol now outdid itself emitting sounds I had never thought a viol could emit. The shutter rattled more loudly, unfastened, and commenced slamming against the window. Then the glass broke shiveringly under the persistent impacts, and the chill wind rushed in, making the candles sputter and rustling the sheets of paper on the table where Zann had begun to write out his horrible secret. I looked at Zann, and saw that he was past conscious observation. His blue eyes were bulging, glassy and sightless, and the frantic playing had become a blind, mechanical, unrecognizable orgy that no pen could even suggest.

A sudden gust, stronger than the others, caught up the manuscript and bore it toward the window. I followed the flying sheets in desperation, but they were gone before I reached the demolished panes. Then I remembered my old wish to gaze from this window, the only window in the rue d'Auseil from which one might see the slope beyond the wall, and the city outspread beneath. It was very dark, but the city's lights always burned, and I expected to see them there amidst the rain and wind. Yet when I looked from that highest of all possible gable windows, looked while the candles sputtered and the insane viol howled with the night-wind, I saw no city spread below, and no friendly lights gleamed from remembered streets, but only the blackness of space illimitable; unimagined space alive with motion and music, and having no semblance of anything on earth. And as I stood there looking in terror, the wind blew out both the candles in that ancient peaked garret, leaving me in savage and impenetrable darkness with chaos and pandemonium before me, and the daemon madness of that night-baying viol behind me.

I staggered back in the dark, without the means of striking a light, crashing against the table, overturning a chair, and finally groping my way to the place where the blackness screamed with shocking music. To save myself and Erich Zann I could at least try, whatever the powers opposed to me. Once I thought some chill thing brushed me, and I screamed, but my scream could not be heard above that hideous viol. Suddenly out of the blackness the madly sawing bow struck me, and I knew I was close to the player. I felt ahead, touched the back of Zann's chair, and then found and shook his shoulder in an effort to bring him to his senses.

He did not respond, and still the viol shrieked on without slackening. I moved my hand to his head, whose mechanical nodding I was able to stop, and shouted in his ear that we must both flee from the unknown things of the night. But he neither answered me nor abated the frenzy of his unutterable music, while all through the garret strange currents of wind seemed to dance in the darkness and babel. When my hand touched his ear I shuddered, though I knew not why—knew not why until I felt the still face; the ice-cold, stiffened, unbreathing face whose glassy eyes bulged uselessly into the void. And then, by some miracle, finding the door and the large wooden bolt, I plunged wildly away from that glassy-eyed thing in the dark, and from the ghoulish howling of that accursed viol whose fury increased even as I plunged.

Leaping, floating, flying down those endless stairs through the dark house; racing mindlessly out into the narrow, steep, and ancient street of steps and tottering houses; clattering down steps and over cobbles to the lower streets and the putrid canyon-walled river; panting across the great dark bridge to the broader, healthier streets and boulevards we know; all these are terrible impressions that linger with me. And I recall that there was no wind, and that the moon was out, and that all the lights of the city twinkled.

Despite my most careful searches and investigations, I have never since been able to find the rue d'Auseil. But I am not wholly sorry; either for this or for the loss in undreamable abysses of the closely-written sheets which alone could have explained the music of Erich Zann. ✳

The Dark Beauty of Unheard Horrors

by Thomas Ligotti

I t is not necessary, perhaps not even possible, for a story to mean just what it says. Beneath the surface utterances of setting, incident, and character, there is another voice that may speak of something more than the bare elements of narrative. The things this other voice has to express must be interpreted for the mind through the strictly conspicuous aspects of the story, though such interpretations are often wildly various. (Religious parables offer the most obvious example of this chaotic phenomenon.) In greater accord, one hopes, are the emotions experienced in the course of reading, since emotion, not mind, is the faculty for hearing the secret voice of the story and apprehending its meaning. Without emotion, neither story nor anything else can convey meaning as such, only data. This, not entirely original, argument goes double, if not more, for stories of the supernatural.

More than many other types of stories, it is crucial that those of the supernatural make their statement of meaning as much as possible by means of emotion, especially the present advanced stage of this literary genre. Years of exegesis have made interpreting supernatural tales into a game that anyone can play, and one finds that gods and demons are quite easily relocated from the dreams in which they were born into some mundane context of sociology, psychology, politics or whatever. The result is pathetic and, in the worst sense of the word, grotesque. One of the noblest and most tragic figures of the imagination was the vampire—damn his soul, and our own. But to see this marvelous, terrifying creature reduced to a plastic Halloween mask for sexual or political repression has been a tedious outrage. The vampire attained his stature through the emotion of fear of a fantastic evil, yet how utterly he has lost it all at the heavy, hammering hands of explication. Rest in peace, Nosferatu, none will ever take your place.

If the vampire no longer raises the emotion he once did, perhaps it is partly his own fault. He lost his mystery because he had so little of it to start. His nature and habits were always documented in detail, his ways and means a matter of public record. Too many laws lorded over him, and all laws belong to the natural world. Like his colleague the werewolf, he was too much a known *quantity*. His was a familiar, most of the time human body, and it was used like a whore by writers whose concerns were predominantly for the body as well as the everyday path in which it walks. Consequently, the vampire was stripped of all that made him alien to our ordinary selves, until he was transformed into merely the bad boy from next door. He remained a menace, to be sure, but his focus shifted from the soul to the senses. This is how it is when a mysterious force is embodied in a human body, or in any form that is too well fixed. And a mystery explained is one robbed of its power of emotion, dwindling into a parcel of information, a tissue of rules and statistics without meaning in themselves.

Of course, mystery actually requires a measure of the concrete if it is to be perceived at all; otherwise it is only a void, *the* void. The thinnest mixture of this mortar, I suppose, is contained in that most basic source of mystery—darkness. Very difficult to domesticate this phenomenon, to collar it and give a name to the fear it inspires. As a verse writer once said:

> The blackness at the bottom of a well
> May hold most any kind of hell.

The dark, indeed; the phenomenon possessing the maximum of mystery, the one most resistant to the taming of the mind and most resonant with emotions and meanings of a highly complex and subtle type. It is also extremely abstract as a provenance for supernatural horror, an elusive prodigy whose potential for fear may slip through a writer's fingers and right past even a sensitive reader of terror tales. Obviously it is problematic in a way that a solid pair of gleaming fangs at a victim's neck is not. Hence, darkness itself is rarely used in a story as the central incarnation of the supernatural, though it often serves in a supporting role as an element of atmosphere, an extension of more concrete phenomena. The shadowy ambiance of a fictional locale almost always resolves itself into an apparition of substance, a threat with a name, if not a full-blown history. Darkness may also perform in a strictly symbolic capacity, representing the abyss at the core of any genuine tale of mystery and horror. But to draw a reader's attention to this abyss, this unnamable hell of blackness, is usually sacrificed in favor of focusing on some *tangible* dread pressing against the body of everyday life. From these facts may be derived an ad hoc taxonomy for dividing supernatural stories into type: on the one side, those that tend to emphasize the surface manifestations of a supernatural phenomenon; on the other, those that reach toward the dark core of mystery in purest and most abstract condition. The former stories show us the bodies, as big as life, of the demonic tribe of spooks, vampires, and other assorted bogeymen; the latter suggest to us the essence, far bigger than life, of that dark universal terror beyond naming which is the matrix for all other terrors. Prominent among the last-named tales is H. P. Lovecraft's "The Music of Erich Zann."

* * *

The most radical form of the unknown, and the least adulterated avatar of mystery, darkness is all-pervasive in "The Music of Erich Zann." In addition to functioning as a natural atmospheric element of the tale, it is ultimately revealed as the primary supernatural phenomenon. The story reaches its pitch of uncanny revelation when the narrator witnesses "the blackness of space illimitable" in place of the reassuring city lights he expected to see through the window of Erich Zann's garret room. There are only two things we can know about this mysterious blackness: first, that in some indefinable way it is both menacing and alluring (a usual, perhaps necessary conjunction in horror tales); second, that it has an important, and once indefinable, connection with Erich Zann and the strange music he plays on his viol. Zann is portrayed as a musician of genius, yet he performs with a "cheap theater orchestra" and resides in a freakishly dilapidated boarding house in the also freakishly dilapidated rue d'Auseil. He himself is described as being physically and psychically deformed in such a way that identifies him with the rue d'Auseil and its crooked, leaning houses. This is his realm, which may be prison or paradise or both, and with his death at the end of the story it disappears from this earth, if it ever was in fact on it. Indeed, neither Zann nor the street was ever part of material reality, for Zann's world "lay in some far cosmos of the imagination." It is to this world that the narrator is unaccountably drawn at the beginning of the story and which he also seeks to recover after he flees the "marvels and terrors" introduced to him by the bizarre German musician.

Just as there exists an intimate correspondence between Zann and the rue d'Auseil, and between Zann's music and the blackness beyond the wall at the summit of that unreal street, there is also an identification between Zann and the narrator. Both of them are victims of "physical and nervous suffering." More significantly, they are each in thrall to the "dread of vague wonder and brooding mystery" of an unearthly music and by extension to the dark doom that this music seems both to conjure and keep at bay. Earlier in the story, the narrator makes an effort to whistle some of the "weird notes" he has heard Zann playing in his crummy garret room, an act that seems to stir *up* certain forces beyond the room's window; later, Zann plays these same notes as if they had some power *against* the advancing blackness. Perhaps that power is one of both invocation and exorcism, allowing Zann to play with another power, namely that of a supernatural music-maker who produces a "shriller, steadier note" than Zann's, "a calm, deliberate, *purposeful, mocking* note from far away in the West." (Italics mine; apparently at the time this story was written, 1921, Lovecraft did not yet perceive the alien forces of the universe as "indifferent," nor had he begun to anthropomorphize what culminated in the Great Old Ones of *At the Mountains of Madness,* who are also called "men" for all their superficial strangeness.) What led Zann into this terrible duet with the dark is unknown, though his perpetuation of this relationship is characterized as something of a vice by the narrator, who observes the performing Zann "dripping with perspiration and twisted like a monkey" and who impressionistically symbolizes Zann's music with visions of "shadowy satyrs and bacchanals dancing and whirling insanely through seething abysses of clouds and smoke and lightning."

Certainly Zann is aware of the temptations of his music, and does his best—or does he?—to quell the curiosity it has aroused in the narrator. But the exact nature of Zann's obsession is left in darkness—the "notes" the Old German composes in explanation of himself, unlike Alhazred's *Necronomicon,* would have been far too unearthly and alien to simple human feeling to survive even in fragments; hence, they are wisely lost to the world. What brought this man who "signed his name as Erich Zann"—as if he had another name, or perhaps none—to that run-down boarding house in the rue d'Auseil? What caused him to remain on that twisted street? Above all, what is it about the blackness and its "shocking music" that so possesses him? (Of course, the identical questions might be asked concerning the narrator, who is in a position to inform us of the answers but, for obscure reasons, is unable to.) Interestingly lucid is the fact that the supernatural aspects of the story—that reverberant blackness which threatens to overwhelm the city beyond Zann's window and possibly the entire world—is exclusive to Zann, and, by some occult transference or predisposition, the narrator. After the narrator flees the rue d'Auseil, he finds that the rest of the city has been unaffected by the fantastic cataclysm that occurred in his old neighborhood. But, as previously established, Zann and the rue d'Auseil were, at the very least, sympathetic entities, a district unto themselves—and when he disappeared into the blackness he seems to have taken the street, which was as old and misshapen as he, along with him.

In the blackness is the secret core of the primary supernatural phenomenon of the story, whereas Zann's music may be viewed as an ancillary phenomenon, a more credible and tangible quality that allows one to grasp, however tenuously, the utterly mysterious. And in the blackness the mystery must remain, nameless and unknown, leaving only the memory of a certain haunting music to suggest, as subtly as possible, its meaning. It is the abstract, elusive form of supernatural horror in this story that may account for its enduring enchantment for certain readers.

"The Music of Erich Zann" was Lovecraft's early, almost premature expression of his ideal as a writer: the use of maximum suggestion and minimal explanation to evoke a sense of supernatural terrors and wonders. It is also among those of his stories that bear the greatest resemblance to the masterpieces Lovecraft most admired and held as touchstones for excellence in the realm of the weird: Blackwood's "The Willows," Machen's "The White People," Poe's "Fall of the House of Usher." Like those tales, "The Music of Erich Zann" ultimately withholds its secrets and preserves its mystery; narrative gives a peculiar shape to perennial enigmas, creating a new landscape at the center of which is the same ancient abyss (and outside of which is the void). Later, in "The Colour Out of Space," Lovecraft fashioned a visual counterpart to the aural mysteries of "The Music of Erich Zann," a pernicious and inexplicable entity that arrives from the black well of the cosmos to blacken the life of our earth. No surprise that Lovecraft conjoined these two tales as his best, setting them apart from those of the famous Cthulhu Mythos which, by contrast, seem to fall into the category of "explained" supernatural fiction after the manner of Ann Radcliffe. In the earlier story, as much as the later one, that secret voice beneath the narrative speaks strongly and stridently, imparting its meaning through feelings rather than facts, singing a song without words on the theme of the nameless horror and strangeness of the universe, that cosmic neighborhood where everything that is, is terrifyingly wrong . . . and at the same time alluring, a place of charming evil.

"The Music of Erich Zann" seems to say: stay away from the rue d'Auseil. In actuality, however, it invites us to make our home there, haunts us, as the narrator of the story is haunted, and inspires us to find again something that was lost, to seek out that blackness and play to it at our peril . . . without ever knowing why. This is a familiar experience for those "sensitive few" whose responses form the foundation of Lovecraft's aesthetic of supernatural horror, illuminating this ordeal which is indulged in for its own sake by aesthetes of the unknown. Jorge Luis Borges has written: "Music, states of happiness, mythology, faces molded by time, certain twilights and certain places—all these are trying to tell us something; that imminence of a revelation that is not yet produced is, perhaps, the aesthetic reality."

The above quotation cannot fail to remind us of so many statements made by Lovecraft concerning those sensations which, as he asserted, alone made his existence endurable. Among such declarations is the following:

> Sometimes I stumble accidentally on rare combinations of slope, curved street-line, roofs & gables & chimneys, & accessory details of verdure & background, which in the magic of late afternoon assume a mystic majesty & exotic significance beyond the power of words to describe . . . All that to capture some fragment of this hidden & unreachable beauty; this beauty which is all of dream, yet which I have known closely & reveled in through long aeons before my birth or the birth of this or of any other world.

In "The Music of Erich Zann," Lovecraft captured at least a fragment of the desired object and delivered it to his readers. Like Erich Zann's "world of beauty," Lovecraft's "lay in some far cosmos of the imagination," and like that of another artist, it is a "beauty that hath horror in it." ✳

In the Rue d'Auseil

by Fred Chappell

We recognize that one characteristic of the genius of Thomas Alva Edison was his willingness to turn customary conceptions on their heads. Before him all attempts to make music by means of machinery had imitated the performance of instruments; there were player pianos, mechanical violins, clockwork drums and harps by the thousands. Soulless, their operations produced in their audiences only melancholy depression or embarrassed amusement or listless boredom. Edison—poor, deaf man!—undertook to imitate the act of listening, the operations of the ear, with his paper membranes and grains of carbon. His results are omnipresent.

But my own interest has clung to the earlier efforts, to the methods that most people now would name irrelevant. I suppose it is quite the grandest thing to flip a switch and hear a recording of Rubenstein rendering Brahms or Isaac Stern undertaking a Sibelius or Stravinsky conducting his own jagged scores. Recordings can give some little impression of the sound and even a hint of the excitement of live performances, though much is lacking and will be lacking always. Yet for me not enough is lacking. The peculiar spiritless performances of the music made by automata are exactly what I seek.

I am the composer Tether; that is the single name with which I sign my works. My choice of *nom de musique* is a matter of self-protection as well as of self-advertisement, for wealthy persons are at risk in contemporary society, and as long as there are mineral springs in Haddon, Arkansas, I shall pursue my admittedly eccentric and expensive interests without hindrance.

I have not written music for live performers for fifteen years. For me the sight of flesh-and-blood men and women whipping away at violins and cellos or torturing drumheads or puffing brass till they grow cross-eyed is irresistibly risible. I prefer the dignity of the figure animated by gears and levers to the untidiness, to the unavoidable ugliness, of spit valves and sweaty handkerchiefs.

My interest at first was in composing for these mechanical figures, a number of which I ordered to be constructed according to my own designs. It was easy enough to find engineers who could build plausible mannikins fingering special pianos and bowing real violins. For a quartet of these all-too-lifelike automata I wrote a suite of four piano quartets called *Esprit autonome.* I composed likewise for flute, double bass, tuba, tympani, and cello—all lifesize robot figures playing actual instruments.

Yet I remained dissatisfied. Robotics has advanced too far as a science and these machines were almost as arbitrary in their execution as human performers would be. It would be easy to design them to play more mechanically, less musician-like—but to what point? You may take a sophisticated robot and deck it out as an old-fashioned mechanical doll, just as you may build a contemporary automobile to look like a T-model Ford, but the falsity of the idea makes the enterprise a silly one.

And so, collecting the ancient automata became my dominant interest. Perhaps I should amend my statement, for I am still driven by an ambition to compose, but I want my work to be played by those older contraptions, the justly famous toys of earlier centuries.

You will readily conceive how expensive this fancy might prove to be. Even I, for whom money is so plentiful, could hardly afford to acquire the most celebrated mechanisms, even if they had been available for purchase. Most of the best of them are owned by state or municipal museums which are legally bound to keep them. I must say, however, that often these lovely machines are not well kept, allowed to rust and stiffen in their workings, their rich finishes dimming, flaking, and cracking because they have so few friends, even among curators and amateurs.

I have managed, however, to purchase several treasures. The first I acquired was a miniature Schubert at the piano, playing the first bars of his "Wanderer" fantasy; this was of Genevan origin, I believe, but the date is uncertain, and—to be truthful—I bought it only as a tentative first step. Putting my toe in the water so to speak; flirting with my destiny . . . I am much prouder of my tambour player by Vaucason, ca. 1780. Originally part of a group that included a flautist and (inexplicably) a duck, the figure stands three-quarters life-size and has required little restoration. My best piece by all measure is a full-size cellist by Jacquet-Droz once exhibited at the court of Louis XVI. There is a well-known nineteenth-century lithograph of this event and there can be no doubt that mine is the genuine article. I am not at liberty to say how it came into my possession and it would be tedious to give an account of the extensive repairs the figure required. But now it looks as unsullied, and performs as perfectly, as the day it emerged from the Droz workshop.

You can imagine how hard such prizes are to come by, and this fact brings us to the matter at hand. My research is painstaking and unending. I pore over the books, the pamphlets and broadside announcements, the catalogs and footnotes, in search of automata the museums and libraries and other collectors have overlooked. When I first read of the group, a piano quintet, created by the Roget frères workshop in 1762, I knew immediately that no museum owned any one of the five pieces. I knew too that they were still in existence, for "Rogets" are treasures avidly sought, and I suspected that the group had been broken up, the violins, the viola, the cello and piano all swept into separate fates. Upon these figures I set my sights.

Even though I could find no pictures, I knew what the figures would look like: all in eighteenth-century dress with the violins in the guise of twin brothers, rather delicate of feature, the viola an older man with strong hands and a prominent jaw. The pianist would be a ravishing woman in silver wig, closely similar to Jacquet-Droz's "La musicienne," which had established the tradition for such figures. The cellist, however, I could not imagine. I ransacked my memory and exercised my fancy to the utmost, but the features and even the form remained imageless.

Yet I knew I would recognize it when I saw it.

* * *

—And now I have seen it and recognized it and to acquire it means the accomplishment of a project whose implications had remained hidden even to myself.

The pianist I purchased first; she still resides in Tokyo. The others are in Basel, London, and Hyderabad. The cellist is—in transit. The tracing of each of them was a separate epic in historical detection and their acquisition would require a financial chronicle of Balzacian amplitude. Yet by resolving one rumor at a time, by sniffing out clue after clue, pursuing wisps of hints, and then by pouring money into my search as if I were trying to displace with it all the water in the Atlantic Ocean, I gathered under my ownership four of the quintet. The cellist eluded me like a wily prey that hears the hounds.

Then, as so often happens in these cases, an accident set me upon the track. I spotted an advertisement in the April 1893 issue of *La Revue Blanche.* It pictured the establishment of a piano retailer, but the photograph also included part of a neighboring storefront in which sat a decrepit-looking figure with a cello cradled between its knees. The posture of the figure drew my attention: it was human but not truly human; it seemed not inanimate but like an animate figure from which all the energy had been drained. The facial features were too small to discern even with a magnifying glass, but already I suspected something.

The address of the piano shop was given as 24 rue d'Auseil and this address sounded a strong echo in my head. In only a moment I remembered that street as the address given by H. P. Lovecraft in his story, "The Music of Erich Zann." I had always taken this address to be fictional, for though we now know (thanks to the assiduous researches of S. T. Joshi and Robert M. Price) that the great horror writer was working from materials found in an actual diary that fell into his possession, the story declares that the locale had disappeared.

You will recall Lovecraft's narrative: an unnamed narrator, a philosophy student, takes a room in a house in the rue d'Auseil kept by the paralytic landlord Blandot. In his room on the fifth floor he hears very strange music being played in the garret above and discovers the source to be an impoverished foreign cellist named Erich Zann. He strikes up an acquaintance and, after some preliminary difficulties, persuades the old musician to play some of this music in his presence. Reluctantly Zann does so, but his performance is interrupted by sounds from outside the garret window. More frenziedly the fellow plays, as if defending himself and his visitor from an onslaught of unknown horror from outside. Then the window is broken, fierce wind extinguishes the candles and discomposes the room, and Zann plays more wildly than ever. When the narrator rushes to the window he finds that the city has disappeared from view; the scene outside has become "the blackness of space illimitable; unimagined space alive with motion and music." He feels, he thinks, another Presence in the room and blunders into the bow of Zann, still working crazily upon his instrument. He discovers then that Zann is dead, "ice-cold, stiffened, unbreathing," yet still playing. . . . The story ends abruptly as the narrator flees in hysterics.

One of the most puzzling details in the affair is the name of the street. "Rue d'Auseil" was no Lovecraftian invention; the name does not occur in the diary that suggested the story, but I had spotted it in the advertisement. Yet there is no rue d'Auseil in present time and none listed in the old directories or found upon the maps. My discovery of the street name in the periodical advertisement was the first confirmation that such a place had actually existed.

The next step was for me a simple one. I turned my datum over to my assistant, Janice Renfroe, one of those thoroughly contemporary young women who know computers intimately and love nothing better than the use of them to pry information from old records, public and private.

In a mere two weeks she was proud to inform me that the rue d'Auseil did indeed exist, but under a different denomination. "It is still there," she said, smiling, her blue eyes twinkling as they always did when she had proved some triumph of her machines. "Only now it is under its true name. It is actually the rue d'Oseille. In English we'd call it Sorrel Street. For a period of months it was misnamed. The city was replacing its street signs and somehow the name was misheard or mispronounced and the error resulted. Then it was rectified, and the maps don't record the temporary mistake. What else do we need to know?"

"Immensities," I replied. "But now we know how to begin. The first step was the most difficult."

Having located the street, we set to work, tracing down business records, finding heirs and descendants, locating invoices and bills of lading, inspecting warehouses, storehouses, sheds and hovels.

Our excruciating efforts were successful. Three weeks ago I flew across the ocean to encounter the thing that had been—and still is— Erich Zann.

There in the farthest corner of the webbiest sub-basement of a disused clock factory in the rue d'Oseille I found the figure of Zann to be unmistakably close to Lovecraft's description: "blue eyes, grotesque, satyr-like face, and nearly bald head." Now, one hundred years later, his "glassy eyes bulged uselessly into the void"—as they will forever. But his appearance differs in some important aspects. He has been dressed up in an eighteenth-century costume—knee breeches, buckle shoes, lace cuffs—that is falling to mildewed ruin. And his face and hands have been painted and lacquered— at some point someone attempted to pass him off as an automaton musician, an achievement of the Roget frères, perhaps their finest, though unfinished in regard to the music it should play. The original mechanical cellist had been lost or destroyed and some entrepreneur of vicious disposition had substituted Erich Zann. The old man whose music served as a passageway to illimitable space and unimaginable modes of existence had been transformed by the power of those Presences to an eerie mummy of adamant which only that particular music can animate.

And that is the music I design to hear.

* * *

I have arranged a concert of my own compositions. The first of these, for my mechanical pianist, violins, and viola, is quite tame in conception, keeping close to eighteenth-century models. By stages, however, the pieces become more radical and at last are truly demonic. I can hear in my head the music that Zann played alone in his garret and I shall reproduce it, with wilder and wilder variations, until the Presences are summoned to the salon of my Los Angeles apartment where my petite soirée is to be held. Then Erich Zann will be brought forth and the apartment doors locked from outside. The Presences will possess Erich Zann once again, that once-human automaton will play the mocking music of the Presences, the unmeasured lines and sardonic harmonies that cause the first hysteria Lovecraft's poor scholar suffered and then the oblivion of irreparable insanity.

My highly select audience will at first struggle against that oblivion but at last embrace it as a refuge from the music of Erich Zann. We shall find insanity a relief—myself, the coolly beautiful Neal Lamson, and Bruno Starker, the stupid blond rough beast with whom Neal betrayed me, for whom he abandoned me. ✳

The Plain of Sound

by J. Ramsey Campbell

Verily do we know little of the other universes beyond the gate
which YOG-SOTHOTH guards. Of those which come through
the gate and make their habitation in this world none can tell;
although Ibn Schacabao tells of the beings which crawl from the
Gulf of S'glhuo that they may be known by their sound. In that
Gulf the very worlds are of sound, and matter is known but as an
odor; and the notes of our pipes in this world may create beauty or
bring forth abominations in S'glhuo. For the barrier between haply
grows thin, and when sourceless sounds occur we may justly look
to the denizens of S'glhuo. They can do little harm to those of
Earth, and fear only that shape which a certain sound may form in
their universe.

—Abdul Alhazred, *The Necronomicon*

When Frank Nuttall, Tony Roles and I reached the inn at Severnford,
we found that it was closed.

It was the summer of 1958, and as we had nothing particular to do at
Brichester University that day we had decided to go out walking. I had suggested a trip to Goatswood—the legends there interested me—but Tony
had heard things which made him dislike the town. Then Frank had told us
about an advertisement in the *Brichester Weekly News* about a year back
which had referred to an inn at the center of Severnford as "one of the oldest in England." We could walk there in the morning and quench the thirst
caused by the journey; afterward we could take the bus back to Brichester
if we did not feel like walking.

Tony was not enthusiastic. "Why go all that way to get drunk," he
inquired, "even if it is so old? Besides, that ad in the paper's old too—by now
the place has probably fallen down. . . ." However, Frank and I wanted to try
it, and finally we overruled his protests.

We would have done better to agree with him, for we found the inn's
doors and windows boarded up and a nearby sign saying: "Temporarily
closed to the public." The only course was to visit the modern public house
up the street. We looked round the town a little; this did not occupy us
long, for Severnford has few places of interest, most of it being dockland.

Before two o'clock we were searching for a bus-stop; when it eluded us, we entered a newsagent's for directions.

"Bus t' Brichester? No, only in the mornin'," the proprietor told us. "Up from the university, are you?"

"Then how do we get back?" Tony asked.

"Walk, I s'pose," suggested the newsagent. "Why'd you come up, anyway—oh, t' look at the inn? No, you won't get in there now—so many o' them bloody teenagers've been breakin' the winders an' such that council says it'll only open t' people with special permission. Good job, too—though I'm not sayin' as it's kids like you as does it. Still, you'll be wantin' t' get back t' Brichester an' I know the shortest way."

He began to give us complicated directions, which he repeated in detail. When we still looked uncertain he waited while Frank got out notebook and pencil and took down the route. At the end of this I was not yet sure which way to go, but, as I remarked: "If we get lost, we can always ask."

"Oh, no," protested our informant. "You won't go wrong if you follow that."

"Right, thanks," Frank said. "And I suppose there will be passers-by to ask if we *do* go wrong?"

"I wouldn't." The newsagent turned to rearrange papers in the rack. "You might ask the wrong people."

Hearing no more from him, we went out into the street and turned right toward Brichester. Once one leaves behind the central area of Severnford where a group of archaic buildings is preserved, and comes to the surrounding red-brick houses, there is little to interest the sight-seer. Much of Severnford is dock-land, and even the country beyond is not noticeably pleasant to the forced hiker. Besides, some of the roads are noticeably rough, though that may have been because we took the wrong turn—for, an hour out of Severnford, we realized we were lost.

"Turn left at the signpost about a mile out, it says here," said Frank. "But we've come more than a mile already—where's the signpost?"

"So what do we do—go back and ask?" Tony suggested.

"Too far for that. Look," Frank asked me, "have you got that compass you're always carrying, Les? Brichester is almost southeast of Severnford—if we keep on that direction, we won't go far wrong."

The road we had been following ran east-west. Now, when we turned off into open country, we could rely only on my compass, and we soon found that we needed it. Once, when ascending a slope, we had to detour round a thickly overgrown forest, where we would certainly have become further lost. After that we crossed monotonous fields, never seeing a building or another human being. Two and a half hours out of Severnford, we reached an area of grassy hillocks, and from there descended into and clambered out of miniature valleys. About half-a-mile into this region, Tony signaled us to keep quiet.

"All I can hear is the stream," said Frank. "Am I supposed to hear something important? You hear anything, Les?"

The rushing stream we had just crossed effectively drowned most distant sounds, but I thought I heard a nearby mechanical whirring. It rose and fell like the sound of a moving vehicle, but with the loudly splashing water I could distinguish no details.

"I'm not sure," I answered. "There's something that could be a tractor, I think—"

"That's what I thought," agreed Tony. "It's ahead somewhere—maybe the driver can direct us. If, of course, he's not one of that newsagent's wrong people!"

The mechanical throbbing loudened as we crossed two hills and came onto a strip of level ground fronting a long, low ridge. I was the first to reach the ridge, climb it and stand atop it. As my head rose above the ridge, I threw myself back.

On the other side lay a roughly square plain, surrounded by four ridges. The plain was about four hundred yards square, and at the opposite side was a one-story building. Apart from this the plain was totally bare, and that was what startled me most: for from that bare stretch of land rose a deafening flood of sound. Here was the source of that mechanical whirring; it throbbed overpoweringly upward, incessantly fluctuating through three notes. Behind it were other sounds; a faint bass humming which hovered on the edge of audibility, and others—whistlings and high-pitched twangs— which sometimes were inaudible and sometimes as loud as the whirring.

By now Tony and Frank were beside me, staring down.

"Surely it can't be coming from that hut?" Frank said. "It's no tractor, that's certain, and a hut that size could never contain anything that'd make that row."

"I thought it was coming from underground somewhere," suggested Tony. "Mining operations, maybe."

"Whatever it is, there's that hut," I said. "We can ask the way down there."

Tony looked down doubtfully. "I don't know—it might be dangerous. You know driving over subsidence can be dangerous, and how do we know they're not working on something like that here?"

"There'd be signs if they were," I reassured him. "No, come on—there may be nowhere else we can ask, and there's no use keeping on in the wrong direction."

We descended the ridge and walked perhaps twenty yards across the plain.

It was like walking into a tidal wave. The sound was suddenly all around us; the more overpowering because it beat on us from all sides. We could not fight back—like being engulfed in jelly. I could not have stood it for long—I put my hands over my ears and yelled, "Run!" And I staggered across the plain, the sound which I could not shut out booming at me, until I reached the building on the other side.

It was a brown stone house, not a hut as we had thought. It had an arched doorway in the wall facing us, bordered by two low windows without curtains. From what we could see the room on the left was a living room, that on the right a bedroom, but grime on the windows prevented us from seeing more, except that the rooms were unoccupied. We did not think to look at any windows at the back. The door had no bell or knocker, but Frank pounded on a panel.

There was no answer, and he knocked harder. On the second knock the door swung inward, revealing that it opened into the living room. Frank looked in and called: "Anybody at home?" Still nobody answered, and he turned back to us.

"Do you think we'd better go in?" he asked. "Maybe we could wait for the owner, or there might be something in the house that'd direct us."

Tony pushed past me to look. "Hey, what—Frank, do you notice anything here? Something tells me that whoever the owner is, he isn't house-proud."

We could see what he meant. There were wooden chairs, a table, bookcases, a ragged carpet—and all thick with dust. We hesitated a minute, waiting for someone to make a decision; then Frank entered. He stopped inside the door and pointed. Looking over his shoulder, we could see there were no footprints anywhere in the dust.

We looked round for some explanation. While Frank closed the door and cut off the throbbing from outside, Tony—our bibliophile—crossed to the bookcases and looked at the spines. I noticed a newspaper on the table and idly picked it up.

"The owner must be a bit peculiar . . . *La Strega,* by Pico della Mirandola," Tony read, "—*Discovery of Witches*—*The Red Dragon*—hey, *Revelations of Glaaki*; isn't that the book the university can't get for their restricted section? Here's a diary, big one, too, but I hadn't better touch that."

When I turned to the front page of the newspaper, I saw it was *The Camside Observer.* As I looked closer, I saw something which made me call the others. "Look at this—December 8, 1930! You're right about this man being peculiar—what sort of person keeps a newspaper for twenty-eight years?"

"I'm going to look in the bedroom," Frank declared. He knocked on the door off the living room, and, when we came up beside him, opened it. The room was almost bare: a wardrobe, a hanging wall-mirror, and a bed were the only furnishings. The bed, as we had expected, was empty; but the mark of a sleeping body was clearly defined, though filled with dust. We moved closer, noting the absence of footprints on the floor; and bending over the bed, I thought I saw something besides dust in the hollows left by the sleeper—something like ground glass, sparkling greenly.

"What's happened?" Tony asked in a rather frightened tone.

"Oh, probably nothing out of the ordinary," said Frank. "Maybe there's another entrance round the back—maybe he can't stand all that noise, whatever it is, and has a bedroom on the other side. Look, there's a door in that wall; that may be it."

I went across and opened it, but only a very primitive lavatory lay beyond.

"Wait a minute, I think there was a door next to the bookcase," recollected Tony. He returned to the living room and opened the door he had noticed. As we followed him, he exclaimed: "My God—*now* what?"

The fourth room was longer than any of the others, but it was the contents that had drawn Tony's exclamation. Nearest us on the bare floor was something like a television screen, about two feet across, with a blue-glass light bulb behind it, strangely distorted and with thick wires attached. Next to it, another pair of wires led from a megaphone-shaped receiver. In between the opposite wall and these instruments lay a strange arrangement of crystals, induction coils and tubes, from which wires hung at each end for possible attachment to the other appliances. The far corner of the ceiling had recently collapsed, allowing rain to drip onto a sounding-board carrying a dozen strings, a large lever and a motor connected by cogs to a plectrum-covered cylinder. Out of curiosity I crossed and plucked a string; but such a discord trembled through the board that I quickly muffled it.

"Something *very* funny is going on here," Frank said. "There's no other room, so where can he sleep? And the dust, and the newspaper?—and now these things—I've never seen anything like them."

"Why don't we look at his diary?" suggested Tony. "It doesn't look like he'll be back, and I for one want to know what's happened here."

So we went back to the living room and Tony took down the heavy volume. He opened it to its last entry: December 8, 1930. "If we all try and read it, it'll take three times as long," he said. "You two sit down and I'll try and read you the relevant bits." He was then silent for a few minutes, then:

"Professor Arnold Hird, ex-Brichester University: never heard of him—must've been before our time . . . ah, here we are."

"'January 3, 1930: Today moved into a new house (if it can be called a house!). Noises are queer—suppose it's only because there's so much superstition about them that nobody's investigated before. Intend to make full study—meteorological conditions, &c; feel that winds blowing over ridges may vibrate and cause sounds. Tomorrow to look round, take measurements, find out if anything will interrupt sounds. Peculiar that sound seems to be deafening in certain radius, relatively faint beyond— no gradual fading.

"'January 4: Sleep uneasy last night—unaccustomed dreams. City on great mountain—angled streets, spiraling pillars and cones. Strange inhabitants; taller than human, scaly skin, boneless fingers, yet somehow not repulsive. Were aware of me, in fact seemed to await my arrival, but each time one approached me I awoke. Repeated several times.

"'Progress negative. Screens on top of ridges did not interrupt sound; undiminished though little wind. Measurements—northwest ridge 423 yards . . .' Well, there's a lot more like that."

"Make sure you don't miss anything important," Frank said as Tony turned pages.

"'January 6: Dreams again. Same city, figures as though waiting. Leader approached. Seemed to be communicating with me telepathically: I caught the thought—*do not be afraid; we are the sounds.* Whole scene then faded.

"'No progress whatever. Unable to concentrate on findings; dreams distracting.

"'January 7: Insane perhaps, but am off to British Museum tomorrow. In last night's dream was told: *Check Necronomicon—formula for aiding us to reach you.* Page reference given. Expect & hope this will be false alarm— dreams taking altogether too much out of me. But what if something on that page? Am not interested in that field—impossible to know in normal way. . . .

"'January 9: Back from London. Mao Rite—on page I looked up— exactly as described in dream! Don't know what it will do, but will perform it tonight to find out. Strange, no dreams while away—some influence existing only here?

"'January 10: Didn't wake till late afternoon. Dreams began as soon as sleep after rite. Don't know what to think. Alternatives both disturbing: either brain receiving transmissions, or subconsciously everything— but wd. sane mind act thus?

"'If true that transmissions external, learned following:

"'Sounds in this area *are equivalents of matter in another dimension.* Said dimension overlaps ours at this point and certain others. City and inhabitants in dream do not appear as in own sphere, but as wd. appear if consisting of matter. Different sounds here correspond to various objects in other dimension; whirring equals pillars & cones, bass throbbing is ground, other varying sounds are people of city & other moving objects. Matter on our side they sense as odors.

"'The inhabitants can transmit whole concepts mentally. Leader asked me to try not to make sounds in radius of point of connection. Carried over to their dimension. My footsteps—huge crystals appeared on streets of city. My breathing—something living which they refused to show me. Had to be killed at once.

"'Inhabitants interested in communication with our dimension. Not dream-transmission—frequent use of Mao Rite is dangerous. *Translator* to be built on this side—enables sound to be translated into visual terms on screen, as in dream, but little else. When they build counterpart, link will be effected—complete passage between dimensions. Unfortunately, their translator completely different from ours & not yet successful. Leader told me: *Look in* The Revelations of Glaaki *for the plans*. Also gave me page reference & said where to get copy.

"'Must get copy. If no plan, all coincidence & can return to normal research. If plan, can build machine, claim discovery of other dimension!'"

"I've been thinking," I interrupted. "Arnold Hird—there was something—wasn't he asked to leave the university because he attacked someone when they disagreed with him? Said he'd return and astonish everybody some day, but was never heard of again."

"I don't know," said Tony. "Anyway, he continues:

"'January 12: Got *Revelations of Glaaki*. Had to take drastic measures to obtain it, too. Plan here—book 9, pp. 2057-9. Will take some time to build, but worth it. To think that besides me, only superstitious know of this—but will soon be able to prove it!'

"Hmm—well, there don't seem to be any very interesting entries after that. Just 'not much progress today' or 'screen arrangement completed' or here 'down to Severnford today—had to order strings at a musical shop. Don't like idea of using it, but must keep it handy in case.'"

"So that's it," Frank said, standing up. "The man was a lunatic, and we've been sitting here listening to his ravings. No wonder he was kicked out of the university."

"I don't think so," I disagreed. "It seems far too complex—"

"Wait a minute, here's another entry," called Tony. "'—December 7.'" Frank gave him a protesting look, but sat down again.

"'December 7: Got through. Image faint, but contact sufficient—beings aware. Showed me unfinished translator on their side—may take some time before completion. Few more days to perfect image, then will publicize.

"'December 8: Must be sure about weapon I have constructed. *Revelations* give reason for use, but way of death is horrible. If unnecessary, definitely will destroy. Tonight will find out—will call Alala.'"

"Well, Frank?" I asked as Tony replaced the diary and began to search the shelves. "Crazy, maybe—but there are those sounds—and he called

something horrible that night where the diary ends—and there's that peculiar stuff all over the bed—"

"But how will we know either way?" Tony asked, removing a book.

"Set up all that paraphernalia, obviously, and see what comes through
on that screen."

"I don't know," Tony said. "I want to look in *The Revelations of
Glaaki*—that's what I've got here—but as for trying it ourselves, I think
that's going a bit far. You'll notice how careful he was about it, and something happened to him."

"Come on, let's look at the book," interrupted Frank. "That can't do
any harm."

Tony finally opened it and placed it on the table. On the page we examined diagrams, and learned that "the screen is attached to the central portion and viewed, while the receiver is directed toward the sounds before
attachment." No power was necessary, for "the very sounds in their passing
manipulate the instrument." The diagrams were crude but intelligible, and
both Frank and I were ready to experiment. But Tony pointed to a passage
at the end of the section:

"'The intentions of the inhabitants of S'glhuo are uncertain. Those
who use the translator would be wise to keep by them the stringed sounding board, the only earthly weapon to touch S'glhuo. For when they build
the translator to complete the connexion, who knows what they may bring
through with them? They are adept at concealing their intentions in
dream-communication, and the sounding-board should be used at the first
hostile action.'

"You see?" Tony said triumphantly. "These things are unfriendly—the
book says so!"

"Oh, no it doesn't," contradicted Frank, "and anyway, it's a load of
balls—living sounds, hah! But just suppose it *was* true—if we got through,
we could claim the discovery—after all, the book says you're safe with this
'weapon.' And there's no rush back to the university."

Arguments ensued, but finally we opened the doors and dragged the
instruments outside. I returned for the sounding-board, noticing how rusted
it was, and Tony brought the volume of the *Revelations*. We stood at the edge
of the area of sound and placed the receiver about midway. The screen was
connected to the central section, and at last we clipped the wires from the
screen to the rest.

For a minute nothing happened. The screen stayed blank; the coils and
wires did not respond. Tony looked at the sounding-board. The vibrations had
taken on a somehow expectant quality, as if aware of our experiment. And then
the blue light bulb flickered, and an image slowly formed on the screen.

It was a landscape of a dream. In the background, great glaciers and crystal mountains sparkled, while at their peaks enormous stone buildings stretched up into mist. There were translucent shapes flitting about those buildings. But the foreground was most noticeable—the slanting streets and twisted pillar-supported cones which formed a city on one of the icy mountains. We could see no life in the city brooding on a sourceless blue light; only a great machine of tubes and crystals which stood before us on the street.

When a figure rose into the screen we recoiled. I felt a chill of terror, for this was one of the city's inhabitants—and it was not human. It was too thin and tall, with huge pupilless eyes and a skin covered with tiny rippling blue scales. The fingers were boneless, and I felt a surge of revulsion as the white eyes stared unaware in my direction. But I somehow felt that this was an intelligent being, and not definitely hostile.

The being took out of its metallic robe a thin rod, which it held vertically and stroked several times. Whatever the principle, this must have been a summons, for in a few minutes a crowd had formed about the instrument in the street. What followed may only have been their method of communication, but I found it horrible; they stood in a circle, and their fingers stretched fully two feet to interlace in the center. They dispersed after a short time and spread out, a small group remaining by the machine.

"Look at that thing in the street," said Tony. "Do you suppose—"

"Not now," Frank, who was watching in fascination, interrupted. "I don't know if it'd be better to switch off now and get someone down from the university—no, hell, let's watch a bit longer. To think that we're watching another world!"

The group around the machine were turning it, and at that moment, a set of three tubes came into view, pointing straight at us. One of the beings went to a switchboard and clutched a lever with long twining fingers. Tony began to speak, but simultaneously I realized what he was thinking.

"Frank," I shouted, "that's their translator! They're going to make the connexion!"

"Do you think I'd better switch off, then?"

"But suppose that's not enough?" yelled Tony. "Do you want them to come through without knowing what they'll do? You read the book—for God's sake, use the weapon before it's too late!"

His hysteria affected us all. Frank ran to the sounding-board and grabbed the lever. I watched the being on the screen adjusting his machine, and saw that it was nearly ready to complete the connexion.

"Why aren't you doing anything?" Tony screamed at Frank.

He called back: "The lever won't move! Must be rust in the works—quick, Les, see if you can get them unstuck!"

I ran over and began to scrape at the gears with a knife. Accidentally the blade slipped and twanged across the strings.

"There's something forming, I can't quite see," Tony said—

Frank was straining so hard at the lever that I was afraid it would snap—then it jerked free, the gears moved, the plectrum cylinder spun and an atrocious sound came from the strings. It was a scraping, whining discord which clawed at our ears; it blotted out those other sounds, and I could not have stood it for long.

Then Tony screamed. We whirled to see him kick in the screen and stamp ferociously on the wires, still shrieking. Frank shouted at him—and as he turned we saw the slackness of his mouth and the saliva drooling down his chin.

We finally locked him in the back room of the house while we found our way back to Brichester. We told the doctors only that he had become separated from us, and that by the time we found him everything was as they saw it. When they removed Tony from the house Frank took the opportunity to tear a few pages out of *The Revelations of Glaaki*. Perhaps because of this, the team of Brichester professors and others studying conditions there are making little progress. Frank and I will never go there again; the events of that afternoon have left too deep a mark.

Of course, they affected Tony far more. He is completely insane, and the doctors foresee no recovery. At his worst he is totally incoherent, and attacks anyone who cannot satisfactorily explain every sound he hears. He gives no indication in his coherent periods of what drove him mad. He imagines he saw something more on that screen, but never describes what he saw.

Occasionally he refers to the object he thinks he saw. Over the years he has mentioned details which would suggest something incredibly alien, but of course it must have been something else which unbalanced him. He speaks of "the snailhorns," "the blue crystalline lenses," "the mobility of the faces," "the living flame and water," "the bell-shaped appendages," and "the common head of many bodies."

But these periods of comparative coherency do not last long. Usually they end when a look of horror spreads over his face, he stiffens and screams something which he has not yet explained:

"I saw what it took from its victims! *I saw what it took from its victims!*" ✳

The Last Show at Verdi's Supper Club

by Stephen Mark Rainey

H elen looked positively glamorous as she made her entrance that night at Verdi's. I saw her eyes, wide beneath the long black lashes, searching the restaurant for a sign of her friends. When her glance fell briefly upon me, she smiled and gave me a small wave. She was wearing a sleek, black satin gown, her dark hair neatly stacked, ramrod-straight; in her high heels, she truly stood out above the crowd. She began gliding toward the far corner of the room, having caught sight of Dean or Suzie, her head barely bobbing with each elegant step.

The thing in my head moved suddenly, and I jerked upright in an involuntary spasm. The episode passed quickly, and the chills that accompanied it faded away rapidly. But I knew then that this was to be my final show.

Helen was moving to Washington, D.C., and this, her farewell celebration, had brought the whole crowd out from under their rocks. The theme was 1940s, and appropriate fashion was required for admittance; Helen's idea, and I loved it. I'd decked myself out in a dark gray pinstripe suit, with a black shirt and white tie, topped by a gray, feather-brimmed fedora. There was no tommy gun in my guitar case, though—merely the instrument. It rested beside me on the stage, waiting for me to begin the first set, which I dared not delay much longer.

Off to the right, I saw them all sitting at the long table they'd reserved: Dean, Bob, Scott, Suzie, Anna Lee, Mike, Cathy, and a few people I didn't know, all resplendent in their antique finest. Helen, the star of the evening, sat at the head of the table, surrounded by her court. Glasses were raised, cheers voiced, beer and liquor downed with exuberance. Helen remembered me on stage, and lifted her glass toward me, though I doubted she could actually see me beneath the darkened stage lights.

Verdi's was frequented almost exclusively by the senior set. The Glenn Miller Ensemble had dibs on the stage four nights a week; the Lake Geneva Swing Brigade owned Fridays, playing the Dorseys and Duke Ellington with unabashed, sloppy abandon. Saturdays, though, were for me: solo, with guitar, giving the house the pure melancholia of American and European folk. No contemporary stuff here. Verdi's roots lay deep in the past, and even the occasional Elvis tune the Brigade covered seemed a rude intrusion of modern times, hideously translated as it was by sax, trumpet and trombone.

I took a long swallow of beer, took my guitar from the case, and gave the steel strings a tentative strum. She was tuned impeccably, a veteran performer to this crowd and many others over innumerable years. The chatter from the audience stuttered as several pairs of eyes glanced my way, expectantly, waiting for the spotlights to come up and the music to begin.

Agee, my sound man, gave me a thumbs up from his hidden corner at the back of the room. I heard the hollowness of the speakers activated, then rolled my pick over the strings, playing a lush C chord. The beer had wet my lips and throat, and drawing up a breath, I invoked the musical spirits.

> "Hey, look—yonder up in the sky.
> Hey there, look—yonder up in the sky.
> Buzzards circlin' around my head
> Must know I'm bound to die.
> Take my hammer, carry it to the cap'n. . . ."

I didn't have to think about playing or singing; the words flowed from the background of my consciousness. My thoughts were mortal tonight, and directed toward my friends in the audience. To bid them farewell would be hard, yet I had no choice. I could not say they were family; I hadn't had one in my living memory and thus had no understanding of the concept. Yet I liked most of them. Some of them I even loved, like Helen, and Dean, and Mike and Cathy. I'd known them the longest, and shared a lot of life with them. Then there was Anna Lee, whose soul was paper thin, her every motivation purely selfish. Yet even she was innocent in her own way, and I'd miss her.

Their eyes were on me, most shining with appreciation, many already glazed from alcohol. They were by and large a sincere crowd, satisfied by life's simple things. But in recent years, cynicism had begun its inevitable creep as the world became a heavier burden, and too often their graciousness seemed forced. These nights at Verdi's were medicine, rejoining them with the simplicity of their youth, a thing not long gone; the oldest of them all, Mike, was thirty-six.

A young man that I'd never met before was sitting next to Helen. My voice had become a thing of its own; I didn't need to listen to it. I listened to what the room had to say.

They were passing a piece of cake.

"Would somebody eat this?" Helen asked, her voice low and delicate. "I don't want it."

A round of small laughs, a few polite refusals. Dean and Suzie each took a forkful as the piece came their way. It finally settled in front of the young man next to Helen. "Yes, I'll take it," he said, glancing at her as if seeking approval.

"It's good," she said. "But I'm not hungry."

In the distance, I heard my voice.

> "Dig my grave with a golden shovel
> In that land, Great God, where I'm bound.
> Lay me down, so slow and easy,
> Ball and chain there by my side."

The young man looked almost guiltily at the cake before scooping up a piece with his fork. When he took the bite, chewed and swallowed it, I saw his face glow with momentary delight. I felt a sudden, unexpected pang of heartfelt sorrow, seeing such joy result from this tiny, human act. Tears began forming in my eyes, and my pick missed a beat. A few glances turned my way, but I simply cranked up the pace and growled the words to cover the choking feeling in my throat. The song ended, and the applause came, as it always did, yet this time with a definite poignancy, as if everyone knew tonight had special meaning.

I didn't address them. I merely went into the next song.

> "To preach of peace and brotherhood
> Oh, what might be the cost?
> A man he did it long ago,
> And they hung him on a cross.
> Long ago, far away. . . ."

Again, I let the room become my focus, and the song played itself. My vision swam momentarily, and the corruption upstairs asserted itself another time. I had no wish to succumb, yet the years behind me left me no choice. Within a short time, the music would have to change.

I tried to console myself with the knowledge that none of these people believed in the truth. If a one of them did, there would be no place for someone like me. In our times together, we would talk of pain, and the insanity of the world, and ask each other why brains and ethics and honor and religion couldn't overcome the spiritual cancer eating up the nations of man. Yeah, we'd wonder, I as much as the rest—really! I pretended nothing. We'd say, yes, it's foolish to think that man requires God to establish a higher moral order; ignoring the fact that the proof to the contrary exists from the subatomic level to the realm of the stars, right in front of our eyes.

Alas, it's all a matter of interpretation, as Dean was so fond of saying. No one will ever know the whole truth, so why bother looking? In good conscience, I can't argue against that, but I will say that experience breeds wisdom, and I *have* been around. As I said, I loved these people, all things more crucial to universal truth notwithstanding. Despite their excessive foibles, these were valuable souls, and I was originally drawn to them for that reason.

My song came to an end, and again, I segued into the next one without my traditional greeting to the audience. A few faces registered surprise, but of an agreeable kind. They wanted to hear me play. They could listen to me talk anytime.

I began to play one for Helen: a wistful ballad of romance—just the sort of thing she'd never admit to liking, though I knew she did. I watched her features brighten almost ecstatically, then quickly return to a passive mask of pleasurable acceptance. She wouldn't look at me now. The little nodding of her head was priceless; she wouldn't realize she was doing it.

"She carried the water from Wellenbrook Well.
Setherwood, sage, rosemary and thyme.
'Twas there she left me without a farewell,
Saying 'you cannot be a true lover of mine.'"

It moved again, this time urgently—angrily. I saw the walls of the room begin to expand and contract, as if they were breathing. The illuminated EXIT sign over the front door left a wavering trail as it appeared to float out of my field of vision. I managed to keep playing, but I could hear my voice straining, coming out too coarse for the song. They were starting to notice.

The moment was at hand.

My fingers stopped moving, and my voice faltered and died. Helen stood, realizing something was wrong with me. Maybe at first they thought it was alcohol, for several empty beer bottles rested next to my stool. But when I rose to my feet, gripping the guitar like a rifle, my stance was rock-steady, though my head spun like a dreidel.

I truly did not want this.

Dean and Mike began making their way toward the stage, and I could hear their words to each other:

"Something's happened to him."

"God, I hope it's not a seizure or something."

"Is he a diabetic?"

"No."

The rest of the audience looked on with vague disinterest. All my focus was on my friends' table. The voice of the thing in my head, unheard for decades, began to mumble, at first distantly, indistinctly, then with increasing clarity.

"Let them know truth."

My fingers gripped the guitar strings and twisted them. A harsh, dissonant noise poured from the sound box: the opening notes of the Zann fugue. Dean and Mike were stopped in their tracks, and the rest of the group gaped in bewilderment as the sounds began working their effect. No one could rise or speak, and those who were not to take part in the composition were struck deaf and blind, suspended in time, their memories stolen. The thing exulted; its cry echoed from my own mouth.

First, the young man who had eaten the cake. I gazed into his shocked eyes, telegraphing my sorrow and regret to him. He read me, all right, for he relaxed slightly, as if to say, "I don't understand, but I trust you." The betrayal stunned him. In the next moment, his back arched, and I felt his pain as the thing began gnawing his soul. I screamed with him, and felt the fire beginning to lap at my feet, working upward to my groin. As it burned, my fingers spun the steel strings into a frenzy, each staccato then playing counterpoint to another. White agony flashed in my brain; then it was over—for the moment. The body drooped, hitting the table with a thunk. Helen and the others gawked, eyes wide and disbelieving. Dean yelled my name.

My attention was involuntarily drawn to him. His soul opened to me, and it was tarnished—God, nearly black. Yet a child remained there, and to my mind, he should have been spared accountability, if there was ever any mercy. My role pre-ordained, I was overcome by the corruption, which spread from the guitar, flowed with my voice, and entered Dean, despite my own pleadings. He fell, crying out in surprise and fear.

The thing flayed him, spurred on by the music. Again, I felt it as keenly as if my own nerves were being ravaged by steel blades. But my body being only a tenement house, it remained steady, my hands mere performance machines for the arcane sonata. My friend's body died then, but his soul screamed on, joining the other in a bitter harmony.

Mike came next, and within moments, a third voice joined in the chorus of blood. His wife Cathy leaped from her seat in slow motion, struggled past the chairs that separated her from her husband. I felt myself growing weaker, but I was not to be released, not until the show was over. My senses joined with hers, and when she realized what was about to happen, she glared at me with unconcealed hate.

I understood her feelings. She'd always liked me, trusted me. She would have thought me incapable of harming her, or any of our friends. Deep down, her greatest fear was that her fragile concept of reality might one day be shattered, and now, it was happening. Hate was the only familiar ground remaining, and she clung to it with desperation, still knowing in her heart that it could not save her.

Her voice added a new dimension to the music. Higher pitched, saturated with feminine passion, it complemented the bass tones of her husband's voice. The thing in my head rejoiced in the new sensation, while I wept and wished my tears would blind me to the accompanying visions of suffering. They would not.

I was made empathetic to every individual's contribution to the music. Anna Lee followed, her egotism lasting to the end; up until the moment our eyes met, she believed she was to be an observer only, not a participant. From her, a magnificent contralto solo shone above the chorale, rising an octave with every beat of her heart. When at last it burst, her voice mellowed, as if she had resigned herself to the truth she had always so vehemently denied. Unlike Dean, she was accountable, in my view. Still, those vestiges of innocence I'd previously seen in her glimmered like candles doomed to highlight her iniquities. And so they would burn forever.

Iä. . . Iä. . . .

Finally, the time came to take Helen. Here was my truest sorrow, perhaps the deepest regret of my whole existence. I had to live with the fact I'd chosen these people. When my eyes turned to hers, she swooned, having dared to hope that this event might pass her by. I'd never seen such horror reflected on human features, for I'd never allowed myself to get so close to anyone, even before the corruption. She couldn't understand what was happening, or how the thing she perceived as me could be doing it. I would have called to her, told her, "No, it isn't really me," except that my voice was not my own, and indeed, I *had* chosen this role, freely, a long time ago.

Her head jerked back, and the finale commenced. Her torment was mine; we felt the hot stab of steel between our legs, thrusting upward into our abdominal cavity. The air grew hot, and every inhalation drew burning coals into our lungs. White sparks flowed from our fingertips, blackening our flesh as the fire proceeded up our hands, to our wrists. The music slowed, paradoxically, softening into a melodic ballad, as if to underscore the horror with a note of supreme sadness. Helen's voice quavered with anguish, as though manipulated by my strings.

Now, the thing played her for a puppet. Invisible hooks burrowed into her flesh and tugged, opening jagged wounds from which blood splashed and sizzled. Her eyes bulged, and I felt my own expanding in their sockets in continued empathy. Her body was nearly spent, yet her limbs jerked pathetically with each deliberate twist and pull of the monster's will. I could hear her voice echoing through my head.

Stop it stop it please oh God it hurts IT HURTS . . .

As her agony zoomed toward eternity, her once divine body slid to the floor, and my legs suddenly turned to rubber. My head spun, and I felt the thing inside finally settling down to rest. Sated for some unknown period of time, it pumped life into my limbs, saturating my blood with oxygen, renewing my ancient heart. It kept its promise to sustain me.

Now came the most awful part. With a soothing, crooning voice, the thing filled me with comforting warmth, caressing me, assuring me the event was over. Soft music washed away the pain that had wracked my body. It tried to make me forget, though it never would. Still, the memory of what I'd done grew dim as if it had happened a long time ago. The voice sang to me:

"It's all right now. Everything is all right now."

Somehow, I still wanted to believe the lie. I wanted to deny that I had allowed this thing to come inside me in exchange for an all but endless life—so many destroyed souls ago. *No, I could not be some vampiric thing, sending men and women into the damnable heart of Azathoth so that I might live!* It was the corruption inside me. The parasite.

The child of the Black Goat.

I had once lived with no remorse, no empathy with those who participated in the music. But for my conscience's sake, sometime in the late nineteenth century, I had resolved to acquaint myself with those I selected, as if the shared agony might somehow absolve me. In my heart I knew it would not. I have only one role: that of executioner. I cannot minister to those who simply do not wish to see the truth. So I wander and sing and draw to me these poor souls whose only crime is the shallowness of their humanity; these who, for their own reasons, fail to set their sights on the sublime realms above and beneath the material.

At Verdi's, the lights came up, and I stood on the stage, guitar in hand, to the applause of an appreciative audience. I didn't have to look around to know that Helen and Dean and Mike and Anna Lee and the others would all be gone, and that the remaining crowd would have no memory of their ever having been there, or of the performance. The soul-eater worked cleanly. I could feel its satisfaction in the warm reaction of the listeners.

Seating myself again, I began to strum a melancholy refrain. Perhaps if anyone saw my tears they'd attribute them to an overly sentimental heart. My voice didn't crack as I began the next number.

> "This world is not my home.
> I am bound across the river.
> Just a poor, wayfaring stranger.
> Roll along. . . over Jordan. . . .
> Roll along."

The chords were slow and haunting. My voice drifted like a ghost across the room. Everything seemed unreal, as it always did for a short time following a performance, as my body and mind regained their balance.

Tomorrow, Helen and the others would be missed, I'd be gone, and any number of associated lives would find themselves in turmoil, until at last there would be acceptance, and the missing souls would become mere memories, even for me. So it had been for ages that the corruption had preserved my body. It might be years before it came time to repeat tonight's performance, and maybe next time would be the last.

Oh, yes, I've said that before. As of yesterday, tonight was to be the last, and the time before that, also the last. Indeed, I'd let Helen touch my heart unlike any other person ever had. It wasn't a romantic or erotic relationship—far from it. I'd come to know her as a person, and I'd allowed her to see as much of me as anyone ever could. When her company planned to transfer her to Washington, I'd encouraged her to go, hoping I might force her out of my life. But the thing came first, and would not allow it.

No, it doesn't have a name—at least one that I might ever know. It appeared to me in those days when the Earth was young and tempted me, and I succumbed, and probably would do so again. For I am human, and I would have gone the same way as my friends had I not allowed it to join with me. How could I have refused? I can dissolve the partnership at any time. I retain my will. However, the day I order it gone, it will go with my soul, and I will accompany my friends into the depths of torment, where a million years is only a teardrop in the vast ocean of time. My few moments of shared agony will never serve as atonement. Is it any wonder I cannot shed this burden, knowing what lies in store for me? The monster does not reward loyalty.

That night ended like all past such nights. To the sound of applause, I left the supper club, where people gathered and ate and drank, and whose tiny moments of happiness, like eating a piece of cake, meant nothing in the face of universal truth. I began my wandering anew, carrying my guitar, leaving a trail of tears that stained the earth like blood.

That night, as I took in a little sleep, the corruption showed me mercy: I saw in dreams the torment of my friends, bound in the heart of the blind, idiot god of eternity; heard their screams, tasted their horror . . . and languished in the assurance that, as long as I performed, I would be spared their fate. ✳

Water Music for the Tillers of Soil

by Tom Piccirilli

Fugal toccata of a sanguine tide washed over the depleted world. Sections of ancient sea vessels rolled atop reefs, the gliding sharks and tumbling bodies of emaciated faithless performing an exquisite ballet in the roiling surf. Valeria laughed and clapped like a child, took my hand and pulled me to the ocean's edge until we stood knee-deep in the boiling red froth.

Most of the trenches had been cleaned out for the day, all the dead rolled down the muddy hills into the waves breaking on the shore. Barracuda and corpses slung up against our legs, sand littered with silver coins and unsightly jewelry cast from the cargo holds of the rotting ships. She removed her sleeveless cobalt evening gown and carefully folded and placed it on a boulder, then danced forward into the whitecaps as the faithless worked the vast inhospitable stone- and moss-covered fields of the Jesuit gardens, carrying rock, pulling weeds, and scratching for fungi.

She swam out beyond the reef giggling wildly the entire time, wine and expectation shifting her mood from her usually sullen disposition. She waved for me to join her as black fins and bloated faces broke the surface and circled her. I shook my head and kept an eye on the extravagant carriages riding down the glazed brick cliff-side caravan routes, depositing more revelers to the citadel.

From over the parapets and towering keeps came the first alluring strains of Patrick leading the orchestra into "Requiem de Aegir Variations in G Minor." He had a taste for reverent music and remained technically proficient, with a commanding drive for tympani, but didn't know how to correctly decrescendo the violins, and his brass always proved top heavy.

Still, there were so few who would notice besides myself: Tien-Hou, perhaps even Mama Cocha. And, of course, Montague.

Val rushed out of the foam and dove into my arms—blood ran from dozens of small wounds all over her sleek and glistening body. Slashed by dorsal fins, the crush of rocks, snap of eels' fangs, and splintered bones of the flailing dead, she tried to force my mouth down to her cuts.

Her eyes burned with lust and expectancy. "You feel it, don't you?" she said. "The storms are coming. The chasms open. Our season is on us."

"Yes," I said, though I felt nothing. Or at least wasn't sure of what I felt.

Full of seaweed and salt, Valeria's dirty blonde tresses hung in her heated glare and draped across her breasts. Her jaws clenched and unclenched, the spiked sound of her teeth clicking together reminding me of just how much she enjoyed biting. With the dwindling sunlight streaming off the green metallic necklace, the key of release swung with each of her fierce movements. The pounding of the requiem seemed to buffet her over every edge she'd ever stood at, a time of judgment at hand. She rushed up the hill in a mad charge and I sprinted after her, realizing that she actually could perceive the storms coming closer now, the chasms gaping in the ocean, feeling all of it within her.

Dropping to her knees at the edge of the nearest trench, Val reached down into the mud and pulled up a gaunt youth of about twenty, his wiry arms loaded with stones. She drew the key from her necklace and unlocked his chains. Her smile barely dropped an inch, even when she hissed with all slick teeth and lips. "What's your name?"

He dumped the rocks and showed none of the fear that some of them do when Val approaches. Instead, he very nearly smiled, a sorrowful grin jabbed into his features. "My name is Eric." He appeared to enjoy the anguished look of craving and unhappiness in her, and even crossed his arms in elegant repose or a carefully designed act of disregard.

In a moment I knew why he had such great discipline. Montague shambled forth from the trench, his legs and arms rattling the three sets of chains as he stood and watched calmly, covered in the fungi that he reaped to keep their babies alive.

Val lunged and beat Eric until he slid semi-conscious to her feet, but he never got rid of the grin. She eventually coerced him to his feet and led him to the shore, and made her love to him in the shadows of the sharks. His arms flapped as the surf sped over and swallowed them. Perhaps he fought for a few moments right then, or perhaps he sought only to match her urgency, or to meet his own god. Eventually she finished and dragged him through the dirt and left him lying there with a mouthful of soil, wasted and murmuring. She beckoned to me.

I drew my dagger and tossed it to her. With a well-practiced action, she snatched it spinning from the air and cut his throat with one precise slash.

He must've known what was coming—they had all seen it before, many times, a ritual she seldom varied. And still the sorrowful grin, dozens of hours of Montague's lessons in that dying, wry grimace. She worked on him for a while as the requiem swelled on the winds, and drew out his abdomen, spilling viscera which she carefully piled. Valeria enjoyed believing she possessed the gift for divination, and poked through intestines and flipped over the liver with a piece of driftwood, turning to smile greedily out at the ocean.

From the Jesuit gardens rose the usual sounds of despair as the trenches filled with sea water, slowly drowning the weakest of the faithless. Someone hit a low C with a cooing contralto at the exact same moment a corpse's spine snapped against the reef. The contrapuntal melodies caused goose flesh to rise on Val's arms and she shivered with delight, the fresh blood of her gratuitous offering steaming in the cool sand.

Montague drifted from the trenches again in a cloud of peat smoke and kneeled in the soil, hands clasped—it appeared as if he were praying, but I knew he actually listened to the music drifting down the cliffs, his wrist occasionally rising and falling as though he held a baton, our Maestro once more.

"Will you lead the orchestra for the last piece?" he asked me.

"No, it would be rude to Patrick."

"The rains are almost here. Is your final composition ready?"

"Not yet," I admitted.

"It will only destroy you." Fingers twined in his beard, indicating meter and tempo, as if in charge of them again and signaling entries of the winds, the brass, communicating all his interpretations the way he once had. How he loved the requiems. "All of you."

"So you say, from the dirt."

The small gods had tempted me for a time. For those months and miles in one of our rainiest seasons I put on chains and tilled the soil all over this desolate land. I spoke to the perishing Christians and Jews and Wiccans, watching fires in the night of the full moons, when the tide rose and crashed and filled the hollows. I listened to the followers of Shinto and Islam, reformed Druidism and Confucianism, watching the Hindus and Zoroastrians perform their rituals without means, and eventually sat with the Jain and atheists. I transcribed some of their prayers and stories, and with my blistered hands comforted dying pregnant women and their screaming children.

I learned to despise them all.

And at this moment, some of them dug for fungi and moss, trying to grow their vegetables again; others carried the stone to build our great amphitheater that would free the spirit of Earth. The quarries had long since been emptied of their value, so the rebuilding of ruins and new additional wings to the castle and abbey had to be constructed from the smallest rocks and thinnest mortar.

When Val finished feeding pieces of her forfeiture to the sharks she still had the bloodlust, and made a slow crawl across the soil, up the muddy hill again towards Montague. He didn't move at all, except for his hand and chin as he listened, and stared for a moment and closed his eyes. She reached and grabbed hold of his beard, pulled his head back to expose that wrinkled gray throat, my blade catching the fading crimson sunlight in full.

I caught her arm and backhanded her to the ground. It made her snigger hideously, and I struck her again more viciously, as she rose growling.

"Damn you," she said.

"Shut up and get dressed."

Val and I climbed the dripping, greenish stone blocks of the crumbling stairway back up to the citadel as the final notes of the requiem swelled on the whirling wind and echoed into oblivion.

Montague called, "It's obvious Patrick is your protégé. You always had the same poor decrescendo of violins, and your brass too was always top heavy."

I wondered why I hadn't let her cut his throat.

In an alcove off the majestic ballroom, as the musicians rested and humbly accepted compliments from the exalted guests, Abbott Gogel spoke with Mama Cocha about the stars. They held out their weather and tidal charts, the celestial, astral and stellar maps, reconfiguring their equations as they'd done for a decade.

I loved to watch the two of them move, always enacting with drift and rhythm. I heard songs when they were pensive and flustered, given to pointing and throwing their arms in the air, and especially when they kissed with their tiny, aimed pecks. In tandem, their collective half ton of flesh shook and jolted, covered with similar colorful robes and flowing vestments, the same hand-crafted golden girdles and sashes about their waists. They never drank liquor for fear it would impede their calculations, but delicacies remained another matter; tonight the table stood heaped with sweet cakes and pastries from all the bakers of the remaining castles.

Wiping sugar paste from her mouth, Mama Cocha fixed her gaze as I stepped into view. A frown not meant only for me crossed her wide, dark face. The calendars held down by plates of tortes had stains and deep creases, as though she'd worried them a great deal in the past hours.

"Ah, Maestro!" said Abbot Gogel. "At last!"

To my shame, in his exuberance he actually fell back a step and began to clap for me. Slowly at first, and with a smile that grew in its sincerity even as his eyes glazed over with his visions of eternity, he soon stood clapping in a frenzy. The royal visitors, following suit—perhaps in dismay or possibly with respect—also began applauding, until everyone in the entire gallery spun from Patrick and his orchestra and gave me ovation. With a sneer, Valeria joined and whispered, "Bravo," her breath acrid with the blood she'd swallowed.

No amount of gesturing on my part could stop the applause or ease Patrick's suffering as he gaped at the backs of those who'd turned from him. Despite his genius, for years he'd endured the tiny torments of those who patronized or hazarded to mock him. In his muteness, there were some who thought him mentally impeded as well. Patrick cared too much for himself and the audience's admiration to ever be an extraordinary maestro. He remained a jealous lover of the music, who swam inside the euphony and consonance to his own delight. Occasionally, he even achieved orgasm on the stage during a particularly powerful allegro or allegretto, so that his body trembled and hands twitched, sending the musicians off tempo, so many of the women smirking.

He stood taller than he should have, a towering six foot six, which also caused the orchestra confusion over his nominal signals and indications, with his hair a sweat-tossed frenzied black-and-silver mane that whirled like tendrils. His thin fingers took too long to instruct, wild motion of his arms leading to off timings. Still, he could command—no one who actually looked into his fiery sapphire eyes ever dared consider him anything but the most dedicated of conductors. In all truth, he should have remained orchestra master, at his station of first violinist. At my right hand.

Mama Cocha though, as always, proved the most single-minded of us, never swayed by laudation or the sublime. When the diplomats returned to their champagne and cheeses, she asked, "Is your composition finished, Maestro?" Her manner, unlike her jouncing body, never shifted in the slightest, always so succinct and pertinent.

"No."

The Abbot's smile fell into fragments, his lips writhing, eyebrows curling like burning worms. "I thought you'd have it completed by now. But you said so, you said so. I thought you were *already* done. What's wrong?"

"Nothing," I told him. "The work is a slow process, translating such ancient musical and liturgical texts. You know how long it takes to garner the proper choral inflection, for these prayers need to be sung. Certain instruments had to be created anew as well, with rare woods not easily found."

A chilling hint of desperation threaded through his voice, as he looked at his pages of notes, the new calendar, parchments of stellar and astral empirical formulae that would save us all. His rustling whisper both alarmed and excited me; the depth of the everlasting ocean on my shoulders. "Will it be ready on time, Maestro?"

"Of course, it will be finished."

Patrick—seeking to prove his worth, but only proving my own instead—held out a fife as constructed by those of the drowned city of Ib, one with self-contained glass tubes filled with the stagnant white waters of the moon-bog. From my directions, he'd made a perfect reproduction of the instrument, as seen in the surviving vellum scrolls, and the strange lilting croaks that escaped it would prove a perfect counterpoint to the heavy percussion. He played a few mournful notes, and Mama Cocha, having heard the sounds in her dreams, turned to me and sagely nodded once. Abbot Gogel grinned like a fool, but peered at me suspiciously throughout the rest of the night.

With the moon at its zenith, brilliant pale light igniting the glazed black brick, Tien-Hou entered the gallery. The entire room took a collective gasp, as it always did. Her sable hair fell to perfectly frame her heart-shaped face, those lips a natural red deeper than the crimson finery of high born ladies. She wore a black sleeveless silk gown cross-laced down her entire back, exposing every muscle, hew, freckle, curve, and scar from my teeth and nails. Patrick could only make one sound, a half-gurgled grunt that held more passion than any word. The same noise escaped my throat.

Valeria, still bleeding and raw in places, snarled and reached out at the nearest man—a duke of the west ponds—without truly looking at his brittle face, and led him away down the corridors while his wife blithered about the quality of moss in her province.

Aristocrats, patricians, noblemen, and baronesses of all the lagoons, bays, and lakes each bore witness as Tien-Hou came and took my hand, and allowed me to escort her outside to the great turret. She did not entertain. She would not accept flattery or praise. She refused to listen to prattle, and her diffidence had grown legendary. Her beauty was eternal, but her features somehow ephemeral, one moment to the next drifting from the peaked Asian elements to the harsher European angles. So many at once that she stood comprised of them all, changing but immutable, a myriad of remnants left from a world when continents and nations existed and mattered.

My Tien-Hou, mistress of the zills. She'd perfected an art that mankind no longer recognized as art: the silver zills upon her fingers, tiny cymbals barely audible but always sensed by the soul. She flawlessly struck them at the decisive instant, adding another layer of ardor and disposition to the symphony.

From the turret, we looked out at the endless stream of faithless carrying stone and mortar from the trenches, engineering the spacious amphitheater and aqueducts below. The exhibition area where the enormous spectacle of my composition would be held waited half-completed, encircled by dozens of tiers and thousands of seats rising gradually outward from its center, ascending higher than the abbey steeples.

"How does it feel?" she asked. "To have the hopes of a world resting in your measures and melodies and croaking piccolos?"

She'd asked me before, with more sympathy, in the night as she lay back upon the pillows, stretched out as she will always be stretched in my mind. Asking again later, whispering from the darkness, when she believed me asleep.

"Why are you here?" I said.

"What kind of a question is that?"

"An obvious one." I stood behind her, and traced her scars with my fingertips. "Why aren't you out with them? In your heart you hate me, you hate all of us—you despise even the music. You compose but burn the pages. You've been pregnant, yet abort. Is everything so transitory?"

She sighed mournfully, as though antiquity itself drew that breath. "It's late."

"Why are you here with me?"

"Maestro, my maestro. You ask and ask the dark, and sometimes it answers. But not now." She took my hand and pressed it to her chest, and I trembled and worked it beneath her gown, nearly gasping now. "I pursue, exactly as do you. We are tempted and seduced, we are shaped and influenced, as harmonies must rise and fall. I'm here with you because it is warm and the food is good. No one should writhe in the mud."

Her beauty haunted, enticed, even appalled me. Perhaps I loved her, or merely the intangibility of her. Despite our entwinings, I'd never truly touched her, not even with my music. "I'm doing this for you, Tien-Hou, not for the world." Her lips, even now, in spite of all that would soon be flowing forth, or had ever occurred out in the barren terrain, with the death of the earth and ten thousand millennia of music running through my skull, only her lips had any meaning. "Will it work?" I asked.

She spun, and those eyes, with all the nations of mankind tangled in her visage, regarded me with an amused but rueful stare, her mouth passionately sealing against my own. "Perhaps."

For her, even such a hint of hope surged like a squall, leaving implications as vast as the foundation of my life. I kissed her again and said, "Montague taught you well."

"My father is an idiot. Now, to bed."

* * *

Overseers on horses irregularly threw fish and bread down to the starving faithless. Their gods couldn't feed them and ours could. There was usually little argument or debate with them, although the abbot and his priests walked the Jesuit gardens daily, always willing to discuss the dying world and lurking or lost deities. Even the faithless architects who constructed the amphitheater and aqueducts often had tea and exotic liquors with the monks and acolytes of the ocean, so long as the conversations were worthwhile and polite. Once, in a foolish show of martyrdom or insanity, an engineer spit upon a monk. The next morning one-third of the Jesuit gardens were razed and salted, which I considered more childishly spiteful than retaliatory, though no less awful for the destruction of what little flora remained. I heard that Montague himself had strangled the insolent engineer, but never thought to ask him if it was true.

In the trenches, he led them in song, monastic chants and well-cadenced arias. He developed talent even in the dirt, and invited all to join. Sometimes the guards would stand at the brim of the ditches and sing with the faithless, or simply listen, openly weeping and praising Montague.

He showed real concern, resting a hand on my shoulder as the chains rang like Tien-Hou's zills. "And what of you?" he asked. "Even if your composition accomplishes what you seek? You'll drown in their black waters, or sink further in your own oblivion, and they'll feast on your empty remains." I believed in his words more than anything else in my life, but still did not believe enough. "Though you were raised in these circumstances you're only a lackey, a traitor to your race. You enjoy using the misnomer, disregarding us as faithless. Your parents served a different god, as you did when you were a child. I took you to church."

I couldn't remember.

"The guards have orders," I said. "If you change your mind, whenever you wish, tell them so and you'll be escorted and welcomed inside."

"When you're ready, Maestro, simply join me in the earth."

* * *

And so we rehearsed the music of eternity. Symphony of the frozen depths and molten currents of lava, as volcanic islands surfaced and withdrew every day all over the world. We could only perform small sections of the composition at a time, portions of prayers and oratorio. No sentences completed, or consecutive suites played, lest we dare the stars and chasms to yawn too soon. Congregational liturgical verse spoken with the right plea would flow like the deepest of our deities swimming up to meet us.

I had consulted with organ virtuosos and calliope builders for the most faultlessly eloquent, alternative, contrasted music fused into a concerto unlike any heard before in history. Crashing tides sang to me among my nightmares—choral segments flowed with alternating recitatives and our new church cantatas. The coda would be expanded until the very end, even during our one and only performance, amidst the rebirth of all life.

It would call Bokrug the water lizard, and fertile Philistine Dagon, the nine daughters of Aegir, Tethys, the Nereids, Thulassa and Vatea and all the other tiaraed fish gods from the sea to come join with us, the most faithful of followers, in our love and salvation of our dying planet.

In a farcical faux pas, the abbot had taken ten of his finest pubescent singers and turned them into castratos, which he'd thought would surprise, please, and inspire me. But our gods would cherish procreation above all else, and sterile children must appear as an insult to them. I murdered the mutilated boys one by one with poison and blamed the plague, and if anyone proved the wiser they said nothing aloud.

* * *

I unlocked his chains and gave him the key that would set his people free.

"Go."

He stared at the greenish metal in his hand, then at me, and finally gazed out at the ocean. He turned and turned, and spun once more, his rags whirling in the wind, as he looked up and down the length of the trench, watching the other faithless digging, dying, and loving.

"What is the meaning of this?" he asked.

"There is no meaning. Go."

But of course there was purpose and intent, whether known or unknown. "You want me to leave? Abandon them?"

"No. I told you, free them all."

He knew the truth but could not accept it. "But what is the meaning of this?"

"There is none."

"There is always a meaning."

For the first time since he'd become a tiller of soil, I felt no respect for him. We are tempted and seduced, we are shaped and influenced, as harmonies must rise and fall.

He had no hymn anymore, and threw the key in the dirt.

Hours later, when I glanced up, my fists wet and chest still aching from the awful sobs and harrowing truth, Abbot Gogel and Mama Cocha were staring at me, a wide-eyed overseer pointing.

"Stop this wallowing in the mud," Mama told me. "Guard, roll Montague down the hill into the surf."

"No," I said. "I'll bury him."

* * *

Three hundred and seventeen musicians, every one elated and terrified, but playing for the love of music, and the love of the world. These faithful enacted upon passion and reaffirmation of soul. My composition had no name or title—it spanned concerto, grew beyond the dirge and threnody of the dying, greater than requiem. Full oratorio, augmented sonata to incorporate as many voices and instruments as were left in the world, and so few at that: double reeds, drum, coronet, piccolo, clavier, harpsichord, strings, brass, flute, organ, mandolin, dulcimer, balalaika, even zithers and uds, the intoxicating shofta, and, of course, the zills.

The amphitheater filled now exactly as the Colosseum of Rome had filled, just as the house of Dagon had filled with three thousand lords of the Philistines on its last night. Noblemen of the lakes and ponds, the moon-bogs and lagoons, swamps, bayous, and quagmires, all came pouring in. They remained the kings and queens of the globe, dressed in their finest gowns and waistcoats, their capes swimming behind them, frocks and other richly garments on show as they moved among the tiers paved in onyx to their tinted marble seats. Children sat awkwardly on the laps of their parents, gazing at the carvings and inscriptions of the ocean, intrigued and thrilled by the floor made from mosaics of lapis lazuli, and the slime already beginning to drool from the aqueducts.

The mouths of the completed waterworks and straits gaped wide, waiting for the high night tide.

I stood upon the stage.

After a minute, there thrummed a silence more complete than any other throughout memory.

I lifted my baton, feeling the gush of nervous energy rise to peak, and then . . . float off. I took command, indicating meter and tempo, in charge and signaling entries of the winds, the brass, our organ virtuosos, communicating my interpretation of the texts and the missing words and pages I had filled in myself.

A single mind leading their love.

It should have been Montague.

And what of you?

The orchestra followed excitedly, the lords already gasping, ladies swooning. Congregational singing rose around us as pure rapture. Patrick poured his heart into my piece, both of us immediately drenched in sweat as we madly called up the divine to embrace us. Tien-Hou, still perfectly radiant and indifferent, performed magnificently. The zills always there, hardly noticed but all-important, like my pulse.

And what of you? My hands moved in patterns from out of the dawn of our belly-crawling forefathers, dripping with the slime of deliverance. Polyphonies kept every nerve concentrated, each thought and emotion focused, the oratorio beautiful but absurd; side by side with our harpsichord, the fifes of Ib coughed out their bloated noises. Harmony upon harmony, differentiated but toiling together, unified and drawing at the sea as strongly as the full moon. *And what of you?* Anticipation grew. People fainted in their

seats, some disrobed and began to make a violent love. Mama Cocha and the
abbot held hands, prepared to live forever in the abysses at the bottom of the
roiling green, wet world.

This song belonged to me as much as it did our gods and their other
worshippers, who returned to the sea ten thousand years ago.

Music filled the farthest corners, spanning the gulfs of time.

And now . . . working towards the crescendo, the earth rumbled as tec-
tonic plates shifted beneath the citadel . . . cliffs crashing into the boiling
waves as monoliths suddenly rose out of the ocean covered with bloated
frogs and bones of the faithless. The amphitheater shook, brackish water
and brine whipping through the canals and trenches, drowning the faithless
where they lay . . . high tide filling all the tunnels and channels, sluicing
through the aqueducts, and now seeping into the amphitheater.

I lowered my hands and let go of the baton.

But the song still played without me, musicians continuing in their
faith. Patrick ran forward and finished, or tried to finish the piece, his mouth
agape like a fish. He wheeled to confront me, raised his fist but had no time
to strike as pandemonium completed our ritual.

The lords and queens tumbled from their lustrous seats, and started
swimming and laughing as the first of their gods writhed among us, an
impregnable smile scrawled into its needle-toothed slit of a mouth. Others
followed, dozens tumbling from the tunnels, teeming hordes swimming
amidst bobbing heads, whipping arms, and behind poured more of them,
wriggling with serpents and fish. They scrambled up the tiers, loping, hop-
ping, and shambling forward in their endless squirming.

Mama Cocha and Abbot Gogel kissed, oblivious or simply understanding the prices paid to eternity as the coliseum continued to flood.
Often the gazes of our gods' white eyes met with mine, and their strange
brows furrowed with curiosity, understanding that I was the Maestro, and
yet I did not follow the music.

Val laughed in my face. "I knew you didn't believe." She grasped and
tried to hold me as I fell back a step, about to run. "I knew it!" Her hideous
gloating nearly brought me to my knees, and unable to break her grip, I
reached for my blade. Perhaps she even wanted it this way, unbelieving herself but no longer caring, as I plunged the dagger upward once, not even a
killing stroke. I left the blade sticking from her hip, and she laughed and
fell into the water, where ten of the white slithering eels with doubled
human faces fell and wrapped around her, dipping their fangs almost lov-
ingly into her flesh.

I reached for Tien-Hou but she left me standing alone, shrieking. I
watched as she finally grinned at me—in pity or somehow in glory—and
dove into the maelstrom.

And: the behemoth, the behemoth, and still the behemoth as if it would never stop its entrance, dragging itself and bellowing like thunder underwater, barely squeezing into the spacious arena. Dagon, most assuredly mighty Dagon, slithering past or crushing all others as it moved directly for her, and she to it. I wailed and bore witness to Dagon's lust and love, its fibers, claws, lips and cilia surrounding her at once like swallowing the nations of the world, slinking down her throat, into every pore—encompassing my Tien-Hou totally within and without yet leaving her alive and protected, as one with the immortal, great behemoth.

I turned away from the mad throng and swam for safety until I reached the highest arcs of stone and held on with all my strength . . . fearing for my life, my sanity, my soul, of course, but not my love. I hung there, neither faithful nor faithless, until the amphitheater finished its submerging, and the surface of the water lay clear and calm and silent.

Only I remained lost . . . utterly, and forevermore, alone.

                                         * * *

I return every night.

I swim in the flooded coliseum, or sometimes in the ocean, until my body is heavy as stone and I can barely do anything more than press my face below, sinking farther down into my own oblivion, listening.

Last night, as the composition played again in my head, something rose from the churning depths to brush against my lips. And somehow, above the peals of the behemoth, and never-ending screams of joy in the drowning and rebirth of my brethren—the water music of the fathomless ages—stretched out as she will always be stretched in my mind, I can still hear the zills. ✳

Shallow Fathoms

by M. Christian

I'd seen the low, single-story, heavy brick and corrugated iron building every day for five years. I passed it as I wound my way up and back down busy, commercial Bay Street to Saint Anne's, but I'd never thought of stopping. All but invisible against Bay's corroded and abandoned warehouses, Quonset huts, and scrap metal yards it was wrong in several ways I never could really pin down. Many ways: it nagged at me, a regular puzzle—a sad old building on a traffic moaning city street, a dull fascination when it flashed by my driver's side window.

It was a distraction—one I could depend on every day I drove from my quiet and empty little house in Van Nuys to the antiseptic halls of Saint Anne's. The building was something I depended on to chew on with my tired mind, so I wouldn't have to think about the wards. I had a choice: to try to translate the sign in the clouded and humidity-unfocused window or think about eyes like boiled eggs, fecal masterpieces on padded walls, fresh wounds from incessant scratching, or childish pleas for help against the bugs, "daddy" or the usual, enduring, monsters. So . . . was it Chinese? The characters, at one time probably elegant and refined but now just fragments dimly seen through streaking humidity, looked different than any I've ever seen. At one time they were probably very ornate, gold-leafed, full of strange accents and backward (Cyrillic?) characters. The foot high letters running just over the single window on a faded and cracked wooden strip could have been one word, or a whole elaborate sentence. Okay, I admit I don't know Mongolian from Czech but it was still something totally unfamiliar from what I'd seen on other stores' signs and restaurant menus. There was something about the sign that was just sideways, out of kilter from any other sign I had ever seen. I'm sure you've probably had the same kind of experience, hearing someone talking in a language you're completely unfamiliar with, something that sounds (or in my case, with that sign, looked) like you should be able to pin it down but you just can't—the words slipping right out from under certainty, even possibility.

Much like the words I heard almost every day, the language the patients used to try and tell me of their terrors, obsessive desires—why they bit an orderly, wouldn't take their meds, or quietly wet themselves in the day room.

I had no idea what the place sold, or, at least, what exactly the place sold. I could definitely tell you that it was a store—in the window below that puzzling, incomprehensible sign was a very ordinary, though equally grimy and fogged from condensation, OPEN. The name of the store might not have been common but if you've ever been inside a hardware store you've seen OPEN. This place was always open, they never closed. Graveyard, swing, whatever the men and women of Saint Anne's demanded of me I could always depend on that place being as available as I was. Though I had no idea, once again—exactly, of what it was making available.

Below the heavily fogged and condensation-streaked single narrow front window, above the sign leaning against the glass (OPEN), the place softly bubbled and, at night, glowed through water. I never have completely understood people's fascination with fish. Yes, I hate them. Yes, when nothing more stimulating was on television, I would watch some expedition to the dark and quiet Atlantic and Pacific but I never could understand why someone would own one, let alone several. I knew people bought them, raised them, called them pets, claimed they calmed them, but I really couldn't understand the attraction, the fascination.

Day or night, summer or winter, whenever I looked in as I drove by— or, when the signal in front of the place was surprisingly red, stopped—I never, ever saw even the smallest traces of fish in that tank in the window. The building was old, brick with a corrugated roof burgundy with rust, and shadowy holes that emitted a haze of heat and steam on cold mornings. One window, one door: dirty, streaked from heavy drops of condensation, blurred along its bottom edge like a flood had touched it once. Like the rest of the place, the door also had traces of a virulent green moss. It grew inwards from the corners just as it creeped in from the corners of the building; a very faint verdant edge, all but invisible unless you saw the place like I did, every day, for five years.

Mary liked to pull at her eyelids. She liked it so much, in fact, that we had to rush her to the emergency room one day to have the right one reattached. Billy was frightened of the dark. After we had a short blackout we had to reset three of his fingers when he tried to claw his way through a wall. Jessica went through hell, from three till child welfare took her away from her mother at twelve. Her mother saw the devil in her little girl, and tried to get him out of her with hat pins, knitting needles and darning needles through her ears, stomach, and, of course, everywhere between her legs.

Five years of seeing it: five years of disinfectants, shit, piss, and blood; of screams ending in hysterical vomiting; of limbs quaking with unrelenting tension; of the patients, of all of them, every day.

I parked on the street, looking closer and longer than I ever had. The moss or lichen was more yellow, I noticed, leaning out my driver's side window and staring, than green. I could see, too, that it was wet—in the dimming sunlight over the harbor and the other buildings on Bay Street—I could see it glistening like the whole place had recently been hauled out of the sea. The roof, too, I saw was more holes and less substance. In the heavy evening I could see the purple night sky through huge gaps in the rusted iron sheeting that hung on massive struts and braces, the air waving wildly above from hot air escaping, blue-white lights showing from inside. The sign was still a puzzle. The tank in the window still bubbled without company but I could finally see, from the lights glowing through from inside, that the bottom was neatly covered by a thick layer of gray gravel, and that the inside was fuzzy with irregular patches of sickly green algae.

The door was warm against the palm of my hand, almost hot. I pushed and walked in, leaving the drying air of a typical, ordinary, Pacific coast afternoon (dropping to evening) behind.

It was humid, hot. I felt like I'd walked into a damp, heavy blanket. My clothes instantly shrunk around my body, becoming, at first, just too warm but then more like fashionable lead. Then, right then—opening that door and going inside my little, casual curiosity—I wanted to turn and walk back out. Social pressure: I didn't want to wander into somewhere where I wasn't wanted, where I didn't know the language, the lingo. But I didn't leave. Mostly I told myself that all I needed was a break, and the little indulgence of satisfying my curiosity about that strange place was a nice little treat for myself—a look inside the box that I'd been scratching my head over. Now, though, thinking back on it . . . no, I might think it but I won't write it down, not even if no one ever reads these ridiculous notes. Leave it at that, I was treating myself to solving this bit of discontinuity. I had made the decision, yes, to go in and walk around. No one else was involved. Only I had made the decision to go inside. Just me.

At first I thought it was very dark—but that had just been my eyes adjusting from the cooling sunlight outside to the dimness inside. High ceiling above, purple to deep same as the sun set through meaningless constellations of rusted holes. Through one of them, I remember (don't ask me why) seeing a brilliant star just starting to shine.

Below the rusted ceiling were flickering banks of failing, failed, and hesitant fluorescent lights covered with sheets of discolored green plastic, bathing the interior with a lush—no, gangrenous glow.

I was standing on a wooden grill, spongy and black, above a glistening and mildewed concrete floor. A desk, green and institutional, like the ones I had written endless reports on, was on the left, in front of the window, the tank next to it. Behind it, the wall was covered with calendars (one date I saw, was able to make out against the murk: 1955), photographs of fish, octopi, squids—all glistening from the humid atmosphere, looking more like fungi than Pacific maps and charts, clippings for fish foods, and chemicals.

The rest of it, the main entirety of the place, consisted of the tanks. Walking in I faced them and they faced me, a claustrophobic corridor of bubbling, churning blue and bilious green aquarium tanks. There was movement in the first one, so I walked on the soft, decomposing grating up to the tank. It was big, I remember that very clearly. No, I didn't know the hobby of exotic fish, but I knew enough to know that it was a ridiculously huge tank—at least six feet long, three feet wide and maybe five feet deep. Like the tank in the window, it had been clouded with a brilliant verdant green and seemed, at first, only home to cloudy algae. Looking up, I noticed steam rising from the top of the tank, making it look more than anything like it had been a churning vat rather than a place to store precious aquaria.

I went over to it and looked in.

Something looked back.

The size of the eye was what startled me, at first. It was at least human-sized, deep purple and brilliant, surrounded by a halo of faded gold scales. Already nervous, I took a wide step back and felt another tank, wet, hot, and heavy press against my shoulders. No more than five feet in front of me, the fish moved slowly past the clear spot I had looked through. The fish was big, maybe three feet from mouth to tail. Slowly, lazily, it swam back and forth, pacing the confines of its small watery cell. Its movements were almost clockwork, pedantic and automatic: two strokes of its tail, turn and back. Maybe my imagination, but the eye seemed to watch me—to focus on my presence.

Taking too rasping breaths of humid air, I moved back to it, feeling humiliated at being startled by something I had eaten, no doubt, in many restaurants. Getting closer, though, just changed the quick shock to disquieting unease. If the store sold the exotic, then its reputation must not have been a good one. Even I, unfamiliar with fish, could tell that it wasn't healthy. Bulbous tumors hung from it, sprouted from its back and side. Its scales were discolored, gray and cloudy. As it swam, it trailed streamers of faintly yellowish putrefaction. Around its still-staring eye, its body seemed to be methodically, glacially dissolving.

I turned and walked on. In the next tank, also deep-water green and churning from oxygenating bubbles, another coolly swam. It, too, was huge to the point of being disturbing. Its design was very similar to koi, a giant goldfish—but pretty and ornamental no more (if it had ever been). This one was even farther along in its illness: most of its fins were either missing, frayed or holed like leaves gone after by a hungry worm. It swam very sluggishly and with less control and, as it turned to pace back the other way, I saw that its other eye was missing—instead a vacant hole stared back at me, ringed with discolored gelatin, thin streamers of decay receding from it.

The next, and the next . . . tank after tank. I wandered backwards, the air growing warmer and warmer and even more humid. Now steam lazily rolled from between some of the tanks. Every one held fish, two in some, three in others. Some only one. Some were smaller, like they were younger. Others were huge and obviously cramped in their tanks. All were sick. One was almost dead, floating sideways with what seemed to be the last sluggish movements of its fleshless tail. Blind, it solely seemed not to take some kind of interest in my presence. The others—all of them—watched me with what I realized was a kind of sad longing—as if unhappy that I was walking about, healthy and free, when they were not.

I had begun to feel a fermenting revulsion at this place. It was a discomfort that went beyond the heat and the humidity, the sight of the ugly and diseased inhabitants of the tanks. Something about the place made me fear and hate it at the same time. I didn't know what it was, precisely, or why the feeling should have been so insistent. But it pressed more and more heavily upon me the longer I remained under the building's roof.

"Rarities?" said a voice. I had wandered deep into the building, into an especially dark and oppressive corner, and had started to realize that it must have been incredibly huge, impossibly vast. The tanks there were against a very solid-looking retaining wall and the last glow of the sunset was coming in from a row of very narrow windows high up along a far wall—the back of the building, I supposed. The voice seemed to come out of nowhere, weak in volume but with a command, a kind of presence. I turned to try and find its owner and, I guessed, the owner of the place, but all I saw were steaming billows, more eyes watching me from the confines of their tanks.

"Exotics," he said, stepping out from between two of the aquariums. "Priceless." He was short, maybe only five feet tall, and his movements, the way he walked and swung his arms as he stepped out from between the tanks, made me think that he was handicapped in some way. He moved . . . wrong, like he had to force his arms and legs against their own natural rhythms to go where he wanted them to. I'd seem similar in MS patients and, of course, in the corridors of Saint Anne's, but in his case it seemed to have been taken to an extreme. As he came towards me, I noticed that he had to reach down and pull one of his own legs up and forward like he was hauling it out of capturing mud. It was a clumsy move but one that he seemed very deft at, had a lot of practice with.

He was wearing a simple green jumpsuit, stained so much that, as he got closer, I saw that green could have very well been a long, long way from its original color. "They fascinate, do they?" His voice was as odd as his movements, his gait. Like the lettering outside, I couldn't place it. In California, we are bombarded by all kinds of accents yet I couldn't place his—in some ways he seemed to use accents and lilts like those in Chinese but in others he seemed to lean towards almost a Pacific Islander's tone.

"Always interested in fresh," he said, stepping closer. "They last, but not long enough. No—"

I was preparing an answer, a non-committal something that could, perhaps, lead me to apologize and get myself out of there as quickly as possible, but he, simply, stepped out of the patch of some less-green and brighter lighting.

"—they last, but never long enough. But more, I find. Always more," he motioned, if I could call it that, and started to walk away from me, towards the darkened recesses of the building. "Must, and I do."

I followed, captured by a desire to get out, to work my way out of the place. I didn't know if he was leading me down his own path through the tanks, maybe to the front door, maybe to some smaller corner of the building, but it was better than staying there in its hot depths with the fish and their diseases, their eyes watching my movements—and much, much better than staying there, with the too-bright light above shining down on me, revealing him much, much too vividly, with too many details.

He moved slowly, in his forced and clumsy way but, luckily, we didn't have far to go. Maybe not in distance, but much in change. First we walked down a long hall again lined with tanks and their putrefying occupants, then through a thick iron door that seemed to have been added clumsily from the rusting remains of some old ship, stuck into an existing concrete and brick wall. Passing through, we walked down a short hall choked with sweating steel pipes vibrating with the muscular convulsions of massive pumps. It was like we'd taken a left turn and wandered down into the core of some huge mechanical heart. Even the same rotting wooden grills on the floor bounced and vibrated from the power of hidden, ceaseless motors.

In the space of something like twenty feet we walked from tanks and humidity to rusting, but firm, iron and steel, and bleak, bitter cold. There, as he walked and I tamely followed, the only mist that wandered through the air was from our own breaths. At the end of the pumping corridor yet another door. Again he leaned against it with the polish and habit of someone long used to the route, and we walked in.

Another tank. A vast, vast tank. Its sides must have been inches thick, plates of reformed steel, slowly leaking fingers of chill water. The curve of it said that it must have been fifty feet across. It was tall, maybe ten feet—just three short of the tall concrete ceiling. In a room ringed with more humming, pulsing pipes, it sat—heavy and obviously pressurized. This was where he was going.

I don't know why he showed me. He did, though. He showed me. With his same almost-useless gait, he walked around the curve of the huge tank leading me along behind till he came to a porthole in its side, ringed with heavy steel bolts. Looking in, he slowly turned away and backed away. I looked in. He spoke.

Heavy water, pressurized. Dark—a kind of darkness from hundreds of feet down, thousands, miles probably. Still and as quiet as glass. Minuscule fragments drifted in it, caught in its strange eddies.

"Last, they do. Long enough. Always need more, but can always catch. Reach out . . . as they sleep and catch more. Easy to catch, that way, lines when they sleep and dream. Bring them in. Always need more, but easy to catch with dreams . . . and bait."

His voice, still broken and toned with his puzzling accent, droned as I stared inside, looking for whatever I knew must be in there. Slowly, my eyes expanded against the powerful black, trying to look beyond the pressurized water.

I couldn't see his face, but I had. "Exotics, but easy to catch. Much easy. He catch them and I keep them—alive so he can have them when he needs them. Fhtagn—" The word was wrong, clumsy even on even his misshapen and deformed lips. It didn't ring like a mangled English word, and it didn't sound like a word from even his own language. It was too unusual, too reverently spoken. His eyes, I knew from the tone, must have glistened, sparkled as he said it—no, I corrected myself, the one eye, the one not clouded and distorted, bulging from some kind of internal, diseased pressure. That one must have feverishly sparked when he said it, then repeated it . . . "Fhtagn. . . ."

Something massive moved in the darkness of the tank. Something disturbed the turgid darkness.

"I keep till he rises, till he wakes. He in his young, here. Sleeping, too, but here—hungry. Bring them from R'lyeh, down deep. Bring them here so even sleeping can see, and eat." Face bulging and swollen, shrunken and callow. Mouth crooked, puckered—showing teeth disheveled and dark. Skin alternatively greased, yellow, dry and gray. Reflections, spots like a spray of . . . scales, must be scales . . . on his cheeks and on his disease torqued hands.

Inside, something huge swept by the porthole. Something massive and cabled, a squid's tentacle beyond any known size yet with the glow and texture of human skin, moved within. Beyond it, something glimmered, shone from the dull light coming over my shoulder, penetrating the pressurized darkness.

"Till wakes, till moves stones of R'lyeh—"

Then I saw it. Huge, piercing with intensity. I knew it slept, but beyond any means to say how I knew. It slept but still with the concentration of its awesome gaze. It looked at me through the darkness, the weight of pumped, concentrated water and saw all of me, the totality of me, even beyond what we could ever call sight.

I turned away quickly and caught his face in the room's dim light, saw the fever, the brilliance in his solitary eye—mirroring for a moment the brilliance, the incessant hunger of the eye in the tank. I saw and knew the familiarity of the tanks, the almost comfort I felt in the presence of the sick and dying fish in those other tanks. I knew and felt it as a physical thing, a burning panic in my arms and legs. I smashed at him, struck at his disfigured and cancerous face, his tumor-choked features and ran—down the thumping hall of pressure-pipes, down the mildewed and steaming corridors of the tanks, the eyes of the fish watching me as I fled, and then, impossibly, through the maze and to the door.

Out. Night. The drone of traffic speeding by on Bay Street. My car. I climbed in, started the engine and drove. At first I let my fear lead me away, in any direction but back towards that building. I drove all that night and most of the next day—till collapsing in a motel room out near where the desert first begins, close to the dazzling lights of Las Vegas.

That's where I write this, now. Tomorrow, I will travel on—far from the sea and the smell of salt water, humidity, and the deep oceans. Maybe somewhere hot and dry. Start over, reclaim, hopefully, a part of myself that wasn't shaken to hysteria by that place, that building on Bay Street.

I'll never go back, to either Los Angeles, Bay Street or even the patients of Saint Anne's. How could I, after seeing that place—seeing those tanks that, I knew with absolute, chilling certainty, held dying, diseased fish that had stared at me with pleading sorrow, helpless misery out of eyes I recognized: the eyes of Mary who liked to pull at her eyelids, Billy who was scared of the dark, Jessica who had discovered that her mother was a monster? All of them, all of the patients of Saint Anne's, a part of them was trapped there—held and slowly, inexorably, drained.

Till the father of the beast wakes fully and can feast on his own, unaided. *

How Nyarlathotep Rocked Our World

by Gregory Nicoll

He stood motionless in the door of our practice space, blocking the light of the naked 40 watt bulb that flickered in the hallway. The shadow cast by his slender body fell over the big red Dew drumkit and creeped up the wall, obscuring the *Shock Corridor* and *I Shot Andy Warhol* posters we'd hung there. Ann and Jeff had been toking some major weed, but from the instant the old Egyptian appeared, the musky hemplike aroma of their doobie was overpowered by a smell deeper and more earthy, with an overriding sourness. It was like something a Roommate From Hell might have left in the back of your refrigerator and that you didn't discover until eight months after he moved out. Our visitor looked like Boris Karloff in *The Mummy*, complete with long flowing robes draped over his skeletal frame and a red fez atop his bony skull.

His name was Nyarlathotep.

And from the minute he arrived, I felt a disturbance in the Force, planets accelerating in their orbits, and the sense that whatever we were, all we had ever been—and everything we ever would be—were all about to change. Nyarlathotep was that kind of person.

We didn't really know who he was or what he was, but he told us he came from the Land of Pyramids a long time ago, and sometimes when we walked through the streets of Little Five Points with Nyarlathotep, towelheads and Rastafarians would drop to their knees before him and call out in strange languages, as if praying before a deity of unparalleled power. Even the hardcore punkers—with their freakish mohawks, their tattoos and piercings, with their army boots and their Charles Manson T-shirts—even they would pause in their demands for spare change and cigarettes, watching with a curious sort of respect whenever Nyarlathotep walked by. We didn't know him very long, but he rocked our world.

I'm not sure how he got wind of us, but from the moment he appeared, Dew was his band. Maybe he was in the crowd during our long set last year at the Candler Park Festival, or he could have turned up at the Star Bar one night when we were too stoned to notice. We're really not sure. Jeff and Ann remember talking to him while they were drinking pints of Deadman's

Ale at the Vortex one night, though they both later swore to me that they never told him how to find our practice space. But somehow, some way, the crazy old Egyptian with fire in his eyes schmoozed his way into our inner sanctum. And once he arrived, there was no stopping him.

Nyarlathotep was at every practice session, standing motionless in the doorway, watching with his almost unblinking stare as Victoria hammered out the beat, as Ray laid down the low notes on his Fender bass, and as Jeff and Ann worked ethereal magic on their guitars. The sounds those four kids made were out of this world, an all-instrumental psychedelic head trip like some weird-beard merger of the Shadows and Mermen, under the direction of George Harrison, Ravi Shankar and Jerry Garcia while those three day trippers were doing the heaviest magic mushrooms a terrestrial human's central nervous system could possibly withstand. With the music surrounding us, transporting us, and the dense reefer smoke altering our already altered states, it was easy to forget that the big, bony Egyptian was there. He never said a word and hardly moved at all.

But sometimes, like when we stopped to change a broken guitar string or rearrange a song, I got a creepy feeling about him. It was a weird sense of something different, something not quite right, and something eerily familiar. It took weeks for me to place it, but I finally remembered. You see, when I was real little, my dad had lost his foot in Vietnam. He used to tell me stories about the "phantom pains" he still felt, weird sensations that his foot was still there and was hurting him something powerful—as if a dozen Asian wharf rats were gnawing on his toes. I had some really bad dreams about those stories, dreams which didn't stop until a few months after Dad died the next year; but during my teens I'd managed to put those awful memories behind me and get over them. But sometimes, being around this creepy old Egyptian, I'd start to get that same feeling I got when Dad was drunk and told me those scary stories about his missing foot. And, for the first time in my 38 years, I really understood why Dad drank so much.

Speaking of drinking, the Egyptian refused all the beer, Jack Daniels and reefer we offered him, although from time to time he'd pull a tiny handful of some fine green crystals from a pouch at his side and rapidly inhale them. Hey, different strokes for different folks. . . .

And Nyarlathotep, he was different folks.

Things got the most different of all, though, when he finally flipped all the cards and made his move. I guess it had been about two months or so that he'd been making every practice session, always arriving a minute or two after the last of us five had appeared, blocking the door until practice was over. I honestly think the band was at their best during those weeks, as if his presence had energized and inspired them. Ray was new to the group, a replacement for our last bassist who had quit to move out west, and the

big guy had learned all the old songs in the band's repertoire by then. I had
booked them some shows for the following season, and the foursome was
playing really, really tight. Which meant that it was time to start working
up some new material. Thinking about it now, after all that's happened, I'm
sure this is exactly why Nyarlathotep waited as long as he did to reveal his
intentions toward us. He also waited until one night when we were pretty
deep into the weed.

"Play this," he said, thrusting a cluster of dusty parchment rolls at me.

Had I heard him speak before? I don't recall. Surely I must have heard
him say something across all those weeks, but his voice came to my ears like
a hot, sudden wind, unexpected and stinging. But did I actually hear it, or did
I just imagine I heard it, as if an inner voice spoke to me? I leapt up from the
unpadded metal folding chair where I usually sat observing whenever the
band practiced. In an instant Nyarlathotep's dry, coarse, wrinkled parchments
were in my hand and I was passing one of them to each musician.

Jeff nodded his bald head in apparent gratitude as he took the scroll
from me. Ann bowed gracefully as she accepted her copy, and Vicky said
nothing but immediately unrolled hers across the top of her floor tom and
began studying the score inscribed on the crinkled parchment. Only Ray
hesitated. He unslung his bass, propped it against his amp, and shook his
short black hair. "I can't read music, man."

What happened next gave me a serious case of the creeps. I was starting to tell Ray that I'd coach him through it, that I still know my way
around both sheet music notation and the neck of a bass guitar from my
days in the Deep Six, but I never really got the words out. I was looking
Ray right in the face, so close I could see my own reflection in both lenses
of his eyeglasses, and suddenly there he was—Nyarlathotep, his complexion like a bad mud mask and his breath as fragrant as an open sewer—with
his face pressed right up beside Ray's. He'd never moved from the doorway
before, and how he crossed 14 feet of sticky carpet in the time it took me
to say, "No sweat, Ray," I'll never know. The little tassel hanging from his
fez wasn't even swaying.

But there he was, leaning into Ray's ear and whispering, "I'll teach
you. . . ."

What followed was out of this world.

Dew's music had always been a head trip, but Nyarlathotep's song,
well, it was the living end. It started with Vicky hacking out a weird, loopy
beat that sounded like a three-legged horse at full gallop. Then Ray added
a snaky, tremolo-heavy bassline as sinuous as a speeding cobra. Jeff hunched
over his Gibson, picking out a melody that could have been rooted in the
Gypsy, Middle Eastern, or Hispanic tradition—maybe all three at once.
Then Ann laid into her hollowbody Gretsch with a strange new aggression,

dropping tight minor chords into Jeff's melody with a percussiveness that suggested drums, alternating with a fearful sustain that sounded more like a horn section. It was the craziest, most offbeat, and downright spooky music I ever heard. And it went on and on and on. . . .

After about five minutes they stopped glancing at the sheet music and kept playing. Another five minutes passed, then ten, then fifteen. The strange tune continued, building strength and speed, until I thought they would jam on it straight through till morning. But Nyarlathotep stopped it with a single gesture, raising his thin bony white hand in the air. Instantly Vicky ceased the drumbeat and the other three muted their strings.

The silence was deafening.

And Nyarlathotep was pleased.

"You have done well," he said, and a trace of a smile curled at the edges of his dry, crusty lips. Then, turning to me, he asked, "When is the next public performance?"

"Uh, it's on Thursday, a week from tomorrow," I answered, "at The Point." I gestured at a large paper calendar hanging on the practice room wall, with the date circled in red marker.

Nyarlathotep stepped forward and examined the calendar, his unblinking snakelike gaze paying particular attention to a tiny symbol in the corner of the date box, an icon showing a half moon. We all watched, baffled, as he pulled a little brass disc from a pocket hidden in the folds of his robe. It was about the size of a beer coaster, but it had weird markings that looked like some Middle Eastern language written all over it. He turned several movable dials on the face of the disc, then looked up coldly at me.

"That is too late," he said firmly. "It must be two nights before—on Tuesday, at midnight."

If anybody in the band had said that, I would have laughed out loud. Tuesday at The Point was the night that the beginner bands—groups with no real following yet, often playing their first show—would perform for free just to get the exposure. It was a night when the club didn't even charge the usual $5 cover and hoped they'd just barely make back the cost of staying open by selling oversized bottles of Newcastle to the tattoo-and-piercing set. It was a night when losers of all shapes and sizes, all colors and creeds— kids, drunks and burnouts who were too broke to afford to pay to see a show elsewhere—would crowd into the club's narrow confines to watch equally pathetic musicians strut and fret their hour on the small stage like the poor players they were.

It was not, I told Nyarlathotep emphatically, a night when Dew would be playing.

But he nodded his head and said solemnly that these conditions made it perfect. He smiled. At least I think he did.

And then he left.

Without a word Vicky rolled out the drumbeat, Ray picked up the bassline, and Jeff and Ann joined right in. They played "Nyarlathotep's Song" until past 3 a.m., even after we ran out of reefer and Jack—the longest practice in the band's history.

* * *

The next day I awoke groggily, rising with sticky slowness from some damn dream about men with dog's heads living in a city buried under the desert sands. It was the unholy hour of 4:30 p.m., and what ended my whimsical fantasy was the sound of the little VW Beetle telephone beside my bed. There aren't many folks who have that number—even my weed source uses the pager—so I picked it up right away.

It was Ann, telling me that she and Jeff had just heard that our friend Robb Causey, who used to have a great little local rock group called ScumBunnyTrail, had been found dead out behind Savage Pizza. Apparently he was dumping the lunchtime garbage when something happened and he got his head knocked in. The theory was that he'd climbed inside the dumpster to crush down the piled-up trash, and that the lid had closed suddenly on top of him.

Ann was taking it pretty well, and after a bit we started talking about doing a memorial or benefit show for Robb, when right about that time the telephone squeaked its little call-waiting beep in my ear. I put Ann on hold and took the other call, which turned out to be Rich from the Point. He asked me if I knew about what happened to Robb, which of course I did, and then told me that Robb had put together a new band called Rabbit Eggs who were scheduled to play The Point next Tuesday. Obviously that gig was off, so they were turning Tuesday's show into a memorial concert.

He wanted to know if Dew would headline.

I said sure, we'd be honored to play The Point on Tuesday.

Nyarlathotep, it appeared, was gonna get his wish.

* * *

The Point didn't open their music room doors on Tuesday until 10 p.m., with the show scheduled to start at 10:30, but by 8:15 the upper bar was already crowded with musicians drinking themselves senseless and fans were lined up for a block down Moreland Avenue waiting to get in. Turns out that Robb had even more friends than we'd planned. Tuesday turnouts are generally among the week's weakest since the local weekly entertainment newspaper doesn't come out until Wednesday, making it especially hard to publicize a schedule change like the one we were experiencing tonight; but with radio stations pounding the tribal drum, and with me and Nyarlathotep walking the streets of Little Five Points for half the weekend putting up posters, the word had gotten around.

I sure wish I knew where that crazy, smelly old Egyptian had come by that poster design. It was really eye-catching, and I immediately wanted to find the artist who designed it and hire him for some more work. Beneath a huge holographic day-glo eyeball was this weird, complex jumble of lines and loops forming some kind of architecture like one of those nutty M. C. Escher prints—only, come to think of it, these were more like one of those underground cities I'd been dreaming about. Anyway, it was a visual knock-out, and we had to put up twice as many as normal because the kids kept yanking them down and stealing them. No fool, though, I had 200 extra ones printed up for the night of the show, and I got the band to sign them. We stacked them up at our T-shirt table, and asked $10 a piece for them. I sold the whole pile before the first group even played.

The Point is a mighty interesting club which is shaped, as the name implies, like an arrowhead. The stage is up at the tip and the audience gets kinda funneled toward it along the narrowing walls. The "backstage" area is at the rear, behind the soundboard, which means you gotta wrestle your gear through the crowd when it's time to play. The place is all concrete and cinderblock, with big pillars holding up its ceiling, and it feels a lot like a dungeon even though it's on level ground with windows open on both sides. Capacity's about 250 persons, although I lost count at 290 that night. Damn, but it was packed.

Normally the guys who run the place, Rich and Ernie, can be kinda slack about getting the bands started on time; but tonight somebody really lit a fire under those cats. The No-Nothings kicked off the action at exactly 10:30 with a short set of hard-drivin' alternapop, ending with a quick medley of ScumBunnyTrail tunes. Then the surviving members of Robb's ill-fated Rabbit Eggs project got up there and played some of his newer stuff that no one had heard, and Chad from ScumBunnyTrail filled in on guitar as they did a tribute of sorts by playing the songs off the B-sides of all three of ScumBunnyTrail's indie 45s.

It's pretty hard to describe the mood of the room that night, and to give a sense of my increasing anxiety as I realized that our set—which included no plans for playing any of Robb's songs—might come off as majorly anticlimactic. The crowd was really diggin' it, totally groovin' on hearing Robb's old stuff. You could see them smiling, even the ones who were crying, and the club was doing nearly twice the usual amount of liquor business back by the bar.

Well, I started sweatin' it.

And as I watched from back behind the T-shirt table, I began wondering if there was any way I could talk Dew into working one of Robb's compositions into their instrumental jams. I had a tape of a ScumBunnyTrail show in my car and, maybe, I thought, I could let them listen to it up in the dressing room and pick up the riff of one of the better known tunes. . . . At the time, really, it seemed like the only way Dew could top what was already happening on that stage, and damn me but, ever the manager type, I was sure we'd have to get an even bigger rise out of them if we ever wanted to get booked here again.

So, I figured, it was worth a shot. I found one of Vicky's butch friends to watch the table while I hauled for the door and made my way across the parking lot. My feet made a lonesome, crunchy sound on the gravel, and it was oddly quiet as I pushed down the long row of moonlit cars. I finally got to the end of the aisle and dug around in the glove box of my van, finding a whole buncha other stuff I'd been missing, and finally I turned up the tape, in a little black box labeled (a bit ironically) "ScumBunnyTrail—Live at The Point." Then I started back toward the club.

Damn, but it was spooky out there. My eyes weren't really adjusted for the darkness anymore because I'd turned on the big bright overhead light in the van, and a couple times I stumbled around in the dark, losing my way in the rows of cars as if the parking lot was a huge maze or something. The big bright moon was up high and, even though it was only about a half moon, it shined down pretty bright on the lot, only somehow the aisles where the cars were parked seemed all twisted around or something. I dunno. Something felt wrong. It was really confusing for me. . . .

And that's when I saw him.

It was Nyarlathotep. He was standing in the center of the parking lot, facing the moon, with his arms spread out wide. And man, did he look crazy.

I guess maybe he'd been snorting s'more of that weird green powder that we saw him take sometimes, but from the look on his face you'd have thought he'd been highdiving in the stuff. His cheeks were all sunken in and his black eyebrows were arched like the signs outside McDonald's in Hell. That scabby James Woods mug of his was all twisted up in a scowl, and he was staring up at that almost half-a-moon up there as if he was in a contest to draw the best map of it later.

"Hey, Ho-ho Tep," I called. "You gonna be moongazin' all night or are you comin' in to watch the show?"

He didn't say anything. Didn't even flinch. So I walked up close to holler in his ear, and that's when I noticed that his feet weren't exactly making contact with the ground. I mean, I knew the dude was tall, but something sure did seem more than majorly out of order as I got near to him,

and when I looked down at his feet to see if he was standing on a guitar amp
or something, not even the sight of that little brass astro-lab toy of his—
which was down on the pavement, spinning like a pinwheel—could distract
me from the fact that the old Egyptian was levitating himself offa the earth.
I couldn't have been more surprised if the tassel on his fez stood straight up,
like Akbar's in a "Life in Hell" cartoon.

Well, I got so spooked that I ran back to the club and almost knocked
over the big bald bouncer guy who was checking IDs at the door to the
upper bar. "You with Dew?" he asked.

"Uh, yeah," I muttered, more than a little relieved to be suddenly
wrenched back into the real world.

He nodded in the direction of the music room. "Their set got moved
up. You better hustle in there and help 'em get their gear on the stage."

Apparently Rabbit Eggs had finished way ahead of schedule. It was
almost midnight, the lights were down, the crowd was pumped, and we
were expected onstage now.

* * *

I remember those next few minutes as a haze of amplifiers being bumped
and rolled down a beer-splattered stone staircase, of fighting our way
through the packed, sweaty, hollering crowd with a hardshell guitar case
held aloft before us like the Ark of the Covenant, and of struggling in semi-
darkness to untangle a basketball-sized knot of guitar cables and amplifier
cords so hopelessly interwoven that Alexander the Great woulda thrown his
hands in the air and fallen promptly on the point of his sword if faced with
such a challenge. Ernie fussed with the microphones and monitors and
somehow, despite inky darkness, the noise of the crowd, and all the sticky,
smelly puddles of spilled beer and wads of old duct tape grabbing at my feet
like the tentacles of some hungry octopus, we got Dew ready to play.

They opened with "The Dog Who Dances With Lava" off their first
CD, and after the mob finished roaring at Ray's bass intro, the whole band
locked into groove and played their ever-lovin' hearts out like I hadn't seen
'em play in a looooong while. Ernie had the soundboard set perfectly, with
just the right balance between Jeff and Ann's guitars, and whatever genet-
ically-favored grandson of Albert Einstein was running the lights that night
shoulda got a special award from the governor for setting a new standard of
excellence for public performance. The whole joint came unglued as they
roared into "Holidays and Famous Dead People" and for once I was—
briefly—at ease again. With or without any of Robb's songs, we were gonna
go over just fine. Hell, I'd've bet the van on it.

But my comfort didn't last long.

During the fourth song of the set, as I was selling the last of our official Dew "Sing Monkey Sing" T-shirts to a girl with jugs the size of dumbecs and three rings pierced in her left nostril, and just as I was about to try my patented "sniff-sniff-do-YOU-smell-gold?" pickup line, I heard a rapping gently tapping at my chamber door. Actually it came from the window on the right side of the club, and somehow I knew as soon as I heard it who it was. The girl sporting the Valley of Lost Wedding Rings vanished into the crowd, and I found myself looking up into the cold ice-blue eyes of Nyarlathotep. He was outside the window, his face pressed almost up against the glass, and as soon as our gazes met, he gestured toward the stage and opened his mouth, his caked, crusty lips forming an emphatic one-word command which I knew we must obey.

Though I couldn't hear him through the glass, or over the cascades of music, I am certain what he said was, "Now!"

As chance would have it, right about then Vicky looked over at me from behind the drums and I quickly pointed to the window. I guess the message hit her as hard as it hit me, because she hammered the song to a halt as expertly as a diesel driver gearing a runaway truck down to a full stop. Ann, Jeff and Ray all turned around to look at her, kinda pissed off since they'd been enjoying the jam and didn't wanna end it just yet, but they got the point real quick when she pointed both of her Pro-Mark hickories at the window. The three of them all whirled on their heels and, with a group coordination so smooth and effortless it looked like we'd rehearsed and choreographed it that way, they started playing Nyarlathotep's music.

Little Vicky pounded out that crazy three-legged gallop and Big Ray rolled out that rattlesnake bassline. Ann used the sustain on her Gretsch to make those strange horn-section sounds while Jeff twanged out that creepy Arabian Nights melody. To my amazement, the whole room fell into a hush, with everybody staring forward to watch and listen. The cinderblock walls radiated a sharp evening chill and the room smelled of beer, bourbon and reefer, but from the stage came something warm and powerful, something comforting as a wool blanket but stronger and more intoxicating than any drink or any drug I've ever known. It was the music of Nyarlathotep.

Yeah, I'd heard it before. But it was different tonight. Something to do with the alignment of the stars. It wrapped around all of us and became part of us, and it was good. Man, was it good. . . . That is, until the light show started.

Here's where things got the weirdest of all, and I'm not really sure if I remember all of it, but somehow Nyarlathotep was inside the club and right up at the front of the stage, and he raised up his arms so his long, boney body formed the shape of the letter "Y," and just then in the air over his head—the dead center of the stage—a translucent red pyramid appeared. It rotated slowly at first, like one of those motorized displays in a jewelry store window, but getting up to speed like a carnival ride. I guess the red pyramid was about seven feet tall, and it looked like it had four sides, each with some kinda movie playing on it like a drive-in theatre screen, only you couldn't quite make out what the picture was until you were looking straight at it, and by then it had almost turned all the way away. Dew kept on playing, driving the tune faster and faster, which seemed to increase the speed of the pyramid's spin.

But even though it was going really fast, I swear that on one of the sides, for just a flash of a second, I saw images of our friend Robb getting hit hard by what looked like the head of a cane. And not just any old cane, either, but a dark brown eagle-headed walking stick like one I used to have myself—the one my dad had used after he got home from the war, a very long and very heavy one which I'd kept in Dew's practice space for a while, till it disappeared a coupla weeks after Nyarlathotep started visiting us. I never could figure out why whoever broke into the space took that stick—and our drugs—but didn't snatch all the guitars and equipment. Anyway, I only glimpsed that image for a second, because then the pyramid started turning so fast that it looked more like a giant ruby traffic pylon up there.

Nyarlathotep then did his levitating trick again, floating himself up over the pyramid and then easing himself down inside it till he looked sorta like a goldfish in a bowl. The music kept on playing, and Nyarlathotep beckoned to the kids.

"Come!"

I don't know if he actually said the word or if he just thought it really, really loud, but suddenly it was like he was the Pied Piper or something, and the kids started scampering up on the edge of the stage and diving into it with him.

Only, instead of staying inside it like he was, they just disappeared.

Vanished.

Gone.

At first I thought it was some kinda magic trick. I mean, I know The Point has a small, little-used side door on the left side of its stage, a door that opens out onto the street, so at first I thought the kids were being sneaked out of that. But then I realized that when we set up we'd moved Ray's amp up against the door. The amp was still there, blocking it. No way those kids could be going out the side. Nor was there any way that so many kids could fit up on that stage.

Something weird was happening—something too weird. And it suddenly came to me that everybody else in the place was too drunk or stoned or stupid to realize it. Because I'd been so busy and had been sweatin' so many different things tonight, I hadn't toked any weed or drunk anything other than a Diet Pepsi. I was clean. I was straight. And I was the only one who could shut down the freak show. So I tried.

God help me, but I tried.

Shoving my way up front, I hopped up onto the stage and blocked the next kid in line from jumping into the pyramid. However, one of the little cusses a skinhead wearing a Crash Kills Five shirt and with a spider tattooed over his ear—dived under my spread legs and hopped on in. I caught ahold of his Doc Marten boot just as he vanished inside and I looped the fingers of my left hand under the laces. The kid was stronger than me, though, and he started dragging me into the pyramid with him—or at least my arm, anyway.

God, was it ever hot inside there. . . .

Well, Vicky kept drumming, and Ann and Jeff continued zoning out on their guitars, but Ray saw the fix I was in and decided to help. He unslung his bass, propped it quickly against the wall, and came over to give me a hand in the tug of war. Ray's a big guy—tall, that is—but thin and not particularly heavy. Damn if the skinhead didn't drag him all the way in there.

About this time I noticed two things.

First, the pyramid was starting to change shape—it didn't look much like a pyramid anymore, in fact.

And second, Nyarlathotep was not pleased. He was shouting, but it was in some strange language we couldn't understand. I figured out later that what he wanted was for Ray to get back to playing his music, because without its snaky bassline, the tune didn't sound right. Maybe that's what was making the pyramid change shape. Right now it looked like an octagon or something, and then it started irising smaller like the aperture on a really fancy camera or something.

Well, Ray couldn't get back to his bass because by now he was pulled all the way into the big ruby shape. On the plus side, though, he'd managed to get the kid's feet shoved back enough so that I could almost get my fingers undone from his bootlaces.

But then, well, that's when it was all over.

With Nyarlathotep screaming himself senseless in Egyptian—or whatever language it was—the big ruby shape sorta imploded on itself. It collapsed, folded up, and vanished.

So did Ray.

And so did those kids inside.

* * *

It's been really tough the past few months, getting used to everything. Dew's finally got a new bassist and is playing out again. They're doing pretty good, actually, though I haven't seen them much. The police and the tabloid reporters don't bother them anymore, and they've managed to get on with their lives and their careers.

I wish I could say the same for myself. After some physical therapy and counseling I've become a pretty good one-handed typist; I'm certainly grateful that, when the pyramid collapsed, it was my left hand and not my right hand that got folded up and taken away inside it. The emergency room doctor said mine was the cleanest amputation he'd ever seen, one that had somehow instantly cauterized itself. I heard he wrote a paper for one of the medical journals about it, and was looking into duplicating the feat as a surgical procedure with lasers or something.

Physically speaking, I'm coping just fine now. What bothers me is the phantom pains.

You see, I keep remembering what my dad told me about that foot of his, the one blown off by a landmine in Vietnam, and how he kept on feeling it like it was still there, and like something was trying to hurt it.

I can't sleep at night now, for all the dreams. You wouldn't believe the drugs I have to take, prescription and extracurricular, to cope with those. The cities under the sand, with those dog-faced men walking around, hunting for me every night just as they hunted the screaming, fleeing children. . . . And lately I can hardly face the waking hours either, at least not sober or straight, for the thousand exotic Eastern ritual tortures I feel inflicted on my defenseless, missing hand. For the strange tongues and teeth I feel worrying it, and for the wet, squishy sensations of things surrounding it, feeding on it. . . .

Nyarlathotep, wherever he is, must be very, very angry with me. . . .

Yeah, I own a gun—dad's old Army .45—and more than a hundred times I've considered sticking it in my mouth and painting the ceiling. But I don't think that would solve anything. See, I know Nyarlathotep will be over there on the other side, waiting for me whenever I get there.

With an evil army of his own.

And when my torments in this world end, my real tortures will be only just beginning. *

Listen

by James Robert Smith

OCTOBER 17

Listen. I went up to the house. I went up there and stood and looked and could see that there was something sinister about it.

OCTOBER 18

Since I was still settling in, I didn't have time to do more than stand at the bottom of the overgrown drive and look up the hill at it. My own new house was less than a mile away and I had just been curious about that old and overgrown track. I'd thought it was just another logging road gone back to pines and broom sedge once the trees had been hacked down and hauled away. But it didn't really look like a logging road. It wasn't rutted and there was lots of gravel and rock visible under the leaves and small trees. Right away I figured it had been a much used road once, and from the girth of the pines growing in it that it had been abandoned for only about five years. So I walked up there.

The road was a driveway. It slabbed along the slopes of Keener Ridge. A nice walk, I figured as I hiked along, looking down into some really steep hollows full of mountain laurel and wild azalea. If it had been June or early July instead of October I would've seen a blaze of flowers and color instead of turning leaves. The fall colors were kind of drab, though.

What was left of the road curved with the contours of hillside and took a steep climb to the ridgetop and then there was a long, gentle rise up to that house. It was a creepy looking place. I don't mind saying it. The sight of it gave me a chill.

Someone spent what must have been a lot of money on it, once. A classic Victorian. Tall. Three floors of windows staring out. A big porch going along the front and round the side and going toward the back. I thought that it probably continued on to the back of the house. I didn't go back there to look. It was in very nice shape to have been out of use for so long. There was no outward sign that anyone had been walking in here on a daily basis, much less driving in. I wondered what kept the vandals away.

I felt a chill and went back down to the county road before it got dark.

OCTOBER 19

I couldn't stop thinking about that house. I really should have gotten my own stuff in place before hiking around the country. But almost everything was unpacked and shelved. My new job didn't start for two weeks, so they weren't expecting me there. I liked it way out in the woods. The people weren't terribly friendly, but there was a Methodist church about three miles up the county road. The gravel ends there and the pavement begins. I had decided that I should go on Sunday and start to make friends so people wouldn't start looking at my place as an unguarded target. The job was a half-hour's drive into Arkham and the place would be alone most of the day with me thirty miles away.

That house up on the ridge didn't seem to have been vandalized, though. All that window glass was unbroken and the door looked solid. I had to go back and have a look.

OCTOBER 20

I went back. I was frightened by what I saw. I had to tell someone. I was afraid to tell anyone.

As I cowered in my house, I wondered if I would be safe there.

I had hiked back up the ridge for a look. At first, I told myself that I was just going for a walk to see if I could spot some deer sign. It's really amazing how far out in the sticks this place is. Nearest neighbor is two miles away. The nearest phone is three miles, but the phone company had said they would put a party line in. Had a hard time dealing with that concept. A *party line,* in this day and age. I found myself wishing that was still the strangest image I had encountered.

About a half mile down the road is where the drive comes down to the grade. The sun was heading up toward noon and the woods were still and quiet and the sky was really blue. Not a cloud anywhere. So I went back.

This time I went right on up to what used to be the front yard. There were lots of flat stones that someone must have dug out of the local fields and put down to make a walkway. I saw tough little oaks and hickory trees wedging up between them, but it must have been really pretty once. Seeing something that caught my eye, like a parade of worms frozen on the rock face, I knelt to see strange *signs,* letters in some other language, perhaps, carved into some of the paving stones. Touching them, there was the slight sensation of something slick in the grooves, as of damp algae. Shuddering, I wiped my hand on the tough denim of my pants, reminding myself to wash those when I got back.

Like I'd thought, none of those windows were broken. A house all alone like that should have been *asking* for the local kids to heave rocks at it. Those windows should have been full of holes or without a single unbroken pane. But all that dingy glass just soaked up the light and stared back at me, deadlike.

I went back and forth, checking the place out. I halfway expected someone to come out and ask me what the hell I was doing on their property. No one came out. No one came out.

For some reason, I couldn't make myself go all the way to the back. I still didn't know if the porch wrapped all around. Instead, I walked over to a little hillock about a hundred feet from the house and I stood there: it went up about the same height as the third floor and I could see partway down the other side of the mountain. Miles and miles of woods that way. No roads. No houses. Just the woods; the colors a poor drab, scabby brown.

Then, I did it. I gathered my courage and just went on the porch and put my face right up to one of those dingy windows and peeked in. I just peeked, is all.

He was staring right back at me, there, just inside the house. White face. Like bone. Eyes like that dingy glass. His mouth was slack. Loose, as if it had no jaw.

I didn't stop running until I got home. It was safe there. I thought. I didn't like being alone like that and it was getting dark.

OCTOBER 25

It wanted to talk to me. Face to face, and not in my dreams like it had been doing the past few days.

I had to go back up there because it wouldn't leave me alone and if I didn't let it have its say I'd never sleep. I'd never rest. I had to go. No choice at all. For days I had curled up in my small house, wrapping myself in sheets and blankets and covering my head and screaming soundlessly, trying to make him go away. But it wouldn't go. And *those images*. Of. Things.

Never mind that the best part of the day was gone before I cranked up my courage and headed down the road. I even thought about taking the pickup truck to the house, but I didn't think it could make it through some of those trees. I'd probably puncture the oil pan trying. So I just walked. I knew a confrontation was the only way.

The door stuck when I first tried it. It stuck and then it gave a half inch and stuck again and then it heaved in when I pushed.

A sheet of old dust and wood shavings eased down from the doorjamb. It had been years since anyone had opened that front door. 'Five years,' he told me, his voice whispering like old, browning paper rubbing quietly, crumbling. I had figured five years. His eyes scared me. His eyes were dead, like that smeared glass and he spoke to me even though his mouth just hung open, stuck like that door had been stuck; but his voice came out. He was cold. He was alone. I think he just wanted someone to hear.

Facing him like that instead of just hearing him screeching in my nightmares, my courage faded and I know my face screwed up with fear.

I ran again. He screamed at me, all along the way back and even there in my own house, with the lights all on and the television blathering away and me sitting there trying not to hear. He wasn't going to let up until I went back, but I couldn't. Not in the dark. I could hear him from all the way up on the mountain. I wish I hadn't gone.

He wants me to go back. He wants me to say those words. Make *those sounds*. But I won't do it. I *can't* do it.

OCTOBER 27

He was alone, like me. But I think there was something sinister about the ghost. Was it just that he was like me? I don't know. To make him stop screaming I had to go back. So I had to go back. He was driving me crazy. I couldn't even make a phone call. At a nearby grocery I tried to call the office, where I would be working and afterward Mr. Grindstaff must have thought there's something wrong with me. I couldn't get that screaming out of my ears. I didn't know what to do.

OCTOBER 30

I went back.

He spoke all day to me there in the front of the house. I tried to make myself go past the foyer and into the den where he claimed those things were said to him, where he was threatened and frightened and no one could see him because the house is so isolated. I know he wanted me to go in there but I was afraid of what I would see so I just cringed right there in the foyer with the door still open and the light not really coming in but making a blue-white glow where I could see the sky if I peeked out of the corners of my eyes so I didn't have to look in his face. I kept waiting for someone to come walking up the drive or out of the woods. A hunter. A hiker. A local kid. *Anybody.* But nobody did even though I prayed. I said the Lord's Prayer right there. Right in his face but all he did was tell me his story so I quit praying and listened to him.

He made me listen until the light began to fade and the night came down like a huge fist. I opened my eyes once to peek out the door but it looked like there was this big form, like a fat man much bigger than I am, blocking the way out. And *his* face stayed right in my face, almost like his slack jaws were opening wide enough to take in my whole head so I would *have* to hear everything he said. And the night went on and I had to listen. It got cold. My shoulder hurt where I was laying on it and my left leg got sore and stiff where I was curled up on the hardwood floor. He told me what happened to him there. God, I hate it. I *hate* that story.

I was afraid to move so I stayed.

OCTOBER 31

Listen. That room is where it happened. He showed me.

The den is not so bad. It is terrible, but not like the room upstairs on the top floor there in the attic.

He whispered in my ear all night, until the sun came up and I could see light trying to come through the front door again. This time it was trying to seep in under the crack in the front door because the door had shut in the night. I don't know how.

It took me a long time to unbend myself from where I was lying where he preached to me. But I did and I started up the stairs because again the screaming would not stop until I did what he asked, what he *needed* me to do. I reached out and felt the first step under my fingers and then the next and so on until the front door was just a thin line, a tiny sliver of light seeping in under the bottom from way up at the top of the stairs. And by the time I was there, at the top, the light faded out and I knew it was night again.

He told me.

I went in there at the room under the eaves. There is a stout beam there. There is dust there and you can see where the rope went and where the wire was nailed down. And you can see where *that book* was, where it was lying when. When.

There in the wall you can see the nail still holding the wire down. And I reached up with him standing with me his face white like bone, white like a goddamned light there in the pitblackness under the eaves where everything was silent except for his screeching voice telling me how it was done and then *damned if I couldn't feel something in my hands.* 'Hemp,' he said it was. 'Hemp.'

And then he was screaming. I thought it was screaming but really he was laughing. At *me.* He was laughing at *me,* but I don't know why he laughed because that was the *only* thing he did not tell me before he began to squeeze down like a thin bundle of white clay, like a slim pencil of white light that vanished in a pale slurry down the woody grain under the eaves of that house.

He shut up, then. Then it was quiet again.

So now, do you hear me? Do you hear what I'm saying?

It was *here!* It was *right here!* I'm telling you! Why do you screw your face up like that when I'm looking at you? Why won't you *listen?* Listen to me! Don't run.

It will do no good to run. ✳

Mud

by Brian McNaughton

I had spent two years in the trenches when a terrible truth was revealed to me: Jerry was merely the noisiest, most numerous and most vexatious tool of our real enemy, and that enemy was Mud.

In his proper state, a man walks upon solid ground, drinks pure water and breathes clean air. In the most improper state where we soldiers had been thrust, men crawled and fought and slept in the same foul substance they drank and breathed.

To call it by so plain a name can give you no idea of its capacity for mischief. It was no mere compound of earth and water like the honest mud of the countryside, but a complex organism of earth and water and blood and waste, seasoned with foul chemicals and thickened with the rotted flesh of men and beasts. This malign entity clutched us always in its soggy grip, seeping through our clothing, staining our bodies, flavoring our food, clogging our nostrils, stopping our mouths, fouling our weapons and ultimately claiming our lives.

I do not believe we created this being with our murderous war. I suspect we unwittingly freed it from a prison fashioned by far wiser men in the dim past, men who had most unwisely neglected to tell us what combination of words and actions, what volume of human corpses and human suffering was required to break the seals they had put on this Mud of primal chaos.

The war had nothing to do with some absurd quarrel among kings and ministers or some brainless tangle of treaties. No one understood why the war began or why it continued. No one could stop it. No one wanted it . . . except the Mud.

This revelation—so simple, really, so obvious—came to me one morning after an all-night barrage. Those of us who still could crawled from our dugouts to see Jerry advancing through the mist. But were they in fact men? Their uniforms were not grey, their faces were not white. They were brown all over, brown as the ground they slogged through, brown as I was.

I looked about me. The formerly coherent lines and angles of the trench had been eroded, rounded . . . muddied. This amorphous mass concealed my absent comrades and fed upon them, gathering strength and size by a geometric progression. The surviving fools were all firing, hammering even more Huns into the Mud or falling into it themselves and being sucked down.

I wanted to explain my vision to Captain Bennett when he seized me by the shoulder and swore a blasphemous oath. "What are you playing at, Sergeant?" he screamed in my Mud-clogged ear. "Shoot! For God's sake, man, shoot!"

One look at the crudely-sculptured face of this brown Mud-man told me he would not understand. I gestured at the mound beside me: Wilkins, my feeder, who had tangled the ammunition belt when he sank. The captain retrieved the belt and fed muddy rounds into the gun. I fired and Fritz fell, a dozen, a hundred, two hundred. I couldn't miss them at this range. But why? Dead men made Mud.

The captain professed to believe that I had held my fire to lure as many of the enemy as possible towards my gun-position, and that my "steel nerves" had foiled their attack almost single-handedly. He later gave me a sealed message that, he said, contained my recommendation for a D.C.M., and he ordered me to convey it to the rear along with a small contingent of the wounded.

Such was my state of mind at this time that I suspected the message I carried might be an order to execute the bearer for having stumbled upon the truth behind the war. This may have been why I led my charges astray.

I believe, however, that I was beguiled by the unfamiliar song of a bird to investigate a sunken lane between flowering hedges, a lane of moist but solid earth that promised to lead to a dryer, cleaner place.

Surely neither reason would have consoled the two men who died, denied the treatment they might have received upon prompt delivery to a field hospital. But I don't regret their deaths, as we were able to bury them in the honest earth of a meadow. I thought they must have been grateful.

The bird continued to pipe its song as I recited the appropriate words over the shallow graves. I resisted an unseemly urge to cut short the ceremony and follow it. Its song was not unlike "La Folia," the weird folk-melody that bemused C. P. E. Bach, the elder Scarlatti, and so many other eighteenth-century musicians whose works I had played before I was thrown into the Mud, but it was not quite the same. As soon as was decently possible, I tried to whistle the tune and analyze the difference as we marched—more properly, as we hobbled along.

"That's a rum tune, Sergeant," Atkins muttered. "What is it?"

"That bird—" I began, but the bird had chosen to embarrass me by holding its peace. Atkins began to bleat a spirited version of "That's the Wrong Way to Tickle Mary," and the others joined in. I silently cursed them for scattering my concentration.

The lane led us to a mediaeval town of narrow lanes twisting between thick walls of stone, where nothing met our eyes that would have puzzled Scarlatti himself; although he too might have commented on the antiquity of his surroundings. The utter peace was seductive but disturbing. Without the cries of children and animals in the thickening dusk, without even the incessant, quarrelsome, Gallic jabber, with no smoke at any chimney nor light in any leaded window, the peace seemed less that of the civilian world than of the grave.

As an oppressed hush fell on the men's music-hall renditions, the bird sang again from a shadowed eve, but I was distracted by a new sound, an urgent clangor of human industry. At least two men were plying sledges against metal and stone with a vigor and rhythm reminiscent of the Nibelungs' workshop in Wagner's *Ring*.

The simile that came so readily to my mind may have been an omen, for no sooner had I thought of Wagner than I found myself face-to-face with a pack of Huns. They were a bigger and better-fed version of Jerry than one finds in the trenches nowadays, fitted with their new chamber-pot helmets, and with not a spot of the Mud on their loose, storm trooper uniforms. I leveled my rifle and called on them to surrender, but I wadded myself into a doorway as I did so.

They seemed oddly *annoyed*, as if we were more of an irksome hindrance to their purpose than a dangerous enemy, but they were clever as cockroaches, and we were able to kill only three of them before they had vanished into previously unimagined nooks and crannies in the stone facades. For their part, they took down Williams, who had been blinded by a phosphorus-shell, and the stiff-legged Robertson, who had been guiding him.

I called on them once more to surrender, but was greeted by a snarling diatribe that outstripped my linguistic skills.

"What's the bugger on about?" I asked Collins, our scholar from Dublin, who crouched under a farm-wagon directly opposite.

"Let them pass, he says, and they'll do the same for us, if we're foolish enough to go farther."

"Tell him that's not how war works," I said, but I delivered the message myself by loosing a round at an unsteady shadow where I had marked the voice, and I was rewarded with a shrill cry of, "Scheiss!"

I instantly regretted that, for Fritz marked my own position and opened up. I cringed against a stinging hail of stone splinters as bullets hammered the lintel. But my own men returned the fire—I believed there were no more than five on either side, now—and Fritz soon forgot his special animus against me.

As in so many French towns, we had just turned a corner in a remote village and come upon a cathedral worthy of a capital city. It lay across an open square of hard-packed earth at the foot of the street, and it had apparently been the site of all that Wagnerian racket as the enemy looted artifacts or engaged in vandalism for its own sake. Guttural cries and sustained gunfire came from that direction as more of them emerged from the cathedral.

I believed we were goners then, but Collins, who had a better view of the square, called, "They're mad, Sergeant! They're targeting their own men."

I thought at first this might have been a typical case of military confusion, but now the men in hiding returned the fire of those in the square, keeping up a lively dialogue all the while. We resumed firing, too, and the deadly crossfire soon brought that queer internal dispute to an end.

"Go away, Englishmen!" cried a voice from the square. "This is none of your concern."

"A peculiar attitude, surely," I remarked to Collins. "How many are there?"

"Three outside, an officer and two lads stripped to the waist."

"See if you can pick off the head Hun."

He missed, and the three vanished into the cathedral. Hugging the walls, we—only Collins, Liddell, Atkins and I, now—descended to the square, where Fritz welcomed us with a burst of machine-gun fire. We found crowded shelter behind a stone trough.

"Bloody hell, Sergeant, let's give it up!" Atkins said. "What's all this in aid of? Why are we even here, then?"

"Because God made us to share His everlasting happiness in Heaven, and because the king wants us to kill Huns. See if that lot were carrying anything useful."

Atkins may have thought my answer flippant, but it seemed true enough. The purpose of the war was clearer now that I could fight the enemy without making more Mud. It became dreadfully clear when, peeking out to survey piles of dirty laundry I had seen bandaging the base of the cathedral, I identified them as human bodies, men, women, priests in soutaines, even children, that the beastly Alleymen had lined up and shot.

Atkins returned with five potato-mashers. One never knew about these things, but I doubted Jerry would have been carrying booby-trapped grenades. I hesitated only a moment before twisting the handle of one and leaping up to hurl it at the door where the machine-gunner lurked.

"Sergeant!" Collins protested. "That's a bloody church!"

"Bloody, indeed," I said, ducking as the gunner stitched the top of our trough. "When—" my order was interrupted by the explosion, then by a renewed burst of machine-gun fire. I began again: "Take the rest of these and spread out to toss them when I begin firing."

The bird sang. I had come to see it as my good-luck charm, and I stood up to empty my clip through the door. I saw too late that the gunner and his helper crouched to one side on the portico. Fortunately for me, they were distracted by the sudden emergence of my men. I slapped in another clip

and shot the gunner just before a well-thrown egg blew both men and their
gun out to further defile their civilian victims.

"Now—" Incredibly, the idiot officer was firing at me with an automatic pistol from inside the church, a hopeless shot. Unable to see him, I
fired in the hope of keeping him down as I ran forward and waved on my
men. Both of them.

Crouching at the door of the church, we kept up a brisk exchange with
the officer, who managed to bring Collins down with a shot through the
lung before he announced his surrender.

"I have no more ammunition," he said, tossing his boxy Mauser out the
door and advancing as if to accept a medal. Atkins and I exchanged a look
that had become common, the look of Englishmen confronted with the latest
outrageous example of Hunnishness.

"I am Hauptmann Walther, Graf von der Hiedlerheim, a great-nephew
of Queen Victoria and a graduate of Oxford. I salute your gallantry and
determination, my former foes."

In a posh accent that must have recalled fond memories of sculling on
the Isis to the sod, I replied: "I never expected to meet so grand a person-
age, my dear Graf, and can only regret that our acquaintance must be so
brief. I am Sergeant Miller, great-grandson of Miller the gallows-bird, and I
must advise you that you should have surrendered *before* using the last of
your ammunition to kill my men."

I then blew his head off.

"Beautifully put, Sergeant," Collins wheezed.

* * *

We carried Collins inside the cathedral, where my hands began to shake so
badly as I tried to undo his tunic that I stepped back and told Atkins to tend
to him. He would have assumed my tremor was a common reaction to the
skirmish, but it was inspired by terror. The blood from the Irishman's sucking chest-wound had liquefied the caking of the fabric. The Mud had
returned; it stained my hands, it seeped through my own stiff tunic when I
urgently wiped them. Striding jerkily, I ventured deeper into the dark cathedral in search of any distraction as I tried hard not to scream.

Our grenades had made a fine mess of the place, blowing out most of the
stained-glass windows, but one that was nearly intact gave me pause. It
seemed less an image of a saint than of an ancient fertility goddess from the
Levant, all brown breasts and bum, but wearing a pair of hairy black trousers.
It might have passed muster for decency if one didn't inspect it closely, but I
did, and this garment did little to conceal her swollen pudendum. It would
have done even less had the labia not been black as the surrounding hair. I saw

8

0 Song of Cthulhu

that these were not trousers at all, but body-hair, foresting her loins and creeping up her extraordinarily swollen belly to the point where a navel might have
been. Her nether limbs were concealed by the curls as they spread out to
merge with a foreground of black murk shot with brown eddies.

Venus Emerging from the Mud might have been an appropriate name for
this nonesuch, but she was identified as Ste. Nigoureth. She held a misshapen flute between her prodigious breasts, but her hollowed cheeks suggested that she was sucking rather than blowing it. I doubted that Collins
would be able to identify this saint, probably the goddess of a Gaulish tribe
who had been grafted onto the local liturgy without papal sanction; nor
could he have done much with the Latin inscription, if Latin it were, for it
was remarkably deficient in vowels. I was distracted from my attempts to
pronounce it by a sudden recurrence of that bird-song, shockingly loud, as
if it were inside the cathedral. A fanciful man might have suspected that the
music came directly from Ste. Nigoureth's instrument.

"He won't make it," Atkins said at my shoulder, making me jump, but
I doubt he noticed as the window seized his attention. "Bloody hell! I knew
her sister in Liverpool. You had to clap your hand over your mouth and try
to finish fucking before you could start spewing."

* * *

I would have thought we had traveled a hundred miles behind the lines, to
say nothing of a hundred years, but a map retrieved from the dead officer
showed that the front was less than ten miles away. Even carrying Collins,
we could leave at dawn and make the railhead at St. Azedarac, our original
destination, by mid-morning. Our victory over Huns who had massacred
the citizens of a peaceful village would deflect whatever criticism I might
have faced for meandering through the countryside.

A prisoner would have been useful, though, to explain what Jerry
thought he had been playing at. Why would he infiltrate a crack
stormtrooper detachment behind our lines for no other purpose than to
murder children and loot a church? After we had supped on Jerry's barkers,
along with bread and wine from the sacristy, and lit all the candles and coal-
oil cressets we could find in a vain attempt to drive back the gloom of night,
we inspected their work.

They had broken into a crypt beneath the main altar and all but
unsealed a lead coffin whose lid was sculptured into what could have been a
slimmer and more decorous version of Ste. Nigoureth. The resemblance
didn't even occur to me until we had torn it open and found that it contained nothing but a replica, or perhaps even the original, of the queer flute
pictured in the window.

"I know they ain't half-fond of music, but even for Fritz, this does beat all," Atkins breathed as I lifted the grotesque pipe and turned it over in my hands. "Is *that* what they wanted?"

A dual bulb at the bottom suggested a gourd, although I believed the instrument had been carved from a single piece of very heavy, black wood. Curving upward from this, a thick shaft was perforated with holes that seemed too large and awkwardly spaced for human fingers. These were ringed with gold, and the mouthpiece was of gold, too, but that couldn't account for the value the Huns had put upon it. The hole in the mouthpiece itself seemed too narrow to inject a sufficient volume of air to make music.

I was seized by an irrational urge to try playing it. Yet some of the unpleasantness of the image in the window clung to it, deterring me.

"Give us a tune, then, Sergeant," Atkins urged, noting my fascination. "None of your weepy dirges, either, a nice tootle of 'Pack Up Your Troubles.'"

"Have a go yourself."

He didn't hesitate. His cheeks puffed out and his face reddened as he tried to force air into the mouthpiece, but not one sound came out of the flute. Then he tore it from his mouth with a look of shock and loathing, and he would have dashed it to the floor if I hadn't caught it.

"Why, what—?"

"It *moved!*" He spat. "Bloody thing wriggled like a . . . like a snake."

I didn't believe this, but his horror was clearly unfeigned as I put it to my own mouth and, imitating the saint's technique, sucked on it. This produced such a sudden and unprecedented surge of euphoria that I thought the pipe must contain the still-active residue of an ancient drug. If I had been thinking clearly I would have put it aside instantly, but I could no longer think clearly. I felt exhilarated, as if some cosmic secret were coyly dancing to the dark fringe of my consciousness, about to unveil itself fully in the next instant. The aches drained from my muscles, my limbs shed their weariness, all the unutterable nastiness of the war faded to become merely a rumor of another man's dream.

I fingered the pipe to produce the notes of "La Folia" as best I could, even though I knew that was the wrong tune. Rather eerily, I heard the music, or thought I heard it, not from the pipe itself but from the black vault high over our heads. I suddenly recalled the notes the bird had sung; and when I attempted to reproduce them, I heard them ringing clearly, triumphantly through the cathedral. But once again, the music seemed not to emanate from the pipe I held, but at once from all the shadows of the ancient building.

"Good Lord," I said, reluctantly taking the flute from my mouth. "What was that?"

Atkins answered cryptically: "Rain. You've whistled up a wind and no mistake, Sergeant."

I strode to the door and was driven back by a wet blast. The darkness outside was total, but it was obvious that the skies had opened. Even in the trenches, rain had always brought a clean smell, however brief, and I anticipated this with pleasure. But the wind that now howled through the vaults and rattled the remnants of the windows carried an odor more foul than any I had ever known.

I recognized it, though. In an undiluted and nearly unbearable concentration, it was the stench of Mud.

* * *

All night long the rain hammered down, the stench persisted. Our lamps and candles blew out, making the frequent lightning all the more jolting. I soon learned to avoid looking at the window depicting Ste. Nigoureth, her form seemingly twisted to a new and more disquieting posture by each flash, but indelible after-images of the creature capered on malformed legs in all the shadows. Collins didn't help matters by muttering deliriously throughout the night of a black goat, although most of his ravings were spat and croaked in an unfamiliar tongue that might have been Gaelic. Whatever it was, it recalled most disturbingly the tangled consonants from the saint's window.

I didn't dare touch the pipe again. I didn't have to, for that damnable tune always seemed to hover just beneath the roar of the wind and rain. I felt that something terrible was going on around me, all the more terrible because I couldn't say exactly what it was, and that I had somehow provoked it by piping the melody.

Atkins didn't share my apprehension. He curled into a pew and snored through the night. I'm not sure that he had even heard the music of the flute, but I refrained from questioning him about it for fear of seeming mad. I suspected that I was indeed going mad. Why should a little rain and a foul smell and illusory music—the latter probably brought on by too much exposure to shellfire—so unman me, who had sometimes slept as soundly as Atkins through the very real dangers of a German barrage?

I had no answer, but I fought against sleep. Whenever I began to drop off, the music grew far clearer; it progressed through a series of insane variations to a chaos of tuneless piping, heralding the sinuous approach of Ste. Nigoureth and her vile embrace. In my dreams I welcomed that embrace, and each time—more times than I had imagined possible, more times than I could bear, until the throbbing of pleasure progressed through increasing degrees of agony—I was woken by the pulsing of a seminal emission. The

Mud extended its slimy domain over my loins until I began to fear that I was spending blood to feed it.

* * *

The roar of the storm faded with the dawn, to be replaced by a rattle of gun-fire in the distance that grew steadily more intense. I ran to the door. As nearly as I could tell, and I had a good ear for such things, Jerry was deal-ing a massive punch against a narrow section of the front, having omitted the customary warning of a barrage.

This seemed almost unimportant as I gazed around me in a prickling drizzle and saw that the Mud had followed me, found me, and was now lay-ing siege to the cathedral. The bodies around the wall had sunk into it. The houses across the square seemed to be subsiding into it. The narrow street leading down to the square ran sluggishly with it.

Atkins stumbled out to my cry, but his oath of disbelief was lost in a sound like the gods ripping up their blankets. Shells from our own batter-ies were passing overhead. A steady crump-crump-crump soon rolled toward us from the site of the attack.

Into a brief letup, he said, "I think Fritz is coming this way."

"Where else?"

I was spared an explanation that would have sounded deranged, I'm sure, as our batteries opened up again. The captain had not returned with the flute, and so a large part of the German army was coming to get it. The cost didn't matter. My night-terrors had suggested to me that it was a weapon of fearful virulence, a device for summoning the Mud and its guid-ing demon.

Before I could stop him, Atkins stepped into the square and immedi-ately sank to his knees. His struggles to lift his feet only drove him deeper. I was somehow able to wrench him free, but only after the Mud had claimed both his boots.

* * *

Two men could never have defended the cathedral. A speedy departure was in order. Armed with Jerry's hammers and pry bars, we smashed up the pews and whatever other wood came to hand for makeshift duckboards and stretched them across the Mud in a queasy line.

We made a litter for Collins from the intricately carved panel of a con-fessional screen, overlarge and unwieldy. The poor chap objected as vehe-mently to this as if we were trying to lay him on a hot gridiron, but we assumed he was lost in his delirium and tied him down. Once he was secured, I noted that the screen's carving bore a weird motif of goat-horns

and hoofs in a riot of fantastic foliage, and all of it fit somehow with
Collins's ravings:

". . . it's more than a thousand children she has in the wood, you know,
and the wood wouldn't be same as the wood that would the greenwood . . .
the Wood at the World's End, Gram called it, lying astride this world and
the world of the *sidhe,* where the Black Goat pipes. . . ."

"This is going to be tricky," I told Atkins, but only knew what a
damnable understatement that was when I had taken my first step onto
the tilting boards with my arms awkwardly supporting Collins's litter
behind me.

We had got nearly halfway across when the wounded man redoubled
his struggles, thrashing and bouncing as if determined to make us lose our
slippery grip. He cried hoarsely that *she* was here, that *she* had come to get
him, and when I looked over my shoulder I saw that he was craning his neck
to stare, bulgy-eyed, at a bubbling eddy in the Mud beside him.

"Chub, you bleeding bugger!" Atkins shouted, struggling to keep his
balance. "Put a sock in it!"

Thus distracted, I lost my footing and fell to one knee. I threw a hand
out to brace myself against the unsteady board, releasing my hold on the litter. Atkins stumbled at the same time, and it was all over for Collins. Litter
and all, he slipped over the edge and vanished into the Mud as neatly and
quickly as a man buried at sea. In a flash of recovered lucidity, he cursed us
bitterly for having tied him down.

"No!" I screamed as Atkins flung himself flat and plunged both arms
to the shoulders into the Mud.

"Give us a hand, Sergeant! I've got—I think I've got—*good God, it's
got me!*"

Trembling on the unsteady planks, more like a shipwrecked sailor on a
raft than a soldier on duckboards, I watched helplessly as Atkins disappeared.
His legs scissored wildly in the air as he was upended and pulled down.

I crawled forward on my belly to the point where thick bubbles rose
and popped sluggishly. Having witnessed the fate of Atkins, I could no
more have put my hand into the Mud than I could have put it in a caul-
dron of boiling oil, but I told myself that I must, and I was trying to screw
up my courage when something broke the surface at a surprising distance
from the boards.

"Something," I say, because its contours had been so distorted by clinging Mud that I didn't recognize it as a human head until its clogged mouth
opened and it gabbled, in a voice very like Collins's, "She's got me, Sergeant,
you bastard, she's sucking me into her hairy—"

And he was gone.

Bubbles no longer broke the surface where Atkins had disappeared, but I at last forced myself to reach in with one arm while keeping a death-grip on the board. The Mud was unexpectedly warm, it slithered around my hand, and I told myself this was evidence that Atkins still struggled down there.

Another distorted face rose, this one directly beneath mine, and I swear it was not the face of Atkins. The soldier from Liverpool was bald as an egg beneath his helmet, but this head flowed with long curls, or with Mud that clung to long curls. I recoiled in terror. The arm slung around my neck was bare and soft, but its grip was like iron as it dragged me down.

This wasn't Atkins, it wasn't even human, it could only be Ste. Nigoureth herself, but it felt like human bone and teeth that my fist smashed as I hammered it again and again until it gave up its grip and sank.

* * *

Crouching in the thinner Mud beyond the square, I drifted away from the war for a time. I seemed to drowse in a country garden where bees murmured, and I wondered why they should be so active in such wet weather.

It took me an unconscionable time to tumble to the fact that someone was shooting at me.

Hastily taking cover in the mouth of an alley, I peered out to behold a sight that hadn't been seen at the front since the earliest days, Huns on horseback. They had called up their long-idle cavalry to exploit the breach and retrieve the hellish pipe, and now a cluster of them sat their horses on a low hill beyond the cathedral. Faced with the new lake of Mud before them, they seemed at a loss what to do next, but two or three had hit upon the pleasant diversion of trying to kill me.

Jerry's murderous intentions seemed almost irrelevant when I looked up and saw the thing that entangled the spires of the cathedral. It was a cloud, I suppose, but it was far darker than the remaining mass of cloud that pressed low on the village. It roiled and folded upon itself, expanded and exfoliated in ways independent of the surrounding atmosphere. Lurid flashes illuminated it from within at odd moments, but I heard no thunder. I thought at first it must be pouring rain on the Mud, but I came to the uneasy conclusion that the Mud was popping and spurting upward from some inner force as it yearned to join the cloud.

The more I stared at this anomaly, the more strange details I observed in its depths: eyes, tentacles, horns, random bits of human and bestial anatomy, none of them holding steady long enough to convince me that I wasn't using the cloud as a blank canvas for my fevered imagination.

This vision was so alien, so menacing, and so damnably real that I conceived an urgent desire to open fire on it. Only then did I discover that I had lost my rifle somewhere along the way. Without intending to, I had retained the pipe, however.

I had no doubt that I had called up this thing. But if it could sit on a whole church full of crosses and ikons and holy water, how could I possibly lay it? The archbishop of Canterbury might have offered helpful suggestions, or possibly Mr. Aleister Crowley, but neither of them was available.

All this while I had been tempted by a strong urge to put the pipe to my lips and play the tune it wanted. I could forget about the cloud, forget about the Huns, and recapture the sweet euphoria I had known last night. I feared that this was surely the path to my destruction, and I impulsively tried smashing the pipe against the stone wall beside me, but it seemed indestructible. Worse, my efforts provoked a sudden, angry expansion of the cloud, a more frenzied eruption of the Mud.

Jerry was up to something. No longer firing, the horsemen were shouting in unison—at me? No. A shift in the wind brought their peculiar cries to my ears, and it seemed they were chanting a variation of the saint's foul name: "Iä! Iä! Shub-Niggurath!" The flashes in the cloud began pulsing in time to this chant, displaying colours unknown to honest lightning.

I put the pipe to my lips. A hymn—but no hymn that came to mind would be a match for the otherworldly power of the theme that even now the German horsemen were bellowing. All other melodies seemed to have been driven clean out of my head. I clutched the pipe until my fingers bled in an effort to keep it still.

As cellist in a string quartet before the war, I had known a hundred melodies, a thousand, but none of them . . . and then I remembered the very last thing I had played before the Mud flowed over the world, the final theme of Bach's *Art of Fugue*. All his life he had used his work to praise God, but in that last work he had dropped the mask of Christian humility and taken all the credit with a flourish: I, Bach, a mortal man, did this. If there were any antithesis to the power of Primal Chaos, it was to be found in the greatest musical mind of all time. I attempted the four simple notes.

Once again I had no idea where the music came from, but it filled the air as if the stone walls of the village sang. The Mud cringed back towards the central lake, flowing around my feet so rapidly that I was hard put to keep my footing. Anticipating some spectacularly unpleasant effect, I backpedaled against the tide as hastily as I could, playing one part of the Bach fugue all the while. Oddest of all, I heard the other parts clearly, as if all Nature were joining me in an assault against the Unnatural.

Flashing and boiling all the while, the cloud condensed, darkened, and pressed down more heavily on the cathedral. The solid stones of the edifice wavered and began to flow downward, as if it had been nothing but a structure of Mud. Towers lost their clean contours and toppled. Buttresses melted away, the roof collapsed, the great walls folded in upon themselves.

Despite this monstrous addition, the lake didn't grow. In fact it shrank more and more rapidly as a vortex developed in the boiling Mud where the cathedral had fallen. Thinned to a pale mist, retaining nothing of its otherworldly imagery, the former cloud fell to the Mud and was absorbed.

I had forgotten the enemy. Understandably chagrined, they had left off posturing and chanting and were devoting their full attention to killing me.

They very nearly succeeded.

* * *

The army believed that I had done something remarkable, since Jerry's attack had recoiled at the very point where I was found barely alive. According to the official version, my small detachment had defended the cathedral so determinedly that the Huns had vindictively shelled it into oblivion. I did nothing to correct this, maintaining that my severe head-wound had produced amnesia.

No one mentioned the flute to me, and I suspect that Jerry managed to retrieve it, poor devil. The sudden collapse of his monstrous war-machine, the famine and plague and anarchy that seized his homeland, suggested forces even more sinister than human incompetence and confusion.

And now this Hitler chap—he does tend to rave on, doesn't he, even more rhapsodically than Kaiser Bill did, about blood and soil? We know what that combination can produce. I fear he may believe that Germany's last attempt to regress the human race to primal slime failed only because not enough blood was added to the mix.

As for the flute of Ste. Nigoureth . . . last night Jerry had the effrontery to interrupt a Mozart recital with his damned bombs. We musicians were sheltering in the underground with our audience when our guest artist, Herr Kreisler, said to me, "Did you notice that odd harmonic in the air-raid sirens? It sounded uncannily like 'La Folia,' didn't it? Except—"

And here he raised his violin to demonstrate the melody he believed he had heard.

Much can be forgiven a wounded war-hero, I have learned, but assaulting a world-famous violinist and smashing his Stradivarius underfoot may be a bit over the mark. I suspect that my musical career has suffered an irreparable reversal. ✳

Paedomorphosis

by Caitlin R. Kiernan

Nasty cold for late May, rain like March; Annie sat on one of the scrungy old sofas at the front of the coffeehouse, sipping at her cappuccino, milkpale bittersweet and savoring the warmth bleeding into her hands from the tall mug. The warmth really better than the coffee, which always made her shaky, queasy stomach if she wasn't careful to eat something first. Beyond the plateglass, Athens gray enough for London or Dublin, wet Georgia spring hanging on, Washington Street asphalt shimmering wet and rough and iridescent stains from the cars passing by or parked out front. The rest of the band late as usual and no point getting pissed over it, baby dykes living in their own private time zone. Annie lit another cigarette and reminded herself that she really was cutting back, too expensive and no good for her voice, besides.

The door opened, then, and the cold rushing in, sudden rainsmell clean to mix with the caffeinated atmosphere of Bean Soup, air forever thick with the brown aroma of roasting beans and fresh brewing. Jingled cowbell shut again, Ginger and Mary and Cooper in one soggy clump, stupid happy grin on Mary's face and Cooper sulking, wet-hen disgust and she set her guitar case down beside Annie.

"What's with this fucking weather, man, that's what I want to know? I think my socks have fucking mildewed."

"Maybe if you changed them every now and then," Ginger sniggered and Mary giggled; Cooper groaned, shook her head and "These two have been sucking at the weed all afternoon, Annie," she said. "It's a wonder I finally pried them away from the bong." Mary and Ginger were both giggling now.

"Well, you know I got all day," Annie said over the steaming rim of her mug, and that was true, three days now since she'd quit her job at the diner, quit before they fired her for refusing to remove the ring in her right eyebrow.

"Yeah, well, I'm about ready to kick both their stoner asses, myself," and another hot glance back at the drummer and bass player, Ginger and Mary still blocking the doorway, sopping wet and laughing. "I'm gonna get some coffee. *You* see if you can do something with them."

"Okay, ladies, you know it's not nice to pester the butch," and of course that only got them laughing that much harder, and Annie couldn't help but smile. Feeling a little better already, something to take her mind off the low and steelblue clouds as cold and insubstantial as her mood.

"She's such a clodosaurus," Mary said, tears from giggling and stuck her tongue out at Cooper, in line at the bar and her back to them anyway. "Hey, can you spare one of those?" and Mary was already fishing a Camel from Annie's half-empty pack.

"No, actually, but help yourself," and Cooper on her way back now, weaving through the murmuring afternoon crowd of students and slackers, Cooper with her banana-yellow buzzcut and Joan Jett T-shirt two sizes too small to show off her scrawny muscles. Annie still amazed that their friendship had survived the breakup, and sometimes, like now, still missing Cooper so bad it hurt.

"Thank you. I will," and then Mary bummed a light from Ginger.

Cooper sat down in a chair across from them, perched on the edge of cranberry naugahyde and sipped at her mug of black, unsweetened Colombian, plain as it got, no decaf pussy drinks for Cooper.

"They still going at it down there?" and Cooper stomped at the floor like a horse counting, and Annie nodded, "Yeah, but I think they're winding up."

And *"See,"* Ginger said, mock-haughty sneer for Cooper, "it's a *good* thing we were late. The sad widdle goffs ain't even done yet," and Cooper shrugged, "Unh huh," and she blew on her coffee. "We gotta find another fucking place to practice."

* * *

Honeycomb of identical rooms, gray cubicles beneath Bean Soup rented out for practice space, but down here the cozy scent of fresh-ground espresso replaced by the musty smell of the chalkwhite mushrooms they sometimes found growing in the corners, the mildew and dust laid down like seafloor sediment.

Concrete poured seventy or eighty years ago, that long since the sun into this space, never mind the single hundred-watt bulb dangling from the ceiling. Something painful bright but not light, stark illumination for the sickly little room so that they could see to tighten wing nuts and tune instruments, so Annie could read lyrics not yet memorized from her scribbly notes. Ten feet by ten, or that's what they paid for every month, but Annie had her doubts, maybe a different geometry than her idea of ten square. But at least the steel fire door locked and the pipes that laced the low ceiling like the coffeehouse's varicose intestines had never broken. Enough electrical outlets (when they'd added a couple of extension cords) for their monitors and Mary's dinky mixing board.

Thick layers of foam rubber glued to the walls, Salvation Army blankets stapled over that, and they still couldn't start practice until Seven
Deadlies had finished. No way of shutting out the goth band's frantic
nextdoor drone and "Those assholes must have the bitchmother off all sub-
woofers crammed in there," Cooper had said more than once, an observation she must have thought bore repeating. Sound you could feel in your
bowels, bass to rattle bones and teeth, that passed straight through concrete
and the useless sound-proofing.

Complaints from some of the other bands, but Annie thought it was a
shitty, pointless thing to do, bitching about another band playing "too
loud," and besides, the complaints all summarily ignored. So TranSister
always waited until Seven Deadlies were done for the afternoon before they
started. Simpler solution and no toes stepped on, no fear of petty reprisals.

One long and narrow hall connecting all the cubicles, cheapest latex
maroon coming off the walls in big scaley flakes, and TranSister's space way
down at the end. Passing most of Seven Deadlies on their way out (eight of
them, despite the name), painful skinny boys and girls, uncertain androgynes
with alabaster faces and kohlsmudged eyes. Pretty in their broken porcelain
ways and usually only the most obligatory conversation, clash of subcultures
and Cooper sometimes made faces behind their backs. But one of the girls
waiting for them this time, tall, thin girl in fishnets and a ratty black T-shirt,
Bauhaus and a print Annie knew came from *The Cabinet of Dr. Caligari*, tall
girl with her cello zipped snug inside its body-bag cover.

"Hi," she said, shy but confident smile, and Annie said hi back, struggling with the key and she could feel Cooper already getting impatient
behind her.

"I'm Elise," she said, was shaking Mary's hand, and "Would you guys
mind if I hang around and listen for a while?"

Immediate and discouraging grunt from Cooper and Mary said, quick,
"I don't know. It's really pretty close in there already and all . . ." and Elise
countering, satin voice and smile to melt butter and "I don't take up much
room, honest. And I can leave this in our space," pointing to her instrument.
Before another word, "Sure," from Annie, and to the others, "She can sit in
the big chair, okay?"

"Yeah," half a snarl from Cooper, "She can sit in the big chair. Right,"
and pushing her way past Annie, unlocking the door and inside, Mary and
Ginger pulled along sheepish in her wake.

* * *

Five times through the set, a couple of the newer songs more than that, only
three nights until they opened for Lydia Lunch and Michele Malone at the

40-Watt Club and everyone was getting nervy. Finally too tired for any more and Annie too hoarse, Ginger's Sailor Moon T-shirt soaked straight through so you could see she wasn't wearing a bra. Cooper and Mary dripping sweat, dark stains on the concrete at their feet. Annie had left the door open, against the rules but hoping that some of the stormdamp air from above might leak down their way.

Cooper sat on the floor and lit a cigarette, smoke ring aimed at the light bulb, and she pointed a finger at Elise.

"Damn, girl, don't you fucking sweat?" and getting nothing but that mockshy smile back, Elise who'd sat quietly through the entire practice, legs folded in a half-hearted lotus on the broken-down recliner, slightest shrug of her black shoulders.

"Well, *I* do," said Mary, propping her Barbie-pink Gibson bass against the wall, static whine before she switched off her kit. "I sweat like a god-damn pig," and she made loud, oinking noises for emphasis.

"Well, whatever, but you can fuck this heat," Cooper calling it a night, so time for a beer at The Engine Room; hazy, cramped bar next door to Bean Soup, pool tables and Mortal Kombat, PBR by the pitcher half-price because Cooper once had a thing with one of the bartenders.

Annie sat on the arm of the recliner next to Elise, top twisted off her water bottle and she took a long swallow. Bottle that had once upon a time held water from "wild Canadian springs," but recycled from the tap in her apartment time after time and now it tasted mostly like warm plastic and chlorine. Something to take the edge off the dryness in her throat, at least; she glanced down at Elise, had glanced at her a lot while TranSister had punched and yowled their way through carefully rehearsed riot grrrl anger. And every time, Elise had been watching her too, enough to make Annie blush and maybe she was starting to feel horny for the first time since she and Cooper had called it quits.

"What about it?" she asked Elise. "Wanna go get a beer with us?"

"I don't drink alcohol," and Ginger, rolling her eyes, squeezed herself out from behind her drums and past the big chair. "Well, they got Cokes and stuff, too," she said.

"Hey, we'll catch up with you guys in a little bit, okay?" Annie said, braver than she'd felt in months, the rest of the band exchanging knowing looks, but at least they waited until they were all three in the hall to start snickering.

"Sorry about that," when they were gone and feeling like maybe they'd taken her new boldness with them, so another drink from the bottle because she didn't know what else to do.

"That's okay. I understand," and Elise's voice cool and smooth and sly as broken glass.

"Thank god," and Annie sighed, relief and now maybe her heart could slow the fuck down. "I was afraid maybe I was making an ass of myself."

"Nope," Elise said, up onto her knees now and her lips brushing Annie's. "Not at all. Want to see something neat?"

* * *

The space where Seven Deadlies practiced like a weird Xerox, the same four walls, the same pipes snaking overhead, same mushroomy funk. But these walls painted shiny black and draped in midnight velvet (or at least velveteen), a wrought iron candelabra in one corner and plaster saints in the other three. Dusty, threadbare Turkish rug to cover the entire floor, a hundred faded shades of red and orange and tan, the overall design obscured by speakers and keyboard stands; a wooden table made from two saw horses and an old door, crowded with computers and digital effects equipment.

"Shit, did one of you guys win the Lotto?" and Elise laughed, shut the door behind them. "Jacob, our vocalist, comes from money," she said. "The old Southern type," and "It comes in handy."

Annie nodded, "With all this gear, no wonder you guys can make such a racket."

"Mostly we're working with MIDI programs right now," Elise said, standing just behind Annie and for the first time Annie noticed the heady, sweet reek of vanilla off the girl, and something else, something wild that made her think of weekends at her parents' river cabin when she was a kid.

"You know, Sound Forge and some other stuff. Lots of sampling," Elise was saying, "on Jacob's Mac."

"I don't know shit about computers," Annie said, which was true, not just a line to get away from shop talk and Elise smiled, another kiss on Annie's cheek. And that smell stronger than before, or maybe she was just noticing it now.

"Anyway, I wanted to show you something," and Elise stepped past her, past the computers and she was folding back a section of the velvet (or velveteen) curtain. "Down here."

Annie followed, six steps to the other side of the room and she could see the crack in the concrete wall, a foot wide, perhaps a little more where it met the floor, stooping for a better view and *This is where it's coming from,* she thought. The waterlogged, mudflat smell of boathouses and turtles, and she wrinkled her nose at the dark inside the hole, the fetid air drifting from the crack.

"Man, what a mondo stinkorama," trying to sound funny and Annie realized that she was sweating, cold sweat and goosebumps and no idea why.

Something triggered by the stench from behind the wall, a memory she wasn't quite remembering or something deeper, maybe, primal response to this association of darkness and the rotting, wet smell.

"Oh, it's not that bad," Elise said, taking Annie's hand and she slipped through the hole, gone, like the concrete wall had swallowed her alive and nothing left in the world but one arm, detatched, silver bracelet and ragged black nails, one hand still holding Annie's tight.

"Aren't you coming?" she said, "Don't you want to see?" Elise's voice muffled and that speaking-in-an-empty-room quality to it now, sounding much further away than she should've, and "No," Annie said, "Not really, now that you mention it." But a tug from Elise and she almost pitched forward, one hand out so she didn't smack her forehead on the wall. Sweatcool palm against cold cement and a sudden gust or draft from the crack, stale pocket dislodged by Elise, and Annie was beginning to feel a little nauseous.

"I'm *serious*," she said, tugging back and Elise's white face appeared in the crack, irked frown for Annie like something from an old nightmare, like the sleepwalker on her T-shirt.

"I thought dykes were supposed to be all tough and fearless and shit," she said.

Annie shook her head, swallowed before she spoke. "Big ol' misconception. Right up there with the ones about us all wanting dicks and pickup trucks."

Elise was crawling out of the crack, dragging more of that smell out behind her, dustgray smears on her black shirt, dust on her Doc Marten's and a strand of cobweb stuck in her hair.

"Sorry," she said, but smiling now like maybe she really wasn't sorry at all. "I guess I just don't think about people being bothered by stuff like that. My dad's a paleontologist and I spent a lot of time as a kid crawling around in old caves and sinkholes."

"Oh," Annie said and sat down on the rug, grateful for something between her and the concrete. "Where are you from, anyway?"

The loose flap of cloth falling back in place, once again concealing the crack, and "Massachusetts," Elise replied, "but no place you've probably ever heard of."

"Yeah, like Athens is the white-hot center of the solar system," and a dry laugh from Annie, then, sound to make herself feel better and she fluttered her eyelashes, affected an air-headed falsetto, "'*Athens?* Athens, *Georgia?* Isn't that where R.E.M.'s from?'"

"And the B-52s," Elise added, sitting next to Annie. "Don't forget the B-52s," and "Yes," Annie agreed. "*And* the stinkin' B-52s." Both of them laughing and Annie's abrupt uneasiness fading almost as fast as it had come, only the slimmest silver jangle left in her head and Elise bent close, kissed her and this time their tongues brushed, fleeting, teasing brush between mouths before she pulled away.

"Play some of your stuff for me," Annie said and when Elise looked doubtfully toward her cello, "No, no, no. A tape or something," and she motioned toward the black cabinets and consoles, row upon numbered row of dials and gauges. "With all these cool toys, surely you guys have put something down on tape by now," and Elise nodding, still doubtful but *yes*, anyway; she stood, began digging about on the door *cum* table, loud and brittle clatter of empty cassette cases and a moment later slipped a DAT cartridge into one of the machines.

"Jacob would probably have a seizure if he knew I was fucking around with this stuff," she said.

And nothing at first, at least nothing Annie could hear, and then the whisperchirp of crickets and fainter, a measured dripping, water into water. Elise returned to her spot on the floor next to Annie, an amber prescription bottle in her hand and "You *do* get stoned, don't you?"

The crickets getting louder by degrees, droning insect chorus, and Annie thought she could hear strings buried somewhere in the mix, subliminal suggestion of strings, but the dripping still clear, distinct *plop* and more distinct space between each drop's fall.

"Mostly pot," Annie said and Elise had popped the cap off the bottle, shook two powder blue pills into her open palm. "This is better," she said. And Annie already feeling like a pussy for not following her into the hole in the wall, accepting the pills, dry swallowing both before she had a chance to think better of it.

"What are they?"

Elise shrugged, "Mostly codeine, I think. One of our keyboardists gets them from her mother." Then three of the tablets for herself before she screwed the cap back on the bottle, tossed it back onto the table.

"Okay, now listen to this part," and Annie's attention returning to the tape: the crickets fading away and there were new sounds to take their place, a slow, shrill trilling, and then another, similar but maybe half an octave higher; a synth drum track almost as subtle as the strings.

"Are those *frogs?*" Annie asked, confused, wishing she had her water bottle because one of the mystery pills had stuck halfway down, and Elise shook her head, "No," she said. "Toads."

* * *

Later, but no sense left for her to know how much later, wrapped up tight in the twin silken embrace of Elise and the pills, time become as indefinite as the strange music that had swelled until it was so much bigger than the room. Understanding, now, how this music could not be held within shabby concrete walls. Feral symphony and Annie listening, helpless not to listen, while it took her down and apart and Elise made love to her on the shimmering carpet like all the colors of autumn lying beneath still and murky waters. Held weightless between surface tension and siltdappled leaves; the certain knowledge of dangerous, hungry things watching them from above and below, but sanctuary in this girl's arms.

And the second time Elise offered to show her what was on the other side of the wall, Annie didn't say yes, but she didn't say no, either; dim sense that she'd acted silly earlier, afraid of the dark and getting her hands dirty. Elise still in her shirt, but nothing else, Annie in nothing at all and she followed, neither eager nor reluctant, scraped her shoulder squeezing through, but the pain at least a hundred harmless miles away.

"Watch your head," Elise whispered, library whisper like someone might overhear, "the ceiling's low through here."

So hands and knees at first, slow crawl forward, inch by inch and the muddy smell so strong it seemed to cling to Annie's bare skin, scent as solid as the cobwebs tangling in her hair. A vague sense that they were no longer just moving ahead, but down as well, gentle, sloping descent and then the shaft turned sharply, and Annie paused, "Wait," straining to see over her shoulder. Pinhead glimmer back the way they'd come, flyspeck of light like the sun getting around an eclipse and a sudden, hollow feeling in her gut that made her wish they had stayed in the warm pool of the Turkish carpet, tadpole shallows, drifting between the violins and keys, the twilight pond sounds.

"It's so far back," she said, the compressing weight of distance making her voice small, and "No," Elise said, "It's not much further at all."

* * *

Finally, the shaft opening wide and they could sit up, the impression of a vast and open space before them and the unsteady flame of the single pillar candle Elise had brought from the room revealing high, uneven walls to either side, old bricks wet and hairy with the colorless growth of some fungus or algae that had no need of sunlight or fresh air. "Be careful," Elise said and her arm out and across Annie's chest like a roller coaster safety bar, and she saw that they were sitting on a concrete ledge where the crawl space ended abruptly. Short drop down to rubble and the glint of water beyond that.

"Where are we?" and Annie heard the awe in her voice, little girl at the museum staring up at a jumble of old bones and daggerteeth awe; Elise pointed up, "Right beneath the old Morton Theater," she said, "But this goes on a long way, beneath most of downtown, and *that* way," and now she pointed straight ahead of them, "that way goes straight to the Oconee River. Old basements and sub-basements, mostly. Some sewer lines. I think some of it must be pre-Civil War, at least," and Annie wished halfheartedly she wasn't so fucked up, so she could remember how long ago that was.

And then Elise was helping her down off the ledge, three or four feet to an unsteady marble slab, and then showing her the safer places to put her feet among the heap of broken masonry.

"I never had any idea this was down here," she said and realized that she had started crying, and Elise kissed her tears, softest flick of her tongue as if salt might be too precious to waste and "No one ever has any idea what's below their feet," she said. "Well, *hardly* ever, anyway."

Misstep, ankletwist and Annie almost fell but Elise there to catch her. "Are you okay?" but Annie only nodding her head, guessing she must be since nothing hurt. A few more careful, teetering steps and they were already to the black water, mirrorsmooth lake like glass or a sky without stars or moon. And Annie sat down again, winded and dizzy, a little queasy and that was probably the pills, the pills and the smell. "How deep?" and Elise smiled, Elise holding the candle out above the surface and the water stretched away as far as they could see. "That depends. Only a few feet right here, but a lot deeper in other places. Places where the roofs of basements have fallen in and the structures below have been submerged."

"Shit," Annie muttered, her ass cold against the stones and she hugged herself for warmth.

"There are a lot of cool things down here, Annie," and Elise was crouched right at the water's edge now and one hand dipped beneath the surface, spreading ripples that raced quickly away from the candlelight.

"Things that have gotten in from streams and rivers and been down here so long they've lost their eyes. Beautiful albino salamanders and crayfish," she said, "and other things." She was tugging her T-shirt off over her head, the candle set carefully aside and it occurred to Annie how completely dark it would be if the flame went out.

"Want to swim with me, Annie?" Elise asked, seductive coy but Annie shivered, not the damp air or her nakedness but remembering now, swimming with a cousin when she was nine years old, a flooded quarry near her house where kids skinny-dipped and thieves dumped the stripped hulks of cars and trucks. Being in that water, beneath glaring July sun but not being able to see her feet, dog paddling and something slimy had brushed fast across her legs.

"I'll wait here," she said and reached for the candle, held it close and the flame shielded with one hand, protective barrier between the tiny flame and any draft or breeze, between herself and the native blindness of this place.

"Suit yourself," and a loud splash before Elise vanished beneath the black surface of the pool. More ripples and then the surface healing itself, ebony skin as smooth as before and Annie left alone on the shore. Every now and then a spatter or splash that seemed to come from very far away, Annie feeling sleepy and the pills playing with her sense of distance, she knew. Trying not to think of how filthy the water must be, everything washed down sinks and toilets and storm drains to settle here. But Elise would be back soon and they could leave, and Annie closed her eyes.

* * *

Sometime later, a minute or an hour, and she opened them again, headachy and neckstiff, the nausea worse; Elise was there, dripping, and her hands cupped together, something held inside them for Annie to see. Something fetal, the pinkwhite of an old scar, floating indifferent in the pool of Elise's hands, and she said, "Isn't she wonderful? She looks a little like *Gyrinophilus palleucus,* but more likely she's a whole new species. I'll have to send one back to my father."

And then the salamander released, poured from her hands back into the lake, and she bent to kiss Annie. Slick arms around Annie's waist and lips so cold, so wet they might be a drowned girl's, drowned Ophelia risen, *And will 'a not come again, and will 'a not come again;* faint and fishy taste passed from Elise's mouth, and she pulled away, was reaching for her T-shirt, lying where she'd left it on the rocks.

"I really hope you didn't get bored," she said, and Annie shook her head, "You should have come."

Elise lifting her arms, and Annie saw the crimson slits where her armpits should be, the feathered edges bright with oxygen-rich blood, gasping slits like twin and puckered mouths, and then the Bauhaus shirt down, and Annie almost made it to the edge of the water before she vomited.

* * *

The last week of June and TranSister moved their gear into a new space across town, a big loft above a pizza place, the rent too high but they were sharing the cost with two other groups. And the wet weather passed into the blistering swelter of early summer, and Annie stayed away from Bean Soup. There were other coffeehouses, and when she saw Elise on the street she smiled, polite recognition, but never spoke. A few prying questions from Mary and Ginger, but she only had to tell them once to shut the fuck up.

And sometimes, late at night and especially when the summer storms came riding high and swift across the land and the sky rumbled like it was angry at the world, she would lie awake in her apartment on Pulaski, trying not to remember the throbbing, amphibian voices threaded into the fabric of Seven Deadlies' music, *Elise*'s music, trying not to think about the vast and empty spaces that might sprawl somewhere beneath her. And unable to think about anything else. ✳

> *There are strange things living in the pools and lakes in the hearts of mountains . . .*
>
> —J. R. R. Tolkien

Intruders

by Hugh B. Cave

When his wife died and his kids called him a stubborn old man, retired police captain Tom Carter only shrugged. His son and daughter were probably right, he conceded. But they should try to look at the problem from his point of view.

"If I sell this big old Hancock County house and move to Atlanta to be closer to you two and your families," he said, "I'll just make your life and my own miserable. I'll grant you I ought to move into a smaller house that I can take care of by myself, but it has to be a *house*. With your mother gone, I'm lonely, kids. I need things to do like mowing a lawn and puttering about in a garden. Staring at a TV screen all day long in a two-by-four apartment just won't cut it."

So he found a smaller Hancock County house, one more suitable for a widower, and they helped him move into it, and he thought he had the problem solved. The house was on a short, quiet street in a pleasant little town, with fine big *Magnolia grandiflora* in the front yard and room for a vegetable garden in back. It had a spare bedroom and an extra bathroom, in case any of his old friends wanted to pay him a visit and stay awhile. And he had some interesting neighbors.

The ones across the street—Kempton was their name—were about his age and had a divorced granddaughter and her small son living with them. The lot of them walked over to welcome him the day after he moved in. On his left was a young couple with nine-year-old son who would call out, "Hi, Mr. Carter!" if Carter happened to be in his yard when the boy came bounding out of the house or jogging home from the school bus stop. And on his right, in a house about the size of his, was a woman close to his age whose husband had died only a few weeks before Carter moved in. Millicent Armer was attractive, with a fine figure and lovely red hair.

Like Carter, Mrs. Armer enjoyed gardening, though her taste leaned toward flowers rather than vegetables. Almost every time he went out, he would see her on her knees with a box of garden tools beside her and, there being no fence between them, they would exchange a few words about this and that.

Before long they ceased being "Mr. Carter" and "Mrs. Armer" and became a more neighborly "Tom" and "Millie."

Though lonely with his wife gone, Carter was in good health except for having a bladder that interrupted his sleep two or three times a night. Fortunately, when that happened he had only a few steps to go to the bathroom off his bedroom. The window there was fitted with a kind of frosted glass, and the only time he could see out, or anyone could see in, was when it was open.

This was September. Air conditioning could be dispensed with and the window left open at night to provide fresh air. So when he went into the bathroom at night he could see into Millicent Armer's back yard, because she had a floodlight over her back door.

In fact, most of the townspeople had installed floodlights by now, believing—or hoping—they afforded some protection. All over the United States of America, in small towns and big cities alike, newspapers reported a rash of nighttime break-ins. For the most part, those committing the crimes were drug-addicted teenagers, desperate for money to support their habit but unable or unwilling to work for it.

So . . .

One night when Carter got up to go to the bathroom about three a.m.— he had a small alarm clock with a luminous dial on his bedside table, so he was certain of the time—he happened to glance out of the window, and as he was standing there, he saw someone at Millicent Armer's back door.

Oh-oh, he thought. *A lone prowler at three in the morning?* So he didn't flush the toilet when he was finished—with the window open, the caller would have heard it—but just stood there in his pajamas, in the dark bathroom, looking out.

And realized, with a shock, that the prowler was a woman. And not a real woman, but one quite extraordinary.

In fact, though she wore some sort of white dress or gown, Carter could see the door and the doorframe quite clearly through it—and through *her.* That she actually was female there could be no doubt, of course. The gown and the shape of the body beneath it were both quite clearly defined. Yet he could see the doorway as though nothing at all were standing in his line of vision.

And there was something else that didn't seem real. Along with the vision of a ghostly woman, he was hearing something. Something he recognized, because he had always loved classical music and had quite a collection of it.

What he was hearing was a sort of ghostly version of *The Miraculous Mandarin,* by the Hungarian composer, Béla Bartók.

He took in a sharp breath of astonishment. Unfortunately it caused him to cough.

Spinning around to look at Carter's bathroom window, the lady apparently saw him standing there. And vanished.

Didn't walk away, or float away. Simply vanished, disappeared like a blown-out candle flame.

Carter stood there, waiting to find out if she would return. Stood there for nearly half an hour, actually. But she didn't. So he finally went back to bed, to lie there wide-awake and wide-eyed thinking about it. Twice more that night he got up and went into the bathroom—not for the usual reason, but to look out of the window at Millicent Armer's back door. But nothing was there. At least, nothing he could see. Nor did he hear the Bartók music again.

At daybreak he got up, dressed, and had a cup of coffee. Then at eight o'clock, when he felt Millie would also be up, he went across to that same back door and knocked on it.

She was wearing a blue dress with white dots on it that morning. Very pretty with her lovely red hair and blue eyes. Carter said he had something to tell her, and asked if he might step in for a minute.

"But of course!" she said with a welcoming smile. "I'm just having a cup of tea. Come and join me."

He hadn't been in her kitchen before—only in the front room by way of the front door. It was a nicer kitchen than his, with paneled walls and all sorts of cupboards, and a breakfast nook containing a handsome oval table with four chairs. Millie and he sat there at the table, with tea in front of them, and he began the conversation by saying, "You know, of course, Millie, that I can see your back door at night from my bathroom, because of your floodlight."

"From your *bathroom,* Tom?" said she, sort of frown-smiling.

"When my window's open. Which is now every night unless we're having rain or a lot of wind."

"I see."

"What you didn't see last night, I'm sure," said he, "was someone at your back door about three a.m."

Her reaction startled him. The smile vanished. All the color fled from her face.

"Someone—at—my—door?" she managed at last. "And did you—did you hear any music?"

"Why, yes, I did! From *The Miraculous Mandarin,* by Bartók!"

"Oh, God," she whispered.

Carter reached across the table to touch her hand, which lay there palm down, like something that had just died, next to the teacup for which she'd been reaching. It was cold as ice. He let his own hand rest upon it, hoping to make her feel she had a friend who wanted to help. "You mean you've seen this woman before?" he asked gently.

Millicent slowly nodded, as though even that little effort caused intense pain.

"Often?" he pressed.

"No, not often," she said. "Once before Arthur died. Twice since."

"You know her?"

"I wasn't sure. But if you heard Bartók . . . yes . . . I'm certain."

Carter waited. There was something she wanted to tell him, he felt, but the color had not returned to her face. The look of apprehension, fright, terror—whatever it was—still remained. She seemed to be fighting to regain control of her emotions, and it might take time.

He gently withdrew his hand from hers and they sat there in silence for a time. Then she spoke in a voice so nearly inaudible that he had trouble hearing her.

"I need someone to talk to about this, Tom. Can I look upon you as a friend?"

"You know you can," he replied, reaching for her hand again.

"I must tell you about my husband. You won't mind?"

"I won't mind. Of course I won't."

"How I met him, I mean. How I married him. It's—have we known each other long enough for you to want to hear about this?"

"Talk to me, Millie," Carter said.

"Very well. I lived in Atlanta and worked as a receptionist for a pharmaceutical firm. My name was Osborne then. I was a widow. My husband, Jim Osborne, had died in a car accident. Arthur Armer, the man I'm telling you about, represented a supplier of ours based here in Hancock County, and lived in this house—*this* one, here, where we are now—with his wife. And every time he came to Atlanta, he—well, he let me know that he found me attractive." She paused, shaking her head and letting her breath out in a kind of sigh. "Must I go into details about that part of it?"

"Of course not," Carter said.

"I told him no," she went on. "I told him I didn't go out with married men, ever. And never would."

The silence came back between them. Carter was the one who broke it. "And then his wife died?"

She nodded. "Then his wife died. And because I liked him, I began going out with him. And ended up marrying him, giving up my Atlanta apartment and moving in with him here."

Carter thought about it for a bit, then said, "So he and his wife both died in this house?"

"Yes, both of them."

"What caused her death?"

"A heart attack. At least, that's what he told me."

Carter did some thinking. "Did you ever make inquiries? Other than asking *him,* that is."

She shook her head.

"Do you have a photo of his wife?"

She got to her feet in silence and left the room. Returning, she placed on the kitchen table between them a color photograph of a woman.

Though he might well have, Carter did not blurt out, "Good Lord! This is the woman I saw at your back door last night!" What he actually said, after frowning a moment, was, "Millie, tell me something. Or perhaps you've already told me, and I haven't got things in their proper order yet. This woman, Arthur Armer's wife, died of a heart attack?"

"Yes."

"Then her husband married you and *he* died."

"Yes."

"Just how did he die?"

She didn't reply at once. Again for nearly a minute she only looked at him. Then, closing her eyes, she said, "I went shopping. He was fine when I left, sitting at his desk in what he called his workroom. The desk is still there. But when I drove into the garage and beeped the horn to let him know I was home and needed some help with the groceries, he didn't come. And when I walked into the house and called out to him, he didn't answer. That frightened me, so I ran to his workroom, where I'd left him, to see if something was wrong."

"And?"

"He was sitting there at his computer, staring as if he were writing something. A letter, perhaps. But when I touched him on the shoulder he fell sideways and I saw his face, and I screamed."

"Screamed?"

"His eyes were wide open, and the look on his face—well, the whole shape of his face was changed by it, but I knew it was a look of fear. Or terror. As if he'd seen something so awful it changed his whole appearance, making his eyes bulge out and his mouth fall open and the rest of him freeze into—into—an obscene position, as if he had died trying to fend off something horrible that was attacking him."

She paused to look at Carter, and he saw tears welling in her eyes. "And all at once," she said, "I realized I was hearing music. *Her* music, the Bartók. He had told me it was her favorite, one time when I came across a recording of it and would have played it. He took the CD out of my hand and smashed it."

"You found him and heard the music," Carter said, scowling. "Then what? You called nine-one-one?"

She nodded. "But it was too late. Even before I called, I knew he was dead. When they got here, there was nothing they could do."

"Millie," Carter said, "there's something going on here. This husband of yours—you wouldn't marry him while his wife was alive, but she died and you became his wife. Then *he* died. Now she—his dead wife—shows up at your door in the middle of the night, but she isn't real, and I hear a piece of music he told you was a favorite of hers. Would I be way out of line if I suggested you come over to my place at night until we find out what's happening? I have a guest room you can use."

"I have a guest room *you* could use, Tom," she said.

"That would suit you better? If I came over here?"

With her eyes still full of tears, she moved her head up and down.

"All right," Carter agreed. "I'll come back here tonight when it gets dark."

He stood up. She did too, and they looked at each other across the table. Then, with a little sob, she came around the table into his arms, and he held her until she stopped trembling.

"When it gets dark, Millie," Carter said then, and went home.

* * *

Two disconnected events of importance happened that night. The first occurred in Millie's house before Carter and Millie retired to their separate bedrooms.

They were in the living room, talking. Mostly they talked about the strange death of Millie's husband, and about the woman in white whom Carter had seen at her back door the night before. And, to a lesser degree, about his having heard the Bartók.

"I have a theory," Carter said. "It may be completely crazy, but then again, I've been a policeman most of my adult life and have seen some strange things over the years." He paused, suddenly afraid he might be on the verge of saying something that would put an end to their friendship. He didn't want their friendship to end.

Millicent only looked at him and waited, though frowning a little as though slightly puzzled.

It had to be said, Carter decided, and leaned toward her to say it, very much aware of how pretty she was in the soft light of the lamp beside her chair.

"You told me your husband—before you married him—came onto you pretty strongly, as the kids might phrase it today, even though he was married," Carter said.

She nodded.

"In fact, you had to tell him you didn't go out with married men. Ever."

"That's right," she replied almost inaudibly.

"Then his wife died. Of a heart attack."

"Yes."

"He worked in pharmaceuticals, you said. So he knew about drugs, poisons, that kind of thing. He had access to such stuff."

Millie's eyes widened. Her face took on an expression of shock. "You think he killed her!" she whispered.

"It's at least possible, isn't it? And it would explain her coming back. You say you saw her once in this house before he died and that when he died he had—how did you put it?—such a look of terror on his face that you think he may have been frightened to death."

Millie only gazed at him in silence, with one hand half lifted as though in protest.

"You say you saw her twice *after* he died," Carter went on. "And now she's here again. Which could mean that she thinks you were his accomplice. That you and he planned her death together."

"No!" The word shrilled from Millie's lips with such force it made the windows shudder. "If he killed her, I had nothing to do with it!"

Carter threw up his hands. "Good Lord, I'm not accusing you. I only said she might *think* you planned it with him, Millie. She's avenged herself on him. Now she may be seeking vengeance on you."

"Wait." Millie put her hands on the arms of her chair and pushed herself unsteadily to her feet. "Wait, please," she said again, and all but ran from the room. "I won't be a minute!" she called back as she disappeared down the hall toward her bedroom.

It seemed more than a minute to Carter as he sat there rigid, waiting, hoping to God he had not wrecked their friendship by stupidly putting forth an unprovable theory that he should have kept to himself.

When she reappeared she was calm again. Walking across the room toward him, she extended her right hand and there was a white envelope in it. "Read this, Tom," she said.

He took from the envelope a hand-written letter addressed to Millicent Osborne and signed by one Arthur Armer. A letter from her husband, obviously written to her before she became his wife. It told in sad detail the passing of Arthur Armer's wife, of a heart attack, and how the writer hoped that she, Millicent, would understand his grief.

Finishing the letter, he frowned and looked expectantly at Millie.

"So you see," she said. "I was not his accomplice. If he murdered her, as you suggest, he did it without my knowledge."

Carter slowly nodded. *But does the ghost of Armer's murdered wife know that?* he asked himself.

It was something to think about. Assuming, of course, that he was right about the woman's death in the first place.

* * *

The other important event that happened that night took place across the street. The Kemptons, who lived across from Carter, were robbed.

As mentioned, the Kemptons were people about Carter's own age who had a divorced granddaughter and her small son living with them. And they were nice people—nice enough, at any rate, to have come over to welcome him to the neighborhood the day after he moved in.

About seven in the morning, in Millicent Armer's guest room, Carter heard strange sounds from over there and went to a window to see what was happening. He saw two police cars in the Kemptons' driveway. They left soon afterward, and about nine o'clock, after Carter had returned to his own home, Alan Kempton came across the street and rang his bell.

"I suppose you wonder what the cops wanted, Tom," said Kempton, a small, wiry man with a forthright way of talking. "Thought I'd better tell you, so you'll be on guard."

Carter invited him in, and they sat in Carter's living room.

"We were robbed," Kempton said. "I didn't hear them break in, mind you, but about four-thirty I woke up and realized there was somebody in the house, and got up to investigate. There were three of them, and they'd opened a kitchen window—with a special tool burglars have for doing that, the police said—and they had guns and told me they'd shoot me if I made a noise."

"What kind of guns?" asked Carter.

"Those semi-automatic pistols you hear so much about these days. Glocks, I think they're called. Anyway, they're awesome. And I wasn't about to argue with anything that deadly, believe me."

"Of course."

"So they took our TV and other things, and made me give them what money I had in the house—about a hundred and eighty dollars. Then one of them hit me with his gun and knocked me out. It was after six when I came to and was able to wake my wife and the others and call nine-one-one."

"Three of them?" Carter said, scowling. "What did they look like?"

"They were teen-agers. The oldest couldn't have been more than eighteen and had one of those Indian haircuts—you know, with a ridge of hair

across the top and the rest of his head shaved? The others were maybe fifteen or sixteen, and all three were high on something—you could tell by
their eyes, which were too big and too bright. And they'd have shot me, I
know they would, if I hadn't done what they told me to."

Carter nodded. "Thanks for coming over to warn me," he said. "If I
can help . . ."

"No, there's nothing you can do to help. I just thought you ought to
know, so you'd be on your guard."

Carter frowned. "I wish to God we knew what to do about these teens
and their drug-addiction problems. It's tearing the country apart."

"You ask me," his caller said with a long face, "it's because we haven't
been nearly tough enough on the creeps who sell the damned drugs. Cops
risk their lives catching them, and smart lawyers get them off or idiot judges
turn them loose to keep on doing it. The whole country is heading straight
to hell if we don't wake up and do something."

Shaking his head and muttering, he trudged back across the street.

* * *

In the days and nights that followed, former police captain Tom Carter came
to know the home of his neighbor Millie Armer quite intimately. He continued to occupy the guest room at night, of course—he was that kind of
man—but there were assorted things that needed doing or fixing around
Millie's house, and he knew how to do them and fix them. He and Millie
did things together, too, often spending time on their knees, side by side, in
her flower garden and his plot of vegetables.

They did not talk about his "theory" again. But Carter knew where she
kept the letter from Arthur Armer, informing her of his former wife's death
by heart-attack. And that bit of knowledge was to come in handy.

It happened in the third week of their "relationship"—if such is the
word for the loving but not-quite-intimate life they led. Millie had retired
early that night, tired after a long day of shopping for both of them.
Carter was about to go to his bed in the guest room after the eleven o'
clock news on TV when he saw a strange glow outside one of the living
room windows.

Striding to the window—he was still young enough to stride, in fact
was still young enough to serve as a captain of police had regulations permitted it—he saw something at the same back door where the nightlight
gleamed. The door at which he had seen the woman in white that first time,
from the window of his bathroom.

All right, he thought. *Let's confront this and see what happens.*

Reaching the back door, he snapped the deadlock back, then jerked the door open. And there she was: the woman in white whom he had seen before, but diaphanous, transparent, so much a nothing that he could see his own house, his own bathroom window, as though she were not there at all. And he was hearing the music again. Béla Bartók's *Miraculous Mandarin*. Not clearly. Not as though he were hearing it at a concert or even from a CD player, but as though it were a faintly shimmering, quivering part of the night itself.

He took a step backward. Nothing in his police training had prepared him for a face-to-face encounter with a creature such as this, who brought her own weird music with her!

She took a step forward and was suddenly inside the house, with the door wide open behind her. And then, so swiftly that Carter felt he'd been struck by a bolt of lightning, she changed.

The music persisted, but no longer was Carter face to face with an attractive young transparent woman in a white dress. The thing confronting him was straight out of an incredible, blood-chilling horror movie: a creature with the face of a fiery serpent and hair made up of writhing minor serpents all hissing at him.

Carter thought of Millie's description of how her husband had looked when she found him dead in his study. As though he had seen something terrifying, something awful, that frightened him to death. "My God!" he cried out. "Wait! You don't understand."

The monster-thing put out a hand—now a tentacle—and thrust him aside with such force that he slammed into the wall and sank to his knees in agony. It surged past him. But he knew its destination and was on his feet, scrambling down the hall to get past it, before it reached the door of Millicent's bedroom.

Somehow—he never afterward could explain it—he managed to hurl himself past the intruder and reach the bedroom ahead of it. Somehow—he could never explain that either—he clawed his way to the chest-of-drawers and yanked open the second drawer and snatched the letter out and whirled in his steps to thrust the letter up in front of the night-walker before the creature could reach the bed where Millicent Armer lay sleeping.

"*Look!*" Carter yelled. "*Look* at this, for God's sake! Read it and you'll know she wasn't part of any plot to kill you!"

The intruder stopped in mid-stride. Every eye on those dozens of swaying tentacles focused on the letter. It didn't take long. Certainly not as long as it had taken Carter to read those same hand-written words. Reaching out a tentacle, the creature took the letter from Carter's hands and held it close to the bigger eyes in its head, and seemed to read it again. Then, letting the letter fall to the floor, it turned away.

And right then, right there, something else happened. Three young men—the same three young men who had robbed the Kemptons' house across the street—found the back door open and crept into Millie Armer's house to strip it. And all three of them were armed with the semi-automatic pistols—smaller, more powerful, even deadlier than ordinary weapons—that their former neighborhood victim had described when telling Carter how his home had been broken into, weeks before.

Well. They made a noise when they pushed wide the already opened back door and thrust it against a wall. They didn't care. With weapons of such power, they could have announced their arrival with a brass band. Bursting into the house, they came storming into the very bedroom where Carter and the other intruder stood.

Carter and the creature turned to confront them. Faced with such weapons, Carter, of course, was helpless. All he could do was turn to look at the still-asleep figure of the woman he now knew he hoped to spend the rest of his life with.

But the monster-thing, the ghost of the murdered wife of the man Millie Armer had mistakenly married—ah, now, that was different.

That awesome horror-shape turned to face the three teenage intruders, obviously indifferent to the firepower of the semi-automatic pistols they brandished. As they skidded to a noisy halt in front of her, she extended her long, quivering tentacles toward them. From their lips came cries of terror as they tried to back away, but the tentacles grew longer to block their retreat. And a hissing sound, as of angered snakes, filled the room and the night.

No music now. No *Miraculous Mandarin*. Only hissing.

Nothing more need be said, really. When Carter called nine-one-one half an hour later and the police came, the three intruders were on the floor, staring at the ceiling as though they had looked into the depths of hell and would never forget what they saw there. The creature who had brought them to that condition had long since vanished. Carter and Millie, their arms about each other, admitted the police at the front door and told what they could.

Had Tom Carter been a less highly admired police captain, he might not have been believed. But he had a reputation. His report was not questioned.

The three intruders were buried with that ghastly look of terror still on their faces.

The word went out. The number of nighttime break-ins dramatically declined.

Tom and Millie, now sharing the same bedroom, have not seen the woman in white again. But they found something a while ago that makes them wonder. When Millie married Tom and moved into his house, putting her own up for sale, Tom spent some time cleaning out the attic of her house and discovered a box of books up there that apparently had belonged to the dead wife of Millie's former husband. At least, her name was in most of them.

One was a book of witchcraft. One was a large, thick book on the occult. And a third, very old and worn, was by someone named Abdul Alhazred, who, the introduction noted, had authored an earlier volume called the *Necronomicon*.

Which seemed to suggest, Tom and his new wife decided, that the woman who loved Bartók may have spent some time of her own delving into more ancient and even deeper mysteries. ✻

Chant

by Robert Weinberg

It was nearly 2 a.m. and I was out of ideas. Sprawled across the living room sofa, I stared with bleary eyes at the TV screen, searching for inspiration. My agent had been hounding me for weeks, begging me to put together a proposal for a novel dealing with the millennium. *Something scary and yet totally believable,* she had demanded in our last phone conversation. *Write a book filled with paranoid conspiracies about the end of the world. You're good at that type of stuff.*

Believable yet paranoid. Lori knew exactly what she was talking about. I *was* good at writing that type of stuff. Six novels, three of them best-sellers, proved that statement the old fashioned way. With money. Lots of money. But, now, my publisher wanted a new book focusing on the millennium. My agent had assured them I would deliver a proposal in just a few weeks. And my mind was as empty as a congressman's promise.

Whenever I came up blank, I channel surfed the cable TV networks for ideas. To me, television represented vast unexplored jungles of modern American thought. Cable channels were filled with the most outlandish and bizarre dreams of the working man. And woman. TV was the place where reality and fantasy merged and nothing was too outrageous to be dramatized or sold.

My books were hits because they took the most familiar imaginings of television and gave them new and unexpected twists. I thrust the pop icons of modern culture into crazy-quilt adventures filled with manic suspicions, half-truths, and urban mythology. The larger-than-life heroes and heroines of my novels fought a desperate, never-ceasing, battle against the huge, many-headed beast known as the System. Sometimes they won, sometimes they lost. But, they never quit. And just like the television shows from which they came, my plots always came to a satisfactory conclusion on the last page of the book. My audience, like television viewers across the country, preferred their stories nice and tidy. All plot threads were resolved, with no loose ends. My novels imitated drama, not real life. Cable was God for middle-America and I was its humble prophet. For the right price, of course.

Thus, *Gilligan's Island* served as the basis for *Castaways,* a paranoid thriller about secret genetic testing on a Pacific atoll. *The Dukes of Hazzard* was transformed into the ghoulish *Hell's Night Riders.* And, *Lassie* underwent a startling metamorphosis into *The Dog from Hell.*

Eyes weary, I stared at Rhoda and toyed with the idea of making her into a vampiric creature, feeding off Mary Tyler Moore's goodness. It seemed plausible enough, but how then would I explain Lou Grant? As Nickelodeon switched to commercials, I reached for the remote control. My thoughts were going goofy. Time for bed and rest. Tomorrow, a full day's schedule of reruns and cartoons hopefully would provide the impetus necessary for my new plot. And keep those fat royalty checks coming.

My eyes were turned from the set, so I heard the voices before I saw the singers. Deep, powerful, sonorous tones filled the living room. A chorus of men's voices, chanting in some unknown tongue. Harmonizing together, repeating again and again, a phrase like no other I had ever before heard. *"Ph'nglui mglw'nafh Cthulhu R'lyeh wgah'nagl fhtagn."* Stark, dramatic, intense singing, the sound sent chills racing up my spine. It felt as if someone, to use the old folk expression, was walking across my grave. I shivered, wondering the identity of the language of the chant. It was definitely not Latin, the usual tongue of such invocations.

I turned my head and stared at the TV screen. A dozen men, dressed in hooded crimson robes, stood clustered in a semi-circle around a large stone altar. A diverse group, white, black, brown and yellow, they stared at the camera with serene, composed expressions. No question that these were monks of deep, abiding faith. Behind them, though mostly blocked out by the singers' bodies, stood the walls of a massive stone church. Obviously, the commercial had been filmed on location, at some out-of-the-way cloister or abbey in Europe.

"Cthulhu, Cthulhu," sang the men a second time, but this repetition the sound was much softer, as a voice-over provided the expected product pitch.

"From the ancient halls of Exham Priory comes the most enthralling, the most captivating CD you will ever hear," declared the unseen announcer. "The voices of the Brothers of the EOD raised in harmony in their magnificent rendering of the old tongue religious litanies, *Cthulhu R'lyeh.*"

The announcer droned on, listing the dozen chants on the CD, while the red-clad monks, each now shown holding a long yellow wax candle, continued their chants in a language that was not Greek. There was no background music of any kind, no accompaniment, and yet the sound of the dozen voices was enough. The joyful sound of their singing was complete in itself. The strange words seemed to take on a meaning all their own, as if sending a message to me directly from the singers. The chant was more than a chant. It was a summoning, a calling, an urging for completion. As I watched the pictures on the TV screen, my body swayed almost hypnotically in time with the mystical adoration. It was a spooky, unexplainable feeling.

I knew without question, I had found my story.

"Send for your copy of *Cthulhu R'lyeh* today," urged the unseen announcer as the voices swelled once again in song. "Available on CD for only $6.95, on cassette tape for only $3.95. All shipping and handling charges included."

A fulfillment company's name and address flashed on the screen. Hurriedly, I copied the words on my scratchpad. A post office box in New Orleans. A guarantee of complete satisfaction or your money back from The Starry Wisdom Association, located in Los Angeles. My thoughts were racing as I wrote. It was an incredibly low price for a CD, half of what such recordings usually cost. No extra charges for shipping or state sales tax. The offer was an unbelievable bargain. Almost too good to be true. A perfect opening for my novel.

"An insidious cult of devil worshippers scheming to control the world through the use of subliminal messages planted on a seemingly innocent CD," I murmured to myself as Valerie Harper shrilly returned to my TV screen. "Disguising their hidden commands in lines of otherwise meaningless babble." Yawning, I put down the pad and pencil and clicked off the television set. Enough for tonight. I had my idea. Already, my mind was racing through dozens of possible scenarios and plot devices. Writing this book was going to be a snap.

It was time for sleep. Tomorrow, I'd begin my research. A smart writer left nothing to chance. I wanted to know the real reason the CD was so cheap. And what actual language was being sung by the monks.

Who were the Brothers of the EOD? Ditto, the Starry Wisdom Association? The Los Angeles address hinted at some fringe group, possibly one of the innumerable cults that dotted the southern California landscape. Maybe the language they used was some sort of pseudo-Atlantean tongue. Or based on supposed Lemurian thought records. It didn't matter to me. In my years as a writer, I had learned long ago that despite claims to the contrary, truth was not stranger than fiction.

In my novel, EOD would stand for the Exotic Order of Darkness. The Starry Wisdom Association would be a cabal of black magicians, seeking to rule the world for their master, an unspeakable entity from another dimension. Much different, I felt certain, than the guiding principles of the real organization. Fortunately, libel laws did not apply to religious groups.

Still, I fully intended to learn all I could about the EOD and their beliefs. The last thing I wanted was to offend some oddball religious cult. Devils and demons made good copy but they didn't frighten me. I wasn't superstitious. I worried more about real horrors—lawyers and libel suits. Though I was always extremely careful disguising the source of inspiration for my books, it never hurt to take an extra step. Tomorrow, I'd make some phone calls. And find out the truth about the EOD and Starry Wisdom Association.

* * *

I slept the sleep of the satisfied author and woke the next morning feeling the best I had in weeks. After a hearty breakfast, I dialed my agent, Lori Smith in New York, with the good news. Proposal humming, it would be on the way to her in a week. Paranoid but believable. Based on current news. Without any question, the best book I had yet written.

She sounded quite pleased and promised to relay the news to my publisher that afternoon. "If the book's as good as you say," Lori declared, "we'll ask for double the advance we got for your last novel. Millennium books are hot."

"Sounds fine to me," I answered, grinning. Considering that I had received $500,000 for the previous book, we were talking big money. A million dollar advance put me in the company of King, Koontz and Rice, the superstars of horror fiction. "Let me know what they say."

"Definitely," said Lori. "You have a name for this epic? Something catchy?"

I did. It had come to me in my sleep. The perfect title, mystical and enticing, yet simple and familiar. A one word title that I felt certain would resonate in the minds of my readers long after they finished reading my story. *"Chant,"* I told Lori.

"The book's titled *Chant."*

"There's a popular CD by that name," she said. "The one by those monks. . . ."

"Can't copyright a title," I replied. "Besides, my book's about a pretty similar group. Only they're not priests. Just the opposite."

"The opposite of monks?" said Lori. "Pagans?"

"Devil worshippers," I replied, then said goodbye.

Now, firmly committed to the book, it was time for me to do my research. And hope that I hadn't stuck my head into a noose. As always, I went first to the most complete encyclopedia and reference guide in the world. The Internet. Logging on, I called up Infoseek and punched in the words, *Starry Wisdom.* In seconds, the search engine displayed 847 sites on the subject.

Number one on the list was "The Starry Wisdom Association Home Page." I clicked on the address and waited for my computer to make the connection. The site was a large one but downloaded fast. In less than a minute, I was staring at the same dozen red robed monks from last night's commercial. In dark black headlines, the page's banner proclaimed THE STARRY WIS-DOM SITE. Beneath, in smaller letters, were two lines in italics.

That is not dead which can eternal lie,
And with strange eons even death may die.

"Nice work if you can get it," I murmured and scrolled down the page. The Starry Wisdom Association obviously had money and knew how to use it. Their web page was totally professional, done with panache and style. Reading it answered most of my questions. But the information raised new queries, equally troublesome.

Under Frequently Asked Questions, the language of their *Cthulhu R'lyeh* CD was listed as *the old tongue*. I assumed it was a cross between Lemurian thought records and Atlantean gibberish. The chant used in the commercial translated into "In his house in R'lyeh, dead Cthulhu waits dreaming." How someone could be dead and dream, I didn't understand. But, then again, religion was never one of my real interests.

The Starry Wisdom Association was described as a non-denominational free-thinking religious order, dedicated to spreading the Gospel of the Ancient Ones. Little was actually said about what those beliefs might be, nor was there any mention of their background or past history. To me, it all sounded very New Age, very California. The organization came across as the usual scam, a pseudo-religious cult aimed primarily at leeching money from unsuspecting members.

None of my business. I was no crusader. If the idle rich wanted to pay big bucks for their chance at heaven, who was I to say no? The preamble to the Constitution guaranteed everyone the right to "life, liberty, and the *pursuit of happiness*." Not happiness, just the *pursuit* of happiness. I wasn't looking to save my fellow man. Just sell them a book.

At the bottom of the page was a phone number and post office box number for those who wanted more information about the association. I copied both. While contacting the group would probably be a big mistake—no cult likes to hear a writer is interested in their activities—it was better to be prepared than not.

There were no links connecting the Starry Wisdom page to any other sites on the net. So, I went back to my search engine list of all sites that mentioned the two key words. Patiently, I scanned through each page. While I had my basic concept and plot for my novel, I was hoping to find a few juicy details that would round out the story, give it some needed depth. Somewhere on the Internet, there had to be some dirt on the Starry Wisdom Association. And I wanted to find it.

The first two dozen entries were worthless. Home pages for people who were entranced by the music CD. A few sites for very strange people, filled with gibberish phrases like "The Hounds of Tindalos," "The Book of Eibon," and "The goat with a thousand young." California cult silliness. There was even one page of photographs of the night skies, with the words "The stars are right," in big bold red letters superimposed over the pictures. Since when were the stars ever wrong? Maybe the Starry Wisdom

Association was involved in astrology. I didn't know, but vowed to check on the possibility later.

I was intrigued by the title of the twenty-ninth page in the web search listing. "They're All Actors." The actual contents of the site proved equally interesting. A die-hard fan of singers who worked for commercials had reproduced the photo of the Brothers of the EOD on his page, and beneath each red-clad monk had posted the man's real name. Evidently, none of the Brothers were actually monks at all. They were professional background singers, men with melodic voices who did backup work for soundtracks, commercials, and music videos.

Further down the page were biographies of each singer, along with a list of other credits and in some cases, even a contact phone number. Shaking my head in amazement, I copied down several of the names and numbers. So much for the sincerity and deep religious feeling shared by the Brothers.

I bookmarked the search page on the Starry Wisdom Association and exited the net. My eyes were starting to hurt from staring at the computer screen. It was time for me to make a few phone calls.

In my novel, all of the people who worked for the demon worshippers of EOD would be dead, killed in the most gruesome manner I could imagine. Of course, those murders would be the clue that would convince my hero that something terrible was happening. It was a melodramatic happening that made for a good story but was otherwise totally illogical. In real life, a cult would never do anything so foolish. The best disguise for evil was boring normalcy. I had no trouble contacting any of the singers in the commercial.

Larry Daniels answered on the third ring. His voice was rich and mellow, silky smooth. He was not the least bit reticent to discuss his work for the Starry Wisdom Association.

"Great job," he told me. "Nice people, good money, wonderful production facilities. Wish I could say the same about most of my other assignments. You wouldn't believe the crap I have to put up with sometimes."

"Didn't bother you to dress up like a monk?" I asked. "You weren't concerned about deceiving the public?"

Daniels laughed, a full rich sound. "Deception? In a music CD commercial? You must be joking, right? We're talking television, son. Nothing's real on TV. So what if we dressed up in those silly red cassocks? Nobody's come looking for me to tell me their confession. No worse than those old geezer actors suckering people about health insurance for the elderly. Or the faded rock stars promoting those oldie CDs. The music's the only thing that matters. And that wasn't faked. It was us singing. We recorded the entire CD, then did the video commercial."

"Then you have no idea what the Starry Wisdom Association is all about?" I said.

"Not a clue," said Daniels. "They put an ad in *Variety* looking for commercial artists with experience in religious and choral music. Interviewed hundreds of people. Wanted men who looked the part. I was lucky enough to be one of those chosen. Spent six weeks in a studio, working on the CD. Paid well, with no hassles. Best job I've had in years."

"In a studio," I repeated. "What about Exham Priory, that huge stone church behind you?"

Daniels' deep sigh was audible even over the telephone. "Son, you're awfully naïve for a professional writer. We recorded the CD in a studio in Los Angeles. The commercial was shot in a studio fifteen minutes off of Sunset Strip. They backdropped in photos of that old abbey. I think I heard someone mention it was located in England. Nice touch." The singer laughed. "Candles were real, though."

"Thanks," I said, feeling stupid. "You have a contact name, someone from the Association I could talk to, find out a little more about the group? I'd make sure not to mention your name, keep it secret how I found him."

"No worry on my end," said Daniels. "After all, those people are members of a religious organization. Try Charlie Newsome," and he gave me a phone number in Los Angeles. "He directed the whole commercial. Nice guy. Though I doubt if he'll be able to tell you much more than me. Got the impression he was being paid to do a specific job. Nothing more."

"Nobody on the set from the EOD?" I asked. "Watching to make sure everything was strictly accurate?"

"Not a soul," answered Daniels.

I thanked the singer, hung up, and dialed Charlie Newsome. He proved as cooperative as Daniels and equally ignorant.

Newsome had been hired by the CD manufacturer to produce the music infomercial. They selected him on the basis of previous commercials he had done for similar products. He had never met anyone from the EOD or the Starry Wisdom Association. He did what he was told and collected his paycheck. It had been an easy job.

Newsome put me in touch with the recording company who actually produced the CD. The woman I spoke to was cool at first, until she connected my name with my books. Turned out she was a fan. A promise to send her an autographed copy of my last book and she gave me all the dirt on *Cthulhu R'lyeh*. There wasn't much.

The entire CD had been arranged by a legal firm in the Valley. The lawyer, Norman Marsh, had sent the music, lyrics, and a dreadful tape of a man singing the strange words using the correct pronunciation.

"Dreadful meaning unearthly or horrifying?" I asked.

"Dreadful as meaning the singer was tone deaf," said my fan, Rita Gladney. "My boss later told me he was convinced it was the lawyer, Marsh, singing. Crazy, huh?"

"Definitely," I answered. From the story, it seemed likely that Marsh was the man behind the Starry Wisdom Association. That the entire CD was his baby.

The cheap price was a marketing gimmick. Or so Marsh had claimed. The singers were relatively cheap, the studio didn't cost a lot, and the video was done in one shot. With little overhead and minimal charges, the CD was supposed to make money on volume sales, not markup. "Marsh said he wanted to sell more than a million CDs," said Rita. "That the Starry Wisdom Association was convinced that with the right promotion they'd get national attention and make headlines. Personally, I think the whole project's a tax dodge."

It seemed quite possible to me as well. After a few more minutes chatting with Rita, I hung up and tried to locate the tone-deaf Mr. Marsh. And ran into a blank wall.

There was no lawyer named Norman Marsh practicing in the San Fernando Valley. According to a call to the California Bar Association, there was no one by that name practicing law in the entire state.

I debated calling back Rita but decided it would be a waste of time. She had been quite specific on the name, even spelling it for me. Someone named Marsh had paid for the CD to be produced, advertised and distributed. He might not be a lawyer, but plenty of people weren't what they seemed to be in California. As best as I could tell, Marsh had done nothing illegal. Besides, I was no cop, just an author.

Keeping that thought in mind, I dialed the phone number for the Starry Wisdom Association. An answering machine took the call, telling me to leave my name and phone number and someone would get back to me shortly with information on the group. The message suggested in the meantime, I buy a copy of their first CD release, *Cthulhu R'lyeh*. "Play it often," the message concluded. "All truths can be found in its words."

"Modest," I said, breaking the connection. The entire scenario stank like three-day-old fish. An organization looking for publicity who answered their calls with a machine? A CD priced so cheap that it barely broke even? Why run a swindle that lost money? I didn't know the answer, but I intended to find out.

After a quick lunch, I was back searching the Internet. I hunted through a hundred entries on the Starry Wisdom Association, most of them filled with pseudo-religious babble about Old Ones, Deep Ones, Ancient Ones, and *De Vermis Mysteriis,* which sounded like something I had ordered by mistake at a French restaurant once. There was no mention of a lawyer named Marsh. There were six more pages mentioning that the stars were right, three stating that the stars were almost right but not quite yet, and one page saying that the stars were definitely wrong and would not be right for another 347 years.

Growing bored, I switched back to my search engine and ran a new search for the word *chants*. As expected, in seconds, I had over a thousand locations. Hoping against hope, I scanned the long list, searching for some mention of the Starry Wisdom Association. Or *Cthulhu R'lyeh.*

I was ready to conclude there was nothing to be found on the net about the mysterious EOD and their CD when I came across entry two hundred and forty-seven. The title was intriguing. Pulling up the article, I read it carefully. I knew I had found something important. But I wasn't sure exactly what. Four times I read the article. The words remained unchanged. As I stared at them, the feeling I had about someone walking across my grave returned. But this time, the mysterious stroller was doing an Irish jig.

The page was titled *Chants: Opening Strange Doors.* It was written by some guy named Murray Wills from Massachusetts. There was no mention of the *Cthulhu R'lyeh* CD from the Starry Wisdom Association. It wasn't necessary.

"A chant is merely another name for an invocation," began Wills. "Despite the rash of recordings and concerts centered around chants as entertainment, one should never forget such melodies are actually religious prayers set to music. A chant is an invocation, a magic spell, using sound and repetition. Such words can be dangerous."

I liked that line, wondered if I could use it in my novel. "There are worlds parallel to Earth, separated only by rates of atomic vibration. Quite possibly they are home to life forces, beings totally and completely alien to humanity. Monstrous creations, these things are glimpsed only in nightmares or visions. Heaven and Hell are most likely based on such psychic revelations.

"Fortunately, the quantum boundary separating our dimension from another is almost impossible to cross. But, there is a way. Vibrations keep the universes separate. Therefore, vibrations can also be used to form a gateway, a dimensional door."

I wasn't much on quantum mechanics or rates of atomic vibrations. But I had read plenty of science fiction novels about parallel universes and passages from one plane of reality to another. Not that I believed in such stuff. But Wills' writings were convincing.

"Broken down to simplest terms, music is a vibration. A chant is nothing more than an invocation, a summons. The right chant, the right words, sung in a specific manner, can open a gate between worlds. Reading the truth behind the legend, we can surmise that solitary mages in the Middle

Ages were able to use such spells to bring demons, minor denizens of other realities, into our world."

The next few lines were the ones that worried me.

"If one voice, chanting the correct phrases, sung in the proper manner, pronounced exactly the right way, could accomplish this act, imagine the incredible power of a dozen such voices, blending together in perfect harmony. Ponder that. Then, consider the use of modern technology. Postulate copying that sound, that *chant,* so that each duplicate is an exact replica of the original. Imagine what a *million* chants, played at the same time, might do. The vibrations would be enough to bend space and time. *Think of the size of the gateway that would be opened.* Tremble at the thought of what could enter our world from a place outside our universe."

There were no more words. Just a number.

1,257,831.

How Murray had determined the figure I had no idea. But I had no doubts as to his meaning.

I logged off the Internet suddenly feeling very nervous. Dialing the Starry Wisdom Association gave me the same machine, the same plug. "Play it often."

I hung up.

If everyone who owned a copy of the CD played it at the same time, would those chants blend together, merge together into one immensely powerful invocation? Become a summoning that could reach outside of our universe and into another? I didn't know. But somehow I suspected that the Starry Wisdom Association wasn't the least bit concerned about publicity or a profit. That they only wanted to distribute as many copies of *Cthulhu R'lyeh,* their chant, as possible.

I emailed Murray Wills. My letter was short and to the point. *What is dead Cthulhu dreaming about? And where exactly is R'lyeh?*

That was three days ago. I still haven't received a reply. I suspect I won't.

Maybe I'm worried about nothing. Dimensional doors and forgotten languages and chants used to summon monsters. Maybe I'm letting my paranoid fantasies finally get under my skin. I'm truthfully not sure. It could all be a crazy coincidence. Still, I'm scared.

I bought *Billboard* today. To check on *Cthulhu R'lyeh.*

According to a brief mention, sales of the CD are climbing, due to the low price and flashy commercial. It's moving up the charts fast.

Number 57 with a bullet. ✳

Ghoul's Tale

A Narrative from the Necronomicon
Transcribed from the Dee Edition

by Robert M. Price

The nethermost caverns are not meant for the eyes that see the light of day; nay, but the revelations thereof are reserved unto those, for whom darkness has become as light. And such was I, Alhazred, spiritual son of the mage Yakthoob and Opener of the Gate whereby the Spheres meet. I had long since become even as one with the creatures of night and shadow, and it was the smiling of the sun that I cursed. Oft had I ventured into the earth's cancerous bowels in search of the secrets of the grave, and thus it was that I came to delve beneath the ruins of elder Khem into the honeycombed netherworld of Amente itself, wherein sits enthroned for all aeons to come the desiccated shell of the Acheronian sorcerer-king Nephren-Ka. Whispered legends had it that all the destiny of the ages had been vouchsafed unto the Black Pharaoh, and that the secrets of Thrice-Great Nyarlathotep were finely traced upon the copious lengths of yellowed linen that now embraced him. It was this artifact that I sought in my folly. For though many esteemed me master of the eldritch arts, the greater wisdom was that of my novices and acolytes, none of whom dared follow me.

Passage was easily enough wrought, providing one but knew the hidden paths, and such knowledge was mine, for had I not bargained with Those who chart the topography of Hell and of other realms more dreadful still for those unwilling to wait till death should bear them away thence? Like unto the ancient mage-king Solomon ibn-Daud who adorned his courts with apes and peacocks and suchlike, reckoning no cost too great for these gladsome fancies, neither did I estimate any price too dear for the secrets held out to tempt me, as I have related aforetime. I shudder even yet at the fearful tribute of one eye exacted of my Master Yakthoob for the secret of the Elixir of the angels, and no less at the demand of Tsathoggua, the Abomination beneath Memphis, whom naught less than mine own manhood would satisfy. For the knowledge of Irem the City of Pillars ceded I unto foetid Nug a full score of years from the sum of my life yet to come. The price of the map to the throne of buried Nephren-Ka I care not to repeat, save that the leather scroll I scrutinized by the flickering light of my torch was tanned from mine own back. And this was but the beginning of sorrows. But so much and more I judged to be small in exchange for what powers might be mine if I were to gain me that winding sheet.

The hieratic glyphs lining the walls about me, preserved by the arid heat of Aegypt's blazing sands, mutely told forth the first purpose of the shaft I now half-trod, half-slid down at a steep angle. In ages past, the place had served as an initiation hall for those who sought to plumb the deepest mysteries of Set-Typhon and Gol-Goroth, secret Gods of antediluvian Acheron. I scrupled not to defile these holy precincts with my passage, since was mine own errand not a pilgrimage for knowledge? I, too, would possess the secrets of the Ancients.

Hours and days became nigh indistinguishable to me as I made my continual descent. Sorely did I require sleep, but no opportunity was found, and at all events, I had years before bartered the power of restful slumber for some esoteric secret or other. Verily did I commence to fancy that I heard the noise around me as of some foul vermin scuttling just beyond the scope of my vision. But this uneasy fear I sought to dismiss, fancying instead that the sounds be merely those of mine own slow progress downward, distorted and partwise magnified by the peculiar shape of the winding tunnel by which I sought ingress.

In the fullness of time did I gain my sought-for destination. Before me yawned vast doorposts and lintel wrought cunningly of black and polished stone. Glyphs in the tongue of Acheron announced the place for that terrible vault in which the withered mummy of Nephren-Ka, earthly avatar of the Crawling Chaos, did drowse away the ages. Again, scarce could I ignore that uneasy sensation that crafty eyes did trace my movements, but so great was my eagerness to despoil the tomb of what lay unsuspecting within it that I spared thoughts for naught else, waxing bold to enter.

The shadows coating the adytum were doubly thick, and the torch I bore did little in truth to dispel them. Still, the object of my quest was manifest before me. I stepped silently toward the figure seated on a dais at the far extreme of that charnel chamber. But soft! a sound that was verily no mere echo brought me up short. Doubtless, another was with me in the place. I stood still, then turning warily about, and sought to detect my living shadow. I had not long to search, for the silence of the ages was straightway vanquished by the echoing of a voice soft and sly like unto the voice of the Edenic serpent—and it did hiss mine own name! What guardian demon had apprehended me?

"It is I, old friend, thy fellow apprentice, Ibn Ghazoul. I dared not believe mine eyes, but of a truth, thou canst be none other than Alhazred!"

He stepped forward into the narrow circle of fading light cast forth by the torch I grasped. And in the feeble luminescence I saw that the past had forsooth yielded up a ghost I had thought forever exorcised, even that false-hearted betrayer who had seen fit to sell the soul of our Master, the venerable Yakthoob, merely to satisfy his carnal appetites. Seeing him now brought no joy to my heart.

"Praise be to Eblis that thou hast come at last, O Alhazred! Oft have I prayed for deliverance from the curse that hath befallen me. For long have I paid dire penance for the deeds that disgraced me."

I would fain know how the infamous Ibn Ghazoul had happened upon this place, since scarce could I credit his having either sought or gained occult erudition like unto mine during the many years since we had learned together at the feet of Yakthoob (upon whom be peace), for that he preferred the ways of Dionysus to those of Hecate.

"'Twas the merest luck, O Alhazred, that brought me hither, though ill luck, to be sure. Like thee, my brother, I sought the Elder lore among the houses of silence, but I chanced to attract the unwelcome attentions of a pack of meeping feasters upon the dead, even the muzzled children of Anubis al-Ghul. Meseems their pickings to be slim insofar as they have of late waxed exceeding bold so as to pursue the living, there being insufficient carrion to satisfy them. And in my flight I took whatever winding paths and tunnels I might, at length successfully eluding the mangy devils. At yon shadowed portal did they recoil with much yelping and slunk away like unto the craven curs they are. And now, forsooth, I do confess I fear to depart, lest, in their great hunger, mayhap it transpire that they linger, waiting to pounce upon my person."

"O Ibn Ghazoul," said I, "I marvel that these loping feasters reckon thee not among their own number, as thou hast most abundantly proven thyself the most craven of jackals. But then little do they know thee as I know thee. Nonetheless, thou canst readily see how I myself penetrated even unto thine hiding place without molestation, howbeit I did think to hear furtive sounds upon my way. But if what thou sayest be true, how was it they did not beset me?"

Ibn Ghazoul did answer, saying: "That I wot not, O brother in Al-Mousin Metatron! Save that I suspect thine own aura of occult sanctity hath repelled them even as hath that of this holy fane."

Somewhat in this reply pleased me not, and I inquired whether it was in truth mere happenstance which had brought him to the resting place of the avatar of Nyarlathotep. Mayhap he had contrived to steal or cheat his way to this secret adytum, knowing full well the value of that which lay within. Yet his fear was most palpably real.

"If, old comrade, thou hast, by the providence of those Powers we serve, come so far on some errand of discovery, then permit thine humble acolyte to serve thee in this venture. All I shall beg in return is thy protection in passage from this dark place. What sayest thou?"

My torch had now grown exceeding dim. And as the darkness waxed thick, certain shadows commenced to shift and to circle about us twain. The sounds of nameless chittering and cachinnation were henceforth in no wise to be doubted, and for all that did the fear which had haunted Ibn Ghazoul but slim moments before seem to depart the closer did the loathsome ghouls approach.

"Meseems thou hast underreckoned the power of these surroundings to keep yon parasites at bay," quoth I by grim jest. "Well do I now discern thine insidious craft, how, trapped by the ghouls, thou didst bargain with them to spare thine own worthless life in return for thy services in procuring for them human meat. Then would they at length suffer thee to depart with the Shroud of the Black Pharaoh."

"O Alhazred," the traitor mocked, "thy reputed wisdom never faileth! Albeit it may dawn a trifle too late." With this did the coarse forms of the ghouls draw fast about me, as my flesh, friend to a thousand abominations, did nonetheless quail from the loathsome caress of their drooling muzzles. Next did they force me to my knees as Ibn Ghazoul, whose villainy exceeded their own for that it was freely embraced and no necessity of nature, made for the recumbent form of the husk of Nephren-Ka, drawing his dagger with the which he might more swiftly despoil the rotting cadaver of its wrappings and be on his way.

But it was not for naught that, Ibn Ghazoul having wenched and drunk away his energies over the years, I had devoted myself with ascetical ardor to the scrutiny of the Elder Records filched from the very bog of Ubbo-Sathla. Unlike my torch, my resources were far from spent, and I did utter forth the binding spell of Anubis, the totem of those feasters upon the dead. Straightway there concatenated a nimbus of light of no familiar hue. Even as the mongrel hounds of this world do fall back and cringe before the sound that surpasses human hearing, so did the ghouls drop away in agony, and I was free of their noisome clinging.

I was astonished past all measure to behold Ibn Ghazoul halt in his course, as if seized by an unseen hand. Slowly he made to turn, sore racked with pain, but having taken up his evil cackling again. Only now that chilling laughter issued forth from canine jaws, from which poisonous spittle did drip. So Ibn Ghazoul was himself one of the ravening pack! His trap had not been as I surmised, though of a certainty it was nonetheless treachery most foul. That he was not thoroughly whelmed by the magic I had summoned I ascribed to whatever vestiges of his sorcerous apprenticeship he had retained from his former days of tutelage under the venerable Yakthoob. And now therefore I made ready to deal with him.

Only that, as it eventuated, this task was made moot unto me. For all at once did the rangy form of Ibn-Ghazoul fall limp in the grasp of a towering figure looming up from behind him, even, as the fading radiance of mine cantrip shewed, the shuffling lich of the Ebon Pharaoh, whose millennial rest our interloping presence had disturbed! Deep did his bony talons sink, cutting into the leathery flesh of the ghoul-changeling and choking off his blasphemous cackle. Stinking, sluggish blood overflowed the mummy's hands as his ineluctable grip inexorably severed Ibn Ghazoul's head from his neck. I beheld the dead visage regaining its former semblance of human features even as the head dropped to the dusty ground like an overripe fruit.

I stood as nerveless as an embalmed mummy ought by rights to stand, transfixed as the hideous eyeless gaze of Nephren-Ka turned in my direction. He made no sound, but the tiny writing scribed upon his funereal bands was eloquent in its mockery. I knew I should have the lavish boon of the Gods should I escape with the treasure of my own life, if not my soul. And that is what I did, abandoning the tomb of the revenant forever, so do I swear by Al-Illah or whatsoever Gods may yet deign to hear me. ✳

The Next Big Thing

by Rob Suggs

Friday was harvest day for Brother Lucien. As he tilled the soft earth and basketed the fine fruits of the soil, he hummed a canticle to the Blessed Mother and savored the willowy April breeze; rain must be planning a visit.

A springtime chorus serenaded him: wind-rippled wheat, crickets and sparrows; the baritone of a bullfrog. Man and earth sang together, until a note of discord was introduced. Brother Lucien looked up from his labors and pricked his ears to, what? An insect-song, faint but growing. He shaded his eyes toward the horizon, where a lone figure appeared. He was coming from the south, meaning Marseille. Perhaps a ship had brought him in.

Lucien could see the stranger was piping on some small instrument; but the tone was new and peculiar. The tune danced a bit too freely, a mite too rhythmically for God's pleasure and praise. Notes unrelated to one another mingled together, as if they were brothers. After a round, the stranger lowered his pipe to sing a chorus. He was not too far away for Lucien to hear:

> The Ancient of Days, may He rise to reclaim,
> Let the firmament speak the unnamable Name
> Of the One who is dreaming in darkest of deeps,
> But for only a season the Elder One sleeps.
> Let the ocean-spray roar, and the mountains be shaken;
> The Eldersong soar, that the One may awaken!

The hymn, like its melody, carried blasphemous overtones; yet his ears strained for more. Lucien stood gaping, hands brown with earth, as the stranger unlatched the gate and shook free his ragged hood. The birds and crickets had stopped singing, but the chill wind intensified. "Welcome, brother," Lucien offered with a little bow. "Come and rest from thy journey, shake the dust from thy boots, and take refreshment."

The man nodded and smiled as Lucien brought a pitcher and a cluster of grapes from the vineyard. He was swarthy of complexion, his skin cracked and leathery. The eyes glimmered with a light suggesting faraway ports; the sparkle of cold, distant stars. Lucien sat in the shade of an elm and motioned the stranger to join him.

"My deepest gratitude for your hospitality," said the visitor in his smoky baritone. "The enchantment of music is my only coin, but I think you would reject it."

"I am uncertain it is music, if I may say so. Your words and your melody are at odds with the worship of the Lord of creation."

"Perhaps you are right; but is music thus constrained?"

"Yes, such it has always been. The psalmist says, 'Make a joyful noise unto the Lord, all ye lands.' It is His gift for His praise. Surely His ears are displeased by lascivious melodies and blasphemous words; for indeed He does not—as thou hast sung—sleep, nor does He dream!" For contemplative Lucien, this was a considerable outburst, and he trailed off awkwardly. He wanted to look away, but he realized his eyes were locked on the thin flute. The stranger, watching his gaze, lifted it and resumed playing. This time it was a familiar, sanctified song of Cross and Passion, and Lucien smiled in relief (and an undeniable trace of disappointment).

Yet when the refrain came around again, the player introduced odd variations. Lucien lifted his voice and sang the proper Latin phrases, closing his eyes to force the correct notes and tempos. But this proved futile; he found himself caught in the surge of the stranger's tonal torrent, and his voice faltered in resignation and confusion.

Suddenly the stranger was standing, smiling again. "You will forgive me. I should not tempt one so marked by his charity to wandering minnesingers. Besides, I have many miles yet to travel before I sleep. Shortly I will play in the streets of Paris, and in jeweled palaces. But a final word for you, my friend: The world is ever transforming. New melodies spring forth. Disharmony is rendered harmonious. Soon even your holy order will hear with new ears; or your order will return to the dry dust. For the music has its own life and power, and it lives, draws breath, and plots its course in regions beyond your feeble comprehension. It cries out to hearers unknown, beneath, and beyond, just as it calls now to you. Perhaps, dear Lucien, it is not you who sing; but the song which sings you."

Brother Lucien stood at the garden gate and watched the odd, hood-enshrouded minstrel vanish into the distance. Before he was gone, the stranger began to pipe anew his fading insect-song, and Lucien listened, infuriated and infatuated. Soon nature resumed its concert, but Brother Lucien could no longer hear it. His muddy foot was gently tapping a new rhythm to accompany the odd melody flowing through his veins—an inner song the monk would never cast out, nor cease sharing, until he was driven from the order and executed as a heretic six years later.

The music itself fared better. It moved across an awakening continent, just as rats—as if charmed by the piper's tune—emerged to spread their own deathsong. Half of the awakening continent perished in the plague's

onslaught; the survivors saw a strange new era dawning, one full of exploration, new learning, and ancient secrets rediscovered. Madness flourished
too, and its minions bellowed and screeched in their barred chambers, and
raved about things stirring in the earth.

* * *

Johnnie grimaced. Dr. Leo was scratching, scraping, and scrawling on the
dusty blackboard again. He wrote, "Does religion determine the music, or
does music drive religion?" He faced the class, clapping dust off his hands.
"In other words, which came first—the chicken or the egg?" Dr. Leo was a
devout believer in starting the session with a Big Question, regardless of the
resounding apathy he encountered.

Silence. Gum popping. Somewhere, a dog barked. Johnnie would have
to bail out the good doctor once again. "I suppose we'll eventually arrive at
our traditional conclusion that it's 'both/and' instead of 'either/or', but in the
benevolent interest of stretching our young minds toward the joy of learning,
I'll play dumb and say, 'Duh, why religion determines music, of course.'"

Dr. Leo snarled melodramatically and hurled the chalk at Johnnie, who
snapped it out of the air and yawned; all part of their daily act. "I'll stretch
your young mind after class," threatened Dr. Leo. A coed giggled, while
another two or three rolled their eyes and yawned. The course was entitled
"Music and Religion: God's Greatest Hits," and it was the kind of elective
that attracted perhaps nine or ten students in its annual appearance.
Johnnie enjoyed the smaller, more informal classes anyway, but signed up
mainly out of loyalty to Dr. Leo Richter. Johnnie was a bit older than most
college students, and Dr. Leo was younger than most professors. In four
years they had struck up a casual friendship.

Now Dr. Leo, pleased with the two or three minutes of dialogue he had
presided over, was waxing eloquent. "In my stranger moods I've entertained
the idea that it's music calling the signals," he was saying. "Think of it in
terms of power. Church services are built around music, but most of the
music has lost its potency. It's either funeral parlor organ, or some nun
strumming the chords of Peter, Paul, and Mary; not too much in-between.
But leave the service, climb into your car and crank up the stereo. There's the
real deal! Doesn't matter if it's jazz, metal, opera, rap, or that new thing. Just
pull up to a light and watch the people in the cars around you singing with
the radio. Look at their faces. Rapture! Music is religion—it inspires, heals,
transports, rhapsodizes, evangelizes. Studies show that people work better
with music. House plants flourish with Mozart—who knows why? Every
century or so the church rediscovers this truth, and then, like a bolt from

heaven, power surges through religion. People are healed; disciples speak in unknown tongues. But music is always at the bottom of it."

Johnnie found class more interesting than usual; it was obvious the prof was energized by his topic. When the hour was gone, and the others emptied the room, he approached the desk. "You gonna stretch my young mind, or was that an idle threat?"

"Don't flatter yourself. Come back with a mind sometime, and I'll stretch it."

"Well, I've got a question. Research papers are due in a month. Obviously I plan on plagiarizing from some obscure Internet archive the night before it's due. But you're wanting the topic early, right?"

"An Internet leech, my friend, is a hell-spawn abomination upon whom vengeance will be wreaked unto the seventh generation. Yeah, I need the topic next Friday. Why?"

"I have a unique idea, but you'll scoff; it sounds bogus. There's a big music festival three weekends from now, and it has religious implications. I'd like to cover it as a research project. That's it. At the sound of the tone, scoff."

They were walking down the hall now. Dr. Leo grinned contemptuously. "You do think I'm an easy touch, huh? A grade for going to a rock concert?"

"Well, actually, that's the point. It's not rock . . ."

". . . It's R&R. You're talking about Blasted Heath at West Arkham."

"You know about it?"

"Duh, of course. Describe the religious implications, please, sir."

Johnnie lounged in a chair of Dr. Leo's tiny office. "Okay, well, you know that R&R is Rant 'n Rave, of course—a fusion of several streams of popular music from the end of the nineties. As you said in class last week, music divided into all these different sub-genres, and lost its power as a uni-fying cultural force. R&R (actually they're calling it Rant) is both evolu-tionary and reactionary—all the colors bleeding into one. Or so say the music critics as they wet their pants over it."

"Johnnie, my boy, you're stalling. Religion, remember?"

"Okay, geez, I'm getting to it. Rant is the Next Big Thing, right?—and it has exploded over the last few months. And Rant seems to be spreading across the whole dang global village, which is unprecedented in music. It's 'omni-cultural.'" Johnnie grinned self-consciously; he was more articulate than he liked to let on. "So anyway, this festival is on the west side of Arkham, in this infamous old forest. Tons of urban myths revolve around these ol' woods, and you hear about everything from UFO landings there to spirits in the greenery to zombie squirrels. There's a spot called Blasted Heath; a whole family died there a century ago, which started all the stories. Then nothing would grow in the vicinity, or so they say. They cleared it for a reservoir, which, in turn, produced some funky water. They gave up and drained it, and, presto, you've got this big open area ideal for a festival; smack in the middle of The Enchanted Forest, near witch-burning Arkham. It's got Kid Appeal written all over it, i.e., Big Bucks."

Johnnie thumbed one of Dr. Leo's magazines and continued, as the professor tidied his bookshelves. "Now, the big buzz on the festival, and Rant itself, is that it's a Big Satanic Conspiracy. Religious folk accuse everything new of being 'of the devil,' right? There are rumors that the music and the festival are fronts for some kind of occult network. And that kinda talk, needless to say, simply attracts more kids. Get the picture, now: you've got fundie protesters and tract-pushers lined up; and since Arkham has a history with witchcraft, there's a nice local contingent of witches and pagans, who will most definitely put in an appearance, if only to face down the Christians. Picture the color, the pageantry, all with a soundtrack of ranting and raving. See the movie; buy the video game. It's going to be a circus! Don't these journals do a swimsuit issue?"

Dr. Leo snatched the issue out of his hand and shelved it. "So your religious implications are less in the music than the politics around it?" Dr. Leo's words carried a vague note of disappointment.

"Well, not exactly. I think Rant is a spiritual experience for a lot of kids. Matter of fact, some of them really get off on these tunes. It's kind of creepy, if you've been in a Rant bar. But it's a moot point; I'm getting my report off the 'net, remember? I'll probably be tanning in Bermuda."

"And I'll torment you for the rest of your days. Okay, write the paper, on one condition." A moment of silence for impact, then he smiled. "You have to take me along."

"Say what?"

"I earned my doctorate in Arkham, my boy—at Miskatonic. They've got a great collection of old sacred texts, particularly of the occult variety. It contributes to the area's reputation. I'm writing a study for one of the journals, and I need to do some work with the *Necronomicon*. The only way to see it is to use their library. So I'll catch a ride with you, hit the MU library, and catch some R&R at Blasted Heath." Dr. Leo whistled excruciatingly off-key as he rubbed Lemon Pledge onto his desktop.

* * *

The figure strode briskly into the little tavern, and heads turned. The locals knew Ludwig van Beethoven more for his manner than his music. Beethoven scanned the tables until he caught the cool, piercing eyes emerging from the tattered hood in an unlit corner. He paled, and momentarily froze. Then he made his way to the table, whose occupant offered a hand.

Beethoven only studied it, his eyes returning to the face. "Time has not changed you," he murmured.

The man smiled. "Travel is tonic for mind and heart. I choose not to grow old. But you, my friend, are quite altered."

"I was six years old then, Herr Pfeiffer. You disappeared after you had taught me the arts and conventions of music—and some other things. Your training was quite unconventional, and I might say traumatic, for a sensitive child."

"You were an unconventional child, Ludwig; and now, an unconventional man. Your music, however, is quite pedestrian." He took a long draught of his beer.

The young composer glowered. "It provides me a life of prosperity, a measure of fame, and an abundance of friends."

The hooded man was silent for a moment, but his eyes sang a song of contempt which turned Beethoven's blood cold. Finally Pfeiffer asked, "And fulfillment? Creative satisfaction?"

"I'm getting a drink." He rose and attended to that, without returning or even looking back. Instead, he downed his beverage, got his coat and stick, and left. Beethoven needed time to think. He made his way down the snowy street, his heart pounding to the rhythm of his rapid steps. But he knew flight was futile. As he sat at his piano and played a soothing figure of recent composition, the old shadow from his nightmares fell across the ivory and maplewood. It lingered a bit; it spoke: "And this is the state of your art?" It was less question than accusation.

Beethoven's hands continued to work the keys, but with new purpose. The piece modulated to something more darkly exotic; the tempo shifted stealthily, and shifted again. Intensity grew. In a moment he was not so much caressing the keyboard as assaulting it, threatening it, pounding his will from it. He concluded, and turned to face Herr Pfeiffer through a fog of perspiration and tears.

The old teacher smiled. "You were an apt pupil. I knew you had not forgotten."

"How could I? That option was never available to me. Your cacophonous scales and motifs have pursued me beyond the veil of sleep until rest offers no release. When I attend the opera I begin to hear your music superimposed, until my ears—my ears—" He broke off and looked away from Pfeiffer.

"Your ears begin to fail you? The doctors can do nothing for your encroaching deafness, am I correct? My son, your inner ear hears, and it knows, and finally it surrenders, overwhelmed in the presence of Truth. Your deafness is too late to arrest, Ludwig, even if I so willed. Perhaps if you had embraced in your youth the gifts I lavished on you, things would be different. As it stands, you can only bow before the will of the Muse and give life to the wonders she reveals to you—before the hour passes. You might yet be spared a miserable death, or madness at least; it is impossible to say. But your legacy will be far greater than the paltry friends and feasts of your pitiful boasting."

His smirking aroused Beethoven's ire; but what could be done in the face of raw, merciless power? He turned again to the keyboard, closing his eyes and drawing from deep within himself, throwing open those chambers he had declared forbidden. Near-demonic power, raw and unrepressed, came forth through his hands to torment and arouse him, and he played with escalating passion. In the streets, candles appeared in windows and dogs howled. A few sensitive souls noticed slight tremors of the earth in Vienna and environs. When he was finally spent, late the next morning, Herr Pfeiffer was gone.

His Third Symphony was banned at Prague's conservatory. In whispers, of course, he was hailed as a genius who had found his voice. But Beethoven knew this was the least of what he would unleash on the world. What must be done, must be done slowly—safely. The music would grow darker, deeper, more dissonant with the fading years. He would hear less and less of it, until white silence sheltered him from the madness of his musical sensibilities. But Napoleon heard, and Nietzsche too, and finally Hitler. All drew from Beethoven's well of inspiration.

* * *

The stranger traveled on, offering a farewell to the sleeping city of Vienna as he arranged his hood. He thought again of Paris streets, where blood had flowed like wine and the Bastille had become a charnel house for peasants and aristocracy alike—democracy indeed! He had made beautiful music. And with such magic, the best was always yet to come. He drew a battered old flute from some hidden pocket and rendered a tune for the moon and the tides.

* * *

"Prof? Hey, prof?" Dr. Leo's mouth fell open. He was napping in the passenger seat. Johnnie found a Rant station on the radio, and turned the volume knob about three hundred degrees clockwise.

When Dr. Leo recovered his faculties, Johnnie said, "Prof, I just wanted to ask if you were trying to go to sleep."

Dr. Leo rubbed an eye and mumbled, "I knew this was a mistake."

"You hungry? I thought we could stop, gas up, and grab something."

"Whatever. I don't care. God, what is that?" He tuned the station in more clearly.

Johnnie chuckled. "I guess you haven't heard much of this music, huh? Well, it's an acquired taste. Let me set the stage for you. Rant bands usually have two lead singers, one who is called a chanter, kind of descended from the rapper. He or she chants vague, darkly suggestive lyrics that have an emotional pull. The other singer, the wailer, serves as an extra musical instrument. A multi-octave range is a plus, and the voice can be bluesy, ethereal, maybe even melodic—but more often eerie and disturbing. The singers are accompanied by bands of various combinations, but percussion is by far the most important element. Primal, thundering rhythms are key. I think you can see why the uninitiated start babbling about the occult."

Johnnie saw Dr. Leo's knit brow, and he turned the volume down. "Hey, I've also got some show tunes . . ."

"No, leave it on; I'm interested. I was just thinking about where we go from here."

"McDonald's? I think there's a Pizza Hut."

"In preparing my lectures I've listened to everything from Gregorian chants to Brahms to the Sex Pistols and early Miles. After a while, you can see patterns. The music defines the culture. But what does this—" (he turned the volume up for a second) "—tell us about where we are? And what can it evolve to?"

"I say bubble gum will make a comeback, like that early seventies stuff; something to cool out with after Rant. It all goes in cycles—what goes around, comes around, right?"

"You tell me. Will a satellite that goes around a planet, come around to infinity?"

"No, because it moves just a tad off course each revolution. Ultimately it either crashes in, or flies out into space; right, Dr. Astronomy?"

"Exactly. Art has certain cycles, too. But each time it comes around—each revolution, if you will—the orbit is a bit more distorted. Look at Greek sculpture: when the empire flourished, their art was all about heroes and ideal anatomy. But as they neared the end, the figures in the statues grew hideous and distorted."

"So you think Rant is hideous and distorted?"

"Well, it's all relative—to a point—but we've come a ways from Gershwin and Porter and moon and June. Remember, too, that I've been looking at the ancient Scriptures—the really ancient ones. The Bible is hot off the press compared to some of these."

"This is the stuff you're going to dig up at Miskatonic?"

"Yeah. But I've already been around the block a few times with these writings. We're talking prophecy here, and a different take on space and time. I think some of the ancients expected what we're hearing in modern music. You passed a fast food exit."

"On purpose, too, because you're scaring me. Is this whole thing leading up to Nostradamus, and the punch line is that he foresaw Elvis? Because this isn't the Dr. Leo we all know and love."

"Nostradamus was a fool. I'm talking about wise men—and some totally insane ones; maybe one or two that weren't men at all. They passed on ancient rumors, from the very dawn of history and a page or two beyond, about earth's prior occupants. These Elder Gods are very much alive, but for various reasons they're in remission until 'the stars are right,' or whatever it takes to awaken them to rightful redomination. And I've been thinking about music as the key to the lock."

"It sounds like someone needs to be separated from his Lovecraft editions."

"Just remember Lovecraft was a journalist, Johnnie. More of his work was journalism than his readers care to admit."

"So what's the Elder God Rock 'n Roll Conspiracy Theory? Because I think I saw the movie on cable."

"It's this: that music began as a primitive instrument of sacrifice, orgy, fertility, and invocation. It connected us to awesome powers we've long since forgotten; and it evolved with everything else to its lofty peak of elevator ambience. But in all of its orbits, the path has veered inward with each revolution. At every opportunity, it has attempted to lurch backward—or inward—to its real roots, to chaos and darkness and rage. They thought Mozart was dissonant, then Beethoven, later Stravinsky. Elvis was the Antichrist, then they burned Beatles records in Alabama, and rap was supposed to be the mother of violence and anarchy. 'Same song, next verse, same as the first.' Though culture encapsulated and neutered every one of those, this force is the Thing That Won't Stay Dead. It simply gets up off the floor and keeps coming, morphing into some wild, new sound that attacks our sensibilities yet again. Don't keep passing these exits, I have to go to the bathroom!"

"Just talking about this stuff does something to your biological urges, doesn't it? So, what's the bottom line?"

"That it's not all relative. Ultimately, there must be a final orbit: a style that can't be neutered. In musical terms, it would be a kind of primal crescendo; I (and a few others) would expect a convergence of primitive powers. Chaos would reign supreme—but that might be the least of it: if I'm reading the ancients correctly, this crescendo could reawaken some sleeping dogs we'd best leave lie. Bottom line? I'm saying that music has become the gateway for crawling chaos."

* * *

Under a southern moon, two headlights surveyed the darkness. The old car pulled up slowly and paused, its motor wheezing, and spat out Robert

Johnson. As the auto rattled into the distance, reclaimed by the night, he considered pursuing it; this no longer seemed such a wise idea. Instead he stood at the crossroad and fingered the neck of his guitar, the only love that sustained him.

The sky was as black as only a country sky can be, and every bit as unquiet. The wind whispered, and as he finger-picked a tune the trees swayed like lady listeners at the juke. The wheat field rippled with unseen presences; Johnson decided not to think about that as he worked the strings and sang one of his favorites, "There's a Hell Hound on My Trail."

Something flew across the red moon, then a cloud passed over it. When the eerie light was restored, the dark man stood before Robert Johnson.

His skin was dark, but Johnson could never decide whether he was a Negro. All that mattered was that the man had stood on the opposite corner today, the barrel house corner, and stolen his crowd cleanly. After he'd caught a few bars of the "Walking Blues," Johnson had stopped to listen; then time itself had stopped. Nothing else mattered now but the chords, and the fingerings, and the stringed ecstasy that had claimed his soul on a street corner at noon. Now it was a minute past midnight, the hour of revealed secrets.

"Do I call you Mr. Scratch?" said Robert Johnson, studying the stranger. "Do I offer you my soul?"

"Your soul is no prize," said the man, lighting a cigarette. "Only the music matters. Do you want it?"

"I want nothing else."

"It brings misery and madness."

"I'm already mad and miserable. I might as well be a mad, miserable, damn fine blues player."

The stranger smiled. "In the great symphony, yours is a short movement, though important enough. Your torment will not be sustained. I believe you were playing 'There's a Hell Hound on My Trail.' Hear its true sound. Open yourself and take it in." And Robert Johnson watched the hands, if hands they were; for they seemed more like claws as they commanded the strings. Even the bottle neck was merely another digit; it appeared to emerge from the hand like a sprout; strange fruit indeed. It was as if those hands were speaking a timeless, forbidden language with the guitar as their tongue. He listened with heart, mind, and soul. He "opened himself," as the stranger had ordered, and his own fingers began to hear and understand that primal language with its timeless secrets. And he knew with assurance that, in the past, he had been neither mad nor miserable after all; not like he would be from this night forward.

The night Robert Johnson died, several years later, witnesses said he was on his hands and knees, howling like an animal. The only actual death-witness, however—the man who signed the certificate—would never be found. No one could place the name. Various stories circulated, none of them supported by evidence. All that seems clear is that the latter-day Robert Johnson was a creature of darkness and mystery, and that the record he cut transfigured the art of the guitar, which in turn transfigured twentieth century music. Hendrix would listen, before unleashing his chaotic, dissonant feedback and succumbing, like Johnson, to the demons he had freed.

Even as Robert Johnson delivered the new musical truth, something broke the surface in the South Seas; but none could say what befell the New Zealand ship and its crew. Strange stories circulated about the port city of Innsmouth, while other rumors involved an expedition in Antarctica. Trends of distortion and abstraction fascinated visual artists, and lunacy flourished; sometimes one couldn't tell which was which. Simultaneously, the stock market crashed, and men of distinction leaped from skyscraper windows on Black Friday, for they could not bear the looming vision of the new Dark Ages.

* * *

Johnnie's old Prelude rolled into downtown Arkham late at night. Despite the hour, the two wanted to cruise the boulevard before checking in at the little motel ten miles or so beyond the city limits (Arkham was not designed for huge crowds, and rooms were scarce). "Is this the Arkham you remember?" Johnnie asked.

"Not exactly. There were never this many people on the streets at noon, much less midnight. Then again, there were never any pop festivals here; it's basically a sleepy university town."

Excited non-sleeping concertgoers were to be expected. But the figures milling around the dark storefronts seemed oddly out of place. For one thing, the vague silhouettes didn't necessarily suggest teens or twentyish folk. They skewed a good bit older, and in some cases, distinctly elderly. They shuffled along the sidewalks slowly. Neither Johnnie nor Dr. Leo could get a good glimpse of a face. Then Johnnie realized what he was seeing. The strollers were turning away from the lone car, and its headlights, as if from years of habit. At the moment he pulled parallel with two or three figures, they would turn to look into a dark store window.

The Prelude's twin beams of light also revealed that their dress, far from being the T-shirts and halters of youth, tended toward the baggy and the over-covered. It was a warm night, but short sleeves were hard to find. Some of the wardrobe reflected other cultures: an Indian scarf here, a kimono there, bright African colors on another. But what the two travellers noticed most was the limping, the shambling, and the disfigured or missing

limbs. Neither of the pair spoke the rest of the way to their destination—
the Shady Arms Motel.

They had come a day early, opting out of Friday classes. This gave Dr.
Leo a chance to get some work done at Miskatonic, and Johnnie an opportunity to wander around and take in some of the concert atmosphere. They
met, by design, at the makeshift box office near the entrance to Arkham
Westwood. It was a lovely, Robert Frost kind of forest—or it looked like it
had been before the gods of commerce found it.

Attendance overwhelmed all expectations—and Arkham preparations,
of course, underwhelmed. The highway was two-lane and traffic was backed
up for miles. Kids were deserting their cars and partying on the highway
shoulder. Dr. Leo remembered a few obscure shortcuts and managed an
end-run, miraculously appearing only an hour late.

They staked out a spot perhaps fifty yards from the stage. It was certainly
an odd assembly. The midnight crowd from the boulevard was in full
strength; and given their appearance, odor, and a few disturbing intangibles,
their close proximity was undeniably disturbing. Teens and twenties were
there, too, but even these did not constitute your average concert audience.
While Rant was all the rage, its core audience still seemed to draw from the
fringes: some skinheads, cyber-cultists, vampire fetishists, and plenty of general down-and-outers. So the behavior of the crowd was unpredictable. Many
of the fringe groups, along with the occult and fundamentalist delegations,
had set up booths on the perimeter, and any number of skirmishes, shouting
confrontations, orchestrated demonstrations, fistfights, and miscellaneous acts
of weirdness were in progress.

Pre-concert music came over the megalithic speakers, eclectic in repre-
sentation of the streams converging to form Rant. There was late rap, techno-
pop, some 1960s R&B, a touch of blues and gospel, even a Beethoven sonata.
The final piece, as the lights went out, somehow transfixed the crowd. It was
a simple Gregorian chant from medieval times, and it seemed to inject an odd,
ethereal charge into the moment. Lightly, then with increasing volume, a
wailer airily and eerily accompanied the monks. Steady, nearly dissonant
streams from a synthesizer were then introduced. A Brazilian drum began to
beat with a suspenseful, steadily building rhythm; after a while, the monks
had been drowned out. Then a lone spot revealed the pale, deep-shrouded
chanter, who began with a whisper:

> You better open yourself,
> you better give up your mind,
> You better harken to the darkening—
> as worlds unwind,
> You better look to the stars,

and the alignment of Mars,
within the earth is the rebirth
of what will swallow mankind,
and if the mountains are shakin',
and the crust is a-quakin',
and the ocean is in motion,
We've a notion He'll awaken!
—Let his light be shined!

Suddenly the huge stage was flooded with red illumination, and smoke drifted before the footlights. The drums and percussion were now pounding furious counter-rhythms. Guitars and synthesizers soared to acoustic clashes. A choir of chanters from the various groups joined the lead:

O Ancient of Days, the One we're coming to raise,
As we attune to the moon and the stars and their phase,
So may our whispers and screams,
Conspire to enter your dreams,
And as the opening eyes
Of the awakening wise
Realize you must rise.
—WATCH THE SKIES!

With a cymbal crash, an incredible combination of fireworks and laser technology awed the crowd. Johnnie smiled and shouted, above the din, in Dr. Leo's ear: "Contrived but cool, huh?" Dr. Leo made no attempt to reply. He just continued to goggle at the apocalyptic Arkham sky.

The music went on well into the wee hours, but the biggest groups were scheduled the following night. The professor and his student slipped away a bit early to beat the crowd. Back at the Shady Arms, Johnnie wound down by channel-surfing, while Dr. Leo tapped intently at his lap-top computer, checking news across the world. But it was a quiet night on the wire.

* * *

Next day it was impossible to move anywhere close to the stage. Thousands had camped out on the grounds, and the setting resembled pictures of Woodstock from the history books. Many of the kids wore little or no clothing, and sexual activity was commonplace (except to the fundamentalist protesters, who recognized a sure sign of Armageddon). But the boulevard bunch was subdued, whispering among themselves and huddling sweatily inside their baggy suits and dresses.

When Johnnie and the prof arrived in the late afternoon, they noticed the bizarreness quotient had increased around the perimeter. A KKK group, complete with robes and hoods, had set a great cross on fire. A number of African-Americans were assembling, and counsels of war seemed to be in progress on both sides. A man with a Bible stood atop a beer pavilion and continued to shout for Holy Ghost revival, even after he had been bloodied by a volley of rocks and bottles. But the sun was going down, and attention was increasingly drawn to the stage, where the rising, charismatic symbols of the new music came on to perform.

There was a peculiar charge in the air as the night wore on and the full moon seemed to cover the sky. It seemed to Johnnie that traditional concert trappings—the hit medleys, laser shows, and guitar solos—were being discarded, and that the nature of the event was shifting. The bands were no longer playing identifiable album cuts; they were broadly improvising, with the wailers working themselves into hoarse frenzies, and the chanters spitting out rambling, primal invocations from the heart of darkness, urging on the crowd and unseen forces.

The relentless drumming was slowly dismantling the audience's defenses, and many began to succumb. There was sex of every variety including gang-rape in both genders. Violence broke out between individuals and groups. All of it moved to the pounding rhythms of the bands—chaos in cadence. Johnnie could see a crowd clustered around one of the victims, appearing to come to the man's aid; then he realized they were fighting for scraps. Despite the music's amplification, the air was filled with shouts, screeches, chanting, and howls surely not human. Stage smoke drifted through the crowd, and colored spotlights revolving through the audience offered fleeting glimpses of primeval savagery. And the vast, blackened forest around them seemed to harbor scurryings and stifled screams.

The contingent of police and security would have proved inadequate for the most ordinary of concert events. In the face of what transpired, they were impotent; some were trampled or tortured, though not a few joined in the revels.

Midnight approached, and various band members from earlier in the evening returned to the stage to form a superband. The songs, which had given way to one massive Song, built and built to some inevitable, unthinkable crescendo. Johnnie pulled Dr. Leo to the safest corner of the grounds he could find. The professor seemed just short of acquiescing to the madness. His pupils were dilated, his teeth were clenched, and he was breathing rapidly.

Onstage and on the grounds, the orgasmic crescendo had arrived. The music was a frenzy of rapturous white noise, in which guitars, keyboards, percussion, and voice were indistinguishable. In the audience, full lighting now displayed the aftermath of a death-orgy. Human debris was everywhere. A boy in a bloody Dartmouth jersey stood atop an ex-torso, shrieking mindlessly and waving some oozing memento of carnage. The flash of a camera revealed two Methodists, taking turns posing with a headless witch. Ecstatic poets gibbered in tongues ancient and inhuman; they danced until they collapsed, hands raised to the moon. The KKK's cross had been planted, though now it held a body. And at some obscure signal, the odd midnight boulevard delegation finally spun into action, emerging from their wraps to reveal scales, misshapen limbs, claws, and appendages best not described— all variously combined with human features. The sounds they emitted offered the night's weirdest music, as they scurried throughout the grounds for a joyous feast of the quick and the dead.

Johnnie stood back, looked around him and tried to assess the evening as musical concert and religious experience. What should his research paper say? He chuckled. In the words of the old American Bandstand, the melody was lame but it had a nice beat and was good to dance to. He would give it a B-plus. Whether the true purpose of the evening was accomplished, only tomorrow's headlines would tell—if there was a tomorrow. Johnnie's guess was that there was still work to be done. He let go of Dr. Leo's shoulder and let him slide to the ground, trembling and weeping. His mind was shattered, poor fool. If he hadn't been so familiar with the ancient books, his sanity might have survived the evening.

As he arranged the tattered hood on his parka, Johnnie took one last, lingering glance at the natural beauty around him: oaks and elms, darkness and light, a canvas of carnage. Time for these hooves to be wandering. Perhaps one more song for the road. He removed a guitar from a dead hand and began picking out "Walking Blues."

The woods were lovely, dark, and deep; "but I have promises to keep," he whispered, fading into the crowd and the centuries. "And miles to go before I sleep." Somewhere down that road lay the Next Big Thing, which couldn't sleep forever. *

The Flautists

by Edward P. Berglund

And none may know
the lurker at the core:
a leasher of the light of suns,
a trapdoor spider of the stars.
——Keith Allen Daniels, "Singularity"

Gordon (never Gordy!) Larson looked down the dark alley. The only noticeable light in the darkness was the neon lights two hundred feet down the alley, which flickered on and off, staying off longer than they stayed on. He looked back across the street where he had parked his car, locked of course. Was it worth it coming to this seedy part of town on the whim of the assistant editor of the *Rose City Register?* He could be mugged, his car stripped down. But what choice did he have?

He had practically begged Saul Borski to give him an assignment off of the society page. Well, "good ole" Saul had come through for him. If he didn't follow through with this assignment, he could kiss his chosen career goodbye anywhere in the state of Oregon. And then what would become of his mother, whom he had had to put in a nursery home two years ago? He was just barely making ends meet as it was.

A wind came out of nowhere and its coldness went right through his clothing and almost made his bones ache with its harshness. *God! It's only September! At least it's not raining!* He put his notebook under his arm and pulled the collar of his jacket up around his exposed neck, which didn't seem to make him any warmer. He looked at the streetlight on either corner, swallowed, and stepped into the alley.

Several feet in from the entrance to the alley, something screamed behind him. He jerked around as something wrapped itself around his lower leg. A cat scampered out of the alley entrance before him. Larson looked down at his leg and he breathed a sigh of relief as he pulled the newspaper page from around his leg. Before he threw it on the paving, he noticed the headline. Another body found in the warehouse district. The warehouse district began at the other end of this alley, he thought. He turned back in the direction he had been heading and hurried to the patch of lighter dark that denoted a doorway beneath the flickering neon lights. They flickered back on just before he entered the doorway and he looked up at them.

The Green Oyster.

What a name for a nightclub. But this is the place!

As Larson entered The Green Oyster, he reached up and turned his collar back down. He then smoothed his hair down, thinning already at twenty-six. As dark as the alley had been, it still took his eyes a few moments to adjust to the dimness of the nightclub. It was a few minutes before eight and the club was already filled to capacity. The noise of people conversing was at an acceptable level to Larson. He looked over at the bar, where he could just barely see through the smoky haze three bartenders busily filling the orders of the waitresses. He made his way through the press of people to the end of the bar and leaned back against it, as there were no empty chairs in sight.

"What'll it be, Mac?" a voice rumbled from behind him.

He turned and saw one of the bartenders standing there.

"I'll have a . . . a beer, please. Any kind."

With a surety of movement, the bartender leaned to the right and had a cold bottle of beer and a glass sitting on the counter before Larson. Somehow, in the bartender's movement to the right and back again, he had also found time to uncap the bottle. Larson was impressed. He took five dollars out of his wallet and handed it to the bartender. Pouring some of the beer into the glass, he turned and resumed his leaning position on the bar, oblivious as to whether he ever received any change.

Somebody had turned the lights up at the front of the club, revealing a bandstand. There was a set of drums on the rear of the bandstand, with three guitars equally spaced in front of the drums. In front of each guitar was a microphone with a fourth microphone right at the front of the bandstand. It must be show time, Larson thought. *This had better be good, Saul.*

As he watched, four clean-shaven young men and a young girl, with long black hair, came out from the wings and assumed their respective places. They were dressed in comfortable jeans. The men had on long-sleeved shirts, rolled up to the elbow; the girl wore a light sweater that emphasized, rather than covered, her exquisite figure. There were amplifiers at each side of the bandstand, their little red eyes showing that they were ready to rock. As the drummer settled onto his seat, Larson noticed the lettering on the bass drum head—The Changelings. There was something about the band's name, something that tickled at his memory. He had just about latched on to the elusive memory and then, all hell broke loose.

Oh no, not heavy metal! Larson groaned to himself. The band went into their first number. Larson tried his best, but he couldn't recognize a beat to the music. Hell, he couldn't even recognize whether the noise that assaulted his eardrums even had a melody. He could just barely hear the band's voices above the music. The men seemed to be able to carry a tune, which was more than he could say for the young girl, who seemed to be screeching. *Maybe she was an owl!* he thought.

Larson stood there with his untouched glass of beer. The waves of sound washed over him, around him. He watched the people on the packed dance floor, unable to determine exactly who was dancing with whom. And the sound drew his eyes back to the band. The sound that pulsed, ebbed and flowed, until it had matched the pounding that grew behind his eyes. He didn't know if he could take much more of this . . . this music.

And then the absence of sound surrounded him, the perspiration cooling on his forehead and upper lip. The first set was finished, and so was he. He turned, put the glass of beer back on the bar, and made his way to the entrance to the nightclub.

Outside, he waited a few moments for his eyes to adjust to the darkness. He heard a cat growl from the direction of the warehouse district, turned to his left and hurried back to his car. He got in and locked the door, opened the glove compartment and took out a bottle of aspirin, dumping three in his hand. He tossed them in his mouth and swallowed, the bitterness almost making him forget his headache.

When he arrived home, his headache had subsided somewhat. He turned on his computer, typed in his review of the opening night of The Changelings at the Green Oyster, and emailed it to Saul Borski. *Maybe I'll get something better next time,* he muttered and went to change clothes.

When Larson came out of the bathroom in his pajamas, the little letter icon on the bottom of the computer screen was blinking at him. He had some email. He clicked the icon to bring up the letter and hastily read it.

He couldn't believe what he was reading. Saul had written, "Gordie, the review was great and Mr. Dexter, The Changelings' manager, enjoyed it as well. Mr. Dexter wants to meet with you at The Green Oyster at seven-thirty tomorrow night. He has a proposition for you. Do me proud, I owe Dex one."

"What'd Saul do, call Dexter up and read him the review?" he said aloud to the room around him. Wonder what kind of proposition? And Saul owed Mr. Dexter one what? *Oh, well.*

He turned off his computer and the lights and went to bed.

* * *

Once again Gordon Larson found himself in The Green Oyster, but this time he got to sit down. One of the bartenders saw him enter the club, came out from behind the bar, and escorted him to a table near the bandstand. The bartender said that Mr. Dexter would be with him shortly, and left him sitting there with a bottle of beer and a glass on the table.

Nothing had changed since he had come into the club the night before. It was still dim, still smoky, and still noisy. He poured some of the beer in the glass and took a sip. It was almost as bitter as the aspirin he had taken. He couldn't help wondering why this Mr. Dexter wanted to see him. He would just have to wait and find out. After all, he had arrived fifteen minutes early. And he could get up and say to hell with it and Saul could kiss his . . . But then, Larson's mother would enter his memory. If he wasn't working, he wouldn't be able to afford to keep her in the nursing home. And he couldn't take care of her!

"Good evening, Mr. Larson." The greeting startled Larson, as he had not even seen the man sit down across from him. The man was dressed in an expensive dark suit. He had a slender build and a full head of hair that reached to his shoulders. His face was thin, the bone structure emphasizing the eyes, which were a piercing blue.

"Mr. Dexter?"

"Yes, Mr. Larson. May I call you Gordy . . . no, that's not what you prefer." He studied Larson for a moment before continuing, "You prefer Gordon. Then Gordon it is. I am Nathan Dexter, the manager for The Changelings. You can call me Nathan, but all of my friends call me Narly."

What a strange nickname, Larson thought. "Why, thank you, Nathan . . . uh, Narly, is it?"

"Saul Borski, the *Register*'s assistant editor, was kind enough to read your review of the opening of The Changelings. I thought it was rather refreshing, having a review done by someone that doesn't normally do them."

"I'm sorry . . . Narly . . . but heavy metal music is just not my forte. To be truthful, I'm a fan of the big band era of the forties. I don't really know anything about modern music. And . . . heavy metal is just a lot of noise."

"Don't sell yourself short, Gordon. For someone who doesn't understand the current trend in music, you managed to write a very objective review without showing your bias. And, in the case of The Changelings, your review was a positive one. It really helped us."

"Well, thank you. But I still don't understand why you asked me here. Saul had already told me that you liked the review. And he said something about a proposition . . . ?"

"True, but he owed me a favor, a rather large favor for services rendered." Dexter paused and Larson couldn't help wondering what kind of services Saul received from Dexter. Saul didn't like heavy metal music either!

"You see, last night's opening was just a warm-up for tonight. Tonight The Changelings will be in full regalia, so to speak. And this will be their last night here in Rose City. They're going on the road tomorrow. I wanted to get your impressions of how they will go over, with their costumes, the lighting, and the special effects. With your first review of their music and the review that you will write of their presentation, why, we can send these on to their bookings so they can build up the interest in The Changelings."

"Special effects?"

Dexter ignored Larson's question as the overhead lights in the nightclub went out. The only light, dim as it was, came from behind the bar.

Larson looked across the table to where the other man sat. His eyes must be playing tricks on him in the dim light. He would swear that Dexter was wearing a cloak with a cowl, which he had pulled up over his head. He could not see any features of the other man's face, except the eyes, the blazing red eyes that seemed to bore through him and into his soul, leaving behind an empty coldness.

He rubbed his hand over his eyes and looked back across the table. The outline of Dexter was as he had expected it to be, a normal man, without a cloak. But what about the eyes? And then he remembered the ready lights on the amplifiers at the side of the bandstand. He reached up and ran his finger across his upper lip, wiping the perspiration off.

And then light appeared on the bandstand, an eerie greenish light that seemed to emanate from the simulated fog that covered the floor to a depth of three feet. It just barely illuminated the headstones, with microphones extending from their tops, that marked the positions of the three guitarists and the lead singer. There was something written on the headstones, but he couldn't make out what it was through the swirling fog.

A solitary rim shot on the snare drum jerked his attention to the rear of the bandstand. He could just barely make out the drummer sitting behind his equipment. Two more rim shots and a double thump on the bass drum, and the other members of The Changelings rose up out of the fog without a sound. They stood there while the greenish light intensified enough that their faces could be seen.

Larson had trouble swallowing as he looked at the band members' faces. Their skins were a pale green, including their lips. The eye sockets had been blackened, which emphasized the whites of their eyes. The contrasting colors and the lighting effects brought a sense of strangeness to the band. It almost didn't look like makeup, it looked so real, especially when they smiled and displayed their sharpened teeth. They seemed to radiate an evilness beyond anything Larson could imagine.

He nervously licked his lips and looked over at Dexter, who just smiled and said, "They would make a good study for Pickman, I think."

And then the music started. Not by the band members, for the music seemed to emanate from everywhere and it was not music that could be made with guitars. It was a high-pitched sound that could only come from a flute; no, there were two flutes. The sound of one flute sailed and swirled around the sound of another. There were notes that he had never heard produced by a flute, sometimes above the range of the instrument and sometimes below. When the flutes were playing the same melody, each was distinct, interweaving into a perfect harmony, but then they would go off on tangents, the melodies becoming discordant.

Larson looked over at Dexter and said, "Flautists? With a heavy metal band?"

"Oh," Dexter began, "it's something my father suggested. Something that was required for the sending."

Sending? Larson thought, fear trickling down his spine. He made to get up and Dexter laid a strong hand on his shoulder and glared at him, his piercing blue eyes changing to the intense red he thought he had seen before. He slumped back down onto his chair and looked back toward the bandstand.

The Changelings joined in with a feverish intensity, practically drowning out the sound of the flutes. The notes from the bass guitar set up a vibration in Larson's bones, while the lead guitarist fretted the sounds from his guitar at such a high pitch, that they made his teeth ache. The lead singer seemed to be doing nothing more than moaning, the sound rising and falling with the beat of the drums. But still the melodies from the flutes overlay the whole.

Larson was oblivious to everything around him, including Dexter, except for the uncanny music that washed over him, inundated him. It went on and on and on . . . for what seemed like hours. The Changelings before him gyrated with the music, moving in ways that human bodies were never meant to move. And then they seemed to dissolve, with visions of what could only be madness supplanting normality. Surely this was madness, it couldn't be real.

His eyes were drawn back to the swirling fog on the bandstand. It seemed to have taken on a life of its own, swirling, roiling, boiling, undulating, moving as if it had a life of its own. Minute followed minute as Larson came to realize that it did have a life of its own. That was where the sound of the flutes was coming from! Even as the fog continued roiling, it took on a semblance of solidity and he could now see mouths and eyes and tentacles forming and dissolving with the alien rhythms as the music reached a higher pitch of feverishness.

Dexter said something to him and then laughed. With the noise all but deadening his ears, Larson thought Dexter had said that his father, Azasomething, was really going to enjoy him and the flautists were harbingers of his father.

Larson stiffened as an intense pain raced through his body. It was as if someone or something was tearing his essence, his soul, out of his body. And then he was floating in the air above his lifeless body, but only momentarily.

And then he plummeted upward through the ceiling, up into the night sky over Rose City, and on into space.

He soared at a dizzying pace through space, heading for the center of the galaxy or possibly even the center of the universe. Ever faster he traveled until the mighty stars of the universe became nothing but a blur, their colors intermingling until everything was a blinding white flash to the sides with a blackness dead ahead, a blackness that approached him ever faster. But the "blackness" was not a total black, but more of a complete absence of light. An immense deep, dark hole that he was falling into, moving faster and faster.

He felt himself being stretched until it seemed that he could stand upon the planet that he had just left and still touch the bottom of the dark hole he was approaching. And since time seemed to have come to a standstill, he knew he would be able to ponder what would happen to his mother now. Yes, he would ponder that even more than wondering what awaited him at the bottom of the hole. ✳

Fall from Grace

by D. F. Lewis

There can only be more fear coming with the words. But I simply write them to keep more worrying ones at bay.

"This is where the hinge would have gone," announced the well-endowed woman as she passed her arm up through the hole. A tongue of stone, near the top of the cyclopean boulder, was a protrusion which her demonstration proved was not entirely solid. Judging by the difficulty she had withdrawing her arm, the dimensions of the aperture were evidently not great. I could imagine the wooded pole that was inserted there years ago and the huge gate hung from it across the lane. But why a gate here?

"Why was a gate needed here?"

Somebody else in the group had beaten me to the same question. In any event, "hinge" didn't strike me as the best word, the one the buxom woman had decided to use, but I could not think of a better one. Whilst I was thus day-dreaming, my mind slipped a gear upon this and other pre-occupations—and I had missed the answer to the question. So I provided my own answer: the road once needed to be blocked to prevent the easy transit of things that should not have walked the earth.

I sucked my Polo mint from the middle outwards and trudged after the tassel of tourists as it coiled in the woman's wake. The day was hot, a fact which, based on the summer so far, was quite extraordinary—but ever since I'd arrived for a holiday, the sun had not failed to disperse the desultory clouds. The island was 3 1/2 miles by 1 mile, irregularly ringed with back-breaking climbs down to craggy bays. And the lack of cars was a heaven, despite the few tractors to which it would have been uncharitable not to permit the five hundred inhabitants to have access. The tourists pedaled along the island's dusty lanes on hired push-bikes or clip-clopped around in horse-drawn buggies. The names of the bays rang alien to my English ears, with words I had seen written on the island map, like *Leng, R'lyeh* and *Tekeli-li!*

In any event, the islander woman who chatted with us batches of holiday-makers on foot, as we accompanied her in constituent groups of twos and threes, was an expert on the gossipy sights of the island, including tales of an Occupation, which I took to be the German one during the Second World War. It was strange to believe that some of the old inhabitants had actually been the subjects of the Iron Heel of the Nazis . . . but even stranger to hear said that the oldest ones had submitted themselves to other invading forces which were somehow softer, looser, and paradoxically, crueler.

One sight to which the large woman trooped us along was the very hotel in which I happened to be staying, a hotel that boasted a room where Victor Hugo had once slept. Yet some of the poems she read aloud to us spoke of things like Yuggothian Fungi and were, to my mind, as far from Hugo as it was possible to get.

In any event, the group tagging behind the woman guide was treated to coffee at this my hotel and I was delighted to see that some of the waitresses (who attended my table during dinner in the evenings) were milling about amid the clinking cups and saucers. The waitresses were indeed attractive: one in particular with boyish looks and confident mien, some others in the early blossom of womanhood, a few younger than I would have thought possible in such an occupation, all dressed smartly, if sombrely, from silky shirt to short skirt to black stockings—most with bashful looks on their faces, some more than others. In the evening, one or two of these waitresses seemed to sink back into the shadows of the dining room wall to keep careful watch over us eaters, so that, presumably, they could the sooner clear up used crockery, whilst the other waitresses were in the kitchen making girlish noises to whomsoever prepared the excellent French-style cuisine. The diners themselves were predominantly French and it was a delight to hear the waitresses stutter in neither English nor French but some hybrid of both. Shyness incarnate, those waitresses. Prettiness personified. But I often felt a fear that they were not quite what they seemed: a feeling with no evidence to support it. Even the boyish waitress could not have looked sinister if she tried.

As I finished my Polo mint earlier in the day, I realised indeed that word association had caused me to think of "pole." "Post" was better. Gate-post. I determined to repeat the question regarding the mysterious need for such gates on the island, since I had indeed spotted a few of those stone tongues elsewhere. I hastened after the female guide—but that was when she had, surprisingly, via paths I had not previously traversed, reached my hotel for coffee and for a Victor Hugo so foreign he ceased to be simply foreign.

So, the question of the hinge, ineluctably, faded from the forefront of my mind. I vaguely recall that I dreamed that night of a long snake that threaded the stone hole with the consequent squeezing of a moveable thinner section along its malleable extent. And its snorting noises seemed like a mixture of Welsh, French and German, with backsliding gutturals that belonged to none of those languages.

It was peculiarly difficult to sleep on the island, with its background of silence. This was in contrast to the quietest spots on England's mainland that were endemically infected with an insidious hum of traffic, the most distant of which seemed to be borne in on you by all means of mental and

physical channels. But, here on the island, with the sea's insulation, paradoxically accentuated by the cry of the gull and the waves' watery whispers,
there was silence in its true sense—except for the occasional light footsteps
of waitresses heading to their beds in their hotel annex. Yet sleep, once
established, was all the more powerful in its grip, resulting from its own
satiation on such silence. Sleep was blacker than I ever remembered it on the
mainland, but not without vague hints of impending curses and of echoes
that leapfrogged words whilst retaining some nagging meaning which only
a pukka language could convey.

The pre- and post-prandial drinks in the bar, with which I often tended
to indulge myself when on my holidays, added to the initial restlessness as I
tossed and turned upon the squeaky wooden bedframe—but, then, with a
single click of night's fingertips, I would drift into seamless slumber. The
day's energetic clambering of crags and sunlit rock-pools also enabled the
body thus to slip the mind's sticky spider-web more easily. All of which could
not account for the incursion of that particular dream I later tried to recall
but which, now, I've completely forgotten without rereading the worrying
words I have written above.

When I woke in the morning, peculiarly unrefreshed, I found it troublesome, for the first time during my stay, to meet even the tolerant require-
ments of the hotel's availability of a cooked breakfast in the dining room.
The waitresses were not so pretty in the mornings, I had already noticed—
and their attentiveness was imperfectly maintained. Still, young girls are
infamously inconsistent. The boyish one had her hair cropped even closer
upon her day's leave yesterday across in a larger island nearby called
Guernsey. However, I eschewed mentioning her change of hairstyle—not
that I had ever held any meaningful conversations with her (or with any of
the other waitresses) before this morning, so she probably didn't notice I
was off colour and untalkative. I normally requested more toast after con-
suming the full English breakfast, but not this morning. I overheard the
French conversations mumbling around my central table and, uncharacter-
istically, I did not bother to stumble through a clumsy translation. The difference between hearing and listening, I suppose.

Today, I determined to visit Derrible Bay (thus pronounced in the
French way), one of the very few locations (named on my map) that I had
not yet explored during my stay. I suspected it would be as similar to the
other bays as they were to each other, such as Dixcart Bay (again thus pronounced in the French manner) and, yes, the ones whose strange names I
had forgotten.

One such newly nameless bay had a particularly steep (even for this
island) climb to its sandy cove: close to the causeway that led to a nearly
separate peninsula of the coast, one which reminded me of an annex or, in a

more physiological likening, an appendix. It was almost as if it had been left unsqueezed at the bottom of a shapeless toothpaste tube.

In any event, Derrible Bay was to be my venture today. I would save my visit to the peninsula until my last full day on the island (tomorrow). Even so, I was sure there were other parts of the coastline I hadn't visited even once. But, for the first time, I noticed that the whole island was becoming slightly claustrophobic, yearning, as my subconscious probably was, for a good stretch in a train journey and a refresher course in resorts. A number of bikers nearly knocked me off my feet and I mentally shook a fist at their receding backs, as they pedaled off, no doubt, to the gardens and maze at La Seigneurie. It was then I noticed another of those stone tongues poking from the side of an islander's house. I decided, for no obvious reason, to put my own arm through it, as if, in hindsight, that would complete a circuit between me and the island's heart: an attempt at reconciliation.

The place had seemed so idyllic when I first arrived on the small ferry from St. Peter Port, I had imagined I could stay forever in such a Shangri-La as this island. Now, I wasn't so sure. My arm just fitted the hole in the stone tongue but I could wobble it about, my hand emerging from the top like a five-feathered head-dress on a totem. As previously with the woman guide, it was more difficult to remove the arm than insert it. However, once accomplishing the withdrawal, I touched the outside of the stone that encompassed the hole. It vibrated, I'm sure, echoing my own metabolism. With some reluctance, I continued towards Derrible Bay and my assignation with yet one more alcove of contemplation. I couldn't get certain words out of my head, although, as I write, they have entirely vanished.

The path spiraled down towards the rocks where I could see somebody sunbathing, draped across a rock in what I considered to be a most uncomfortable position. I soon gathered it was one of the waitresses from my hotel, respectably, if scantily clad. This was the first time I had seen a waitress out of uniform and I was surprised at how surprised I actually was at such a sight. So surprised I almost slipped.

Her vulnerability as a human being was particularly striking. I decided to return towards the gull-screeching cliff and leave the poor girl in solitude. Yet, before I could accomplish my escape, she raised her head—and smiled. Simply that. All the waitresses in the hotel had often smiled in my direction, but this smile, in comparison, was more focused—human, yet with an indefinable animal's instinct, if not with a bird's, or even, fish's. Her rearing stance from the rock allowed me to glimpse the tops of her small breasts. I waved, as if to say: "I do recognise you, but it's not fitting for a guest to acknowledge a waitress outside the hotel, especially here, when nobody else is about, not safe, not anything." And I ran all the way back, despite my normal inability even to *walk* such island paths without stopping to catch my breath.

The boyish waitress—whom I later believed to have been that very "crea-ture from the deeps" (as I tend to think of her now) whom I had encountered in Derrible Bay—served me my meal that evening. As I munched through the Duck a l'Orange, washed down with a half litre of dry white house wine, as was my habit, I wondered for the first time why there was no Gideon's Bible in my room (as was the wont in most hotels I had previously visited) but only a strange black-skinned book with Arabic-looking words. I also mused that there had been no yachts moored in Derrible Bay that day—which was strange because I'd never visited an empty bay before on this holiday: being August, there were many such white triangles around the whole island, pep-pered along its coastal outskirts like mosquitoes kissing the waves. Before the duck, I had struggled with a starter of lobsterish fish, described in the menu by a French word I hadn't dared ask to be translated, but it was almost alive, I thought, as I held down its unwieldy tail with my fork whilst forcing off, with my knife, segments of pink meat from the central fan-nerved bone. I cannot recall its taste, but it does somehow dredge up another dream that dis-rupted the deep parts of my sleep that night.

Instead of silence outside the hotel, I heard the trundle of horse-traps and the gentle rumblestrips of bikers. But, surely, that could not be right, it being the dead of night. I dared not move but, in spite of such immobility, the bed squeaked—of its own volition. I dared not move because I simply knew I could not move even if I tried. The boyish waitress walked towards me and I could see as if I saw through her luminous eyes—but then I knew she did not walk at all, for she dragged part of herself behind her, across the carpet, and she held out her arms, with each five-pointed hand like a sculp-tor's about to mould clay into new shapes.

* * *

The next day I could not stir myself to do anything, except for a spot of packing and sitting in the hotel garden reading a Henry James novel. Towards evening the weather finally broke down with doses of drizzly wind. Yet, on the day after that, my spirits returned, as my body returned, as it were, to Guernsey, on the small ferry. I was childishly eager for the bigger ferry that would take me on to England. I now sat *inside* the ferry, in con-trast to my excited sentry-like stance at the bows on the outward journey, waiting for what was then to have been the first glimpse of my holiday island. I tentatively felt all round my neck. Felt the collar bones. And deli-ciously scratched my back on the deck-rail. The break had been at least of *some* benefit. I was decidedly more in tune with my own body, with all that climbing in and out of the craggy bays.

I looked down at the tops of my own small breasts. Yes, no doubt about it, the break had done me a whole world of good. Leaner and fitter, indeed, for the encroaching chills of Autumn. And I relaxed my mind, listening to the other passengers drawl and prattle in words I wouldn't care to translate even if I could. ✳

Drums

by William R. Trotter

Sound the trumpets; beat the drums . . .
Now give the hautboys breath; he comes, he comes . . .
—John Dryden, "Alexander's Feast"

Major Harold Briggs (ret.) eased himself into his favorite rattan chair and switched on the radio on the table beside him, while his wife, Li Peng, prepared a strong scotch-and-soda in the kitchen of their spacious bungalow. As was his habit, he tuned to the afternoon financial report on the government-run station in Kuala Lumpur. Smiling her ineffable smile, Li Peng handed him a cool drink; their hands touched briefly.

The rubber market was booming, as it had been for several years now. That business in Vietnam may have torn the Americans apart, but it had certainly been good for the Malayan economy. Once this season's tappings had been sold, there would be enough profit for Briggs and his lady to make their long-discussed voyage to England. Of course, there had been other bumper crops, other robust profit margins, and somehow, they had never gotten around to actually booking passage. Briggs had not set eyes on England since he had taken a long overdue leave at the end of the "Emergency" in 1960.

Well, there was no hurry. England wasn't going anywhere. Time passed slowly here in the Cameron Highlands, eighty miles north of the capital. Here, unlike in most of the country, there was at least a suggestion of seasons, a fragrant coolness at night. They lived an ordered life of slow rhythms. The long, disciplined rows of the rubber trees were soothing to his eye; he liked to make love to Li Peng while the heavy rains boomed like surf against the rattan blinds of their bedroom; and he liked to sit here, after a productive day, sipping his drink and wondering what strange beauty the land would show to him next. Last week, after a lashing torrent, the sun had poured down on steaming earth and a curtain of butterflies, thousands of them weaving an iridescent sarabande, had come out from the jungle and danced for them, stopping his breath with their loveliness.

What, after all, would he find in England after all this time? A changed society, a few aged relatives whose lives and concerns seemed very distant, the tawdry bustle of London night life, but little else. And what would Li Peng find there? Some painful reminder of the colonial past, when British soldiers who married half-breed girls were looked down upon, if not actually despised? These things had to be weighed, contemplated at some leisure. They could be contemplated better, he thought, with another drink.

But as he rose to go inside, he heard the unmistakable sound of a Land Rover grinding its way up the winding red road that led from the distant lowland highway to his plantation. A moment later, the vehicle hove into sight. It was painted in military colors and bore government license plates. An old soldier's instinct told him that this boded no good, although he could find no rational explanation for this premonition—Malaya had been peaceful and prosperous for more than a decade, even if the rest of Southeast Asia had not.

After the Rover came to a halt in the graveled turn-around in front of the veranda, a spruce, exceedingly fit young man in plain khakis bounded forth and approached with his hand extended in greeting and a salesman's smile on his lips. Behind him was another man: thin, middle-aged, wearing a black, short-sleeved shirt and a clerical collar, his face glazed with perspiration.

"Major Briggs? Major Harold Briggs?" said the young man.

"Retired, but at your service. And you are . . . ?"

"Nicol Puckeridge. Captain Puckeridge, actually."

"Let me guess. Special Branch or S.A.S.?"

"The latter. Your old outfit." Puckeridge gestured toward the cleric. "And this is Father Smythe-Jones, Church of England. He's an up-country missionary, ministering to the aborigines . . . or was, until recently."

"May I get you a drink, Captain? And one for you, Father? I'm having scotch and soda."

After an instant's hesitation, the young officer nodded; the missionary shook his head. Briggs called to his wife, who had seen the vehicle pull up and had already fixed a drink. She appeared, as if by magic, almost as soon as Puckeridge sat down. It pleased Briggs to see that Li Peng made her usual vivid impression, and how could she not, in her red silk sarong with her shining ebony hair down to her slender waist?

After his first swallow, the captain seemed to lose some of the agitation he had shown during their initial handshake.

"It's an honor to meet you, sir. You're a bit of a legend in the service, you know. Parachuted into Perak Province in 1944, made contact with the Chinese Communist bandit Chin Lai, organized with him one of the most effective guerrilla movements in Malaya, harassed the Japanese without mercy. Then, after the insurgency broke out in 1948, you led more than thirty long-range patrols into the jungle, culminating in 1959, when you set up an ambush that wiped out Chin Lai's last effective unit."

"But not Chin Lai himself, of course. You've done your homework, Captain, so you must know that he escaped, along with perhaps four or five

others. Probably into the wilderness near the Thai border in northern Kedah
Province, and from there, who knows? Maybe to China itself."

"Yes, and he hasn't been heard from again."

"Why do I have the feeling you're about to add the words 'until now'?"

Puckeridge flushed and coughed uneasily. "Because I was about to, sir."

"Rubbish. Chin Lai may have been the most fanatically dedicated
Communist I ever knew—and I met many during those years—but he was
only human. Personally, I doubt that he survived. Do you know what the terrain is like up there? If you think the jungle in this part of the country is bad,
you cannot conceive of what it's like in Kedah. Do you know the condition
of his men, when we sprang the final ambush?"

"Ah, no sir."

"Their bellies were swollen with starvation and their legs and arms
were thin as twigs. They'd been living on bananas, tapioca, and, when they
could get it, snake meat. They were covered with running sores, wasted by
dysentery, half of them were malarial, one or two of them had gone insane,
and the stocks of their weapons were almost eaten away by jungle rot. No,
Captain, I'm afraid my old friend Chin Lai died a lingering death in one of
the worst places in all of Asia."

"You called him your friend."

"Curiously enough, he was. The bond between us had been forged during our operations against the Japanese, and even though we stalked each
other for years, and there was a time when we would have killed each other
on sight, he was an old comrade with whom I'd shared hardships and for
whom I had genuine respect. And if he were alive today, he'd be too damned
old to hack it in that jungle—he was several years older than I, and I am
fifty-two. No, Captain, I don't think the government has anything to fear
from Chin Lai—I think his bones are moldering somewhere up there near
the Thai border, and have been for thirteen years."

Puckeridge sipped his drink and stared thoughtfully out over the plantation grounds. Sunset was near—Briggs' favorite time of the day—and ser-
ried rays of light poured through the distant jungle canopy and lit the precise corridors of the rubber trees with golden light, thick and slow and
grainy with pollen. The effect was not unlike viewing the interior of a cathedral. Malay tapping crews, their day's labor finished, walked through the
angled light in their white and flowing robes.

"I would not ask you to leave all this," Puckeridge finally continued, "if
that were true, if we did not have solid evidence that Chin Lai is back and
making trouble. Serious trouble. The truth is, Major, we need your expertise, your insight into his character, your knowledge of the northern
provinces—few men except the aborigines have ever set foot in Kedah."

"For reasons which immediately become clear to you if you venture there. Perhaps you'd better fill me in, starting from the beginning. I promise you, however, that I have no intention of moving from this comfortable veranda and back into that green hell of a rain-forest without good and sufficient reason."

Six months ago, Puckeridge told him, a force of well-armed men had raided a police barracks in Baling, the provincial capital of Kedah and the last outpost of civilization before the jungles and swamps became impenetrable. Propaganda leaflets were left behind, as were the bodies of a dozen policemen; leaflets which identified the raiders as the vanguard of something called "The Peoples' Righteous Sword." Maoists, of course, from the tenor of the writing. One surviving policeman, an old sergeant close to retirement, and himself a veteran of the 1948-1960 "War of the Running Dogs," swore the raid had been led by Chin Lai, whose face he had seen staring out from innumerable "wanted" posters during the Emergency. No one took him seriously at first.

Other raids followed, near Kota Bharu on the eastern coast, and a dozen lesser hamlets in Perak and Kelantan Provinces. And other witnesses came forward to identify Chin Lai. Back in the capital, the Malaysian government's team of crack British intelligence experts began to see a pattern. The United States was winding down its involvement in South Vietnam as rapidly as decency and logistics permitted; the Khmer Rouge was gaining strength in Cambodia; Thailand was racked by periodic riots and coups—the whole vast region was going up in flames. With his cause resurgent, even victorious, what better time for Chin Lai, a Communist legend, to resurface?

For twelve brutal years, the British had fought the Communist insurgents in Malaya, and had finally won, thanks to enlightened political leaders and men like Harold Briggs, who had gone into the jungle and met the enemy on his own ground, his own terms, and slowly but surely broken him. But now, Malaya was an independent state, and England, though still vitally tied to the nation by trade and tradition, manifestly lacked the will or the resources to wage that war again.

If Chin Lai and his revitalized cadre had merely mounted the odd raid, his campaign would amount to little more than a nuisance. But in recent weeks, something unprecedented in Malaysian history had begun to take place: the aborigines had begun to flee the northern jungles and seek protection.

Briggs knew them about as well as any white man did: shy and peaceful, diminutive brown-skinned people, probably descended from some wandering Indo-Chinese tribe that had settled in the jungles a thousand years ago, they seemed indifferent both to the jungle's hardships and to the other cultures that shared the land. They farmed an area until it was exhausted, then moved on, supplementing their diets with whatever small game they could bring down with blow-guns and tiny bows. Briggs had dealt with them on occasion during the fight against the Japanese, and he believed them to be perhaps the most imperturbable people on Earth. They sought nothing from the outside world and in return asked only to be left alone, to live as they had always lived.

Never before had large numbers of them fled their forest home, never before had they shed their treasured isolation and sought anything at all from the town-dwellers.

"How many refugees?" he asked.

"More than seven thousand so far, and more coming in every day," said Father Smythe-Jones, speaking for the first time.

"Good Lord, that's a significant percentage of the total population. What's motivating them?"

"Terror."

"Surely not from Chin Lai. He really believes all that Maoist dogma about fish swimming in the sea of peasants. And besides, I've never known him to be wantonly cruel—ruthless, yes, but not the sort of man who tortures natives or pillages their pathetic little villages."

"The problem doesn't seem to be Chin Lai himself, Major," said the missionary. "From what little we can glean from the aborigines themselves, they're much more frightened of what Chin Lai has unleashed, what he may even have allied himself with."

"I don't understand what you're getting at, Father."

Smythe-Jones watched the sun go down and seemed to be savoring the first cool breath of shadow. He was silent for a long moment before continuing.

"Major, what do you know about the Tcho-Tcho . . ."

Color drained from Briggs' face and his hands knotted on the arms of his chair.

"The Tcho-Tcho are a myth. They don't exist."

Quietly, almost sympathetically, Puckeridge whispered: "There was a time when you did not think so, Major. I've read your report. That mission against the Japanese railway in Thailand, in June of 1945."

"Christ!" Briggs turned angrily to one side.

"As you probably know, Major," the missionary continued, "the aborigines are animists. They believe that everything in their world, from rocks to flying squirrels, is possessed of an indwelling spirit, and they have a deep reverence for those spirits. It's a sound philosophy for them, really, because it covers *everything,* and it's one reason they can live in such harmony with their environment. It's also made them one of God's most peaceful people. But something about the Tcho-Tcho doesn't square with that world-view.

It's as though the Tcho-Tcho, and whatever they are in league with, were some sort of monstrous aberration—something that *should not be*. The aborigines can't handle it, fear it profoundly, and are now fleeing from it in great numbers."

"What do you mean, Father, about the Tcho-Tcho being 'in league' with something?"

"I've lived among the aborigines for four years, Major, and I speak their language as well as any white man in Malaya. When I've questioned them about their fears, however, the language barrier comes up again— they simply can't explain the situation in terms of their traditional beliefs. They fear and loathe the Tcho-Tcho, yes, whom they describe as having filthy and repulsive customs, but they also speak of something called 'R'taq,' which translates, as near as I can figure it, into 'He-who-shakes-the-swamp' and of the 'R'taq-vaht,' which translates as 'Servants-of-R'taq.' Whether this R'taq is some powerful Tcho-Tcho chieftain, or a shaman, or even a mythological creature, I can't say—it might even be a symbolic term for pure evil, in which case we might be dealing with a militant cult, something along the lines of Mau-Mau. I can say, however, that, whatever it is, it's a bad business for the aborigines . . . and for us."

Puckeridge leaned over and gently laid a hand on Briggs' arm. "We need you, Major . . . that is, this country, and England, and the refugees. You're the only military man who has any idea of what we might be up against. We need you to lead a team into Kedah and find out what's really going on up there. You'll have your pick of men, air support, and communications gear you could only dream about twelve years ago."

Briggs was silent, his face a mask of stone.

"Major . . . ?" prompted Puckeridge.

"Gurkhas. I shall need Gurkhas. A platoon should do it."

* * *

Puckeridge had stayed for two more drinks, which, Briggs had to admit, he consumed with the sturdy resilience that had been a hallmark of British colonialism since the invention of gin. Even Smythe-Jones permitted himself a single drink. Li Peng had joined them in the gloaming of early night, her jasmine scent blending perfectly with the framing aromas of wild hibiscus and frangipani. The young S.A.S. officer had cemented their agreement with a handshake as he and the missionary were leaving: Briggs would meet him at the Kuala Lumpur military air base, one week hence, temporarily recommissioned. In the meantime, Puckeridge would plan the coming operation and organize the ground and air forces deemed appropriate for the mission. Briggs had every confidence in the young man's ability to put together a suitable force—military technology had changed greatly since his retirement.

As soon as their visitors were gone, Briggs and his wife ate a spare and disconsolate supper, making forced conversation about rubber prices, local politics, the Yanks' grievous situation in Vietnam, and the stale, provincial gossip that was a mainstay of dinner-time talk within the circumscribed community of English planters and their wives.

These topics were soon exhausted. A shadow now lay across their orderly and generally happy lives. Li Peng did not know, or especially care, about the subtleties of geo-politics. She knew only that her husband's hard-won content-ment, and consequently her own, were threatened. She was also worried by the fact that Briggs immediately began to drink again after their meal, something he rarely did. And by the fact that his hands were trembling, something she had never seen before.

She sat quietly with him as the tropical night deepened around them, believing that, when he was ready, he would tell her what was on his mind. At length, after yet another drink, he did. He could no longer silently endure the sadness that had taken residence in her delicate features since she had realized that he was going away, back into the jungle. She looked so shatterable.

For the June, 1945 raid on the Japanese railway in southern Thailand—a branch line that fed supplies to the collapsing enemy front in Burma—Briggs and Chin Lai had organized their most effective force to date: more than one hundred Chinese-Malays, fifteen S.A.S. advisors and support personnel, most of them veterans of numerous clashes with the Japanese, and two hundred aboriginal porters. They destroyed a trestle bridge, blew up culverts and choke-points, and cut the track in two dozen places, then retreated back toward Kedah Province.

At first, it seemed they had made a clean getaway. A few Japanese planes searched for them, but the jungle canopy shielded them from obser-vation and a week after the raid, they crossed the border into Malaya—or so Briggs and Chin Lai reckoned from their compass readings.

But the Japanese secret service, the dreaded *kempeitei,* had become pos-sessed of the same last-ditch fanaticism that motivated the *kamikaze* pilots. Their agents, too, had infiltrated Kedah and were determined to entrap and annihilate the guerrillas who had plagued them for so long. The war might be lost, but vengeance was still possible. And as both Briggs and Chin Lai knew, the Japanese were no less skilled at living in the jungle than their opponents.

Only three hours after the raiders crossed back into Malayan territory, the drums began. At least, that was how Briggs identified the sound, although it had a menacing timbre unlike that made by any percussion instrument he had ever heard. The sound came not through the air, but up from the black and protean earth of the jungle itself. It began behind their column and gradually surrounded it, until they seemed to walk across a vibrating tympanum. It rolled forth in an odd, disjointed rhythm—just as their ears discerned a pattern, grasped a structure, jagged accents shattered any illusions of symmetry. The sound began to grate upon their nerves in the same way as the fat, gray-black leeches in the swamps grated upon their physical security; they wanted to swat at the noise, beat it from their skins as though it were a cloud of ravenous insects. Above them, swimming in the sweat-soaked heat, the triple-canopied jungle vibrated to the sound, but always out-of-synch with the other rhythms of the jungle, growing more discordant, more grinding, with every hour.

It was as though they were being tracked, their slow, torturous progress monitored, even mocked, by the incessant, growling reverberations. And the aboriginal porters, who had been so silent, stoic, and uncomplaining throughout the expedition until this point, grew more and more uneasy.

At dusk, the drumming ebbed somewhat, receding to a soft, surf-like susurrus. Chin Lai put out twice the usual number of sentries, Briggs made sure their two Bren guns were well sited and their precious handful of flares distributed to steady men; the aborigines were herded, rather roughly, into the center of the encampment. Exhausted now, their nerves worn badly, the raiders pulled scraps of netting over their heads and tried to get some sleep.

Briggs scuttled over to where Chin Lai lay behind an impromptu barricade of roots. He had worked with the Communist guerrilla for more than a year, and they had been in tight situations before; but never before had he seen real fear in the eyes of his Chinese comrade.

"You've been here far longer than I, Chin. What's going on?"

"That sound—drums, maybe, or maybe something else—it means the Tcho-Tcho are near. Once or twice, I have caught glimpses of strange deserted encampments, deep in the jungle, but until now, I did not really believe in them."

In dry, whispered tones, the guerrilla chieftain explained. Little was known of the Tcho-Tcho: why, for instance, they chose to live in a pestilential, swampy part of the jungle that even the aborigines shunned, or where they had come from and when. No anthropologist had ever studied them, few white men had ever set eyes upon them. What little Chin Lai knew of them, he had gleaned from his contact with the aborigines, who were reticent about most things and positively stone-faced when mentioning the other tribe.

Chin Lai believed the Tcho-Tcho had been living here long before the ancestors of the aborigines—thousands of years, perhaps. And while the aborigines, when confronted with modern intruders, preferred to retreat deeper into the jungle, seeking only to be left alone, they did at least have some interaction with the outside world; the Tcho-Tcho had none. When Chin Lai first heard about them, he was inclined to think them a myth—a symbolic embodiment of the rain-forests' darker and more dangerous aspects. After he had spent more time in the jungle, the Communist was not so sure. For there were places in Kedah Province which even the aborigines avoided, and events which those primitive but open-hearted people spoke of only in whispers, and only among themselves.

But how, if the Tcho-Tcho were so secretive, so elusive, had the Japanese managed to enlist them—as now seemed evident from the purposeful, malevolent drumming that had followed the guerrilla column all day—into their service? Chin Lai had his own, rather Marxist, theory about that. When the Japanese had sent soldiers into the jungle to hunt the Communists, and then their British allies, they too had sought to enlist the aborigines as guides, porters, auxiliaries. But when confronted with the tribe's customary indifference to outsiders, the conquerors of Malaya had responded with brutal attempts at coercion. Aboriginal villages had been burned, hostages tortured and slain, women violated. Now, two years after the first incidents, no aborigine would cooperate with the Japanese. But Chin Lai's guerrillas had treated them with patience and kindness from the first, slowly winning at least their passive cooperation.

Now, with the Japanese war machine crumbling on all fronts, the task of rooting out the Allied guerrillas had devolved from the bungling, heavy-handed regular troops into the subtle hands of the kempeitei, the shadowy and much-feared Imperial secret service. Their reach across Asia was all-pervasive; they had organized drug cartels in Burma and China and used them to funnel millions into the Japanese war chest; they had penetrated, and savagely destroyed, every major Allied spy ring set up in the Japanese homeland; before parachuting into Malaya, Briggs had even heard rumors of a kempeitei expedition into Tibet, for the seemingly-fantastical purpose of investigating the secrets of dark magic said to be known to a handful of adept practitioners—much as the Gestapo had sought to find the Holy Grail for Hitler.

But compared to their Japanese colleagues, the Gestapo were mere uniformed thugs. In terms of subtlety, the refinements of "persuasion," and the uncanny ability to confound opponents, the kempeitei were their masters. If there were indeed a way to turn the Tcho-Tcho to the Japanese side, to enlist them as guerrilla-hunters and allies, the kempeitei would have found it.

Such was the extent of Chin Lai's knowledge and speculation. Having learned this much, there was nothing more Briggs could do except make sure his own men were ready for whatever the night might bring.

He and Chin Lai had chosen the best ground they could find before the total fall of darkness: a large patch of swamp guarded their front—squishy slime deep enough to bury a standing man—and most of their limited firepower sited on the flanks. Two hours after sunset, the drumming sounds ceased altogether, and the raiders' imaginations were free to feed on the normal, though always unsettling, sounds of the jungle night. Insects hummed, feral squirrels and monkeys chittered, and occasionally, at a far distance, elephants roared.

At about ten o'clock, a bitten-fingernail of a moon crawled above the tree canopy and bathed their position with shredded, hallucinatory light. Although Briggs had seen no movement in front of his position, his skin began to prickle with unease, for as the moon climbed, the jungle noises receded, leaving him and his comrades in a pool of perfect silence. Whatever was out there, the jungle creatures wanted no part of it and had retreated from the swampy area into the deeper forest.

During the next hour, silent as ghosts, the aboriginal auxiliaries began to slip out of the perimeter and vanish. Neither threats nor entreaties could slow them down. Chin Lai grabbed one of the natives, a village headman who had obviously been a leader, and angrily demanded to know why they were deserting. Briggs, who had by this time picked up a smattering of the tongue-clucking aboriginal language, overheard some of the conversation. The headman's eyes were white with moonlit fear, and his gestures were those of barely controlled terror.

"Tcho-Tcho near!" the man babbled. "He-who-shakes-the-swamp is close! Your guns no good! You run, too!" And then the man was gone, slipping free from Chin Lai's hands and diving into the shadows.

What happened next was a nightmare that seared itself on Briggs' memory for years. The drumming began again, suddenly, as though a conductor had cued an unseen orchestra, louder and closer than before. The rich, decayed earth beneath them thrummed and vibrated in waves as though convulsed by some powerful and menacing harmonic.

Then the Tcho-Tcho were on them, materializing out of the darkness like wraiths. Flares went up, and by their sickly light, Briggs beheld a mass of low, squat figures, armed with spears and stone-age knives, their faces flat, nostrils unnaturally wide, eyes burning, all naked and glistening as though rubbed with the very slime of the swamp, penises swinging like blunt clubs, hocking and coughing thick, guttural cries as they advanced not just on patches of dry land, but, seemingly, on top of the very swamp itself.

Gunfire met them and some of the attackers died, but the range was too close and the fighting quickly became hand-to-hand. Briggs saw Chin Lai stand bravely, crying out to rally his men, a Sten gun flaming in his hands, and then he was submerged in a wave of savage flesh. Briggs looked

to his front, held his own submachine gun out like a lance, and killed perhaps three of the attackers before he was knocked down by a terrific blow
on the temple.

He toppled into a ravine full of creepers, which probably saved his life,
but just before he lost consciousness, he saw—or *thought* he saw—the reason
why the Tcho-Tcho had been able to get so close, had been able to cross the
swamp he had assumed no man could cross: a vast, bone-white shallow
hump, impossibly large, broached the surface, and it was across this that the
attackers charged. Whatever it was, the thing was pocked with cracks and
patched with decay, and whatever it was, Briggs knew that it was alive.

Out of their entire force, scarcely a dozen men survived to see the
morning, including Chin Lai. Most were injured, all shaken to their souls
by what had happened, and none could say for sure what they had seen
emerging from that ghastly swamp, as though *summoned* by the drums.

They were finished as a fighting force. Briggs led them on a nightmare
march to the west, a frightened, ashen, group of skeletons. Three more men
died, one of them, an S.A.S. corporal with compound fractures in his arms
and legs who begged not to be left to the jungle's mercy, slain by Briggs' own
hand. Eventually, they reached the coast, the Straits of Malacca, across from
the island of Penang, where a British submarine was watching for them at a
pre-designated rendezvous. Back at the naval base in Rangoon, Briggs wrote
his report on the operation; he mentioned the attack of the Tcho-Tcho, but
did not mention anything else. The report was duly filed away; the war soon
ended. Chin Lai bade his old comrade farewell and returned to Malaya, only
to emerge three years later as the most ruthless and effective Communist
commander during the Malayan Emergency.

When Briggs had finished his tale, Li Peng was silent for a while,
observing the sweat that had broken out on her husband's brow. Then she
said: "So you think that Chin Lai has somehow managed to do what the
Japanese did—enlist the Tcho-Tcho to serve his cause?"

"I can't think of any other reason why the aborigines have fled in such
large numbers. It would give Chin Lai a base of power such as he's never
had. He's the sort of Communist zealot who simply never gives up . . .
believes history is on his side and all that rot. And if you look at the situation in the countries around Malaya, he has good reason to feel optimistic.
He's a very dangerous man, and whatever he's up to now, it must be
stopped before he gains any more momentum."

Li Peng put her slender arms around him; he breathed the scent of jasmine and bent down to taste her delicate, exquisitely formed lips.

"I'm too old, too out of shape, to go back into the jungle," he said,
laughing nervously. "But that young captain was right—I know Chin Lai, I

know the terrain, and I know, better than anyone, how appalling this situation could be."

A breeze, laden with the fragrance of orchids, caressed them.

"Come back to me," she said, holding him with sudden fierceness.

"I will," he promised, hoping that was true.

* * *

One week later—a week in which he had punished his middle-age body with conditioning marches and more calisthenics than he'd done in twelve years, hoping to get himself in shape for the jungle, but mostly just wearing himself out—Harold Briggs passed through a well-guarded gate and dismounted from a government Land Rover on to the hot tarmac of Kuala Lumpur's military air base. Puckeridge saluted (not absolutely necessary, but Briggs appreciated the gesture) and presented for his inspection a crack platoon of Gurkhas. The platoon commander stepped forward, saluted, and extended his hand to Briggs.

"*Tabek, tuan!*" the compact Nepalese said ("Greetings, sir!"), then introduced himself as Jemadar Mohammed Rafiq. Briggs returned the greeting, then inspected the platoon. It was good to be with Gurkhas again; the best professional soldiers in Asia, Briggs thought—always had been, always would be. Tough, resourceful, disciplined, and deadly in combat.

Also on the tarmac, incongruously clad in camouflage fatigues and carrying an FN-NATO rifle on his shoulder, was Father Smythe-Jones. The Church militant, thought Briggs as he shook the missionary's hand.

From there, Puckeridge ushered Briggs into a nearby room, where he met the S.A.S. team that would be going in to handle communications, air support, and probably a lot more tasks that Briggs was too old to have trained for himself. They were keen young men, extremely fit, and, he was glad to learn, veterans of security operations in Borneo—they knew the jungle.

Then Puckeridge took him to a map and explained the plan of operations. They would be inserted by helicopter near the border of Thailand, Kedah, and Perak Provinces, near the last reported sighting of Chin Lai's force and along one of the main routes of the aborigines' flight. They would carry provisions for five days and plenty of ammo, and could be resupplied by chopper whenever necessary. They would attempt to pick up Chin Lai's trail and locate his base camp. They were not to engage him in a firefight unless absolutely necessary—rather, they were to mark the camp (using any of several electronic devices which seemed strange and marvelously compact to Briggs) as a target. Once that had been done, they had thirty minutes to clear the area. After that, a flight of B-52s, on loan from the Americans, would drop 1000-pound bombs on the target, to clear away the jungle canopy, and an entire squadron of

Malaysian Air Force Canberras would follow with napalm. Mopping up, if it
proved necessary, would be done by helicopter gunships. Upon verification of
the camp's destruction, the team would be extracted by choppers and flown
back to the capital city for debriefing.

"It all sounds very neat and orderly, Captain," Briggs remarked at the
end of his briefing. "I hope it proves that way on the ground. But what if
all these wonderful electronic gadgets fail?"

"Then we do it the old fashioned way: a radio message, code-word
'Conrad,' triggers the air attack. I'll show you how to use the radio once
we're in the field."

"I think perhaps I remember how to do that."

"Um, yes, of course, Major. Now, I'll have one of my men show you
how to use one of these new American M-16s."

"I think I'd prefer an old-fashioned Sterling gun, if you can scrounge
one up. Whatever shooting one has to do in the bush, it's always at close
range, and the Sterling is perfectly adequate for that."

"I think perhaps we can locate one." Puckeridge detailed one of his men
to that task, then took Briggs to lunch.

Two hours later, they were flying low over an unbroken sea of trees. It
took the lead pilot some time to locate a clearing near the drop-zone but
finally he did, at the confluence of two large streams. Their landing was wet,
but otherwise uneventful.

While the Gurkhas secured a perimeter and the S.A.S. men sorted out
their equipment, Briggs, Puckeridge and Smythe-Jones studied their maps.
The missionary was vaguely familiar with the area and pointed to a location, a day and half's march distant, where he thought there had been an
aboriginal village. Briggs marked the spot and then traced a line to the
last-reported sighting of Chin Lai's band.

"They've had time to reach that village, and they'll believe there's no
one pursuing them. My guess is that he'll hold up there for a while, plan his
next move, rest his men. He doesn't love living in the jungle any more than
I would, so he'll take advantage of any small comfort he can find."

"How do you reckon that, Major?" asked Puckeridge.

"I only led teams *into* the jungle, Captain. Once we'd done our job, we
went back to civilization and rested up before going out again. In the early
years of the Emergency, the Communists were secure enough to construct
comfortable base camps in the bush, but after we got the upper hand, that
changed. For the last three or four years of the crisis, Chin Lai was on the
run constantly. The discomfort, the sheer human misery, of his existence was
such that eventually even his most dedicated soldiers began turning themselves in, just to escape the bloody jungle. He once commanded hundreds
of agents—by the time we hit him with that final ambush, he was down to

perhaps twenty men. He's even older than I am. No, he'll seek whatever comfort he can find out there, in between raids. If we're lucky, we might even surprise him at this village—at the least, we'll pick up his trail."

"Well, then . . . We've a few hours of daylight left, so I suggest we push on."

Puckeridge circulated among the men and got them into marching order. Then he returned to where Briggs and the missionary were hunched over the map and handed the cleric a foil-covered package. "Here, Father, put one on."

Smythe-Jones flushed with embarrassment. "Is this really necessary?"

"It is. If you're not properly encased, a leech can get into the head of your penis, wriggle up the urethra, and attach itself to the inside of your bladder," said Briggs. "I've seen it happen, and believe me, you do not want to experience that sort of pain."

"Major? Are you . . . ?"

"All sheathed and ready, Captain. Er, Father, if you need some help . . ."

"Thank you, but I think I can figure out the procedure on my own." With admirable, if somewhat misplaced, dignity, the cleric stepped behind a frangipani bush, turned his back, dropped his trousers, and reemerged with an expression that dared the others to make fun of him.

"Push on," Briggs thought two hours later, was hardly the term for it. "Crawl on," maybe; "struggle on," certainly. God, it was even worse than he remembered it. Humidity like a wet wool blanket, vines and creepers that one did not cut through so much as wage battle against with one's machete, the constant knowledge that—among other unpleasant types of fauna—the Malayan rain forest was home to 130 known varieties of snake. And all around, trees a hundred feet tall, filled with raucous parrots, jabbering monkeys, and exotic butterflies, trees whose canopies were so thick that they walked in almost perpetual gloom, their feet squelching in mire that sucked at their sturdy boots and strained the muscles of their calves, clawed by wait-a-minute thorns every bit as nasty as barbed wire.

And where the jungle did not have full purchase on the land, there were mangrove swamps veined with turgid creeks that had to be forded, sometimes up to the neck, such crossings always followed by a rigorous leech-inspection and the ritual cleansing of those fat, disgusting parasites from arms and chests by means of lighted cigarettes. Near twilight, they spotted a twelve-foot crocodile who, fortunately, was content merely to observe their passage from his unblinking prehistoric eyes.

They camped for the night a few hundred yards from the croc's black tarn—not the ideal spot, Briggs thought, but it would have been madness to press on in the dark. Without orders, the Gurkhas and their British comrades formed a defensive perimeter, slathered themselves with a fresh coat of insect repellent, and settled down for a cheerless night. Using one of his new-fangled electronic gadgets, Puckeridge took a fix on their position and held a map-conference with Briggs under a plastic sheet that hid their flash-lights' beams from anyone who might be in the vicinity.

They had made respectable progress. If they continued at this rate, they should be close to the aboriginal village by late afternoon tomorrow—leaving them time enough to reconnoiter before nightfall. Briggs, who was aching in muscles he'd forgotten he had, hoped they would be lucky enough to catch Chin Lai there and bring the mission to a quick, successful close. There was a chance, at least; so far, the wily old guerrilla had acted with impunity, and perhaps that had made him over-confident.

During the night, a typical jungle downpour smote the camp, lashing the foliage above them and hissing like a million snakes. Dawn came and the jungle steamed around them, as primordial, as untouched, as it must have been in the late Jurassic. Miserably, the men wrung out their clothes and crowded together in whatever thick beams of sunlight managed to pen-etrate the canopy. A joyless breakfast of cold rations, an equipment check, a quick coded radio transmission back to Kuala Lumpur, and they were off once more, spread in a tight diamond formation, two Gurkhas at the point, through lingering clouds of steam and fresh pools of rainwater, already scummed with the bodies of moribund insects.

The rest of the day's march was a blurred nightmare for Briggs. He had not had time to get himself back in condition, and his age definitely told upon his body. Already sore from yesterday's abbreviated trek, the muscles in his shoulders cramped from swinging a machete, his hands and face were scratched by thorn-wounds which burned with sweat, and his legs were numb by noon. Still, his old training kicked in to a certain extent—as did his pride in not wanting to be shown up by these fitter, younger, men—and he continued to keep up, reciting to himself a soldier's mantra as old as the armies of Babylon: one foot in front of the other does the trick, old boy. Concentrate on the sweat-soaked back of the man in front and just keep putting one foot in front of the other.

He hypnotized himself so effectively in this manner that it came as something of a shock when one of the lead Gurkhas suddenly raised his hand and brought the group to a stop. Panting like dogs, the men knelt where they were and stared warily at the ferociously tangled underbrush ahead. Puckeridge slithered forward and exchanged whispers with the point men, then came back to Briggs.

"There's a clearing ahead. I think it's the village. Can you come forward and take a look?"

Time to earn my pay again, thought Briggs, forcing his pain-wracked body into one more effort.

A quick inspection told him that the village was deserted. The aboriginal settlements usually bustled with noise, for they were a cheerful and loquacious people amongst themselves, unafraid to announce their presence to the beasts they shared their homeland with. And even a disciplined band like Chin Lai's, though certainly not as noisy as the original inhabitants, would have produced the smells of cooking fire, boiling rice, roasting game, or gun-lubricants—but the air was preternaturally still and the only scent Briggs' experienced nostrils detected was the slight lingering char of cold cooking fires.

"We missed the bugger," he said to Puckeridge.

"Might this not be an ambush?"

"Unlikely. He won't risk a stand-up fight in a place where we can call in air support. We might pick up his trail, though, if he passed through here."

Puckeridge made hand-signals, and his men spread out in skirmish formation on the edge of the clearing. Jemadar Rafiq led his Gurkhas forward cautiously, then softly called out, "All clear, Tuan."

It had been a typical aborigine village: a sugar cane plot, a couple of small rice paddies, picked-over banana trees, groves of heavy, breast-shaped breadfruit, a few small feral pigs that ran squealing into the bush at the soldiers' approach. In front of crude bamboo huts, roofed with fronds and lashed together with vines, the beaten earth was scored with a dozen cold fire-pits. The force began systematically to scour the huts and midden heaps for any sign of Chin Lai's men. Before long, they found what they were looking for. Last night's storm apparently had not extended this far north—such sudden torrents were often quite localized—and one of Rafiq's men turned up a scattering of footprints made by men wearing boots, a luxury the aborigines did not possess and did not need, so tough were their feet by the time they reached adolescence.

Briggs studied the prints. "Chi-com pattern, all right. Heading northwest, deep into Kedah. My guess is two days old, no more, otherwise they would probably have been rained out. Assume they were moving at about the same rate we are, that would put them at the edge of what we used to call, back in '45, the Great Swamp."

"Map doesn't show such a terrain feature," muttered Puckeridge, studying the laminated chart spread on the ground before them.

"No offense, Captain, but your map doesn't show a lot. No one has ever surveyed this part of Kedah on the ground, and aerial surveys can only do so much, due to the constant cloud cover and triple-canopy. Once you get this far past the province border, your map is not unlike something drawn by an Elizabethan cartographer—'Here be beasties' and all that. Oh, yes, we can get a latitude-longitude fix, thanks to your electronic gadgets, and that should be enough for our bombers to drop their eggs in the right place, but as far as what we'll encounter on the ground, I'm afraid we have to make it up as we go along."

Briggs was silent for a moment, his slitted eyes peering intently at the wall of jungle surrounding the village.

"We skirted the edge of the Great Swamp a few times during those operations against the Japs. God alone knows how big it really is, but it's quite impenetrable. Quicksand and crocodiles and more snakes than I've ever seen in any other region of Malaya. It was a useful terrain feature, though, because as long as we marched around the edges of it, we knew at least one of our flanks was secure. Or so I thought until the night the Tcho-Tcho attacked us. We were on the fringes of it, you see, thinking it would protect us, but the little monsters somehow managed to cross it and hit us right where we least expected them to appear. I can't say how they did it . . . perhaps some sort of secret technique the Japs had invented, like snow-shoes or something."

"And you're thinking that, if that were the case, and if Chin Lai really has enlisted the Tcho-Tcho in his cause, he might have learned what that secret is."

"It's something we have to take into consideration. On the positive side, if that's where he is, he'll feel secure, he won't expect us to come after him. He won't know that I'm stalking him again."

"That's why we brought you along, Major." Puckeridge gave him a good-old-boy pat on the back, and went off to get the troops back in marching formation. Four hours of daylight remained, and he wanted to get every meter of progress out of them he could.

A mile or so northwest of the village, they encountered a wall of vegetation so dense, so baroque in its twinings and counter-twinings, that the men had to throw their bodies against it and hack at it with knives to make any progress at all; there was no room to swing machetes. But their progress was somewhat eased by the obvious fact that other men had cut through here a day or two earlier. Some of the creepers and thorn-vines that had not grown back, with the ravenous, avid fecundity of the rain-forest repairing itself, showed signs of having been slashed and cut. Wherever possible, they followed Chin Lai's trail, which zig-zagged crazily, the logic being that he must have known where he was going and therefore had taken the most efficient route.

Suddenly, an hour before sunset, they burst through the barrier and found themselves in a strange place indeed: a convoluted valley of sorts, filled with raw limestone crags on which the jungle had gained little purchase. Briggs had seen a few places like this before, places where the peninsula's bare skeleton poked through its jungle skin, but he had not seen this particular place before.

"Captain, this is a good spot to make camp. I've stayed in places like this before, and, for some reason, the wildlife shun them and the insects are relatively mild too. We can't get much farther in the jungle tonight, and the men need to be as fresh as possible for tomorrow."

Puckeridge scanned the sharp, knobbed crevices and lacerated out-croppings, the oddly disturbing scarcity of vegetation. "If you say so, Major. I don't mind telling you, though: this place gives me the creeps even more than the jungle."

"Yes, well, if it's creepy you're worried about, wait until you see the Great Swamp—it's the sort of place where you wouldn't be surprised to see dinosaurs grazing."

Briggs busied himself setting up his tent, grateful that the day's exertions were finished. Oddly enough, the rigors of the march had not affected him as much today. Perhaps it was his body getting into shape again. More likely, though, it was the low, continuous adrenaline charge that he remembered from the days when he led long-range patrols against the terrorists in the 1950s. It was a very personal kind of war in those days, a matter of hunter and hunted, of matching wits and skill and endurance against a cunning and determined foe, and despite the hardships and numerous frustrations, it was an oddly honorable sort of conflict. Both the British and the Communists had gone for quick, clean kills—there had been no squalid torturing, no abuse of prisoners. Now Briggs was closing in on the most elusive enemy of all—a man who had once been a comrade, a friend, and a most worthy foe—and his blood was up.

He was startled out of his reverie by the sudden appearance of Jemadar Rafiq. "Tuan, you should come see this."

At the apex of a short narrow deep-shadowed gorge, walled with limestone so eroded that it formed a seemingly fragile filigree, he found two Gurkhas, Puckeridge, the S.A.S. medic, and Smythe-Jones. Sprawled on the ground before them was the headless corpse of an aborigine. The man's skin was oddly bleached and tight; the stump of his neck was curiously puckered.

"His blood's been drained, utterly," said the medic, rising from his examination.

"And the head wound?" prompted Puckeridge.

"You got me, Captain. It's not a tiger—there're no claw marks, no bites—and he wasn't decapitated by a sword or a knife or even an axe. It almost looks as though the blighter's head was *sucked off.*"

Puckeridge turned to Briggs and muttered: "I told you this fucking place gave me the creeps."

"And look there, gentlemen!"

The others followed where Smythe-Jones pointed and saw an opening in the base of the nearby cliff, a black portal framed by squat stone slabs.

"Ever see anything like that, Briggs?"

"No. But as unpleasant as the prospect may be, I think we'd better check it out before we decide to stay here for the night."

At the entrance, the missionary ran his flashlight beam over the dressed stone, its parts as neatly fitted as those of an Inca fortress.

"This is not aboriginal work. They don't have the tools, or the skills, nor do they build permanent temples to their nature-gods. An offering of dog meat hung from a tree, that's about as fancy as their worship services ever get. I must admit to being almost as curious as I am disturbed, gentlemen. Let's push on, shall we?"

Their lights revealed similar stonework lining a passage that was almost, but not quite, large enough for them to stand upright. Water gleamed blackly on the walls and pooled at their feet. As far as the beams penetrated, the shaft went straight, inclining downward at a slight angle, into the heart of the cliff. The three officers drew their sidearms as they advanced deeper into the gloom.

The twilit opening grew smaller and smaller behind them, then disappeared. They were conscious of the ancient weight and age of the rock pressing down above their heads.

After what Briggs estimated to be a passage of two hundred meters, the tunnel suddenly expanded into a chamber large enough for them to stand in. One end of the room was blocked by a still, inky pool of water; whether the tunnel had once continued on its far side, they could not tell, and indeed, their lights played out in the murk without revealing more than a suggestion of a far wall.

"Good Lord, look at these!" cried Smythe-Jones, turning his light against the wall nearest the edge of the pool.

"Stay away from the edge, padre. No telling how deep that water is, or what sort of currents there might be under the surface," cautioned Briggs.

Then he, too, was struck silent by the drawings and hieroglyphs the reverend had illuminated. They were worn with antiquity, and could only be viewed with any definition by angling the flashlight beam so as to limn them with shadows. Briggs saw depictions of other caves, and of small, squat temples surrounded by jungle. Populating the inscriptions were short, brute-featured figures, naked and primitive, with splayed nostrils and thick lips. The Tcho-Tcho. He shuddered.

Here and there among the figures, were other drawings that depicted some sort of gigantic snake-like creatures, their heads reared into the air, their long, boneless bodies humping like obscene inchworms along the ground. Some wore crude harnesses and were dragging trees or blocks of stone, working in concert with, *controlled by,* the Tcho-Tcho.

"'R'taq-vaht,'" murmured the missionary. "Now, where's a picture of 'R'taq' himself?"

As he traced the lines of drawings, Smythe-Jones had gradually moved closer and closer to the edge of the silent black pool. The others were too entranced by what they saw to notice. The first sign that anything was wrong came when the water began to spew and bubble violently.

Briggs reached for the preacher but he was a second too late. From out of the pool rose a pale, mottled worm-shape, thrusting up as high as a man, its bulbous, eyeless head dominated by a great round sucker-mouth filled with a circle of teeth as long as bayonets, like some sort of hideously engorged lamprey eel. Quick as a viper, the creature struck at Smythe-Jones and that dreadful mouth closed completely around his head, cutting off his scream. There came a liquid sucking noise, and rivers of blood streamed from the puckered circumference of the creature's mouth.

Gunfire thundered as all three officers opened up with their pistols. Their bullets slapped audibly into the beast's bloated flesh, puncturing it the way a needle pierces a globe of fruit, and, while not apparently killing it, causing it enough distress to interrupt its feeding. It hurriedly submerged, and the Reverend Smythe-Jones' head came free with a ghastly popping sound, leaving a flopping torso whose neck bore the same wrinkled appearance as that of the dead aborigine outside.

Jemadar Rafiq hurled a hand grenade into the pool and they all ducked as a blasphemous rain of flesh poured down over them.

"Did I kill it?" the Gurkha asked.

"I think so. I hope so," said Puckeridge. "Briggs, what in God's name was that thing?"

"Like the reverend said: it was a servant of R'taq. In more mundane terms, I think it was some sort of gigantic leech."

Puckeridge set up one of his two L7A1 machine guns near the mouth of the cave, just in case. Then they buried what was left of the Reverend Smythe-Jones. Darkness came in a sudden gulp, and the stone-walled valley became utterly silent. The sight of the missionary's headless corpse had unsettled even the stolid Gurkhas. Briggs stood with bowed head as the burial party shoveled the last earth over the cleric's grave—the missionary had seemed a decent chap, and brave, too, after his fashion. Jemadar Rafiq stood beside him, cap in hand. Briggs was startled to hear the Nepalese recite: "The sun's rim dips, the stars rush out; in one stride comes the dark."

"Wordsworth?" asked Briggs out of the corner of his mouth.

"Close. Coleridge, actually."

"Where did you . . . ?"

"I read the classics at Oxford, Major. Before I returned home to follow the family trade of soldiering. Does that surprise you?"

"After today, Jemadar, nothing would surprise me."

Three hours on, three hours off; double the usual number of sentries. No one would get much sleep, but no one complained. Their quarry was near, less than a day's march away, and the night held a palpable menace. Men kept turning their eyes toward the cave-mouth.

Just after midnight, the drums began. The sound was distant, to the northwest, in the direction of the Great Swamp. It was as Briggs remembered it: ceremonial, yet arrhythmic, the basic sound fractured by sudden jagged accents that jarred the nerves, as though its purpose was to deprive them of sleep. Perhaps he knows we're coming, thought Briggs; after so many years in the jungle, his senses would be tuned to the finest quanta of premonition. Perhaps he can smell us, even at this distance. Or perhaps, after all the time the two of us spent stalking one another, he just *knows,* like a tiger sensing game. Or perhaps one of those things, one of the R'taq-vaht, had somehow reported to him our presence. One thing was certain: the nature of their mission had changed. They were in uncharted terrain now, both literally and psychologically, and their enemies were no longer mere men.

But eventually, Briggs did sleep; his old soldier's body knew the rules of the game, and one of them was to take whatever rest was available, whenever it could. His slumber was not deep, however, and his dreams were troubling.

They moved out at dawn. There was no need to consult the map—they had only to march toward the drums.

Just after mid-day, the jungle thinned. The drums were louder now, a kilometer or two away. They had reached the edge of the Great Swamp. Before them was a landscape out of time: a vast dark tarn dotted with mangrove trees like the stumps of rotted teeth. Mist hung like tattered crepe, as though hiding the secrets of the place. Thick and humid was the air, ripe with the smell of profound decay and an undercurrent of char. This unnatural blend spoke to the senses of protean life pulsating dissonantly against pervasive death. It was, Briggs realized in a flash of insight that prickled the hairs on his arms, the olfactory equivalent of the drums' discordant music.

Puckeridge held a council of war before they moved on. The drums marked Chin Lai's camp, which surely would be on dry land on the far side of that sea of muck. If they moved east, skirting the swamp, they would reach it in an hour or so. Once they had visual confirmation, they would mark the target electronically, then pull back and let the airstrikes go in.

It was hard going. The very earth seemed to pulsate in time with the drums, quaking with the consistency of porridge. It sucked at their feet, as though possessed of malevolent intent, as though it too were trying to oppose their passage. Even the landscape was strange and unnatural: there was little of the tangled undergrowth they had hacked through earlier, just soft, semi-solid ground and gigantic trees, spaced with a regularity that seemed almost planned, as though they were walking through some kind of unholy orchard. Briggs, Puckeridge, and Rafiq walked together, just behind the point men, weapons ready, the radioman just behind them. Gradually, they made progress around the eastern edge of the bog. The oppressive, nerve-grinding drums grew louder.

Suddenly, their beat changed into a series of regularly-spaced crashes, a frenzied crescendo. To Briggs, the new sound seemed almost a signal. He gripped his submachine gun more tightly, his eyes flickering right and left, his senses keen and apprehensive.

The drumming reached a climax, then stopped.

And then the giant leeches fell from the trees. Dozens of them, their puckered, fanged mouths wide, their bodies thick as a man's. They landed on the heads of Gurkhas and British alike, crumpling their victims to the ground, striking for their heads. Some jungle-bred instinct caused Briggs to look up just before one the creatures struck. He fired at the leech that was falling toward him, emptying half a magazine of 9mm slugs into the thing's hideous head while it was still in mid-air. The other two officers, taking their cue from Briggs, also responded more quickly than their men, and were able to roll out of danger at the last possible instant, and then to kill the parasites that had aimed at them as soon as the beasts hit the ground.

The three officers reloaded and tried to save their men, but already it was too late. Although they slew a dozen of the leeches, there was no way to reload fast enough to save the screaming soldiers whose heads were submerged in those awful jaws. Briggs saw one headless torso stagger away and flop into the swamp, blood fountaining from the stump of its neck.

It was over in two minutes. The surviving leeches humped and writhed their way into the bogs and vanished, leaving forty decapitated bodies behind, and the three white-faced officers standing together, weapons hot and smoking, surveying the wreckage of their command.

Ahead, just out of sight through the trees, the drums began again.

Jemadar Rafiq wandered among the corpses of his platoon, a stunned expression on his face, unable to believe what he had seen. Briggs knelt down and took deep breaths, trying to control the trembling that wracked his body. Puckeridge—ever the tough, unflappable S.A.S. professional—turned over the radioman's body and salvaged his equipment.

"Let's go get the bastard," he snarled.

But "the bastard" found them first. Ten minutes after they moved on beyond the site of the massacre, a voice called out from behind one of the trees.

"Briggs? Is that you, old fellow?"

Briggs shivered in recognition. He had not heard that voice since 1945, but he recognized it instantly.

"Chin? Yes, it's me. You'd better come out with your hands up. The game's over between us, and you know it."

In person, Chin Lai no longer looked like a legendary guerrilla chieftain. His wiry, compact frame was wasted, his hair white, and his shirtless torso bled from a dozen small wounds. He carried no weapon. He staggered toward Briggs and embraced him.

"I should have known they would send you in to find me. Nobody else could have done the job. May I have some water, please?"

Briggs handed over his canteen, which the Chinese sucked on desperately.

"Chin . . . what's happened here?"

"R'taq. I was foolish enough to think we could control him, just as the Japanese tried to do during the war. There are rituals, incantations—ancient things—that give you the illusion of mastery. The Tcho-Tcho are his servants, and the leeches are the Tcho-Tcho's servants. For a time, they cooperated with us, until they got the idea of fighting their own war."

"Against whom?"

"Everyone. The world. Their souls are as twisted as their bodies. 'Evil' is too mild a word, Briggs. They are darkness incarnate. And they would bring the darkness to everything they can reach. They serve it, even as they serve R'taq."

"What is R'taq?"

"Even I, who have looked upon his shape, cannot tell you that. He has been here since the dawn of time, dreaming terrible dreams, brooding and biding his time. He is vast—I do not know his size, but he lives in the swamp. Under the swamp. He is the Great Swamp. He is the god of the Tcho-Tcho, and maybe he really is a god. At any rate, he's as close to a god as anything you can imagine. And I was crazy enough to think we could manipulate him and his minions, while all the time, he was manipulating me. I sensed the change in things just in time to escape. The rest of my command . . . was not so fortunate."

"I think we've heard enough," interjected Puckeridge, leaning forward and placing the barrel of his weapon against Chin Lai's heart. "One shot, and this mission will be over."

Briggs leveled his own weapon at the captain.

"You can't kill him like that. This man is obviously no threat to anyone now."

"Wrong, Major. I came here to kill him and that's what I'll do."

"May I remind you that I outrank you, Puckeridge?"

"May I remind you that we're hundreds of miles from anyone who gives a shit? I can take you bare-handed, old man."

"But not both of us," said Jemadar Rafiq, stepping closer and raising his own gun.

Puckeridge shrugged angrily. "Stalemate, then. For the moment."

Rafiq took the captain's rifle and sidearm.

"Whatever is over there, beating those drums, needs to be destroyed far more than Chin Lai."

"Rubbish. Monster stories."

"Monsters who just wiped out your entire command," said Chin Lai. "Imagine what would happen if they got out of Kedah Province. And they will, unless you stop them now."

"We have air power on call," said Briggs.

"I rather suspected you would. Follow me, and I'll show you what to bomb."

Until they drew close, taking cover in the last trees before the ground turned into marshland on the shore of an immense area of swamp, they could not hear the screams—the demented drumming masked all other sounds. The Tcho-Tcho village—and, until recently, Chin Lai's base camp—was a collection of reed huts scattered along a few hundred meters of undulating, spongy bank. There were the Tcho-Tcho, in greater numbers than Briggs would have imagined possible for a tribe so primitive, hundreds of them, swarming around their captives while a hundred more pounded on drums made of skins stretched over hollow logs. Focusing through his binoculars, Briggs observed with a shudder that the drum-heads were made from flayed, stretched human skin.

Spread-eagled upright on bamboo poles were Chin Lai's guerrillas, twenty or more. Around them danced the Tcho-Tcho, gibbering and howling, slashing at their helpless victims with sticks and hurling gobbets of mud into their faces. Behind them, like domesticated livestock, sat dozens of giant leeches, some with bridles, some attached to cargo sleds, their hideous blind heads bending slowly in the rank breeze that came from the swamp. They sat, docile as plowhorses, as though awaiting their masters' next commands.

But that was not the worst of it. Seeping out of the marshy ground, undulating in time with the drums, were hundreds, thousands, of ordinary leeches, covering the naked bodies of Chin Lai's men, who writhed and screamed and bucked in their bonds, consumed with horror and loathing. From the waist down, their bodies were covered with a glistening black coat of parasites, which moved slowly upwards toward their faces. Through his glasses, Briggs could see that some of the leeches had already reached the captives' heads and hung, engorged, from their lips and nostrils and eyes, even their tongues.

And in the swamp, just offshore, something moved. It was immense; it filled acres. Even through his glasses, Briggs could not make out its exact shape, which seemed to waver, now coagulating into something almost-solid, now flowing back into liquid form. It was the focus of that disturbing scent of life-within-death. Even from a distance, Briggs could feel the power emanating from it, the wave of sheer malevolence that radiated forth. Chin Lai was right: it was god-like, a life-form from beyond all known coordinates of time and space.

R'taq. Lord of the Tcho-Tcho. *He-who-moves-the-swamp.*

"Seen enough, Captain? Surely even your stunted imagination can envision what might happen if this thing's influence spread to more populated areas. Imagine: every leech in Malaya under its control, responding to its commands."

Puckeridge might not have been the brightest soldier Briggs had ever served with, but he was a professional, and his expression was one of rage and revulsion. No man, not even an enemy, deserved to die the way Chin Lai's men were dying. In a strained whisper, Puckeridge spoke into the handset of his radio, giving the code-word for the airstrike and relaying the map-coordinates.

"All right. We have thirty minutes to clear the area before this place gets turned into the surface of the Moon."

Shaken to their souls, the four men retraced their route, back to the site where the corpses of giant leeches and headless soldiers were already starting to bloat and blacken in the tropical heat.

After a time, they could hear the distant roar of the B-52s, and they began moving more quickly, putting as much space as they could between themselves and the bombers' target. Chin Lai, weakened as he was, began to fall behind. As the planes' drone came directly overhead, Chin Lai called out.

"Help me! I've stepped into some quicksand!"

The man had stumbled into a dark viscid pool and was struggling to free his legs. Briggs turned and went back for him.

Just as he was about to reach out, he saw the pool come alive: a horde of leeches rose from its surface and began to flow up Chin Lai's legs, covering him instantly from the waist down. He swatted furiously at them, knocking off dozens, but hundreds more pressed on, aiming, with terrible *disciplined* intent, for his face.

"Leave him!" cried Puckeridge. "There's nothing more we can do!"

"Yes, there is," replied Briggs, reading the message in Chin's rolling eyes. Briggs aimed his submachine gun and fired a short burst into the heart—one last mercy for an old comrade.

Then he began to run, because all around them, from every pool and creek, a carpet of leeches had begun to roll toward them. It appeared that the soil itself had come alive; all that was soft, viscid, and moist had clotted into quivering life. Where the rolling formations of leeches moved off, the earth beneath them showed black and raw, roots within white as exposed ganglia—

as though the skin of normal reality were being flayed. These steaming, pulpy wounds spread as the leeches multiplied and moved, and the soldiers' ears were buffeted by a howling vibration above the threshold of hearing. As the leeches tore its skin, the very earth had begun to scream.

Seized now by a fear more soul-devouring than any they had known in battle, the three soldiers ran blindly away from the gray undulating mass that flowed in pursuit. Blood flowed from Puckeridge's ears; he began to beat at the sides of his head. All three men were screaming now, helplessly trying to mask the keening crescendo rising from those terrible black wounds spreading across the flayed, agonized earth.

Gradually, distance widened between the fleeing men and the vanguard of that sea of parasites. They plunged into a bank of humid fog, their course gradually carrying them back toward the edge of the Great Swamp. The screaming in their heads suddenly ebbed and with that came a diminished sense of peril. All three stumbled to a halt, lungs raw and hearts pounding like the hammers of hell.

Briggs risked a quick glance behind and through a sudden parting of the mist beheld the mass of leeches frozen in place, their myriad eyeless heads inclined, in reverent expectation, toward the swamp.

Falling back from the sight, Briggs collided with Jemadar Rafiq. Turning to disentangle himself from the tall Gurkha, he saw Puckeridge stagger on a few more yards, feet sloshing into the thick, grainy water of the swamp itself.

What Briggs saw next could have been—*should* have been—a hallucination borne from stress and fear. Through scrims of mist he saw Puckeridge knee-deep in the swamp, shoulders heaving as he gasped for air. In front of the captain, shadows thickened, grew dark, exactly as if a great wave were shouldering its way inland.

Now the great swell hove into view, taller than the captain's head. Puckeridge stared into its sleek-muscled face and understood the dreadful sentience that confronted him. Even as the captain drew breath to scream, the viscid mass changed form; instead of crashing over him, it slid down and engulfed him from beneath, then, with a massive shudder that Briggs interpreted as an obscene gulp of pleasure, it rolled out again, back into the mist. The last thing Briggs saw was the form of Captain Puckeridge, deep inside the awful substance that was both liquid and solid, writhing in slow motion as though entombed in burning acid.

"R'taq," whispered Rafiq.

As though the vanishing of their god were a signal, the army of leeches began to hump forward, inexorable, tireless.

A shrilling filled the air. Recognizing it for what it was, Briggs tackled the Gurkha non-com and rolled both of them into a shallow depression just as the world exploded. Concussion from the 1000-pound bombs buffeted them, sucked the air from their lungs, deafened them. And probably saved their lives, because one of those bombs fell short of the target and landed on the edge of the leech-army that was pursuing them. A torrent of vile, shredded flesh poured down on them as they burrowed into the earth, and when the explosion was over, a vast, smoking, water-filled crater scarred the jungle—full of churned earth and the mutilated remnants of hundreds of leeches. The rest had submerged whence they came.

Amazed to find themselves still alive, Briggs and Rafiq stumbled on, toward the place where they were supposed to be extracted. Later that afternoon, a helicopter came for them and hovered overhead while they used up their last reserves of strength to don the dangling harnesses that hoisted them to safety.

Back at the air base in Kuala Lumpur, Briggs endured a debriefing that was more like an interrogation—an entire platoon of elite soldiers, along with their commanding officer, had been lost, and the authorities wanted to know why. Briggs and Rafiq debated, but in the end, they concocted a plausible story: unexpectedly heavy firefight with the guerrillas, a mis-dropped bomb that wiped out the surviving government troops. A tragic business, to be sure, but Briggs and Rafiq could assure their questioners that Chin Lai and his men had also been annihilated. That fact squared the equation. Briggs was patted on the back, given a bottle of good whiskey, and shown the way to a long, hot shower. After which, he collapsed and slept for eighteen hours straight.

A few hours after waking, Major Harold Briggs was back at home, grateful to resume the life of a gentleman-planter, even more grateful to feel the embrace of his lovely Eurasian wife.

Li Peng asked about the mission, and received only vague replies. But she knew, with a good wife's instinct, that there had been much more to it than her husband wanted to tell.

Because for years afterwards, on the evenings when they sat together on their veranda and drank in the fragrance of the night, Briggs would sometimes lean forward with a strained expression, as though listening for something.

Especially on nights when the wind was from the northwest. ✳

The Enchanting of Lila Woods

by E. A. Lustig

I.

Although I had not heard from Maeve McKiernan in more than twenty years, I recognized her voice at once—it had dropped half an octave, but her words flew at me with the same nearly hysterical velocity. She made quick work of the pleasantries, then asked for my help with what she characterized as "the most meaningful and important endeavor of her life." In spite of my exhaustion—I'd just finished nine months of working sixteen-hour days developing ambiance protocol software for NASA—her enthusiasm engulfed me, and I found myself offering to do whatever I could.

When she came to see me the next evening, I was struck by how little her appearance had changed. She was still an apple-cheeked, bantam woman, and her warm, effulgent eyes were as riveting as they'd been when I first sat in her class. I doubted I had ever looked to anyone as vibrant as she appeared to me.

Maeve had relinquished her chair in anthropology shortly after she was widowed, then spent several years searching for a fulfilling way to apply her expertise. She had found it, she claimed, while working at a rehab shelter for battered women. Then, one day, while going through the inactive client files, she realized that the shelter had failed, science had failed, and she had failed. No matter the therapy or medication, there would always be some who would not heal.

"It was an awful moment," she said, "until I understood what must be done; what *I* could do."

Maeve undertook to establish her own shelter, one which would implement a new approach to treating those "most severely deprived of their portion of happiness."

"I'm not talking about the insane," she explained. "Crazy people are not ipso facto, incapable of experiencing joy or sadness. I'm talking about sane women so badly damaged that they no longer experience *any*thing; for them, life has become something to be gotten through."

Maeve described her pursuit of funding and the process of selecting her subjects—victims of every conceivable kind of violence. Among them were torture survivors from West Africa and South America, sex slaves from the

Far East, refugees from Japanese breeding programs, and a good number of garden variety long-term domestic abuse casualties. All of them in "desperate flight from the 'tremendum' of life," as she put it.

Six months ago, after an exhausting hunt for suitable housing, she signed a long-term lease on "the most perfect place in the world."

Maeve paused to sip the dregs from her wine glass. I poured her a refill, then asked her how I could help.

"I want you to design a web site for us," she said at last. "I need a forum which can accommodate an unlimited number of simultaneous audio transmissions."

"I'm not sure I understand," I said. "For what purpose?"

"Something that's never been tried before," she said.

"Well, there are several virtual orchestra programs I might be able to modify. But unlimited input would eventually lead to unreadable, chaotic data. And bandwidth could be a problem. Maybe if you'd explain what . . ."

"Lila, it broke my heart when you left grad school. And even though you were the most perceptive student I ever had, I'm afraid if I tried to explain, you'd think me quite mad. I'd rather *show* you. You won't believe how lovely and quiet the place is. And we've a wonderfully primitive old house for you to explore. Oh, you *must* come up." She squeezed my hand. "After all, someone will have to install the equipment and teach us how to use it."

"But I'm not a hardware techni—"

"Right now I need 33 units. State of the art stuff. I've hung on to most of the grant money, so bother the cost. I insist on paying you top dollar. Lila dear, will you do it?"

"I suppose . . ."

II.

Three weeks later, I was barreling down a narrow country road which, according to my Triple-A map, didn't exist. Maeve's directions, however, were quite precise: Taconic to State Road 24 east; right on Ringtop Road to St. Anthony's Chapel; Chapel Drive to the fork; left onto Arkham Road; precisely 24 miles to the river bridge; turn right onto the dirt road; when you hit the blacktop, you're 37 miles from the house.

I was on the third "dirt road" I'd tried. Just as I'd decided to give this cowpath another five miles or else I was going home, the car bounced onto a paved surface. Maeve's insistence on confidentiality was understandable; many of the women in her care were in hiding from political regimes or loved ones with murderous intentions. But as the forest thickened, shrouding the road in darkness, I wondered whether she hadn't taken her quest for seclusion too far.

The road grew very steep and the vista changed remarkably. To my right, a sheer escarpment; on my left, I saw nothing but tree tops and sky. I slowed to a crawl, keeping the car as far from the drop as possible. Then the road abruptly leveled off and the crags gave way to a gently rolling plateau. Beyond a low, stone fence, a dozen or so black goats grazed on grass stubble while a postcard perfect August sunset gathered in the west. New England at its best.

I was equally impressed with the house. In scale, it was as grand as any of the great Hudson River mansions. But while those exuded an amiable, lived-in elegance, this place suggested no such geniality. An enclosed parapet of dark stone—perhaps quarried from the very bluffs below—encircled the grounds. Beyond it, loomed Arkham House itself; from each of its five corners emerged a turret which overlooked the flat rooftop where a lattice fence surrounded an enormous black dome. I'd never seen anything like it before—the most forbidding elements from a multitude of architectural styles had been merged to create an effigy of monumental bleakness.

It was nearly seven when I pulled into the driveway. Beside an open door in the stone bulwark, stood a girl with stringy, honey-colored hair. Her head bobbed slightly as she watched me haul my bags out of the trunk and walk toward her. She finally managed a shy smile. Her front teeth were badly decayed.

"What a pretty dressy dress," she said. "And so misty green; like a sick tree frog. You're very pretty too."

I smiled. "Thank-you. I'm here to see . . ."

"I know who. And I guess you're the computer lady they been waiting for."

"That I am. I'm sorry to be so late."

The child—for a child she truly was—took a step back.

"Maeve told me I could come and go as I pleased," she said.

"Is this the way inside?" I asked.

"Oh, there's a lot of ways in; but you'd get lost."

She seemed to have no intention of leading me inside; in fact, I got the impression she meant to prevent me entering on my own.

"Have you lived here long?" I asked.

The girl laughed. The sight of her inflamed gums and the spiked remains of tobacco-brown teeth made me wince. I wondered why in the world someone hadn't gotten this poor child to a dentist.

"I never lived in there. My place is back in them woods. Maeve said I could come and go just like always; like I done before all the ladies came to the mountain." She paused. Her cornflower-blue eyes appeared to darken. "You're not like them, I think."

"What makes you say that?"

She stared at me thoughtfully. "Because," she said at last, "I'm not afraid of you."

The notion that anyone might fear me seemed ludicrous; skinny, five-foot-two, middle aged spinsters, typically inspired only indifference. It seemed equally ridiculous that Maeve, even at her most obsessive, could provoke fear.

Just then, a voice echoed "hello" from within.

Without a sound, the girl scampered up the hillside and out of sight, like a large, timid squirrel.

"Lila Woods!" Maeve said as she emerged from the doorway. "I was about to call the highway patrol."

She took one of my bags and ushered me into the parapet. "I knew you'd gotten lost. Everybody does. I consider that one of the big plusses of the place. An extra measure of security, as it were."

I kept not more than a step behind her as she marched through the dark corridor. "This is quite a fortress," I said.

Maeve chuckled. "We were lucky to get it. Had it been up to old Professor Leiber, the place would have stayed empty in perpetua. But the day after he died, Miskatonic was only too happy to turn it over to us."

She slowed her pace. "Isn't this a nutty bit of business though?" she said as she patted the cool, stone wall. "When we first got here, someone christened the house the 'dark castle,' and this the 'black hall.'"

"Who built this place?" I asked.

"Now that's an interesting story. This mountain and the land around it was granted by George II to Sebastian Arkham—a cartographer and amateur astronomer. It wasn't considered a prime piece of real estate even then, but for some unfathomable reason, Arkham requested this parcel, sight unseen. Unfortunately, the indigenous Indian population believed the mountain was sacred; and they reserved an especially brutal form of execution just for trespassers.

"Arkham finally ran out of patience and, in 1762, hired a hundred mercenaries to 'free his property of hostiles.' Even so, the native holy men fended them off for years. Arkham couldn't take possession until 1768. It took him over twenty years to build the main house. There are still ruins, all up and down the mountain, of the stone cottages which housed the artisans he brought in to do the masonry and so forth. Arkham designed the place himself."

"A regular visionary," I said.

Maeve laughed. "Of a kind. He clearly meant it to stand forever. The foundation goes down I don't know how far—right through solid rock. We've rummaged our way through three sub-levels and found some intriguing artifacts.

"Anyway, while Arkham studied the stars, his wife Sandrine produced six children—all stillborn. When she became pregnant with a seventh, he packed her off to Providence and this time the baby survived. But Arkham never allowed his wife and son to return to the house.

"When the last Arkham—Beatrice—died in 1881, she left the place, lock, stock and barrel, to the Brothers of St. Jerome. At that time, there was no so-called 'black hall.' Perhaps the Brothers didn't feel sufficiently cloistered, because it was they who erected this monstrosity." Maeve stopped walking. "Ah . . . but the Brothers also knew that beauty feeds the soul because . . ." She paused dramatically as she pulled open the door and flooded the corridor with light.

Beyond the door stretched an exquisite, meticulously manicured topiary garden where slender flagstone paths had been woven, like ribbons, into the pattern of the shrubbery. A small stone bench sat demurely at the foot of each of several religious statues.

The sight quite took my breath away; it was so unexpected, so incongruous with the foreboding structure around it and the one which stood at its core.

"Yes, indeed," Maeve murmured as she stepped into the garden. "Makes up for a multitude of architectural sins."

She plucked a small yellow flower, sniffed it deeply, then gave it to me.

"Like lemons," I said.

"I believe it's called *verbena*." She smiled, and after a few moments of reverent silence, continued recounting the history of this increasingly bizarre place.

The Brothers of St. Jerome was an ancient order which had spent nearly a thousand years in ecclesiastic limbo while the Roman Catholic Church debated about its status. Meanwhile, following the example of their patron saint, the monks observed silence, pursued scholarship, and became translators without equal, she explained. They specialized in translating manuscripts written in languages no one had ever seen before. Which, according to Maeve, brought them to the attention of Miskatonic University.

She sat on a bench under the kindly gaze of St. Jerome who cradled a book in one arm, while the other gestured heavenward. The words *Tu, Domine, servabis nos, et custodies nos a generatione hac an aeternum* were inscribed on the base.

"It means: 'You, Lord, will watch over us, and keep us ever safe from the evil days.'" Maeve smiled broadly. "I love this spot. Especially when the light is just beginning to fade."

"What happened to the Brothers?" I asked.

"Gone. The last of them died in 1980. That's when the University got its hands on Arkham House. They wanted to remodel it, turn it into a retreat for burned-out faculty. But old Leiber wasn't having any of it. He got the place put on the historic register so no one could change a thing—ever. The house was left empty. Oh, there were caretakers; but judging by its condition when we got here, they weren't very conscientious about maintaining the house. The garden, on the other hand, had been well tended." She sighed as she got to her feet.

Maeve took a path that wound through a wall of spired boxwoods which veiled the house. We climbed the stairs to the great broad porch from where, it seemed, the whole world could be seen. Above the massive door crouched a disquieting stone sculpture of a winged, goat-like beast—a gargoyle unlike any I'd ever seen.

"By the way," she said, backing away from the door and pointing upward, "those towers aren't safe. There's nothing up there but rotting stairways and a couple of tons of bird poop."

"All right," I said. "Maeve, I saw a girl outside . . . kind of shy, blondish hair . . . who is she?"

"According to the old-timers at the valley store, her name's Rachel Bearfist. Seems everyone assumed that a relative had taken her in after her uncle passed away last year. He'd been caretaker here for as long as anyone remembered. I tried to find other family members, but even the Mormon archives came up empty. That's all I know about her—except that she's always watching us, and she likes to tend the garden. No harm in that."

"Such a shame . . ."

"Her teeth? I know."

"Can't something be done?" I asked.

Maeve stiffened. "Don't you think I've tried? The kid won't let any of us near her. I had to introduce myself from ten feet away. Told her she could come and go as she pleased. I've asked her to supper a hundred times. In all these months, I've never heard her utter a single word." Maeve sighed. "Sometimes I hear her singing though. Nonsense songs. I don't know if she started singing because she heard us chanting, but when she sings I feel she's trying to communicate with us. I've spied her creeping closer and closer to the house when no one's around. We'll have her inside by Thanksgiving, and then we'll see to her teeth . . . and her education. Come on in now, it's getting chilly out here."

I lingered in the doorway to look out over the garden as darkness buried the last wisps of ocherous sky beneath the horizon. The wings of the gargoyle above the threshold seemed to twitch in the gathering shadows. I listened for Rachel, but heard nothing.

In spite of the obvious efforts made to brighten it up, Arkham House was a somber place. There were too many alcoves; too few lights. The ceilings and walls were so thickly laden with sculpted or carved figures and intricate patterns, that even the larger rooms seemed confining. The odor of fresh paint did little to mask an underlying must of decay which suffused the air.

"I wanted you to see this first," Maeve said as we marched to the heart of the house. "It used to be the chapel, but we've redone it for our computer room. The acoustics are exceptional."

In the center of the three-story domed ceiling was an oval-shaped skylight—which looked eerily like an animal's eye. The upper walls were covered with age-worn reliefs of scampering goats followed by goatherds wearing long, elaborately patterned cloaks which seemed to billow and unfurl as their designs were repeated, then interlaced in the richly etched surface of the lower walls.

The tiled floor was a mosaic in hues of gray. In the middle, in the darkest gray, was a blunt-pointed star whose shape was outlined in subtle gradations of gray until, at the place where floor met wall, the tiles were white.

To all of this had been added halogen track-lighting, a narrow, polyurethane counter top which ran all the way around the room, several stacks of black plastic chairs, and a pile of unopened micro-computer boxes.

"What do you think?" Maeve asked proudly.

I nodded. "Nice big room."

"Well, it's more space than we need; but I find it so . . . inspiring." Maeve gazed up into the dome. "This is where we'll heal ourselves . . . and all the others who will join their voices to ours," she said wistfully.

"Interactive cyber-therapy?"

She looked at me and, frowning, slowly shook her head. "Not exactly . . . Tonight, after you've settled in and gotten something to eat, you'll see for yourself." She flipped the lights off and led me down yet another dim passageway.

"You'll be staying on the first floor near the chapel. All the bedrooms are upstairs so I had the old abbot's quarters made up for you."

"You needn't have gone to so much . . ."

"No trouble. Besides, I want you to be comfortable and it's the only room with a private bath. And here we are. Not exactly five-star accommodations, but it's cozy, don't you think?"

"Lovely," I said cheerfully; though, at the moment, I was not feeling particularly cheerful. The room, a large, dark mahogany square with an oppressive seven foot ceiling and two small windows, was clean, nicely furnished, and filled with potted plants and vases stuffed with flowers. But nothing they had done altered its true nature. It was a cell.

Within the half-hour, a tall ebony woman appeared at my door with a dinner tray. I quickly cleared a place for it on the small desk by the window. As she crossed the room, I noticed that she was lame, that the flesh on her

long, thin arms was mottled and pink and drawn tightly over the bone, that
the back of her neck was striated with thick, silvery scars.

"Thank-you," I said, trying not to stare. "It smells delicious."

"Maeve . . . come . . . later," she said. "Okay?"

I nodded. She blinked once, then hobbled away.

I sat down and looked at the steaming curried rice and vegetables, the
crescent of warm, fresh bread curled around a pool of honey, the delicate
china bowl filled with slices of fresh fruit, the tall carafe of sparkling water;
but felt little appetite.

As I studied my gaunt reflection in the dark window, I heard a distant
voice singing. Rachel, I thought. I turned out the desk lamp and tried to
raise the window. It wouldn't budge. Pressing my face close to the glass, I
searched for her in the star-lit garden, but saw no one.

"Rachel," I whispered. "Don't be afraid. It's me. Come inside."

Her mournful song had no discernible melody; and yet, the longer I
listened, the more I came to understand why Maeve had interpreted
Rachel's singing as an attempt to communicate. I sensed that the girl was
pleading with me, begging me to decipher the meaning of the strange lyric
she repeated.

> *Shub Shub Eee-a Eee-a Shub*
> *Vug tla tla gan*
> *Ptabo Shub Ni, Shub Ni*
> *Gur-ath, gur-ath*
> *Ptabo Shub Ni gurath . . .*

I dug pen and paper from my purse, and wrote the words as I heard
them, there in the darkness. They made no linguistic sense, but seemed as
formal, as ritualistic, as a verse from a psalm.

III.

The knock on the door startled me.

Maeve flipped on the lights and noted my untouched meal as she sat
down on the bed.

"I must have dozed off," I said apologetically.

"Did you hear her?"

I nodded.

"Poor kid," Maeve said, shaking her head.

"I jotted down the words she sang," I said, handing her the paper. "Does
any of that make sense to you?"

Maeve read it over several times then shrugged. "Nope. Maybe a per-
version of a Native American dialect? It's not English-based, that's for sure.

It's too purposeful to be gibberish. Seems familiar to me somehow, but I can't quite place it . . ." she said. "Meanwhile, do you feel up to meeting the others?"

"Absolutely," I said with more enthusiasm than I felt. It was only 9:15.

The women stopped talking among themselves when we entered the brightly lit parlor. Apparently they were throwing me a party—light hors d'oeuvres and a delicious white wine. The ladies were attired for the occasion in festive blouses and loose-fitting trousers. They all moved with the same practiced reserve—like participants in a religious ceremony—as they came forward in groups of threes and fours so that Maeve could introduce them.

"That was a lovely tray you fixed me," I said when the tall, black woman was presented.

Maeve smiled. "Lila, this is Solatee. She's quite a wonderful cook."

The woman bowed slightly. "Okay. Thank you," she said.

When the ornate mantle clock commenced chiming the hour, the women fell silent and turned, in unison, toward Maeve, then filed out of the room.

"Where's everybody going?" I asked.

"To the chapel. Lila dear," Maeve said softly, "you're about to witness something extraordinary. Observe; keep an open mind. I promise I'll answer all of your questions later."

She walked reverently and ever so slowly to the chapel where pale yellow candlelight, from a legion of sconces, poured down on the women who had assembled themselves in concentric circles beneath the dome. Maeve took her place at the center, while I remained standing against the wall by the door.

In unison, they drew long, deep breaths, and exhaled in lengthy hisses or in short, rhythmic puffs. Their bodies were rigid, their attention focused on synchronizing these exercises.

As I watched, it occurred to me that I'd seen this all before, long ago; but I couldn't recall where. Trying harder to remember only intensified my irritation—like scratching near, but never actually reaching, a maddening itch—so I gave up.

It was then that the pieces fell into place. Maeve had, at one time, been extremely interested in the cultural aspects of religious ritual—how effectively it mitigated the behavior and attitude, even the physiology, of the participants. Her lectures on the subject were often accompanied by films she'd shot in the field.

I was still an undergraduate when she published an inspired paper which surveyed 300 specific rituals from a myriad of cultures and grouped them according to their purpose. Penance, for example, had precisely the same result whether it was performed through public confession or through self-mutilation.

Communion with the spiritual realm could be as easily obtained through cere-monial cannibalism as through the Eucharist. She postulated that every positive effect of religious ritual was the result of the combined, concentrated efforts of the participants, and therefore could be experienced independent of any set of theological beliefs. In her conclusion, Maeve even suggested that religious ortho-doxy—in any form—might actually curtail the potential of the ritual act to heal, enlighten, or empower the participants.

The women, who had stopped breathing and hissing, now stood in rapt anticipation. I assumed the show was over and that they were waiting to be dismissed. It had been a long day; all I wanted to do was crawl into bed.

And then suddenly, there was music. The first strange, chant-like pro-cession of notes was sung with clearly observable effort. But the grip of con-centration on each face gradually loosened as the individual timbres of their voices converged and became a single voice—sublime, soothing, seductive. *Pacem,* they chanted, *pacem.*

The voice traveled to the top of the scale and back again; ascended by thirds and fifths in rhythmic riddles; descended languorously by half-tones. The chant had no melodic edges, no apparent apexes, no repeated phrases, no hint that it would ever end.

I had no sense of time passing. Nothing seemed to stir but the music. *Pacem, pacem,* said the voice as it climbed from note to note. *Pa-cem, pa-cem,* the heartbeat. *Pa-a-cem,* the breath.

The dome cradled the sound, broadened it, enriched it with the qualities of wood, of stone, of antiquity. Even so, the voice retained its own inviolate distinctiveness; like air that carries scent yet remains, always, air.

The sound was hypnotic. It burrowed through my mind unearthing the hollow memories of too many years passed in long, empty days and nights. I yearned to shed my self and join a sea of kindred spirits.

I wept. I prayed to whatever god still lived—save me. I gazed up into the eye of the dome and saw a pillar of living fire. *Burn me.* The walls shiv-ered and beneath my feet the earth buckled from the weight of too much regret. *Devour me.*

The voice carried me to the edge of madness. Black he-goats stood like men and danced in the flickering light. Their eyes blazed red with feral desire—*take me*—their swollen organs sharp as arrows—*tear me.*

My own unquenchable need quickened, made me dizzy. I wanted to fall, to rise, to die, to savor all the forbidden flavors of hell. I longed to weave scalding ribbons of corruption through my hair, and lavishly drape my flesh in laces of purest evil.

I squeezed shut my hot, moist eyes and giddily watched images of pos-sibility appear in explosions of color—glistening kitchen knives, white-knuckled fists, blue-veined hands, red-tipped razor nails.

I gnashed my teeth until my jaw ached. I was ready to sanctify myself with the blood of thirty-three true martyrs and saints, and lay their putrefying corpses along the pitted road to damnation to cushion my footsteps.

But some errant sinew in my mind—a mote of conscience; a slumbering seed of decency left by a grade school nun; a long-forgotten hope—held me fast.

It was Rachel's hand, however, which dragged me from that unholy place and threw me down on the cool damp grass in the garden. The night air rushed into my lungs.

Slowly my head began to clear.

Rachel gently smoothed back my sweat-drenched hair. A bright sliver of moon hovered over her head like a halo. Her hands were soft and cool.

"Keep breathing," she murmured. "You'll be all right. You're safe now."

She cradled my shoulders and helped me sit. My mouth was dry as cotton. I could still hear the women chanting in the house, but the sound had lost its urgency.

Rachel eventually let go of my shoulders and, as she sat down beside me, gave a long, relieved sigh.

"Too close for comfort," she said. "Nearly got you for sure and always."

"What happened?" I asked at last.

"She got into your head," Rachel said flatly.

"Who did?"

Rachel looked at me incredulously. Then she pointed at the house. "*She* did."

"You mean Maeve?"

Rachel rolled her eyes and shook her head. "No. *She*. The *Shub*. The one who lives way down under that house. You know . . . the beast mother . . . the black she-goat of the woods . . . the *Shub*."

I rubbed my face with my open palms.

"Lord . . . I should never have drunk so much wine. And on an empty stomach."

"It's not the wine," Rachel insisted. "She was after you."

I smiled at her. "Thank you for keeping me from making a fool of myself in there."

"Sure." She shrugged.

We sat quietly for a long time while the muted chanting droned on and on. Finally, she stretched out beside me; she seemed exhausted. I thought she'd fallen asleep. But the moment the singing stopped, the girl hopped to her haunches.

"Listen here, you come stay with me. You ought not be going back in there," she whispered.

"Thank you sweetheart, but I'll be fine now."

"You're not paying attention! It's especially bad when they're singing like that—and I'm sick of it. But She could get you any time . . ."

"Who?" I said. "Yes, I know . . . the Shub."

"Darn right!" she said.

"What about the others? Can't She get them too?" I smiled.

Rachel stood up, brushed bits of grass and leaves from her pant legs, and tossed back her hair. "She'll get to them—they don't know any of the rules. But She can creep into your head any time. And mine too, if I'd let Her."

I held out my hand and Rachel pulled me up. "What makes us so special?"

She sighed. "We're the same, you and me . . . we're not like them. It's easy for Her to take us . . . especially if we're not thinking."

I felt flattered and hugged the child against me. "Tell me, how are we the same?"

She stared up at me; her gentle face, bathed in moonlight, looked beautiful and ethereal.

"We are virgins," she said softly.

I was momentarily stunned. My arms fell limply from her shoulders. I heard a door open and faint footsteps on a porch. Someone was calling my name and coming closer.

"Aren't you chilly out here?" Maeve asked.

Rachel had already vanished.

IV.

Maeve referred to that first night only once during the coming days when she declared that she had never before felt the group "reach such a pitch of intensity" and was thrilled that I'd been there to hear it for myself. And even though I attended no other chanting sessions, I never felt completely at ease working in the computer room—the daytime avatar of the chapel.

All of the women worked hard, doing all the usual chores and learning to use the equipment. When their various tasks were done, they kept to themselves. I had difficulty perceiving them as separate individuals. Except for Solatee and Maeve, they were simply: the women.

Every evening at six I joined them for dinner. Afterwards I strolled the garden and watched for Rachel, or read in my room. Right before ten, while the women assembled for their nightly communion, I wrapped myself in blankets, took to the porch and listened to Rachel's voice wafting through the air . . . *Shub Shub Eee-a Eee-a Shub.* . . . And though I didn't see her, I knew she saw me. I wanted her to see me there.

Maeve encouraged me to explore the house; several times she offered to show me the caverns below, the catacombs where the dust of Indians,

Arkhams and Jeromians mingled. I had learned to navigate from my room to the dining, computer and common rooms, and knew two routes to the garden. Beyond that, I was reluctant to venture. I watched the women carrying stores to and from the cellar, and envied their glassy-eyed indifference. For while I slept in Arkham House, my dreams were filled with images of all the dark horrors which resided below. And when awake, every shadow seemed to breathe.

I noticed subtle improvements among the women—they began to take pride in their work, there was the occasional mention of plans for life after Arkham House, a few even smiled from time to time. Clearly—in spite of Rachel's fairy tales and my case of the shivers—they were benefiting from Maeve's experiment.

By the end of the week, I had finished installing the speakers and had begun modulating the audio transmit feeds—Maeve had insisted on synchronicity, and I was going to give it to her. This was my final task and while I was eager to finish and go home, it was, by nature, slow work, demanding patience and precision.

On the morning of the last day of August, twelve days after I'd begun, I told Maeve the system was ready to boot. She informed the others during breakfast and all through the day their collective excitement mounted. I packed my bags and loaded everything but my overnight case into the trunk of the car. I scrubbed layers of golden pollen dust from the windshield and cranked up the engine just to be sure. I took a long walk outside the parapet and climbed the rocks which jutted over the eastern edge of the mountain top. I looked for Rachel. I was determined to take the child away from here.

I didn't return to the house until sunset. Later, Maeve in her sweater and I in my blanket, sat beneath St. Jerome and watched the moon rise.

"You're leaving first thing then. I'll miss you," she said, trembling against the cold. "I had hopes, you know. Thought you might want to really do something important. Guess this isn't your thing, huh?"

"Maybe not. But Maeve . . . I believe you've found your true calling here," I said, draping my blanket around both our shoulders. "I want to take Rachel with me."

"Have you seen her?"

"Not since that first day. But I've heard her singing in the garden every night."

Maeve sighed. "Well now, I think that's a fine idea. Maybe taking care of her is your true calling." She shuddered against me. "It's freezing; let's go inside."

"You go on. I'll wait here for Rachel."

V.

In my waking dream, Rachel's face is tawny, her teeth white, her eyes lustrous. She runs home from school waving her science report with a large red "A" on the cover. When she finishes her homework, we read together. She can't understand why Ahab didn't take his lost leg like a man, and just get on with his life. I tell her it's his nature, and he's trapped by it. I see her grow up, go to college, marry, have children; and the stream of love between us is always full.

"Is it a good dream?" she asked as she sat down beside me.

"Yes. I was thinking about you. And your future."

"Oh," she said. "You packed up your stuff today."

I nodded. "I'm leaving in the morning . . . and I want to take you with me."

"That'd be nice," she said wistfully.

"I want to adopt you."

Rachel snuggled close to me and considered the matter.

"I can't leave the mountain," she said at last. "Even if I loved you . . . and wanted you for a mother, I belong here."

"But you could visit the mountain whenever you . . ."

She shook her head against me. "No. It wouldn't work like that. I'm the only one left to keep Her where She belongs."

"Oh, sweetie . . . the world is full of so many real wonders; those old tales about the Shub mustn't . . . "

"There's no point in fighting about it."

"Now listen," I said sternly. "You do not belong up here all alone. No one should be left so alone, especially someone who's still a little girl. You need love and looking after; and if your scary stories keep you from getting those things, I say they aren't worth . . ."

Rachel suddenly stood up; she was rigid with emotion. "Just because a person is little don't mean she's a fool, you know."

I reached for her hand, but she jerked it away.

"You and all them in there think you're smart. But none of you know jack about *Her*. When I try to tell somebody something they never listen."

"I'll listen," I said softly.

Rachel took a deep, raspy breath and then, with the efficiency of a familiar bedtime story, told me the legend of an imprisoned demon-goddess.

"The Shub's been down inside the mountain for ever and ever, all alone, sleeping and dreaming," she said. "Then people came. And for a while they were happy—things grew, there was lots of game and the streams were full of fish. So they decided to give thanks to the spirit of the mountain for their good crops and healthy children.

"'Course," she said disdainfully, "they were ignorant and didn't know any better. They piled up stones and everyone got together—singing, dancing, beating drums and stuff. But then . . ." she said ominously, "the Shub woke up. All the rocks shot straight up into the sky and crashed down; and the ground shook so hard that a piece of it gave way—right where that house sits—and opened up into a bottomless pit of green fire."

Like the plagues of Egypt, Rachel recited the horrors which were then inflicted on the frightened people—the Shub loosed a thousand giant, black goats, and demon creatures flew from the fire into the world; Her ceaseless howling and thunderous screams drove people insane.

"And some who'd lost their minds," she said softly, "killed their own kin . . . even little babies."

Rachel paused to ask the time; it was 9:15. Then she straightened up, cleared her throat and continued.

"Did I tell how the Shub was very angry because She was still stuck inside the fire pit? Well, She was. And the people tried everything they could think of to put Her back down inside the mountain—they threw magic potions at the flames, and animals and children, some of them even jumped in themselves. But nothing worked," she said, shaking her head.

"Now there was a woman named Pa'sha'ant who'd almost gone crazy on account of her suffering—all six of her children had been snatched away, one by one, and thrown into the fire. One night she went to the pit and even though the green flames licked out at her, she knelt down and started singing to her poor lost babies."

"A lullaby . . ." I murmured.

Rachel touched my shoulder. "Yes. But she was singing words that no one understood, words she'd heard in a dream; very special words. And she kept singing into the pit—even though she was getting burned. She stayed right there all night long.

"In the morning, the people couldn't believe their eyes. The fire was gone. The Shub had quit her wailing; and the ground was back like God made it."

"And Pa'sha'ant?"

"All of her skin was burned black. But she'd seen things in the fire and saw the hurt and sadness the Shub felt from being trapped all alone for so long. Before Pa'sha'ant died, she told the people the special words so that if the Shub ever waked up again, they could put Her back to sleep. Pa'sha'ant said they should guard the place to make sure no one would go there. She said that as long as the Shub was left alone, things would be all right. But Pa'sha'ant warned them too: if they didn't work hard and keep their minds on their own business, the Shub could send them wicked thoughts. And no one was completely safe—old people were safest because their minds were already filled up with memories; and children were kinda safe because their minds hopped so fast from thought to thought; and grown-ups had their minds on their worries. But virgins had to be especially careful since it was in their nature to have dreams and imaginings." Rachel paused for a moment. "There were lots of other rules, but nobody knows them all. Not anymore."

"Oh," I said with a shudder. "That was a spellbinding story. And you told it so very, very well."

"You don't believe a word of it, do you? Even after what happened to you."

I smiled. "Myths aren't meant to be taken literal—"

"If I didn't sing tonight, and the ground opened up, you still wouldn't believe me, would you?" Rachel petulantly kicked her toe into the dirt. "Who cares what you think. Pretty soon, I won't be able to keep the Shub asleep all by myself anyway."

"What do you mean?"

Rachel folded her arms. "I can't keep up with it. I'm too tired. I'm sick of singing that stupid song. If Maeve brings any more ladies up here . . . well, it won't be my fault if they wake Her up for good and all."

"Sweetie, I don't think Maeve will be bringing in any new people; she's got computers now. And once the Arkham House ladies go on-line, they'll be so captivated by cyberspace, they won't pay one jot of attention to anything else," I said.

Rachel threw her head back and stared at the moon. Anyone seeing her standing there so still in the garden, would take her for a diminutive statue of St. Joan.

"What's Maeve want with computers anyway?" she asked.

"You know how much she wants to help people. Well, with computers, in cyberspace, she can help hundreds, maybe even thousands."

"Like how—exactly?"

"To tell you the truth, I'm not sure I can explain it . . ." I said, and suddenly, the whole undertaking seemed absurd. If Maeve's rhetoric—using the language of science to obscure all that muddled mysticism—had suckered me, then why not hundreds of thousands of others? I felt like the biggest fool at the bottom of a pyramid of fools.

"Try to explain," Rachel said.

"It doesn't matter. She's gotten what she wants. I'll be out of here tomorrow. And you're coming with me. Don't say another word about . . ."

"Shhh . . . listen . . ."

"Stop it!" I said as I threw down the blanket and grabbed her wrist.

Rachel squirmed and tried to pull away. "They've started that breathing . . . please, I got to get closer. I got to sing."

"Fine!" I heard myself shriek; my hand wrenched her stick-thin wrist until she winced. I felt a rush of pleasure and an irresistible thirst for more. And suddenly I was dragging her toward the house. "Let's *all* sing tonight!"

The voice of the women burst, fully formed, from the center of Arkham House. The notes entered me like acid-dipped splinters and I squeezed Rachel's wrist until I could feel the bones begin to buckle. Every nerve in my body prickled with excitement and expectation.

"Lila! Please! You're breaking my arm!"

That was the first time Rachel had called me by name. It was like being plunged into a pool of icy water; my mind was instantly clear. I immediately let go of her.

My tears were cold on my cheeks. "Oh God, I'm so sorry. I don't know why . . ."

Rachel blew on her tender wrist. "Maybe you better go out to the car and wait there until they're done," she said calmly.

"You come with me," I said.

"There's no point in arguing. No time for it."

"I'll wait over there with St. Jerome then."

Rachel ran off toward the house singing. *"Shub Shub Eee-a Eee-a Shub. . . ."*

I felt the eyes of St. Jerome watching with contempt as I wrapped myself, head to foot, in the blanket. I was too ashamed to ask for his forgiveness. With each breeze, I heard another chilling rebuke in the rustle of leaves.

The sound of Rachel's singing floated on the wind, becoming nearly inaudible whenever her orbit took her to the far side of the house. Despair closed around me like a fog—she would never forget my cruelty, my insanity, my anger. And even if she forgave me, she would never completely trust me. Certainly, I could never again trust myself. I wanted the night to do more than simply end; I wanted it never to have been. And I wanted never to have been as well.

Pa-cem, pa-a-cem . . . seeped like lava, from every cleft in the mortar, every minute crevice in the ancient stonework; bleeding heat into the garden. I could feel it. I could *smell* it—the same rotten stench that came from the bowels of the house.

I heard subtle variations as hundreds of faceless voices poured into the mix, and coursed from the speakers. The feed was flawless—the volume remained level; only the tone thickened. The voice intensified, solidified, as more and more singers logged on. It buried Rachel's voice.

The ground swelled in sympathetic waves. The air grew hotter; my blanket was heavy with perspiration. St. Jerome trembled on his base under an ash-blackened sky. And lost somewhere out in that endless darkness was Rachel. *My child.*

But something else was out there too. Something mad with a hunger it could never feed was awakening from its dreams into the torment of that relentless need.

Light in the windows of Arkham House shimmied and dimmed. The building itself groaned. There were screams. I heard the women scrambling to escape; their fear was palpable.

The banks of speakers continued to flood the air with a sound possessed of primal force. The unified, impassioned Voice of the victimized, the brutalized, the enslaved, seeking something beyond vengeance; something transcendent—something darker than night, yet terribly akin to it.

"Lila! Where are you?" Maeve called from somewhere.

"Beside St. Jerome," I said. But there was no reply; only the Voice, resonating with an ever more hideous harmonic, throbbed in the air.

Suddenly, a lucent, green light blasted from the house. The Shub's prison was opening and I knew that Rachel would be there, dutifully singing while her skin crisped on her bones.

As I walked toward the light, four of the women ran at me, almost knocking me down. They linked arms around me, holding me.

"Fire," Solatee shrieked. "Big fire!"

I shouted; I kicked them; I clawed their faces. But they wouldn't let me go.

"We've got to get to the car!" one of them said.

"Stop fighting us," another commanded. "You can't go in there! There's a goddamned volcano under the house."

I laughed so hard I couldn't catch my breath. It startled them and for an instant they loosened their grip. I broke through and ran for the house. Only their terrified screams followed me.

The Shub's thoughts reached out for me; they made me dizzy. I concentrated on the Kaufman Algorithm, repeating each set of subcommands as I slowly felt my way along the hall; clouds of sulfur-impregnated green smoke blinded and choked me. I charted my way by turning always into the heat.

When I finally reached the chapel, I was surprised that the pit itself was not nearly as big around as the room. The flames, however, licked the top of the dome. Many of the mini-units were strewn across the floor, their plastic shells still curling in a slow agony of meltdown. The speakers now hummed with dead air.

But Rachel was not there. Again and again, I called her name. I shouted into the well of liquid fire, commanding the Shub, the demon Herself, to restore my child.

Then up from the depths, came Her reply—an unnatural howl, exploding with such force that it still rings in my ears. I could feel her thoughts on the other side of the algorithm to which my mind clung. In this swiftly escalating muddle of mind and fire and sound and smoke, it was difficult to tell if the small figure which appeared at the opposing door was real or not. It seemed to be moving; it seemed to be dragging something behind it.

I peeled off my blouse and wrapped it around the least damaged unit I saw. I'm not sure if I wanted it for a talisman or a weapon; but having it in my hand was a comfort as I ventured around the edge of the fire and crept toward the figure at the door.

"Rachel!" I gasped.

She dropped the legs of the body she was dragging to the pit and came at me like a rabid cat—all claws and teeth. I could see the blood lust of the beast in her eyes. In one motion, I spun her around and lifted her from behind; her nails sank into my arms and grouted out long strips of flesh. I threw her into one of the small cupboards and latched it. Rachel beat on the door and howled like an animal.

Maeve was alive but unconscious when I got to her. There were signs of Rachel's handiwork on her cheeks and neck. I pulled her out into the hall.

"Don't . . . go . . . back," she muttered weakly.

I wiped the blood from her lips and returned to the chapel. I could feel Kaufman's Algorithm slipping away as black goat-men embraced symbols and numbers and danced off with them.

Only two of the speakers were reachable, and I quickly aimed them into the glowing maw of the fire.

I crouched down near the cupboard; Rachel continued to pound furiously. Whenever the Shub howled, so did Rachel. And the goatmen looked to me less and less like demons.

I unwrapped the unit and quickly booted it and logged on. A few of the keys stuck, aside from that it worked and I was routed directly into the speakers. I shut my eyes and sang only to Rachel, to comfort her and calm her, and to put her to sleep. *Shub Shub Eee-a Eee-a Shub, Vug tla tla gan.* Hush little baby, close your eyes. *Ptabo, Shub Niggurath, Ptabo.* Sleep my child, sleep.

* * *

Maeve did not fully recover from the insanity of that night. She doesn't remember much—except that there was a fire. And there was no point in trying to explain what had actually happened; sometimes I'm not completely clear on the facts.

Most of the women landed in other shelters; a few started new lives in the outside world. Three were never found. Solatee chose to stay with Maeve and look after her. When Rachel and I visited this spring, we helped them plant a flower garden.

Arkham House still stands; amazingly, the fire had inflicted little damage on it. No one goes there. Rachel never even asks about it. She too, has forgotten. Which is for the best, I think.

But now, beneath the chapel dome, there is a bank of heat resistant speakers. At regular intervals, they sing a strange lullaby, with words no one understands, to a demon goddess who must never wake again. ✳

Yog-Sothoth, Superstar

by Thomas F. Monteleone

FAX

DATE: March 3
TO: Garrett Fairfax
FROM: Shirley Zuckerman, The Actors Advocates Agency

Great news, Garrett! I just got off the phone with Michael Morrison (yes, *that* Michael Morrison). He wants you to audition for the lead in a new musical/ rock opera he's going to be directing.

10:00 a.m. This coming Tuesday. The Helen Hayes. It's called *Lovecraft, I Love You!* and I have no idea what it's about. Morrison saw you in Soho. That dreadful little comedy about Saddam Hussein, and thought you'd be perfect for the lead!

Call me as soon as you get this. Congratulations, and give my regards to Broadway!

Shirley

* * *

(. . . so leave your message after the beep . . . beeeeeep!)

Shirley, this is Garrett. Just got your fax and Jesus Christ, I can't believe it! Tell Mr. Morrison I'll be there, and he won't be disappointed. Thanks, kiddo, for believing in me all this time! This is the break I've been waiting for. Jesus, I can't believe it . . . ! Call me and let's catch lunch at Marv's Deli. The reubens are on *me* this time. See ya and thanks again.

(click!)

* * *

April 14

Dear Analia:

So how's my favorite sister doing back in Cincinnati? Are John and the boys doing okay? Last time I heard from you he was taking that new job at American Express. Hope it worked out.

Anyway, you won't believe what happened at the last casting call I went to—I got picked! Not only that, but I got the female romantic <u>lead</u>! That's the <u>best</u> part! I'm playing the part of Sonia, the girlfriend of the hero, a guy named Howard. I haven't gotten my script and songs yet, so I don't know too much about the story. It's a rock opera called <u>Lovecraft, I Love You!</u> and I heard it's about some guy who was a writer in Rhode Island. Sounds kind of boring, but who cares! Your sister is on Broadway! Can you believe it? I'm not sure I do yet.

Don't tell Mom yet. I want to write her a surprise note, okay?

We'll talk soon.

Love,

Estela

* * *

MEMO
TO: Michael Morrison, Director
FROM: Isabel Cortez, Assistant to the Chairman

The Arkham Foundation Board of Directors would like to formally congratulate you on your commencement of rehearsals for *Lovecraft, I Love You!*

Please do not hesitate to contact me for anything you may need during this exciting phase of our production. The Board anxiously awaits opening night.

* * *

(excerpt from *Lovecraft, I Love You!* songbook)

> I don't know why you write those
> Sill-lee stuh-uh-orrrr-eeees!
> And I don't really care . . .
> The only thing I know is that
> I luh-uh-uvvvvv you!
> So you know that ease-a-lee I don't scare!

* * *

June 2nd

Dear Analia:

It's me, your sister. I know I could just call you and just <u>tell</u> you all this stuff, but believe me, the letter writing is very therapeutic. It slows me down. Makes me

take my time. That way, I compose my thoughts and I keep
things under control. Everything in this city is so . . .
high-energy, so frenetic. I need some time when I simply
can't be so UP—know what I mean?

Anyway, it's been more than a month since we started
rehearsals on the musical and I don't know what to think.
I've learned all my songs and my dance numbers, and sister-
dear, I have to tell you—this thing is a squawking turkey.
If we get through opening night with our reputations
intact, we'll all be very lucky. If this show lasts more
than a week, we should start dancing in the streets.

Analia, you know me—I would never bite the hand that
feeds me, and you know I would have probably <u>killed</u> to get
this job (or any job, really), but I have to confide in
you . . . this is the <u>worst</u> show I have ever seen. The
songs are stupid and half of them aren't even written in
English, I don't think. The story (what I can make of it,
that is) is unbelievably dumb. And the main character is
this racist recluse named Howard who writes scary stories
in Providence. He discovered the remains of this ancient
civilization and the names of some of the places and the
people are like . . . unpronounceable! I'm telling you—
it's the dumbest thing I have ever seen. Even our director
(a really famous guy who did <u>Dogs!</u> and <u>Goodbye, Molly!</u>) is
embarrassed by this show.

I don't know why I'm telling you all this, except that I
guess I never thought it could be like this. I always
thought that getting a part in a Broadway show was like
the best thing that could ever happen to you. I never
imagined it could be so . . . so bad.

But that doesn't mean I'm not going to stick this one out.
Some of the other people in the show who've become my
friends, we all say that even if this one's a "bomb,"
we'll all have a "leg up" on the next audition, the next
show. (That's a little theater-talk for you <g>.)

So hang in there, sister. Tell John I said "Hi!" and give
the little boys some hugs and kisses for me. If by some
miracle my show lasts more than a week, I'll send you some
comps. Not that you'll like it, but you should see just to
see how awful it is. You won't believe it. (The worst part
is that it will kind of prove to John that he's right—
that all musicals are dumb.) Oh well.

We still have six weeks of rehearsal before opening (and
probably closing) night. I guess I should wrap this up and
get some sleep.

Love,

Estela

* * *

(. . . and I'll call you back as soon as possible . . . beeeeep!)

Okay, Harvey, this is Michael! Now where the fuck *are* you, man!? Everytime I call you about this show you got me hooked into, you are *NEV-VER* fuck-king there! Harvey, if you're screening your calls, *pick up the phone goddammit!*

(pause)

Damn! I *have* to talk to you about this nutty show . . . Harvey, it's *terrible!* It's career self-immolation! I know I have a contract but I'm telling you—I *can't* stay on this . . . this theatrical *abortion!* So Harvey, I'm telling you—if I don't hear from you tonight, I'm quitting in the morning. I'm calling that Cortez harpy at that bogus foundation . . . and telling her to find herself another director. I'm telling her to get somebody who never wants to work on Broadway again.

Because I can tell you—that somebody ain't me!

(click!)

* * *

```
From: R'lyeh@necronomi.con
Date: Sat, 18 June 23:34:53 -0500 (EST)
To: mmorrison@nymailex.com
Subject: Your Resignation
Mr. Morrison:
```

Your agent, Harvey Goldstone, has just informed me of your wishes to disenfranchise yourself from the project. I am very sad to receive such news. I must take this opportunity to inform you personally of the same thing I said to Mr. Goldstone, *viz.,* you are under contract to the Arkham Foundation and are therefore an indentured employee of the Foundation. You have no choice but to fulfill your obligations. If you read the terms of your employment closely, as I have also requested of Mr. Goldstone, you might notice that you risk dire consequences if you attempt to disregard your contractual agreement.

Thank you for your understanding and expected compliance.

In sincerity, I remain

Albert Hazred, Chairman of the Board

P.S. I am sending this message in duplicate by means of fax, phone, FedEx, messenger, and United States Postal Service as well because it is very important that you receive this warning.

* * *

The New York Times (AP)

It was reported by Lieutenant Detective Thomas Brancuso of the NYPD's homicide division that Michael Morrison, the well-known Broadway director, was found murdered in his Park Avenue South co-op early this morning. "The circumstances surrounding his death are very strange," said Brancuso. "We aren't ready to divulge all the details, but I can tell you this—I've been on the force nineteen years, and I've never seen anything like it." Mr. Morrison was working on a new rock-opera entitled *Lovecraft, I Love You!* He was a native of Painesvillle, Ohio, and was thirty-nine years old.

* * *

(. . . so leave your message after the beep . . . beeeeep!)

Hey Shirley, this is Garrett . . . aren't you *ever* home? Anyway, I guess you heard about Morrison—waking up this morning and finding himself dead. Know what I mean? The rumors are flying around here like feathers in a pillow fight, and I was wondering if you've heard anything or if you might know what's really going on. The one that's flying through the cast and crew is he quit the show yesterday. Not surprised 'cause it was no secret he *hated* it. Got so bad he was starting to hate all of us too. Know what I mean? Bad scene all around. I mean, I gotta tell ya (but *please,* don't tell anybody I said anything . . .), the show's a stinker. If we don't tank the first week or so, I'll be shocked, stunned, and all the rest of that surprised stuff. But a job's a job—especially if it's on Broadway. Know what I mean? So look, give me a call as soon as you can, as soon as you know something, okay? Somebody in the show told me they have a friend at the 84th Precinct and he told her Morrison was like . . . like torn into lots of pieces. Only some of the pieces were missing. . . . So anyway, I'll be waiting to hear from you. Ms. Cortez came by this afternoon and said we'll have a new director tomorrow. I'll tell you who it is when I find out. The show must go on, right? C-ya!

(click!)

* * *

(excerpt from WVXN-FM's *Eye on Broadway* weekly feature)

EOB: There's been a lot of speculation surrounding the new rock opera, *Lovecraft, I Love You!,* which is scheduled to open next week at the

Helen Hayes. I'm speaking with one of the show's leads, Estela Duarte. . . . How're you doing, Estela?

Duarte: Great, Margot, just great!

EOB: Your show has been pretty much of a secret from the beginning, but ever since the tragic death of your director, the legendary Michael Morrison, the producers of *Lovecraft, I Love You!* have *really* put the clamps on, wouldn't you say?

Duarte: Well, yeah, I guess that's true. But I know they've always wanted to keep the whole show under wraps until we actually opened.

EOB: Do you have any idea why they've wanted it like that?

Duarte: Well gee, I don't know. Nobody ever explained it to us. I just know that it's in everybody's contract that we're forbidden to reveal anything about the show until after opening night.

EOB: Wow, then I guess my next question isn't going to get answered—I was going to ask you what could be so exciting in the show's plot that would make it more top secret than the Manhattan Project?

Duarte: *(giggling)* You know, I'm not sure. Why don't you ask me that question next week, after we've opened?

EOB: I certainly will . . . But in the meantime, what can you tell us about the rumors that several other people involved with the show have either died in horrible accidents or have been maimed terribly . . .

Duarte: I'm . . . I'm afraid I can't comment on that. I don't know anything about that.

EOB: Now, come on, Estela—which one is it?

Duarte: *(shrugging, giggling)* Well, I guess a little of both!

EOB: We've also heard there's some huge production expenses connected to this project. Care to comment?

Duarte: Well . . .

EOB: Our spies tell us that there's a scene where an ancient city, buried beneath the deepest part of the ocean, suddenly rises up in a breath-taking display of lightning and volcanoes, and lots of steam and boiling sea foam.

Duarte: *(giggling yet again)* Well, if that's what your spies have told you, I guess you better decide whether or not to believe them.

EOB: Okay, well thanks, Estela! You've got us all curious, to say the least. This is Margot Vanderkelen for WVXN-FM and I'll see you next week with another Eye on Broadway!

* * *

(*. . . after the beep, do your thing . . . beeeeep!)*

Garrett, this is Shirley, calling you back. It's phone-tag again, and you're it! Anyway, sugar, tomorrow's the big night, huh? Just calling to wish you luck, and tell you I'll be there, but I'm going to be a little late. But I'll be there before intermission, I promise. Despite what you think, the buzz is you've got a hit on your hands. With all that hush-hush stuff and all, you've got the whole theater gang pretty excited. I think you're just being too hard on yourself. Oh, and wasn't that awful about Margot Vanderkelen? Anyway, see you tomorrow night! Break a leg!

(click!)

* * *

July 20th

Dear Analia:

Okay, this is it. By the time you get this letter, <u>Lovecraft, I Love You!</u> will be a part of Broadway history.

Well, at least, your sister will be over her opening night jitters. Everybody is nervous and some of the people are actually scared, or superstitious at least.

I mean, you probably didn't hear about it out there in Cincinnati, but this lady who does a radio show about all the Broadway shows fell in front of a subway a couple of nights back—right after the interview she did with <u>me</u> (I know, I forgot to tell you about it . . .) was on the air. There was a witness, a homeless guy, who said she didn't fall at all, that she was <u>pulled</u> out on to the tracks by something in the shadows, something that looked kind of like a big octopus.

Pretty silly, I know, but some of the people in the show are a little freaked by the story. Especially after one of the crew got caught in the gears of the hydraulic lift at tech rehearsal last night. I'll have

to tell you all the gooshy parts when I see you next
week. (You <u>are</u> still flying in with John, aren't you?)

So give all the kids a big hug and kiss (each) from
their favorite aunt. I can't wait to see you guys!

Love,

Estela

* * *

(From the *Sunday Times* ENTERTAINMENT Section)

Probably the most anticipated opening of the young season has to have been the Arkham Foundation's production of *Lovecraft, I Love You!* I know this critic had been hearing conflicting reports about the show on the jungle telegraph, and when you combine that with a few mysterious, albeit accidental, deaths of people connected with the show, well, I'd say you have something intriguing in the very least.

Lovecraft, I Love You! stars promising new talents in the persons of Garrett Fairfax and Estela Duarte, who portray the lead characters of Providence writer, Howard Lovecraft and his enigmatic ladyfriend, Sonia Greene. But before going on, I'd better make a small confession: despite the above actors' earnest efforts, I initially found them in a futile struggle to be believable. The show's opening songs and choreographies seemed so . . . *lame* (the only word that springs to mind) . . . that I was about to dismiss the production as a dismal and insulting assault on good taste. Indeed, I sensed a similar displeasure in the audience.

However, something odd and wonderful happened as the show picked up steam. The leaden cadence of the songs began to create a disposition not unlike that created by a selection of Gregorian chants. The overblown lighting and special effects gradually passed from merely tolerable to palatable and finally engrossing. I experienced a transformation not only of mood, but of spirit. To feel my predisposed negative feelings be consummately dispelled was almost a religious, if not transcendental experience.

Another oddly wonderful aspect of *Lovecraft, I Love You!* is its subtle, yet inexorable, revelation of an arcane mythology, which is far too complex to explore in this limited space. Be it enough for this critic to simply say the portrayal of the mythic system is fascinating, engrossing, and almost hypnotic. For an entirely original and exciting night of theatre, don't miss this one.

* * *

(blurbs from the billboards at Times Square)

"Enthralling!" *The New York Post*
"Mesmerizing!" *The New Yorker*
"A religious experience." *The New York Times*
"Subversive and captivating." *The Village Voice*
"Watch out for this one!" *The East Village Other*

* * *

(from a *Newsday* music review)

For the third week in a row the chart-topper CD in the Showtunes category is *Lovecraft, I Love You!* Industry neophyte Necro Records must
have been using a crystal ball on this one. By releasing an original cast
CD of the hit rock-opera only two days after the Broadway opening,
they've enjoyed the marketing coup of the year. This is the hottest disc
in New York these days. No matter where you go, you cannot help but
hear people humming the odd tunes, singing those songs with their weird
and practically unpronounceable lyrics. Subways, buses, elevators, the
streets, and even store clerks as they work. No doubt about it: the city's
pulse can be found in the beat of this music.

* * *

The New York Times (AP)

Dr. F. X. Paulson of Columbia University confirmed the
reports of unusual seismic activity beneath the deep underwater
canyons of the Hudson River and its confluence with the
Atlantic Ocean. "It's very odd," said Professor Paulson. "It is as
if there was something down there, trying to push its way to the
surface. The pressure point is extremely precise and focused.
I've never seen anything like it." When asked what the disturbance could be, the renowned geologist was in a quandary. "It's
easier to say what it *cannot* be, which is an undersea volcano or
a heretofore undiscovered faultline. Rather, these recent quakes
seem to be caused by a solid object being forced upwards
through the earth's crust. Impossible, I know, but that's what it
looks like nonetheless." When asked how big this "object"
appeared to be, Paulson replied with a smile: "Oh, my . . . much
bigger than Manhattan. That is why it's impossible, you see?"

* * *

(from the police report of NYPD Detective Sergeant Rick Sjoerdsma)

After meeting with Officers Charles and Grant of NY Transit Police, plus compiling the accounts of numerous eyewitnesses (see attached) I have been able to piece together the events of the previous two weeks at the Times Square subway station and the connecting tunnels. The picture that emerges is not pretty and it frankly makes no sense. I've talked to people from some of the colleges, and also guys from the health department and nobody can explain why all the rats and even all the bugs have been clearing out. Sewer workers have been reporting the same kinds of things. People who've seen the rats say it's like watching cattle getting herded along the tracks and up the stairwells. Weird, but that's what they've told me.

The transit employees I've talked with all agree that the bums have all disappeared too. Right after the rats started leaving. Only the homeless people didn't pack up and vacate. They just disappeared, like I first said. My men found their cardboard boxes and blankets, their hoards of food and booze. But no bums.

Lots of people have reported seeing a green-glowing fog in the tunnels.

One trainman I talked to (who pleaded with me not to use his name and agreed to talk only when I put that promise in writing) says he saw some kind of monsters in the tunnels, also in the green fog. He said they were big, but didn't look like any animals he'd ever seen, more like weird vegetables or plants with long waving stems or tendrils, really. He said they moved quickly out of the way of his high-speed train, almost melting into the darkness of the tunnel walls. The guy doesn't sound crazy, but what would you think? No wonder he doesn't want his boss to find out what kind of trash he's talking.

The thing that bugs me the most about the commuters who've been turning up missing is that we haven't been able to find a trace of evidence, not a thing. It's like these people never existed.

* * *

MEMO

TO: Isabel Cortez
FROM: Albert Hazred, Chairman of the Board

The Arkham Foundation would like to personally thank you for overseeing the production of *Lovecraft, I Love You!* Your diligence and attention to detail has been as much responsible for the show's outrageous success as its obviously seductive and powerful content.

Please accept as a bonus, a week's vacation aboard the foundation's yacht, *The Innsmouth,* which will be sailing this week for a cruise to selected archeological sites. It will be an experience that would give me great displeasure were you to miss out.

* * *

(from a CNN tape of an-on-the-scene broadcast)

. . . thank you, Bernard! This is Mark Ashton in New York City coming to you live from the roof of the World Trade Center. Behind and below me lies the historic tableau of the city's harbor and Statue of Liberty, whose waters are dotted with the hulls of hundreds of ships. The boats you see are a collection of scientific and military craft, as well as those of onlookers who have been repeatedly warned to keep their distance. The underwater disturbances of the previous weeks in the waters off Manhattan have been closely monitored after it was ascertained that an immense object is rising up from the ocean floor. Just exactly what this object might be has been beyond speculation and the authorities are not talking. The evacuation of the city has been as orderly as could be hoped for. Looting and violence have been sporadic and kept under control in most precincts. As I look towards the west, I see—uh, can you hold on one moment, please . . . ? We have an open channel to the NYPD's Special Task Force Command Center . . . I'm getting something from their spokesperson . . .

(the camera-view shakes violently, the microphone captures a terrible, rolling rumble, like thunder but much longer and louder . . .)

Something is definitely happening . . . What? I can't get all of that! Bernard, our signal's breaking up with the command center, but I can see from our vantage point that something is happening out there on the water. Another series of tremors have rolled beneath the city and the Twin Tower itself is swaying in reaction! I can see something out in the harbor breaking the surface! It's glistening white and—Jesus, it's fucking *huge!*

(another quake rocks the camera-view, this time violently, and the image is tilted severely, then rezzed out, but the audio continues . . .)

Oh-my-God! What *is* that thing?! The ships! The Statue of Liberty—! Everything's going down! We're getting outta here as soon as possible. The building is swaying wildly now! Christ, Gary, get that chopper in here! Jesus, it's big! It's impossi— ✳

ABOUT STEPHEN MARK RAINEY

Stephen Mark Rainey is author of over 80 published works of fiction, including the novel *Dreams of the Dark* (co-written with Elizabeth Massie), the second in the new series of *Dark Shadows* novels from HarperCollins. His short fiction may be found in numerous Chaosium anthologies, including *The Azathoth Cycle, The Innsmouth Cycle, The Shub-Niggurath Cycle, Singers of Strange Songs,* and others. His other Cthulhu Mythos-related stories have been published in anthologies and magazines such as *Miskatonic University, Whitley Streiber's Aliens, The New Lovecraft Circle, New Mythos Legends, Terminal Frights, Crypt of Cthulhu,* and many more.

Mark also edited the award-winning magazine, *Deathrealm,* for over 10 years before retiring it in 1997. His short-story collection, *Fugue Devil and Other Weird Horrors,* was released by Macabre, Inc. in 1993.

He currently lives in Greensboro, NC, with his wife Peggy. His daughter Allison attends NC State University in Raleigh, majoring in veterinary medicine.

THE SCROLL OF THOTH

Simon Magus was a great figure in the Western occult tradition. He is mentioned in the Bible and by Justin Martyr as the sorcerous opponent of Peter. Some refer to him as the heretical father of Gnosticism. He was a contemporary of the living Jesus. Richard L. Tierney's Simon comes to life as a Samaritan magician of deep insight and great power, an ex-gladiator whose keen sword and powerful sorcery allow him to survive battles of will and flesh with Roman emperors, Levantine princes, cunning priests, and horrendous powers alien to this world. In these stories Tierney mixes the flavor of historical antiquity with the Hyborian and Cthulhu myth cycles. The order of the tales in the book follows that of Simon's life.

5 3/8" x 8 3/8", 374 pages, $12.95. Stock #6014; ISBN 1-56882-105-0.

SINGERS OF STRANGE SONGS

Most readers acknowledge Brian Lumley as the superstar of British horror writers. With the great popularity of his *Necroscope* series, he is one of the best known horror authors in the world. Devoted fans know that his roots are deep in the Cthulhu Mythos, with which most of his early work deals. This volume contains eleven new tales in that vein, as well as three reprints of excellent but little-known work by Lumley. This book was published in conjunction with Lumley's 1997 trip to the United States.

5 3/8" x 8 3/8", 244 pages, $12.95. Stock #6014; ISBN 1-56882-104-2.

THE NYARLATHOTEP CYCLE

The mighty Messenger of the Outer Gods, Nyarlathotep has also been known to deliver tidings from the Great Old Ones. He is the only Outer God who chooses to personify his presence on our planet. A god of a thousand forms, he comes to Earth to mock, to wreak havoc, and to spur on humanity's self-destructive urges. This volume of stories and poems illustrates the ubiquitous presence of Nyarlathotep and shows him in several different guises. Among them, his presence as Nephren-Ka, the dread Black Pharaoh of dynastic Egypt, dominates. The thirteen stories include a Lin Carter novella. Selected and introduced by Robert M. Price.

5 3/8" x 8 3/8", 244 pages, $10.95. Stock #6019; ISBN 1-56882-092-5.

THE HASTUR CYCLE
Second Revised Edition

The stories in this book represent the evolving trajectory of such notions as Hastur, the King in Yellow, Carcosa, the Yellow Sign, Yuggoth, and the Lake of Hali. A succession of writers from Ambrose Bierce to Ramsey Campbell and Karl Edward Wagner have explored and embellished these concepts so that the sum of the tales has become an evocative tapestry of hypnotic dread and terror, a mythology distinct from yet overlapping the Cthulhu Mythos. Here for the first time is a comprehensive collection of all the relevant tales. Selected and introduced by Robert M. Price.

5 3/8" x 8 3/8", 306 pages, $10.95. Stock #6020; ISBN 1-56882-094-1.

THE XOTHIC LEGEND CYCLE

The late Lin Carter was a prolific writer and anthologist of horror and fantasy with over eighty titles to his credit. His tales of Mythos horror are loving tributes to H. P. Lovecraft's "revision" tales and to August Derleth's stories of Hastur and the *R'lyeh Text*. This is the first collection of Carter's Mythos tales; it includes his intended novel, *The Terror Out of Time*. Most of the stories in this collection have been unavailable for some time. Selected and introduced by Robert M. Price.

5 3/8" x 8 3/8", 274 pages, $10.95. Stock #6013; ISBN 1-56882-078-X.

THE NECRONOMICON

Although skeptics claim that the *Necronomicon* is a fantastic tome created by H. P. Lovecraft, true seekers into the esoteric mysteries of the world know the truth: The *Necronomicon* is a blasphemous tome of forbidden knowledge written by the mad Arab, Abdul Alhazred. Even today, after attempts over the centuries to destroy any and all copies in any language, some few copies still exist, secreted away. Within this book you will find stories about the *Necronomicon*, different versions of the *Necronomicon*, and two essays on the blasphemous tome. Now you too may learn the true lore of Abdul Alhazred. Selected and introduced by Robert M. Price.

5 3/8" x 8 3/8", 334 pages, $12.95. Stock #6012; ISBN 1-56882-070-4.

THE CTHULHU CYCLE

Millions of years ago, when the stars were right, Cthulhu ruled from his black house in R'lyeh. When the stars changed, R'lyeh sank beneath the waves, and Cthulhu was cast into a deathless sleep, eternally dreaming. He has used his dreams to communicate with his believers, from prehistoric times through to the present day. Cthulhu has been, is, and always will be. Now the stars may once more be right, and Cthulhu may rise from his millennial sleep and reassert his rightful rulership of the Earth. The thirteen stories in this book trace Cthulhu and his influence through the centuries. General introduction and individual story prefaces by Robert M. Price. Winner of the 1996 Academy of Adventure Gaming Arts & Design Best Game-Related Fiction Award.

5 3/8" x 8 3/8", 268 pages, $10.95. Stock #6005; ISBN 1-56882-038-0.

THE DISCIPLES OF CTHULHU
Second Revised Edition

The disciples of Cthulhu are a varied lot. In Mythos stories they are obsessive, loners, dangerous, seeking not to convert others so much as to use them. But writers of the stories are also Cthulhu's disciples, and they are the proselytizers, bringing new members into the fold. Published in 1976, the first edition of *The Disciples of Cthulhu* was the first professional, all-original Cthulhu Mythos anthology. One of the stories, "The Tugging" by Ramsey Campbell, was nominated for a Science Fiction Writers of America Nebula Award, perhaps the only Cthulhu Mythos story that has received such recognition. This second edition of *Disciples* presents nine stories of Mythos horror, seven from the original edition and two new stories. Selected by Edward P. Berglund.

5 3/8" x 8 3/8", 258 pages, $10.95. Stock #6011; ISBN 1-56882-054-2.

THE DUNWICH CYCLE

In the Dunwiches of the world the old ways linger. Safely distant from bustling cities, ignorant of science, ignored by civilization, dull enough never to excite others, poor enough never to provoke envy, these are safe harbors for superstition and seemingly meaningless custom. Sometimes they shelter truths that have seeped invisibly across the centuries. The people are unlearned but not unknowing of things once great and horrible, of times when the rivers ran red and dark shudderings ruled the air. Here are nine stories set where horror begins, with a general introduction and individual story prefaces by Robert M. Price.

5 3/8" x 8 3/8", 258 pages, $19.95. Stock #6010; ISBN 1-56882-047-7.

MADE IN GOATSWOOD

Ramsey Campbell is acknowledged by many to be the greatest living writer of the horror tale in the English language. He is known to Mythos fans for the ancient and fearful portion of England's Severn Valley he evoked in narratives such as "The Moon Lens". This book contains eighteen all-new stories set in that part of the Valley, including a new story by Campbell himself, his first Severn Valley tale in decades. This volume was published in conjunction with a 1995 trip by Campbell to the United States. Stories selected by Scott David Aniolowski.

5 3/8" x 8 3/8", 274 pages, $10.95. Stock #6009; ISBN 1-56882-046-1.

THE BOOK OF IOD

Henry Kuttner (1914-1958) was a friend of young Robert Bloch and a promising writer in his own right. He also became one of the Lovecraft Circle, submitting plot ideas and draft manuscripts to Lovecraft. He had an important impact on the development of the Cthulhu Mythos, especially with his contribution of a mystical tome, the *Book of Iod*. This collection of stories comprises all of Kuttner's Mythos tales (including one cowritten with Bloch) and a story by Lin Carter about the infamous *Book of Iod*. Introduction and commentary by Robert M. Price.

5 3/8" x 8 3/8", 210 pages, $19.95. Stock #6008; ISBN 1-56882-045-3.

THE AZATHOTH CYCLE

At the heart of the universe the mad god Azathoth pulses like a cancer. As with the physical universe it created, no purely reasoned argument, no subtle scientific proof, no brilliant artistry, no human love affects the unyielding will of Azathoth. As an entity it is of transcendent power and unthinking immortal sway. It can sometimes be avoided but never challenged. Here are fourteen tales concerning Azathoth by authors as diverse as Ramsey Campbell, Lin Carter, John Glasby, and Thomas Ligotti. The macabre poet Edward Pickman Derby contributes his immortal "Azathoth", the title piece of his single printed volume. Introduction, exegetical essay, and notes by Robert M. Price.

5 3/8" x 8 3/8", 244 pages, $19.95. Stock #6006; ISBN 1-56882-040-2.

CTHULHU'S HEIRS

"Cthulhu's Heirs" are the literary heirs to H. P. Lovecraft's creative legacy. This book is a window: Throw back the curtains and find more than twenty writers' visions into the landscape of Lovecraft country and beyond. Some of the landmarks are familiar, while others are entirely new. Witness hidden truths and places best left unimagined. Stories selected by Thomas M. K. Stratman. Winner of the 1994 Academy of Adventure Gaming Arts & Design Best Game-Related Fiction Award.

5 3/8" x 8 3/8", 288 pages, $10.95. Stock #6003; ISBN 1-56882-013-5.

THE INNSMOUTH CYCLE

The decadent, smugly rotting, secret-filled town of Innsmouth is a supreme creation of Howard Philips Lovecraft. It so finely mixes the carnal and the metaphysical that writers continue to take inspiration from it. This new collection contains thirteen tales and three poems tracing the evolution of Innsmouth, from early tales by Dunsany, Chambers, and Cobb, through Lovecraft's "The Shadow Over Innsmouth" to modern tales by Rainey, Glasby, and others.

5 3/8" x 8 3/8", 240 pages, $12.95. Stock # 6017; ISBN 1-56882-113-1.

THE COMPLETE PEGANA

Lord Dunsany's fantasy writing had a profound impact on the Dreamlands stories of H. P. Lovecraft. This original collection is composed of newly edited versions of Lord Dunsany's first two books, *The Gods of Pegana* (1905) and *Time and the Gods* (1906). Three additional stories round out the book, the first time that all the Pegana stories have appeared within one book. Edited and introduced by S. T. Joshi.

5 3/8" x 8 3/8", 242 pages, $12.95. Stock #6016; ISBN 1-56882-116-6.

NIGHTMARE'S DISCIPLE

Even in the modern day, horrors arise in Innsmouth. In this brand-new novel the curse of the Marshes falls upon an entirely new generation when a serial killer terrorizes Schenectady, New York. Detective Christopher James Stewart must follow a trail of mutilated bodies and piece together enigmatic clues before the murderer strikes again. Here is a wealth of terror and exuberant scenes, a detailed Cthulhu Mythos novel of the present day. Warning: contains explicit scenes.

5 3/8" x 8 3/8", 400 pages, $14.95. Stock #6018; ISBN 1-56882-118-2.

THE ITHAQUA CYCLE

The elusive, supernatural Ithaqua roams the North Woods and the wastes beyond, as invisible as the wind. Hunters and travelers fear the cold and isolation of the North; they fear the advent of the mysterious, malignant Wind-Walker even more. This collection includes the progenitor tale "The Wendigo" by Algernon Blackwood, three stories by August Derleth, and ten more from a spectrum of contemporary authors including Brian Lumley, Stephen Mark Rainey, and Pierre Comtois.

5 3/8" x 8 3/8", 260 pages, $12.95. Stock #6021; ISBN 1-56882-124-7.

THE ANTARKTOS CYCLE

Writers are drawn to the unreachable places of the Earth—to the greatest mountains and depths of the sea, the most barren deserts, and the white frozen deserts surrounding the north and south poles. In our minds' eyes, the beauty and mystery of the ice descends from Poe to the present and into the future, an infinite realm of wonder—and terror. This collection includes H. P. Lovecraft's "At the Mountains of Madness" and Edgar Allan Poe's *The Narrative of Arthur Gordon Pym*.

5 3/8" x 8 3/8", 578 pages, $19.95. Stock #6031; ISBN 1-56882-146-8.

TALES OUT OF INNSMOUTH

Innsmouth is a half-deserted, seedy little town on the North Shore of Massachusetts. It is rarely included on any map of the state. Folks in neighboring towns shun those who come from Innsmouth, and murmur about what goes on there. They try not to mention the place in public, for Innsmouth has ways of quelling gossip, and of taking revenge on troublemakers. Here are ten new tales and three reprints concerning the town, the hybrids who live there, the strange city rumored to exist nearby under the sea, and those who nightly lurch and shamble down the fog-bound streets of Innsmouth.

5 3/8" x 8 3/8", 294 pages, $13.95. Stock #6024; ISBN 1-56882-127-1.

THE ENCYCLOPEDIA CTHULHIANA
Second Revised Edition

The Cthulhu Mythos was first created by H. P. Lovecraft (1890–1937), a Providence author considered by many to be the finest horror story writer of the twentieth century. His tales are a blend of fantasy, science fiction, and horror, with the latter being especially prominent. He described a pantheon of powerful beings known as the Great Old Ones. Other writers, among them Robert E. Howard, Ramsey Campbell, August Derleth, Robert Bloch, Brian Lumley, and Stephen King read his works, tried their hand at writing similar stories, and added to Lovecraft's pantheon. This book is the first attempt in many years to provide a guide to the "Cthulhu Mythos." Written by Daniel Harms. Winner of the 1995 Academy of Adventure Gaming Arts & Design Special Achievement Award.

5 3/8" x 8 3/8", 428 pages, $14.95. Stock #6022; ISBN 1-56882-119-0.

All titles are available from bookstores and game stores. You can also order directly from Wizard's Attic, your source for Cthulhiana and more. To order by credit card via the net, visit our web site at http://www.wizards-attic.com, 24 hours a day. To order via phone, call 1-800-213-1493 (1-510-595-2443 outside the United States) 9 A.M. to 4 P.M. P.S.T.